PRAISE FOR *SUNLIGHT FINDS YOU*

'Perfectly captures the joy and exquisite pain of first love, and the sacrifices that change our lives forever. I adored it.' Toni Jordan, author of *Tenderfoot*

'Laura Moriarty writes with a voice that grabs you from the first page and delights you to the last.' Tracey Lien, author of *All That's Left Unsaid*

'I couldn't stop reading. I couldn't stop hoping. What an extraordinary novel!' Ariel Lawhon, *New York Times* bestselling author of *The Frozen River*

'Radiant…An intimate, deeply moving story of separation, sacrifice, and self-determination—and of how early love shapes the lives we carry forward.' Christina Baker Kline, #1 *New York Times* bestselling author of *The Orphan Train*

'I can't remember the last time I rooted for a character the way I did for Nora. This isn't just a good book—it's a cancel-your-plans, hold-your-breath, call-your-best-friend kind of book. An absolutely unmissable triumph.' Amy Jo Burns, author of *Mercury*

'*Sunlight Finds You* illuminates the beguiling power of first love through characters whose teenage choices precipitate lifelong consequences…' Sarah McCoy, *New York Times* bestselling author of *Marilla of Green Gables*

Laura Moriarty is the author of the bestseller *The Chaperone* as well as *The Center of Everything*, *The Rest of Her Life* and *While I'm Falling*. She received her master's degree from the University of Kansas and was awarded the George Bennett Fellowship for creative writing at Phillips Exeter Academy. Moriarty lives in Lawrence, Kansas.

SUNLIGHT FINDS YOU

LAURA MORIARTY

TEXT PUBLISHING MELBOURNE AUSTRALIA

The Text Publishing Company acknowledges the Traditional Owners of the country on which we work, the Wurundjeri people of the Kulin Nation, and pays respect to their Elders past and present.

textpublishing.com.au

The Text Publishing Company
Wurundjeri Woi Wurrung Country, Level 28, 2 Southbank Boulevard,
Melbourne Victoria 3006 Australia

Published in Australia, New Zealand and the UK by The Text Publishing Company, 2026
First published in the US by Riverhead Books, an imprint of Penguin Random House LLC, 2026

Cover design by Jaya Miceli
Cover art: *Detail of Love*, 2017, © T. S. Harris / Bridgeman Images
Page design by Christina Nguyen

Printed and bound in Great Britain by Clays Ltd, Elcograf S.p.A.

ISBN: 9781923058996 (paperback)
ISBN: 9781923059849 (ebook)

EU Authorised Representative: Easy Access System Europe—Mustamäe tee 50, 10621 Tallinn, Estonia, gpsr.requests@easproject.com

For the Spirit of Florida, 1949

ONE

1.

I'm named Eleanor because I was born a week after Eleanor Roosevelt came to Kansas City to campaign for her husband. At the time, my parents were living in Rolla, Missouri, and my mother said that even if not for my imminent birth, she wouldn't have made the trip across half the state to wait with the crowd at the airport. But the next day, Rolla's newspaper used a third of its front page to print a picture of Mrs. Roosevelt smiling in front of the little TWA airplane that she apparently wasn't terrified to ride around in. My mother admired her courage.

My father liked the name Eleanor, but worried it would work against me, as many people in our part of Missouri had strong feelings about the Roosevelts, and not all those feelings were good. He suggested they call me Nora for short, and my mother was fine with that.

I didn't know until I met Leonard that the name Eleanor comes from the name Helen, which in Greek means "shining light." Even at seventeen, Leonard had that kind of information just rolling around in his head. But I doubt my mother ever knew what my name means in Greek. She would have been pleased to learn it, as she loved sunlight. More than most people do, I mean. When she came in to wake us, before she even kissed our foreheads, it was always shades up, curtains back. She hated the long nights of winter. Every July, we spent a weekend at the Lake of the Ozarks, and once, while my father was fishing, she had me and my brother climb a slope with her so she could take a picture of the water at sunset. Back home, when she got the film developed, she was disappointed. The sparkle couldn't be captured in black and white.

Another thing I remember about her is that she didn't tolerate lies. She regularly reminded my brother and me that liars died twice in the Lake of Fire, and he who breathed out lies would perish. And to her, Bobby and I both understood, a lie was a lie was a lie. It didn't matter if you were Hitler saying he only wanted peace (a piece of Poland, the joke went, a piece of France . . .) or the woman who said she'd already paid the bill for her laundry when both she and my mother knew she hadn't. Or, it should be said, if you were a particular daughter, tempted to deceive when asked why the bowl containing that week's sugar ration didn't seem as full as it should be.

Because I admired my mother and loved her, and because I didn't want to be punished by God, and because I most certainly didn't want to have anything in common with Hitler, I tried hard not to lie to anyone. About anything. If a friend at school asked me if I liked her new dress and I didn't, I'd pretend I'd forgotten something and had to run back to get it. Or I'd change the subject to something of hers I did like, maybe a barrette or her socks. But if pressed, I'd tell the truth.

In sixth grade, however, I told a blatant lie, and though I obviously didn't perish, I still believe what followed altered the course of my life.

My teacher that year was a Mr. Pile, and from the first day of class, I loathed him. He was nice enough to me, as I was quick, studious, and a girl. But he called Tom Bigby, who was the smallest in our class, "Mr. Littleby," and he kept doing it long after even the worst of us stopped laughing. Ronald Bell, walleyed and slow, was unimaginatively called "Mr. Fish." Peter Schultz sounded as Missourian as the rest of us, but Mr. Pile would only address him as "Herr Schultz," in the thickest of German accents, and this at a time when no American wanted to be thought of as German.

Mr. Pile lectured at us from behind a podium, and he'd made a little sign for this podium that said MR. PILE in spread-out letters, as if he wanted to spell it for us slowly: M R. P I L E. I'd often stare at this sign and think about what it should say, or rather, what it could say. He'd used his fountain pen to make the letters, so nothing could be erased from the sign, only added.

One morning when we were out at recess, I fell off the monkey bars—it was winter, and when the temperature dipped below a certain degree, girls were allowed to wear pants under their skirts, so those were big monkey-bar days for us. I wasn't hurt when I fell, but I muddied the hem of my skirt, and I asked Mr. Pile if I could please go in and rinse off the mud. He gave me permission, and I went in. Some of the younger grades were on a different schedule, and I remember that there were other girls in the washroom, and other students and teachers in the hall. By the time I got the mud out, the bell had rung and the hall was quiet again, though my class had ten more minutes of recess.

I realized I had time to do something I very much wanted to do. Throughout my life, I've seized such opportunities. Sometimes this seizing has very much worked to my advantage. Sometimes it has not.

I ducked into our classroom and closed the door behind me. I found Mr. Pile's fountain pen in his top desk drawer. With a few strokes, I changed the sign to read MR. RUDE, then capped the pen and returned it. When I went back outside, I showed Mr. Pile I'd gotten out the mud, and thanked him for letting me go in.

"You're quite welcome, Miss Nora. You did a good job getting that stain out."

I smiled back, not feeling bad one bit. I hadn't lied. I'd made the sign on the podium more honest.

Once we were back at our desks, it didn't take long for my

classmates to start smiling and looking at one another. But Mr. Pile, standing behind the podium, had no idea what was so funny. I must say, I was pleased to witness how scared he looked, realizing he was being laughed at. Shoe, meet your new foot. The good time went on until Wilma Cooper raised her hand. Wilma believed that because of her faith in Jesus, she had to be nice to everyone, and when Mr. Pile called on her, she sorrowfully pointed to the sign. He came around to look for himself. By then, no one was laughing. We could hear him breathing through his teeth.

When he turned to face us, he raised one finger, and it trembled.

"Whoever did this," he said, "will be discovered."

I wasn't worried. Everyone in our class had been outside with him, except, briefly, for me. And Mr. Pile only knew me as a good girl, well-mannered and compliant, with no reason to dislike him. I have a picture of myself from that era, and I look irritating and prim—my mother used to wrap my hair in rags Sunday nights so I'd have curls like Shirley Temple through the week. In this picture I'm smiling, resting my chin on folded hands, and I have an enormous bow in my hair that looks gray in the picture, though I remember the bow was yellow. I believe I wore that yellow bow in my hair the day I changed Mr. Pile's sign.

He was still breathing like a bull when he gave us a page of math problems and told us to work quietly at our desks. He went out into the hall, and though he left the door open, some of the boys started to turn around and whisper to one another, trying to guess who might have done it. No one thought of me. Mary Pank turned around, waited for me to look up, then whispered, "Mr. Rude!" I smiled just enough to show I agreed it was funny, then went back to work.

Good thing, because Mr. Pile came back in quickly, and when I looked up, he was staring right at me.

"Miss Chesnow," he said.

Terror bloomed, unhelpful. I put my pencil down. "Sir?"

He took a step toward my desk, and then another. Behind me, the radiator hissed.

"When you came inside during recess, did you see anyone coming or going from this room?"

"No sir," I said. It was true. I hadn't seen myself. But I was aware of my classmates watching, and of their fear on my behalf. Mr. Pile seemed mostly bewildered, as if he'd set something down and turned around, then turned back to find the thing missing.

"Miss Chesnow." A vein on his forehead bulged. "I'm going to ask you one last time. Do you know who altered the sign?"

Now the choice was clear. I would confess, or I would lie. For just a moment, I considered revealing myself. It was like standing at the edge of a dock, your body already leaning forward, and deciding almost too late not to jump.

I recently read a book by C. S. Lewis in which he says that

you don't really know what you believe until the truth of it becomes a matter of life and death. It's one thing to have faith that a rope is strong when it's coiled in a box. But would you dangle from that rope over a precipice? In those moments that Mr. Pile stared down at me, waiting for an answer, I was more afraid than I'd ever been in my life. And C. S. Lewis was exactly right. I discovered that I didn't truly believe my mother's warnings of eternal punishment. Or rather, I was willing to bet against them in the face of Mr. Pile's certain, and imminent, wrath.

"*No* sir." I managed to sound indignant. Unpracticed as I was, fear pushed me to excel.

"I see." Shame filled his eyes. "Forgive me."

My heartbeat steadied. I nodded once, an insulted but merciful queen. Mr. Pile retreated from my desk, dabbed at his forehead with his handkerchief, and with a shaky voice, resumed class.

What C. S. Lewis didn't say: After the danger passes, you might go back to not knowing what you believe and start to worry that you chose wrong.

I spent the rest of the day in a silent panic. At lunch, both Mary and Wilma expressed outrage that I'd been unfairly accused. I said nothing, and felt even worse. When school got out, I waited for my brother at my usual spot, watching fat snowflakes fall from the pearly sky, their beauty no consolation.

When I got home, my mother asked me about my day. I said my day was fine. Because why not? In for a penny, in for a pound. She looked up from her ironing, wincing as if in sudden pain. Or that's how I remember that moment. She'd always told me she could tell when someone was lying, and so I held my breath and waited. The look of pain left her face. She smiled, reached out to muss my hair, and said if I changed my clothes and wore my warm hat, I could go out and play.

That night, I was not visited by demons, and I woke to find, to my surprise, that I had not perished in my sleep.

When I returned to school on Monday, I noticed that Mr. Pile didn't call Tom or Ronald or Peter any names but their own. He didn't call on them at all—his pride was too great for that. But at least some decent part of him realized he shouldn't be dishing out what he so clearly couldn't take.

And so my relief turned to jubilance. I didn't care that no one knew I was the one who'd taught the teacher a lesson. Everyone thought Diana Prince was a regular army nurse, but she was secretly Wonder Woman, using her jet and lasso and superpowers to fight evil, near and far. I had no magic lasso, and no invisible jet, but I could lie with eyes of steel, and that felt like a superpower. Over the next few days, I planned an entire career of secretly using this power to take down other villains.

On Friday, the principal showed up outside Mr. Pile's door. He said my name and told me I should gather my things. I could barely strap my books because my hands were shaking, though Mr. Pile himself only seemed surprised. Out in the hallway, the principal touched my shoulder and spoke to me gently, saying my father was in his office. And I knew. My father was a machinist at a metals plant. He went to work even when he was sick. If I was in trouble, no matter how serious, my mother would have been the one to come. I broke into a run, ignoring the principal calling after me. Some of us are like that with what scares us. If we know it's coming, we rush to it. The dread is worse than the thing itself.

When the secretary saw me in the doorway, she looked at me with pity, then glanced at a door a few feet from her desk. I moved past her, opened that door, and there was my father, a giant in a chair made for a child, the laces of one of his boots undone. He'd been crying. And just that, seeing tearstains on my father's cheeks, was like seeing water run uphill. I'd entered a new world, with different rules.

"Oh honey," he said, and held out his arms.

My mother had collapsed while she was hanging clothes in our backyard. I learned later that Mrs. Ritchie next door saw her fall, and she'd had to run and get her step stool so she could get over the fence and try to help. By the time she did, my mother was already dead. An aneurysm, my father said, and I could tell the word was unfamiliar to him as well. But he explained as best he could, putting a fist by his left ear, then shooting out his oil-stained fingers. A burst vessel in her brain. He couldn't understand it. She was the best person he knew, my mother. And there was no family history of any such thing. She was young and healthy. It made no sense, he said, gasping through sobs, his shoulders heaving. No sense at all.

Of course, all of it made sense to me.

If my father had asked me directly why she died, I would have told him the truth, even if he hated me for it. I sincerely believed my lie had killed her, and that if I lied again, my father or Bobby might be taken as well. But he didn't ask me why she died, and I didn't volunteer the information. My whole life, my father had brightened at the sight of me, laughed at my jokes, and advised my brother, three years younger, to follow my example. I'd grown up basking in the warmth of his esteem, and I couldn't bear the thought of losing it. So I let him think that my misery was like his, coming only from grief.

My shame was so great that I told no one of my guilt, though for months it was always with me, an itch under my sweater, burning but unseen.

I wasn't completely irrational. By the time I started seventh grade, I'd noticed that other people told lies all the time, and most of their mothers were still alive. Slowly, I came to understand that our family simply had bad luck, and I hadn't really caused my mother's death.

But by then, I'd lost my eyes of steel. Even with little fibs, the kind that saved someone's feelings, I'd hesitate, and then I'd get nervous about the hesitation, and I'd invariably start to stammer. My friends thought it was funny, how bad I was at lying. But it's a terrible thing to be caught in a lie, or to know that someone is thinking of you as dishonest, and maybe losing respect for you as you speak.

So I returned to my policy of honesty, not because I feared God or punishment, and not because I was especially moral. I stopped lying because I was so bad at it.

I didn't lie again, or even try to, until I was older, and in love.

2.

My father was allowed to grieve in peace for a year, but soon after, relatives and neighbors started mentioning single women they said were nice. The general feeling was that he needed help with me and Bobby, and that plenty of women would want to apply for the job. My father, not yet thirty-five, was considered good-looking, and though he'd left school in sixth grade, he had a natural intelligence when it came to machinery, a trait that had kept him employed during even the worst years of the Depression. He had good table manners as well as good hygiene, and he didn't gamble or drink to excess. In other words, even with two children in tow, he was very much considered a catch.

By the time he was ready to be introduced to some of these women, I was thirteen, old enough to babysit my brother and even make dinner for us both. My specialty was macaroni and cheese with little pieces of hot dog stirred in. Bobby liked this dish as much as I did, and he and I spent many Saturday nights enjoying several servings while listening to *The Shadow* or *Inner Sanctum Mysteries.* But then our father would come home, looking deflated and smelling of cigarettes, though he himself didn't smoke. If one of us asked if he'd had an okay time, he'd usually shrug. Some nights he actually rolled his eyes. Once, after he'd had a beer, he called the woman he'd been out with a floozy, which was strong language from him.

"I just miss your mother," he told us, which Bobby and I understood. We didn't want him to be alone and lonely, but it was hard to imagine him having anyone else for a wife. Our parents had been well suited to one another. He didn't share her religious convictions, but he respected her for her contentment with simple clothes and a simple life, and for her devotion to our family. Her good sense, as he put it. Before she died, and after, he said he mistrusted women who wore perfume, or dyed their hair, or smiled at everything he said just because he said it.

But then one Saturday evening, he came home with a dumbstruck look on his face, and so late that Bobby had already fallen asleep on the couch. He told me that he'd had a lovely evening conversing with a war widow named Mae. I pictured a skinny old woman draped in black, frowning in a rocker. But Mae, who would become our stepmother, turned out to be twenty-six, stout and pretty, with bright red hair that she pinned up in a floral clip. And she had a daughter, Janet, who was three. The first time I met Mae, she told me she'd just put

Janet's crib together when she found out her first husband wasn't coming back.

"I wanted to die as well," she told me, and I liked this, how right away she spoke to me as if I would understand things a child wouldn't. "There was the sorrow for myself, and a greater sorrow for Janet. We've done okay together, the two of us. But I'd love for her to have a daddy who can hug her and help her." Here she paused, flashing her bright smile. "And maybe a brother and a sister as part of the deal."

She could afford to speak with confidence. My father, I found out later, had already proposed, telling her to take all the time she needed. He'd wait.

As much as I liked Mae, I was surprised to see my father so taken with her, as she was, in many ways, the opposite of my mother, despite the fact they'd both grown up on farms—my mother in Missouri, and Mae in Arkansas. In girlhood, they'd both been repeatedly assured that the meek would inherit the earth. But while this promise consoled my mother, my step-mother, who was about as meek as the color of her hair, took the promise to mean she would inherit nothing, and would therefore need to reach for all she wanted herself. She didn't nag at my father or argue with him, at least not in front of us. He wouldn't have tolerated that. But not long after the wedding, Mae was the one who came up with the idea that we should all move to Florida, though she'd never been there herself. She had a friend who'd been in St. Petersburg during the war, and this friend had gone on about the city's wonders, saying it was up-

and-coming, with so much opportunity, not to mention you could leave your snow shovel and boots behind.

A few weeks later, after my father told us we were moving to St. Pete, Mae got out a map and tapped a red fingernail halfway up Florida's western edge.

"See?" she asked. "Right on the water. They call it Sunshine City. Because it's a real city, not a Podunk town. Mark my words, you kids will love it." She leaned close to me and lowered her voice. "Nora, honey. I bet you will, too."

She was right. We arrived in the summer of 1947, when St. Pete had only around a hundred thousand people. But it was growing fast, and to us, coming from Rolla, a ten-story building was a skyscraper. The first time we saw an escalator, Bobby and Janet wanted to keep riding it up and down. As the eldest, I felt I had to encourage restraint, but really, I was just as excited. And none of us had ever seen the ocean, or run a hand down the latticework grooves of a palm tree's trunk. We moved into a flat-roofed rental painted turquoise. Back in Missouri, a house that color would have been embarrassing and strange. But in Florida, just on our block, there was a lime-green house, and two other houses painted shades of pink. Mae planted yellow roses outside the front door, and because the windows were almost always open, I could sometimes smell them from inside.

We lived in the Kenwood neighborhood, not by the water, but the streets were flat and good for biking, and Bobby and I would sometimes take the bus to the long pier on Tampa Bay, where we'd spend our allowance on saltwater taffy or cotton candy or once, a necklace made of sea glass we presented to Mae for her birthday.

I was a little nervous about starting ninth grade in the fall, and not knowing anyone my age. But I was hardly alone. On the first day, the teacher asked who'd just moved in from out of state, and maybe a third of the class raised a hand. I made fast friends with Roberta, who'd just arrived from Illinois, and then Irene, new from Pennsylvania. Roberta and Irene had no love for our new home's humidity. But I even liked that. Florida felt lush on my skin.

People say you can't run away from your problems, but the move to St. Pete eased my grief for my mother, though of course that grief didn't go away. In contrast, I think my brother, under his often brash exterior, remained startled that we'd somehow gone on without her. He was eleven when we moved to St. Pete, and once, when just he and I were with our father, standing at the dock of a city park, a manatee with a pale scar on its back swam up, watching us from under the surface with its dark, sad-looking eyes. From above, the scar looked like the raised stitching on a football, and our father said that the manatee had perhaps survived a bad run-in with a motorboat. He strolled away from me and Bobby then, humming, his hands in his pockets.

"I feel her with us here," Bobby said. He'd spoken quietly. "She's still with us."

I was unsure what to say, for I didn't feel any such thing. I felt our mother's absence, and I felt sorry for her. The last thing she'd done was go outside on a freezing day and hang wet clothes on the line. Her big dream was to have a window over the kitchen sink, and she never even got that.

"If you're right," I said, "she's probably mad we didn't move here sooner."

Bobby laughed with a quick exhale, nodding, and I knew he understood what I meant. At first, our quiet mother would have been bewildered by our turquoise house and the bustle of Central Avenue, and her kids biking by themselves past big hotels to the city pool or a movie theater, and grown women going out bare legged because of the heat. But I think eventually she would have come to love our new home as we did, with all the freedom and promise it offered, the sandy beaches and bright skies, the pelicans and shaggy-headed palms, and oranges so plentiful and cheap you could eat one every morning, with everything around us growing, thriving in the warmth and light.

Looking back, I now realize St. Pete in 1947 wasn't paradise for everyone. On sidewalks, anyone who wasn't white had to walk close to the street. "Giving whites the wall," it was called, and even with the tourists and the postcard shops and everyone smiling, I never saw anyone dare do otherwise. Separate schools. Separate beaches. Separate exits and entrances for movie theaters. Downtown, you had to be white to try on clothes in a store. I know younger people, or people of any age who've never lived in the South, find all this unfathomable. But coming from Missouri, it was all I'd known. I have to be honest and say I didn't really think about it, at least not until I met Leonard, or really, Leonard's mother.

Leonard and his parents were also white, but they'd moved from New York, so they knew a different way of living. Mrs. Lifton told me she liked Florida's weather, and she appreciated that the cost of living was much lower than it had been in Manhattan. She'd even learned to tolerate the bugs. But regarding Jim Crow, she felt the entire state was stuck in the past. She said she'd spent a summer in Paris before the war, and the French didn't understand segregation at all, and wondered how we could live with ourselves. She said when some white American from the South tried to defend Jim Crow, the French said, "*La raison du plus fort est toujours la meilleure*," which meant people in charge can always find ways to justify bad behavior.

The first time Leonard's mother and I really talked, we were sitting out on their main back patio while Leonard changed out of his school clothes. I greatly admired that patio. The back patio of our rental was a concrete slab with folding chairs, but the Liftons' patio looked like another room in the house—it had a roof with a ceiling fan, and nicer furniture than we had in our living room. The Liftons also had a kidney-shaped pool in their backyard, and this was when that was unusual, even in Florida. Beyond the pool lay Coffee Pot Bayou, which was not the color of coffee, but a sparkling blue, or later in the evening, a deep green that softened to gray. On the other side was St. Pete proper. If I squinted, I could see the dock of the city park where my father, Bobby, and I had seen the manatee.

"My guess," Mrs. Lifton told me, "is that it's shaped like a coffee pot, as seen from above." She raised a long, slender arm and gestured at the cloudless sky. "But no one I've asked seems to know for certain. My husband thinks it must be some old inside joke."

When Mrs. Lifton was a younger woman, she'd been a theater actress, living on her own in New York. The second time she and I were out on their patio together, I asked if she had any pictures. I meant pictures of her when she was living there. I'd seen pictures of New York in magazines. She went back inside, brought out a little photo album, and showed me a picture of herself with flowers in her hair, and wearing a long gown. "I was Ophelia," she said.

I had to tell her I didn't know who that was, and she was patient as she explained, saying she liked that I was always so curious. She kept ticket stubs and playbills in this photo album, and she pointed to a playbill for *Othello* and said it was from when she'd gone back up to New York during the war to see Paul Robeson play the lead.

"He got a standing ovation. I'm sure he got one every night. He was brilliant." She sat with her legs tucked up, her bare feet resting on the cushion of that nice couch like it was the ground. "We have theater here, of course, but not the opportunity to see that sort of artistry." She saw she had to explain again, as I didn't know who Othello was, or Paul Robeson. When I understood Paul Robeson was a black man, and the leading lady was not, she said I found that shocking only because of how I'd grown up.

I considered this opinion, I think, more than I would have coming from someone else because I was dazzled by her. I thought she resembled Katharine Hepburn, and when I told her this, she laughed in her musical way and told me she'd actually been Hepburn's understudy when they were both in college in Pennsylvania. She called Katharine Hepburn "Kate."

"It wasn't so thrilling," she added, taking a leaf from the patio's potted lemon tree, holding it out for me to sniff. "She never missed a performance. But she was lovely to me. She still sends a Christmas card every year." She laughed again. "Or her assistant does. Tell me, Nora. Do you smell the lemon on the leaf? I just adore that, that even the leaf smells divine."

But I'm getting ahead of myself, going on about Leonard's mother. She certainly made an impression. But when I went over, make no mistake, I was there for him.

I met Leonard, or rather, I saw him, on the first day of my sophomore year, my first day at the high school. St. Petersburg High was the first high school in the country to cost over a million dollars to build, and it was the prettiest building I'd ever been in, and also one of the biggest. To me, it conjured a

Spanish castle, with white stucco walls and a red clay barrel roof, and bell towers with arched doorways. The front lawn had palm trees and all kinds of flowers. I often had to strain to hear my history teacher over the chatter of birds, as the classroom's Juliet balcony looked out over one of the shade trees in the senior courtyard, which had a little fishpond with a gurgling fountain.

As a sophomore, the senior courtyard was off-limits to me, but I could sit in the junior courtyard, and this was where I first saw Leonard. He sat by himself, reading a book, pink bougainvillea climbing the trellis behind him. Even with his gaze lowered, I could see the angles of his face and, when he shifted his weight, the easy grace of his long body. I thought: My God, who is *that*? And why isn't there a whole kettle of girls trying to get his attention?

I figured he must be new. But before the bell rang, a couple of other boys walked up, and he put his book down to talk with them. One of them said something that made him smile, and well, seeing that, my fate was sealed. I sound shallow, I know, losing my senses because of the way a boy I didn't even know looked when he smiled. But that's what it was, at first.

The other two boys walked away, and "the Beautiful One," as I thought of Leonard then, went back to reading.

"Nora," Roberta chided, "you're staring." But Irene whispered that she could see why, and they both laughed. I pretended to tie the lace of my shoe so I could crane my neck and try to see what he was reading. I couldn't make it out.

After school, I set about sleuthing. Roberta had an older sister, Becky, who was in eleventh grade and usually nice, and the next time I was at their house I asked Becky to get out her yearbook from the year before. I found his picture, and I liked his name. But when I said it aloud, Becky made a sour face and said sure, okay, Leonard Lifton was easy on the eyes, everyone knew that. But he had a bad personality. He thought he was too good for regular people because his father ran the hospital and they lived in a big house on Snell Isle. She said if Leonard Lifton was Catholic, he'd be at St. Paul's, but too bad he wasn't, and he had to trot his high horse over the bridge every day, mixing with the riffraff. And from the way he acted, Becky said, you could see how much this pained him.

"I don't have anything against rich people," she added. "Susan Monters lives on Snell, and she's perfectly friendly. But my friend Gayle waitressed at the country club last summer, and she had to wait on Leonard's family. She said his parents were fine, but Leonard was out-and-out rude. Wouldn't even acknowledge her, though they'd been in classes together for years. All three of them ordered steak. He's an only child, wouldn't you know."

Becky assured both me and Roberta that there were too many quality fish in the sea to waste our time on a stuck-up, boring one like Leonard. She spoke to us with the wisdom of age, as if we were both her younger sisters, though I was probably almost Becky's age. Because of my September birthday, I was old for a sophomore, though because I was short, no one guessed.

In any case, I thought, but did not say, that I was old enough to think for myself. It was true that most every time I saw Leonard Lifton, he was by himself. Because he was tall, he was easy to spot in a crowded hallway, and he just stared straight ahead as he walked. But I'd seen his smile, just that once, and there wasn't anything snobby or high-horsey about it.

I remained fearful of lying, fearful I would always fail at it. But I wasn't a fearful person in general, certainly not socially. So many people were still coming in new to St. Pete, and as I'd already been there a year, I felt it my responsibility to welcome them, especially the quieter ones, as much as I could. I didn't want anyone to feel left out or lonely, and I'd found that most people appreciated my coming up and saying hello. My father once told me that anyone who didn't want to talk to someone as pleasant and pretty as I was must be unwell in the head, and though I understood he was severely biased in my favor, I tended not to take the occasional rudeness to my overtures personally.

But introducing myself to Leonard Lifton was a different matter. He was older than I was, a junior, and he'd been in Florida for longer. He ate steaks with his parents at country clubs, and he lived on some island I'd never heard of. Still, I thought, there was no law against saying hello to a person. The next time I saw him with a book in the courtyard, I went over, sat down beside him, and asked what he was reading. He looked up and stared at me like I was a giant talking wasp.

But at this point, I could see him up close. His eyes were so dark they were almost black. Lifton sounded like an English name, but I thought he must be at least a little Italian. One of his eyes was slightly larger than the other, and just the larger eye had a mournful look.

"I'm Nora, by the way. Nora Chesnow."

Still, he did not speak. I glanced back at Roberta and Irene—a mistake, as they were both watching with wide eyes. I'd said I was going to just go up and talk to him, but they didn't think I really would. Leonard didn't say anything, just kept looking at me like I was scaring him, and I was about to get up and say *Whoops, sorry, I thought you might be a friendly person. Have fun with your horse.* But then I saw that his neck was turning pink, and he was the one in the shade. I glanced down at his book. There was a drawing of an angry-looking pig on the cover. The title was *Animal Farm.*

"It's about animals?" I asked. I thought, snob or not, scared or not, he could answer a question.

He closed his book, lost his place. "It's not about animals." He had to stop to clear his throat. "I'm Leonard Lifton. Nice to meet you."

I could tell he'd learned to talk in the north, his consonants sharp and clipped.

"I mean it is about animals," he added. Under his chinos,

one of his knees was bouncing, bouncing, bouncing. "But not really. It's an allegory."

Progress, I thought. "An allegory for what?"

He looked down at the book like he wasn't sure. I was starting to feel the sun. I wiped my forehead, and he wiped his.

"They're communists," he said finally. The bouncing knee slowed, then stilled. "The pigs, I mean. They're not all bad. One of them is really good." He pointed at the angry-looking pig on the cover. "But the bad ones take over."

Well, that was actually pretty interesting to me, so it was easy to ask him more questions. But I admit the whole time, I was half paying attention to the suntanned skin of his arms. I'd seen in the yearbook that he was on the swim team. It showed in his shoulders, even in his button-down. And there was a softness to his voice I liked.

"Goodness, it's hot," I said. Not exactly breaking news. But he got it. He moved over and apologized for hogging the shade.

"Hogging it like a communist," I said, which didn't make perfect sense, but we both laughed, and I scooted into the shade beside him. "I think I'd like to read it," I told him. Not a lie. "You get it from the library here?" I nodded upward. The school library was behind us on the top floor, dark with oak trim, quiet. Nothing like the rest of the school.

"Oh no." He lowered his voice, which gave me the opportunity to lean in. "It's banned. You can't even get it downtown."

"Why? Why's it banned?" I'd already spoken when I realized

the ban might have something to do with sex, but he didn't look embarrassed for me. Before he answered, I figured it out. "Oh. You said that one of the communist pigs is good. A good communist."

"Exactly," he said. "That's my guess, at least. My dad said 'because it's Florida.' But I think it's the same all over."

I laughed again, a little punch drunk. I could smell the bougainvillea behind us.

"Well," I said. "Now I just want to read it more." Another truth. But also strategic. *One one thousand*, I thought. *Two one thousand. Three—*

"You can borrow it from me when I've finished." He was looking down at the book again. He moved it from hand to hand. Neat fingernails. Clean. "I'll probably finish it tonight."

We agreed to meet the following day at the picnic table. My friends, when I told them, were astounded by my quick success.

"That's like a date," Roberta said. "That's like a date at school."

Irene disagreed. "He's not picking her up at her house. He's not buying dinner or even a Coke. It's an appointment." She paused. "With potential."

I agreed with Irene. The next day, when I went to the courtyard, I brought every book in my locker with me, and I set them beside me while Leonard and I talked. I quickly got the feeling he'd prepared for the conversation, like it was a test he could study for. He started off asking where I was from, and when I said Rolla, Missouri, he said he'd never been there, as if this was a surprise, or something sadly missing from his general education. That made me laugh, which I soon regretted, as his throat turned pink again. His earlobes, too. But we got back on track. I asked him about New York, and he said he didn't remember much about living there, but it turned out he did—he'd been inside the Empire State Building, and every Christmas his parents had taken him and his cousins to ice-skate at Rockefeller Center. They'd lived in an apartment, and the building had a doorman named Lou who was old and grouchy but who once pushed a girl out of the way of a fast-moving car, right in front of their building.

I clapped twice and said, "Okay, Lou!" just before the bell rang. That was my cue. I sighed, looked at all my books, and said I didn't know how I was going to carry all of them to my next class on the second floor.

This was true. I didn't know for sure. But I had a pretty strong suspicion.

"I could," Leonard said. "I could carry them, I mean." He stood and picked them up like they weighed nothing. I thanked him and stood as well. He was at least a foot taller than I was, and when he looked down at me, he was laughing a little, but not in a bad way, not at all. He looked as happy as I felt. He knew what I was up to. He was just shy, not dumb.

On the way up the stairs, we passed Becky and a bunch of other junior-year girls coming down. They stopped on the landing, blocking traffic, looking at us and then at each other. Leonard and I kept climbing, but I turned my head and caught

Becky still watching us. And I was terrible, so cheeky: not only did I wave, I winked.

Leonard's closest friend was Dale Marshen. Dale was even taller than Leonard but terribly thin, with bright orange hair and pale skin that burned so easily he had to wear long sleeves on even the hottest days, and he could only go swimming after seven. When I first started seeing Leonard, Dale wouldn't look me in the eye. I had the sense he was nervous around girls. But I kept being nice to him whenever I saw him with Leonard, asking him questions, and we eventually found out we both liked movies. Not so unusual, I know. But Dale knew all kinds of background information, like who directed what and how you could tell, and I liked learning these things from him. He seemed to appreciate this, and soon enough, Dale and I got along fine.

Leonard was also friendly with other boys on the swim team, but because of his shyness, he wasn't what you would call popular, except with teachers. They were always saying hello to him in the hall, or coming up and asking if he'd read such-and-such. The answer was usually yes, and when it wasn't, Leonard would write the title in his notebook and thank the teacher for recommending it. Because I was a year behind him, I had some of his former teachers, and Mrs. Rose, who taught American Literature, actually took me aside and said she was so glad I was spending time with Leonard Lifton, as he was such a thoughtful and sensitive young man. I figured out the acronym: TASYM, and the next time I saw him, I called him by it. He took the teasing well.

"They don't all like me," he said. "Mr. Bladen doesn't."

Mr. Bladen taught junior-year history, and Leonard said he started the first class with a lecture about how the US dropping the bombs on Hiroshima and Nagasaki had demonstrated our might and our American ingenuity, and that's what won the war. This opinion was received well by the class, as it would have been just about anywhere. But Leonard raised his hand and asked if we could have demonstrated it some other way besides dropping a bomb on a city full of people, and then another city three days later.

"I wasn't trying to be argumentative," he told me. "I was really wondering. He'd told us that some relative of his was connected to the making of the bomb in ways he could only hint at, so he therefore knew more than most people about it. I thought he might know if they ever considered another way to show what a bomb like that could do."

"Like what, Leonard?" Mr. Bladen had asked him. And Leonard could tell that he hadn't liked the question. Other people in the class had turned around to look at him, their faces unfriendly. But Leonard answered. He said if they just wanted to scare Japan, they could have filmed a bomb going off at a test site, or invited somebody high up in Japan to come watch one go off somewhere that wasn't a city. Or if they wanted the people of Japan to see it, couldn't they have dropped it close to a city, and not directly over one? Just close enough that people could see it, how big and awful it was?

Mr. Bladen replied that if someone wanted to get all bleeding-hearted about it, someone might consider all the young American soldiers who would've died if we'd had to invade Japan, not to mention all the Japanese, who would've fought to the bitter end. He said a high school student whose biggest problem was wondering what his mom was cooking for dinner probably shouldn't spend his time second-guessing the US military. No one actually applauded what Mr. Bladen said, but plenty of people snickered.

"He said that because he didn't know," I said. I thought back to Mr. Pile in Missouri. He and Mr. Bladen might have really gotten along. Or they'd just be mean to each other.

"I was so embarrassed," Leonard said.

I was pleased that he'd told me anyway, that he knew he could.

"You're brave," I said. I meant it. Roberta and Irene were always calling me brave, because I could go up and talk to anyone. But I wouldn't have raised my hand in class and asked a question like that, knowing I was going against what most people felt. Even then, I understood. Leonard and I were scared of different things.

3.

Leonard drove a black Plymouth that had belonged to his father, but it didn't look like any hand-me-down car I'd ever seen. It was beautiful, no dents, all shine, with a dark red interior and a wide front seat. If we stopped to eat at Triplett's Drive-In, we'd get out and sit at one of the tables. I didn't mind. If I'd had a car like that, I would have wanted to keep it nice, too. Leonard would go up and order for us, always remembering that I hated pickles, though I just said it once.

He didn't know how to dance when I met him. When I told him how much I loved dancing, he looked a little queasy. I offered to teach him, and he said he would learn, for me.

We went to his house to practice, as there was more space, less chaos. His mother let us push back the furniture in their living room, where they had both a record player and a radio.

Sometimes she'd watch from the doorway and tell us we were looking good. This was in early October, after school, so even with fans going, we would get overheated. It was Mrs. Lifton who told me that if I ever wanted to bring a suit, I could stay for a swim and cool off. I brought my suit over the next time, and she said I should rinse off first, and that I could use the bathroom attached to the master bedroom while Leonard rinsed off in the shower in the hall. I thought, my God, three of them living there, and two different bathrooms. I'd never known people like this. I'd never even taken a shower—every place we'd ever lived only had a tub.

Mr. and Mrs. Lifton's bedroom led to a second, smaller patio, which also had a view of the pool and the bayou beyond. I marveled at this, that they could open a sliding glass door and step directly from their bedroom to outside. Leonard had told me this smaller patio was where his mother liked to sit and read, and once, when I was in his parents' room changing, I rolled back the glass door and went out there by myself. I felt like Goldilocks, letting myself sit on the love seat and look out at the water. There was a bottle of nail polish on the table. The label said *Lucky Rose*, and it was the same shade I'd noticed on his mother's toenails. A book was wedged between the love seat cushion and the wicker, and I slipped it out to peek at the title: *The Sun Also Rises*. I'd heard of Ernest Hemingway, and knew he was considered a serious writer. I was impressed that this was the kind of book she would read on her little sunporch with no one watching, waiting for her toenails to dry.

I didn't feel I could ask her about the book, or even mention it to Leonard, as I didn't want either of them to know I'd been snooping. The next day, I tried to find *The Sun Also Rises* at the school library, and when I couldn't, I asked the librarian, who gave me a scolding look and said it was an inappropriate book for a girl in high school.

"It's full of vulgarity," she added. "Absolutely full of it. Nora, I have to say, I'm surprised."

I assured her I was surprised as well. I couldn't tell if she believed me.

"I saw someone reading it, that's all."

She frowned. "I hope not another student?"

"No, ma'am." I feared she would ask who, specifically.

"Well," she said. "To each their own. But I hope you'll find something more suitable."

I couldn't bring myself to try to check it out at the city library, as I worried I'd be chastised again, perhaps more firmly, and with other people behind me in line. I couldn't even ask Leonard if he'd read it, for he might guess that I knew his mother was reading it, and if he knew it was full of vulgarity, we'd both want to die of humiliation. Someone else might have been able to play innocent in that conversation, but that person was not me.

Still, I hated that I couldn't get my hands on a copy. I had a hard time believing that Mrs. Lifton would read smut, even smut by a serious writer. But if that were the case, I, too, wanted to read it, and be like her in this small way.

Leonard and I made our dancing debut at that year's Harvest Bash, which was really a Halloween dance, but they couldn't call it that because some parents thought anything having to do with Halloween was demonic. Still, the dance was held on the last Saturday in October, and there was a prize for the couple with the best costumes. Leonard and I went as Prince Philip and Princess Elizabeth. I got a little fake tiara from Webb's, and Leonard found a hat that more or less looked like a Royal Navy hat. The real Princess Elizabeth was about to give birth, but we left that part out of the costume.

By then, Leonard could jitterbug as well as anyone. I'd taught him the tabletop and the octopus, and what he and I called the big unfurl and furl-back. It was his idea to practice a move where he'd push me up over his shoulders and swing me around. We had to practice this outside, by the pool, and when his mother saw us through the window she ran out and yelled, "Oh be careful, Leonard! Don't drop her!"

I wasn't worried. The muscles in his back were firm as a tree trunk. Decades later, when I was helping my friend study for an exam in massage therapy, I learned this muscle was the *latissimus dorsi*, the swimmer's muscle, and I thought, oh, yes, I know that.

He never dropped me. Not at their house, and not at the dance. But an hour in, I lost my tiara, and Leonard had lost his hat. No one knew who we were supposed to be. We laughed when people made wrong guesses, and kept having fun. But when the band played "Blue Moon," we danced slow and close, and I knew I didn't want to spend the whole evening surrounded by other people. He felt the same. Long before they announced the winners of the costume contest, we'd already left for the beach.

Before Leonard, when I'd gone out with other boys, I easily played the part of the Guardian of Virtue—moving a hand out from under my skirt or blouse, or verbally reminding my date of the kind of girl I wasn't. With Leonard, I lost all such power, and didn't miss it. In his car, when we were alone, I wanted to devour him. I loved his voice, and the way he said my name. And looking at him, of course. But if I had to pin my weakness with him on just one thing, I'd say it was the way he made it clear, when he was holding me, or kissing me, that he didn't want to be anywhere else, or doing anything but what he was doing. He'd sometimes pull back and look at me, really look at me, like there'd be a test about my face the next morning, and he'd have to draw every shadow and curve from memory.

Also, it's interesting that every boy I knew used the word *necking*, but Leonard was the first to truly focus his attention on my neck. At least without leaving a hickey. He wasn't interested in that. He'd move his lips down one side of my neck while two of his fingertips slid down the other side, then back up to my ear, again and again until it felt like my very teeth were ringing.

When I was alone with him, I felt a humming current between us, a thing in itself, as alive and real as either one of us.

But I could think of nothing more terrifying, or personally calamitous, than getting pregnant. If given a choice, I would have preferred being hit by a car, killed by polio, or eaten alive by a shark. Really. I'd thought about it. At least I'd be remembered fondly.

Night after night, we pulled away from each other, worn out. The misery was new and bewildering. My friends talked of managing lust in their boyfriends, not of being driven mad by it themselves. Leonard didn't judge me for it, not at all. But I wouldn't have wanted anyone else to know.

The night of the dance, we'd been parked at the beach for maybe fifteen minutes when I lost all sense of propriety. I'll just say that if any other boy tried doing to me what I started to do to Leonard, that boy would have gotten slapped.

Leonard took hold of both my hands and whispered, "What are you doing, Nora? What are you wanting?" I understood that all I had to do was say the truth, and it would happen. Terror rushed in. I told him I was sorry, and retreated to my side of the car. I said sorry again. I meant it, for I could tell by his voice, and by the look on his face, that I'd put him in physical pain.

"I'm going for a swim," he said. "I'll be right back."

"Okay," I said. I wanted to cry. He didn't want me to come with him. He got out of the car and ran barefoot across the sand, right into the water. The moon was out, and because of the white pants, I could keep sight of him until the cresting waves reached his waist. I got out and walked around to the front of the car, leaning on the hood as I watched for him, worried, though I knew he was an excellent swimmer. This worry, I knew, was connected to my longing for him, which I understood wasn't, at the heart of it, caused by his physical beauty or the muscles of his back. What I felt was bigger than that. Encompassing.

He emerged from the water and walked back toward the car, rubbing his eyes, the white pants soaked and clinging. He stood next to me without saying anything, but he reached over and took my hand. His fingers were still wet and cool from the sea.

"I won't do that to you again," I said.

"Okay," he said. "I'm not mad, Nora." After a while, he made an L with his left hand, raising it to the moon. "It's waning."

I asked him how he could tell, and he said if the moon sits in your left hand, it's waning, and if it sits in your right, it's working its way to full. I'd never heard this. I let go of his hand and made my own L for the moon to sit in.

"Where'd you learn that?" I was excited to show the trick to Bobby and Janet. Mae and my father would like it as well.

"I read it somewhere."

I had to laugh. I was still getting a handle on how smart he was, and how much he read. Leonard wasn't even a senior, but he'd already taken three classes at the junior college because he kept testing out of what the high school offered. I did all right in school, but not like that.

He took my hand again, and I started humming "Blue Moon."

"I love that song," he said. "I feel like I could have written it."

I didn't understand. "It's a sad song," I said. "He's standing alone, without a dream in his heart. Even the moon is blue."

Leonard shook his head. "But when he looks again, it's turned to gold." He turned to me, looking shy again, like the first time we talked in the courtyard. He took a breath, held it. "Because he's fallen in love."

Oh, that moment. I wanted to grab hold of the night, the stars above us, the waning moon, all of it, and stuff it down into my pocket to keep. Someone could have tapped me on the shoulder and said, *Excuse me, miss? Nora Chesnow? You can exchange this night for a million dollars*, and I would have said, *Keep your money!* I felt like my heart would explode, joy bursting out everywhere. When I told him I, too, was in love, he gave me such a smile, and even his mournful eye looked happy. For a while, all we could do was stand there looking at each other, still aching, still knowing we'd be like a key and lock, but also grateful for what we'd already found, and had.

A few nights after the dance, when his mother and I were alone in her kitchen, she touched my shoulder and whispered, "You've been so good for him." Even as she smiled at me, I could tell she was listening for his footsteps. She wouldn't have wanted him to feel embarrassed.

"He's been plenty good for me," I whispered, also watching the doorway. When he did come in, I could see he guessed we'd been talking about him, though he seemed more amused than anything. What I always noticed, watching Leonard with his mother, was that he didn't just love his mother—he liked her, too. When she said something funny, he laughed. When she was being serious, he listened. Even when they argued, there was real affection between them. That winter, a local theater put on *Our Town*, and Leonard's mother played the part of Mrs. Soames. When she was in rehearsals, she told us it was just a little part. But Leonard told her no, Mrs. Soames had real significance, as she was the one who pointed out that life was both awful and wonderful.

"That's the most important line in the play!" Leonard thumped his hand on the counter, almost knocking over his water glass. "Mom, come on. That's what the whole play is about!"

"Well," she said. "That and death." But you could see she liked his point.

He went to see the play twice—once with his father, on opening night, and a second time with me. Before the curtain went up, Leonard told me, "Get ready. She's so good you might not recognize her," and he was partly right. I mean, his mother wasn't wearing a wig or anything. But I'd never seen the play, and it turned out Mrs. Soames was the town gossip, always getting in other people's business. Mrs. Lifton, playing this woman, seemed like a different person. Onstage, there was nothing elegant about her. You'd never guess she'd lived in France, or even that she was as pretty as she was. When she moved across the stage, she had Mrs. Soames sort of strutting in a way that made people laugh. When she said her big line, it sounded natural, not like words she'd memorized from a script. The same couldn't be said of the other actors, I'm afraid, though I could see they were all trying.

When the play was over, I gave her the flowers I'd brought and told her how much I admired her talent.

"You're sweet, Nora." She sniffed the flowers and squeezed my hand.

"No," I said. "I'm a terrible liar. Ask anyone. If I was just being sweet, you'd know."

She laughed, leaned down to kiss my cheek, and thanked me again for the flowers.

As comfortable as I felt around her, just being myself, Leonard's father was a different story. He worked late most nights, and on weekends, too, so I didn't see him much. When I did see him, he would make polite conversation with me, but not for long, and even when I asked him questions about the hospital, I always got the feeling he wished I weren't there. Mr. Lifton had a low, quiet voice, excellent manners, and, at least when he was talking to me, a smile that didn't reach his eyes. After a while, whenever he entered a room or took his seat at the dinner table, I'd hear Dracula music in my head. It wasn't anything he said.

It was more the way he looked at me, like he and I were old enemies, which didn't make any sense. I didn't know him, and he didn't know me.

For a while, I thought maybe he was just a serious person, not friendly in general. Or maybe he was just too tired at the end of a workday at the hospital to want a dinner guest at the table. But then one evening Leonard and I were downtown with Dale, and we bumped into Leonard's parents. Mrs. Lifton looked even more sophisticated than usual, wearing lipstick and a dress that cinched in at her waist. She greeted all of us, but her husband saved his friendliness for Dale, asking him about his parents and his older brother, who was already away at college in Rhode Island. He might not have been aware of the difference in his manner when he spoke to me and when he spoke to Dale. But I noticed it.

That evening, when Leonard was driving me home, I asked him why his father never seemed particularly happy to see me. He didn't answer, or say anything at all, and I knew it was something he didn't want to say. Leonard put his arm around my shoulder, steering with one hand, and we were both quiet the rest of the way. When he parked in front of my house, I saw my father in the picture window, wearing his old bathrobe. My window was rolled down, and I scooted over to it and gave a little wave. My father waved back, then made a show of checking his watch.

"You should go in," Leonard said. When I didn't move, he sighed and cut the engine.

I turned to face Leonard. "Just tell me."

The knee started to bob. "He doesn't want me entangled."

"Entangled?"

"That was his word. It's not personal, Nora. Nothing against you." He paused. "He doesn't want anything to stop me from going away to school."

I had to laugh. "That's almost two years away," I said. I already understood Leonard would go to college, likely far away, like Dale's brother. Smart as he was, he was already studying for the SAT. He said he had to do well on it, very well, if he wanted to get into an Ivy.

"I don't want to keep you from college," I said. "I don't want to keep you from anything."

He smiled. "I know that. And my mom loves you. She thinks you're great. She doesn't like to argue with him. But she sticks up for you in little ways."

That made me feel better, knowing his mother was on my side. It seemed to me that in time, I would win over his father as well. I was sure my own father was still watching the back of my head, but I slipped off my sandal, stretched out my leg, and hooked my foot under Leonard's knee.

"Entangled," I said, making my voice deep, and we both laughed. But I felt the heaviness of sadness to come. It wasn't really almost two years until he would go. It was more like a year and a half. "Well, I'm glad he assumes we'll still be together," I said. I was trying to look on the bright side. But

Leonard looked at me with pity. I sat up straight and wriggled my foot back into my sandal.

"He knows I'm head over heels," he said.

I checked my watch again. I had forty-five seconds until curfew. It took fifteen to get from the car to the door. I wanted to ask what he wasn't telling me, but I could see he wished I wouldn't. I kissed him good night and got out.

My stepmother had told me that after she got the bad news about her first husband, she worked in a cafeteria by an artillery factory. After Janet was born, Mae's mother looked after Janet at night, and Mae got a job at a bar. So she'd been around a lot of different kinds of people, and she knew about things I didn't, things my friends didn't know either. For example, the summer after tenth grade, Roberta's boyfriend started calling her his little herring, like instead of calling her honey or baby, he'd say, "Hello, my little herring," and we all thought it was sweet but a little strange, as a herring didn't seem like a particularly nice thing to be called. Also, if his friends heard, they'd laugh. When this boy broke things off with Roberta, I mentioned the nickname to Mae. She rolled her eyes and said he hadn't been calling her a fish. He was saying she was like a Herring safe, meaning hard to crack.

Whenever I made this sort of inquiry to Mae, I tried to be careful, specifically regarding who was around to hear. The year I started seeing Leonard, Janet was only six and Bobby was twelve. But the concerns of Leonard's father didn't strike me as anything crude, and I mentioned them to Mae the following Sunday afternoon as she and I sat on the back steps, watching Janet do cartwheels. When I used the word *entangled*, she told Janet she could go inside and get a cookie. As soon as Janet was out of earshot, Mae waved her smoke away from my face and leaned close. "He thinks you'll get pregnant," she said.

I about fell off the steps. I don't think I'd ever heard that word spoken aloud. And this was in regard to me.

"I know that type." She took a drag off her cigarette and slapped at a mosquito. "The father, I mean. They think every girl is after their wallet." She shook her head. "If your daddy knew he insulted you like that, he'd blow his top. I like Leonard. You know I do. But I hope I never meet that father."

I was too embarrassed to speak. I had no intention of getting pregnant, but I wasn't as virtuous as Mae and my father believed. It seemed Mr. Lifton somehow knew—maybe by just looking at me—that I was no Herring safe, and that it was his son, not me, that kept us on the straight and narrow.

"Thank you for explaining," I managed.

"Explaining what?" Janet asked. She skipped down the steps, still chewing at least half of a cookie. Her hair was the exact same shade of red as her mother's, and she had Mae's eyes as well. But her nose was longer and thinner. I imagined it was the nose of her dead father, and whenever I noticed it, I thought of him, and how sad it was that he'd never known his child.

Mae shook her head. "Honey. Swallow your food before you move or say another word."

Janet did as told, then asked again what we'd been discussing. She hated getting left out.

Mae smashed her cigarette tip against the concrete. "Nora wanted to know how many pecks were in a bushel. Four, in case you were wondering."

She said this so coolly that Janet almost didn't think to ask why I'd need to know such a thing. But when she did, she looked at me.

"School," I tried. "Homework question."

Janet watched me with narrowed eyes. She put her little hands where she didn't yet have hips. "Tell me the truth," she said.

I was still rattled by what Mae had said about Mr. Lifton. And now I felt pathetic for my attempt at a lie. Nothing had changed in that department. I fooled no one, not even a child.

4.

For the Harvest Bash dance of my junior year, Leonard and I went as Phyllis and Walter from *Double Indemnity.* He had an old suit jacket so worn out that his mother said he could cut a bullet hole in the shoulder, and she remembered from her theater days how to mix red poster paint, corn syrup, and cocoa powder to make a bloodstain. Bobby let him borrow his old cap gun. I was just going to wear a white dress I already had, but Mrs. Lifton showed me an old gown of hers that looked remarkably like Phyllis's jumpsuit, and she said she'd be happy to take up the hem so I could dance in it. To me, the dress looked and felt like silk, but Leonard's mother said it was just rayon from during the war, and she'd never wear it again. So I only had to spend money on the wig, and that didn't cost much. In the movie, Phyllis's wig looked like she bought it at a drugstore, so that's where I bought mine.

I didn't tell my father or Mae who we were trying to be until the night of the dance; I wanted to see if they could guess. When Leonard picked me up, my father was the one who got it right away, and he laughed so hard he had to sit down. Mae got out her little Brownie camera and took pictures—some of just me and Leonard, and some with Bobby and Janet and even my father, all of us clowning with the cap gun. Even with the cheap wig, I felt so glamorous, wearing that silky dress. I couldn't wait to get to the dance.

We never made it inside. At the school parking lot, as soon as we got out of the car, somebody turned on bright headlights and started throwing eggs. I got hit in the eyes straightaway and saw nothing, just felt the sting of the shells on my bare arms. Leonard steered me back into the car right away, but there was yolk in my wig, yolk on the dress, yolk even in my mouth. I still couldn't see, but I locked my door, and Leonard got in on his side and locked his. He started the engine but said he'd been hit in the eyes as well, and he needed a minute before he could drive. I heard the yipping and laughter of our assailants, though that was soon drowned out by a revving engine.

Leonard reached over and felt for my shoulder. "Are you okay?"

I told him yes, meaning I was still alive. But my eyes burned, as did the skin of my arms. Our costumes were ruined. Our whole evening was ruined.

"I didn't see who it was," he said. "Did you?"

I told him no. I couldn't think of anyone who had it in for

either one of us, and I knew the attack might have been random. It was almost Halloween. For some people, that meant it was time to throw eggs.

"I'll take you home," Leonard said.

It was the only thing to do. But I knew that when I showed up at our door, covered in egg and bleeding, my father would be angry. Not at me, though that wouldn't matter. I'd be in for the night.

"Let me at least help you wash the car," I said. "I'm already all gunky. It doesn't matter."

We went to a service station where an attendant who felt sorry for us gave us rags and a bucket of soapy water. We both worked fast, with Leonard scrubbing one side of the car and me scrubbing the other. When we finished, we stood together, looking at it, and I felt a little better. No permanent damage. And there would be other dances. But Leonard seemed preoccupied.

"What is it?" I reached up and pulled some yolk from his hair.

"My parents are at the Liebermans' Halloween party. They always stay late." He checked his watch. "It's not even seven thirty."

I knew what he was suggesting. But I waited, needing time to think. I'd never once been to the Liftons' when his mother wasn't home. Leonard and I both understood that neither his parents nor mine would allow it. All the times I'd been there, I'd never even seen his room.

"Yo-kay!" I said. And he laughed.

His parents had left the front light on. Inside, the house was dark, quiet. We left our wet shoes in the entry. Leonard said we should both use the hallway shower, as his parents might notice if either of us used the shower off their room.

"You can go first," he said. He told me he'd put his robe outside the bathroom door, and I could put it on and then go back and find something from his mother's closet, something from way in the back that she wouldn't miss. We'd be gone before they got home, and he could return whatever I'd borrowed later.

It was a good plan. We should have followed it. But on the way to his house, I'd been thinking, and I'd hatched a plan of my own.

"We could shower together," I said. "I'll keep my underwear on."

He looked at the floor as if he were searching for something. He looked at the ceiling and rubbed his jaw. He knew he could trust me. And I trusted him completely. As far as I was concerned, there would be no consequence. This gift of an evening would be our secret, ours, and ours alone.

I don't think I ever learned the reason his parents came home from the party early. Because of the running water, we didn't hear the car in the drive, or their entrance into the house. I remember the sudden knock on the bathroom door, my heart stilling in my chest. Leonard put his finger to his lips, but I knew, even in that moment, it was too late for caution. My wet shoes were still by the door.

Leonard turned off the water.

"Leonard." His father's tone was as sharp as the knock. "Is Nora in there with you?"

I put my hands in front of my eyes like a fool, like a child. Leonard started to explain about the eggs, but his father interrupted.

"I'm not interested in any of that. Both of you get dressed and come out."

Leonard handed me a towel. I stepped onto the cold tile and started to dry off. "It'll be okay," Leonard whispered, but I knew that it would not be. His father knocked again, impatient, and I lifted the lid of the toilet because I felt sure I would throw up.

Leonard told him we didn't have dry clothes. There was a pause, and then his father said Leonard should put on a towel and go directly to his room. I should put on a towel, too, he said. Mrs. Lifton—I remember, he called her "Mrs. Lifton"—would be waiting for me in the hall.

She'd dressed as a witch for the party. When I opened the bathroom door, she was wearing a sleeveless black dress with a translucent cape, and she had green makeup on her face and neck.

"Mrs. Lifton," I said. "I'm so so—"

Her hand made a blade, slicing between us. “Don’t,” she said. She didn’t sound like herself. I’d never seen her angry. “I don’t want to hear it.”

She led me to her bedroom. She’d already laid out a white blouse and a purple skirt I’d never seen her wear. While I dressed, she went into her bathroom but left the door open, and I could hear her rustling about. She said nothing to me from the bathroom, and because of that, more than anything, I started to cry. The curtains over the sliding glass door were closed, and I thought of the little patio, and how I would never see it again. I would be banished from their beautiful home, like a dog who’d peed on the rug.

The purple skirt almost reached my ankles. When she saw I was dressed, she said she would drive me home, and she led me out the door and down the hall, past Leonard’s closed bedroom door. I didn’t see or hear him, and I didn’t see or hear his father. In the entry, I found my shoes where I’d slid them off. A witch’s hat sat on the floor beside them. A broom leaned against the wall.

In the car, I was sobbing, wretched, my wet hair dampening the shoulders of the borrowed blouse. She asked me for directions, and I told her we lived in Kenwood, not far from the school. At a stoplight, I again tried to apologize, but she only shook her head, staring ahead at the light. I continued crying, not as a plea for pity, but because I could not stop. At the next stoplight, she reached over and gave me a consoling pat, though still, she did not speak.

When she turned in to our street, it was already quiet, with most porch lights out. An unlit jack-o'-lantern grinned from our picture window. "It's that one," I whispered, and Mrs. Lifton parked. I turned to look at her. I could see, from the glow of a streetlight, that she'd missed a spot of green makeup by her ear.

"Are your parents home?"

"Yes ma'am," I said. My hope was to hurry in and get to the bathroom without anyone seeing my wet hair or the too-long skirt.

"Mrs. Lifton. Before I go in, I really want to tell you how sorry I am." Here, my voice did not falter. My sorrow was sincere.

She put her palm to her chest and took a deep breath in through her nose, exhaling quickly. Then she did it again.

"Ma'am? Are you okay?"

She glanced at me, breathing in again through her nose. "It's an exercise I used to do before going onstage, when I was anxious." She nodded up at my house. "This won't be pleasant for either of us."

I followed her gaze to the house. Until that moment, it really did not occur to me that she would interact with my parents at all. I'd been crying only because I was so humiliated, and so full of regret. Now terror gripped me. I didn't fear my father's wrath in a physical sense—he'd long stopped using his belt for punishment, and these days, he rarely even yelled. But I was certain that if he knew what Leonard's parents had come home to, he wouldn't love me anymore. He might say that he did, and that he was only disappointed. But that disappointment would never go away.

Even now, I know I was not wrong to think this.

"Mrs. Lifton," I said. "Please. Please just let me go in. Please don't talk to my parents."

She continued looking at our rented house, which had always looked cheerful to me. Now, seeing it through her eyes, the turquoise paint looked garish. Even Mae's roses appeared tinselly in the orange glow of the globe light by the door. My father planned to fix the railing along the front steps, but he hadn't gotten to it yet.

"I can't do that." She shook her head. She usually wore pearl earrings, small, but tonight her earrings were shaped like silver bats, one dangling from each earlobe by a little chain. "I have to tell them. And before I do, I have to ask you, Nora. Do you know that you might already be . . ." She looked at me, stricken. She couldn't say the word.

"I'm not," I said. I wanted to slither under the floor mat, under the car. I wanted to disappear. "I won't have a baby, is what I mean. If that's something you're worried ab—"

She slapped the steering wheel. "My God, Nora! Of course that's something we're worried about! And something your parents should be worried about. Something I hope you and Leonard thought about."

"I can't be, is what I'm saying." I didn't think I could get the words out. "Things didn't go that far. We didn't let things get that far, I mean. And we don't. We haven't. I know you're disappointed in me, Mrs. Lifton. But you don't have to worry about a baby. That's not what I want. Not at all."

I watched her take in my face, trying to decide if she believed me. After a moment, I could see she did.

"I still have to tell them," she said. "You're in over your head. If you were to end up in trouble, and your parents knew we hid this from them, we would be complicit. Leonard is our son, our responsibility. And he should not have taken advan—"

"It was my idea," I said.

She leaned back against her window, staring at me. To look at her, I could have been a cobra, coiled and baring fangs.

"I still have to tell them."

"Why?"

She turned to me, angry. "Because I told my husband I would. That's why. Believe me, I do not want to go in there, into your parents' home, and say this thing to them. Leonard is my son, and you were in our home. And do you know why it's me? Do you know why it's me and not Leonard's father who has to go in there? Do you know why he's not here?"

She waited for me to shake my head. I really had no idea.

"Because . . ." She smacked her hand against the steering wheel again, and then again and again as she spoke: "I . . . have . . . been . . . de . . . fend . . . ing . . . you. For I don't know how long, I've been telling John that he was wrong about you, that we didn't have to worry. And that took a lot. I like a tranquil home. I had a tranquil marriage. But I argued with him, over and over again, for you. And for Leonard. I told him he was wrong about you, that you were a nice girl, and good for Leonard." She was silent for several seconds, catching her breath. "Do you see the position I'm now in?"

"I am a nice girl!" It felt like the truth, but maybe it wasn't. There was perhaps something wrong with me, something monstrous indeed. Leonard's father had always known—he'd been able to see it.

She let me cry for a while, then cleared her throat.

"Okay," she said. "I'll make you a deal."

I lowered my hands. I wanted to hug her. I wanted to grab her hand and kiss it.

"Wait," she said. "On one condition. Listen to me. You need to promise you'll have nothing to do with Leonard. Nothing. Do you understand what I'm saying? Break things off completely. No telephone calls. Nothing. Not even at school."

She blurred before me. I shook my head.

"Okay," she said. "That's the only other way." She started to get out of the car.

"Wait!" I couldn't think. "For how long?"

"Permanently." She said this as if it were obvious. "Nora. Even if I take you at your word, and feel satisfied he's done you no harm, we obviously can't trust you or Leonard to use good judgment. Imagine the position we would be in if you ended up in a condition, and your father found out, too late, that we'd kept this from him. I'm risking a lot for you. Including my conscience. So if I hear about you so much as talking to Leonard—tomorrow, next week, next month, next year—I'll have to tell your father why we can't allow it."

I looked back up at the house. Winged insects swirled around the globe light. My father, if he knew, would make the same restrictions. Leonard was lost to me either way.

"You need to promise," she said. "If you can't do that, and if you can't mean it, we should get this over with now. It's my responsibility to protect you, one way or another."

It was over, I thought. All that wonder, all that luck. When I was older, out of the house, I could bear my father knowing. But Leonard would already be gone. I turned back to Mrs. Lifton. It was my fault. I'd done it.

"We'll break things off," I said.

She shook her head. "No 'we,' Nora. You. You stay away, no matter what he says. I know my son. He can be intractable. And impulsive. I need to count on you."

"Okay," I said. I felt an actual pain in the center of my chest, radiating out.

"When I say nothing, Nora, I mean nothing. I don't care whose idea it is. If I hear of you two spending any time together, anywhere, believe me—I will immediately call your father and tell him about that little water party. You'll leave me no choice."

I turned to her. There was pity in her eyes, but they watched me closely.

"I'll stay away," I said. "I'll stay away from him. I promise."

My voice was steady, and I held her gaze. At the time, scared as I was, I believed I was telling the truth.

5.

My father assumed there had simply been a breakup, and because of my general despondency, he also assumed Leonard had done the breaking. Although he'd previously seemed to like Leonard, he now argued that he'd long ago guessed him a spoiled little fool. He told me this while leaning against the door frame of the room I shared with Janet. She'd left the door open, and he'd walked by while I was at my desk, doing homework and crying at the same time. He disappeared for a minute, then returned to offer me an orange, though usually we weren't allowed to eat in our rooms.

"I didn't say anything, honey, but everybody knows a '46 Plymouth is basically the '42 model with a new grille and bumpers." He set the orange at the edge of my desk. "I guess he likes to throw away money."

I understood he was trying his best to comfort me, because

he loved me, or he thought he did. I was certain that if he knew what the Liftons knew, he'd be just as disgusted with me. I thanked him for the orange and said the Plymouth had belonged to Leonard's father.

"Well," he said. "Then his father doesn't have a brain. That never bodes well for the son. You're the one with real smarts, Nora."

My friends rallied around me as well. I couldn't tell Irene or Roberta about the shower, and they, too, had reason to think Leonard had callously broken my heart: any smile I managed that November was brief and unconvincing, and if I saw him in the hallway, I'd turn and go the other way. Irene and Roberta soon grew vigilant, and they did their best to warn me of his approach. I was grateful, for I knew that his mother was friendly with some of his teachers, and I imagined her enlisting them as spies. This of course sounds paranoid to me now, but at the time, I reasoned she would only need to tell them about the shower, and they would agree I was bad news all around, and volunteer to help keep me away. I felt like a contagion, like a flea.

I even wondered, at times, if Mr. Lifton had been right, if Leonard would be better off without me. It seemed to me that Leonard himself might come to believe this as well. Perhaps he already had.

But the day before Thanksgiving break, I was crossing the junior courtyard when he stepped out from the arch of one of the bell towers, and he looked right at me, making sure I saw him before he ducked back inside. I waited until the warning bell rang, then went into the bell tower. He waved me over behind the stairway, where we were almost fully hidden from view. Still, when he tried to hug me, I stepped back.

"I can't stand this," he said. "I won't."

I told him he would have to. He asked how hard things had been for me at home, if I'd been yelled at, or worse. It was only then that I realized: He didn't know that his mother had taken mercy on me. When I told him the deal she and I had made, he leaned back against the bell tower's wall, glaring up at the underside of the stairs. A tiny lizard emerged from a hole near the steps, looked around, then disappeared back into the hole.

"That's interesting," he said. "She's not always so obedient, is she? I should tell him."

I looked at him, alarmed. "Do that if you want to hurt me, too."

He shook his head, and I knew he wouldn't. But I wanted him to understand.

"She took a risk for me, Leonard. She didn't have to do that."

He was unmoved. "She acts as if they're completely in line on this. Her spine disappears when he's around. It makes me sick." He scratched at his neck, agitated. "I can't stand living in that house anymore. You know what he said to me? He said I would thank them some day. He said I'd meet a nice Radcliffe girl, a Smith girl, and forget all about you. He's an idiot."

I said nothing. At the time, I didn't know what a Smith girl or a Radcliffe girl was. Even with Leonard before me, his voice shaking with anger, the fact that I didn't know seemed another mark against me.

"He doesn't care if I'm happy." He walked away from the stairway, pivoting near the bell tower's arch. "He's not interested in getting to know me. He doesn't know who or what I care about. He only cares about what school I get into. So he can brag about it."

I didn't know if it was true or not. I imagined the three of them at the dinner table, Leonard simmering. Or maybe shouting, and his father shouting back. She must blame me, I thought. She must wish I'd never darkened their door.

I expected Leonard to keep pacing, burning off his frustration, but he suddenly walked toward me. "There's a solution, you know. We could get married. We really could. We both only have to be sixteen. That's state law." He kept his eyes on mine and spoke rapidly, as if he had to make his case all in one breath. "And I'm seeing ads for construction workers everywhere. They would train me on the job, and it's good pay. You could get something, too. We could get a little place. We'd be fine."

The bell above us started to chime. I could picture what he was envisioning, the dream of it. That he wanted this with me—or even that he thought he did—made me heady with joy. But I was also thinking about his mother saying he could be impulsive. And here he was, ready to throw away everything he'd worked for, all that studying, to be with me now, because he couldn't wait. Or wouldn't. Part of me was taken by the romance of it, that he would do that for me.

But his mother had also been right in that, between the two of us, I was the one she could count on to think of consequences. Leonard thought he knew what he wanted, and what he was ready to give up. But he might come to regret the decision, and that would make a heavy burden for both of us. I might regret it as well. I'd never heard of a married girl finishing high school. My father had recently pointed out that I was already the most educated person in the family, probably even going back to grandparents and great-grandparents. My report cards left him both baffled and pleased. He said I must have gotten my love of school from my mother, who'd only dropped out because she had to go to work on account of family finances, and that she would be so proud of me, and envious. I felt fortunate, and beholden to fortune.

And so before the bell stopped chiming, I told Leonard no, not yet. He turned his head and studied me with his mournful eye.

"I'm just saying no for now." Hidden by the stairs, I grabbed both of his hands and held them. "Go to school, Leonard. Wherever you want. Do it for yourself. If you still love me at the end of it, I'll be here. I'll wait."

He didn't say anything to that. He wouldn't even look at me. No part of me thought that was the end of our conversation, but he pulled his hands out of mine and walked out into the courtyard. I stayed where I was, skipping class, which I'd never done in my life. I was too distraught to face anyone, for I interpreted his silence to mean that he hadn't really meant that proposal. He was just angry with his parents, wanting to hurt them, and so would not promise to wait for me.

The only good thing that happened that winter was that I got a weekend job shelving books at the public library, a Beaux Arts building painted pink with white trim. From the front lawn, it made me think of a strawberry petit four. Inside, big windows looked out onto Mirror Lake, and the high-ceilinged rooms were so quiet I could hear the floorboards creak under my feet.

I liked the focus the work required. When I slid a book back into its correct home, I imagined it joyfully recognizing its neighbors (*Hey y'all, I'm back!*). I checked out a new book every week. *The Sun Also Rises* was rarely available, and even when it was, I didn't so much as touch it. I didn't want the public librarians to think poorly of me.

I found plenty of other books to check out, though, and I read while I took my lunch breaks, usually sitting on a bench under the shade of the library's majestic, wide-limbed oak. One day, I happened to look up just as Mrs. Lifton's yellow convertible pulled into the library's parking lot. Before she even got out of the car, I'd packed up my uneaten sandwich, closed my book, and hidden myself behind the oak's trunk, though I kept watch as she crossed the asphalt and approached the library's steps. She had her hair pinned under her hat, and she wore dark sunglasses. But if I hadn't seen the car, I would have recognized her, so tall and graceful in her beige sandals, which were the same color as her hat. She held just one book, no purse, and she walked quickly. If I would have stayed quiet, she wouldn't have seen me. But my heart warmed at the sight of her, and before the scared part of me caught up with myself, I called out hello and said her name.

She stopped and turned. An enormous grasshopper landed by her sandal, startling her. "Oh!" she said, and laughed.

"It's nice to see you, ma'am." I managed a smile, but my voice came out shaky. "Everybody okay at your house?"

She didn't answer. But she came toward me, still wearing her sunglasses.

"How are you, Nora?"

"I'm okay," I said. She looked like him, or he looked like her. I felt tears forming, and I clenched my teeth. I couldn't expect her to console me. "I got a job here. Shelving. I'm on my lunch break."

"That's wonderful." She really did seem pleased. "You'll be seeing a lot of me. I'm here at least once a week."

I was surprised that she seemed fine with this. She pointed to the bench where I'd been sitting.

"Let's talk for a bit," she said.

I walked beside her, not knowing what to expect. Once we were sitting in the shade, she took off her glasses. A lone ibis picked its way through the library's lawn, and she pointed at it.

"They have a disapproving look, don't they? Because of their beaks, the way they curve. Whenever I see one, I always feel a little scolded." She paused, still watching the bird. "You asked how things are at our home. Well, I'll be honest with you, Nora. They're terrible. Terrible. It's Leonard's last year with us, and this time is so precious. And he's angry all the time. Angry with us both."

Her voice caught, and I could both hear and feel her unhappiness. I told her, again, that I was sorry.

"I know you are," she said. "And I appreciate that you've been holding up your end of our agreement."

Here, she turned to look at me. I had to look away, scared she somehow knew I'd talked with Leonard in the bell tower.

"I worry you think that I dislike you, Nora. I don't. I was disappointed in you, just as I was disappointed in Leonard." She leaned down and picked a blade of grass off her sandal. "But I was young once, believe it or not. I do understand. So I hope you understand that we're not keeping you apart as a punishment." Her voice faltered. "I hope Leonard understands that one day."

"We love each other," I said. I hoped for her to understand as well.

She dabbed at her eyes, still watching the ibis. "*These blazes, daughter, giving more light than heat.*"

What I heard, first, was the word *daughter*. Then I realized it must be a quote.

"What's that from, ma'am?"

"*Hamlet*," she said. "It wasn't my line. Polonius says it to Ophelia. Fatherly advice about young lust." She turned back to me. "I still feel uneasy that your own father doesn't know about . . ." She waved her hand. "What I want to say to you is that . . . when you start to see other boys, I hope you'll be more careful with yourself."

I shook my head, incredulous. As if she truly believed I might jump naked into a shower with the next boy who took me to the movies. I'd known Mr. Lifton thought little of me. But I saw now that she, too, had no idea what Leonard meant to me, or how I was suffering, still.

"But you're going to have to keep moving forward, away from Leonard. Because that's done." She turned and looked back at the library. "This is such a good place for you to work. To expand your horizons. As much as you can, for now. I hope you'll travel someday, and see other parts of the world."

With that, she stood. She looked as if she wanted to lean down and hug me. But she didn't. She just said goodbye and went up the library's steps. I took my sandwich back out, watching the ibis, who'd been joined by kin or friends with similar expressions of reproach.

I'd seen *Hamlet* by then. The movie starring Laurence Olivier had come out, and I'd gone to see it with Irene, in no small part because of Mrs. Lifton. What I remembered of Polonius was that he seemed to care about both of his children, but he loved his son more than his daughter.

I also remembered he liked to give out advice, usually well-intentioned. Though he himself was a bit of a fool.

6.

Saturday nights were date nights. I told my friends, and any boy who asked, that I had no interest in going on a date with anyone. Most Saturday nights, I babysat. I liked that after my charges went to bed, I had privacy I didn't have at home. Sometimes I just read, but often, I'd get out my drawing pad and sketch Leonard's face from memory. It was the only thing that eased the ache, and with practice, my sketches got better. By December, the week before Leonard turned eighteen, I finished a drawing of him that I was proud of, and it was small enough for me to tuck into a card. The morning of his birthday, I waited in a corner with a view of his locker. I planned to slip him the card as I passed.

He never showed up. I waited at lunch, too, but never saw

him. I found Dale, talking with two other boys in front of the auditorium. I asked if he knew if Leonard was sick at home.

He seemed surprised that I would ask.

"I would think you'd know more than I would." His voice had an edge to it. I waved him away from his friends, and though he did step away from them, he seemed begrudging.

"You know we broke up?" I whispered.

He nodded. "Now he's always busy brooding."

I guessed what he meant. Before we'd broken up, Leonard was always, or often, busy with me. We'd brought Dale along on plenty of outings; still, Leonard's quick change in availability must have been hard for Dale. They'd been friends since seventh grade.

"You know it's his birthday?" I asked.

After a moment's consideration, Dale agreed this was true. "I'll call him later," he said. "I'm sure he's fine, Nora. You can get the flu on your birthday."

But I had a bad feeling, and the feeling grew throughout the afternoon. When I got home, Mae and Janet were off somewhere, and of course my father was still at work. I found Bobby lying on the couch, listening to the radio. I offered him a quarter to call Leonard.

He squinted. "Why can't you call him?"

"Because I can't," I said, and nothing else. He knew very well that Leonard and I had broken up.

"What am I supposed to say?"

I told him if one of Leonard's parents answered, he should ask to speak to Leonard. If he was asked who was calling, he was to say it was Bobby from the junior swim team.

Bobby appeared offended. "Why junior swim team?"

"Because you're in seventh grade, and you sound like it. Listen, even when you get Leonard on the phone, just keep saying you're Bobby from junior swim team, wanting to wish him a happy birthday. He'll know it's you. But they've got two telephones, so one of his parents could be on the line."

"Jeez." Bobby rolled his eyes. "What's the big secret?"

I shook my head.

"Fifty cents," he said. I agreed, and he got up, very slowly. My brother was almost my height now, and though anyone who looked would have guessed we were siblings, he resembled our mother more than I did. He had her sharp, alert-looking eyes.

"Why do they have two telephones?"

"They just do." I wanted to pinch him. I turned off the radio and followed him into the kitchen, standing close as he dialed. I expected to hear Mrs. Lifton say *Good afternoon, Lifton residence*, in her way that almost sounded like singing. To my surprise, Leonard's father answered, his greeting clipped and sharp. Bobby made big eyes at me, but he pressed ahead, asking if he could please speak to Leonard. Mr. Lifton said Leonard wasn't taking calls. He didn't ask if he could take a message. He just hung up.

"Jeez Louise," Bobby said. "Somebody needs some manners."

When I tried to give him the quarters, he squeezed his nose to sound like an operator and said, "No connection. Your payment will be returned," then went back to the living room and turned the radio on. I stayed in the kitchen, staring at the telephone, as if it could explain.

The next morning, I got to school early and again waited by Leonard's locker. But it was Dale who tapped me on the shoulder. He told me that at lunch, Leonard would meet me behind Triplett's, the drive-in across the street.

"Why?" I asked. "What's going on?"

Dale held up his palms. "I'll let him tell you. You won't believe it."

"Just tell me."

He shook his head, walking away. "You won't believe it!" he yelled. His long legs had moved him halfway down the hall when he looked back over his shoulder. "You won't! He's lost his mind!"

At that point, I guessed what had happened, or I thought I did. The only thing that made sense was that Leonard had gone along with his original plan of dropping out of school. Maybe he'd already gotten a job in construction, or he'd started training. Of course that would make his father angry. I was angry, too. Now he was asking me to head over to Triplett's and meet him in broad daylight, when he knew what I'd promised his mother, and what would happen if she learned we'd been talking.

But when the lunch bell rang, out I went, dashing across Fifth Avenue North. Triplett's was always busy at lunch, a car parked in every space, the carhops hustling. I kept my head down, glad to duck behind the building, where it was quieter, though the air smelled like cooking grease, and the dumpster swarmed with flies. Leonard sat alone at a picnic table hidden from the street. He stood and opened his arms to me. I glared and shook my head.

"You dropped out?" I asked.

He put his arms down. It was a cool day, overcast. At the edge of the pavement, the withered leaves of a Pindo palm rustled in the breeze.

"I did," he said. And still I wanted to go to him. He was wearing his green jacket, which I once wore home after swimming. After Janet fell asleep, I'd gotten it out of my schoolbag and slept with it beside me.

"Sit down with me." He gestured to the table. "I ordered you a burger. No pickles."

"Drop back in, Leonard. Your parents already hate me enough."

He gave me a look that suggested I didn't know the half of it. "Please sit with me, Nora. I need to tell you something. You're going to get upset, but it'll be okay. Just hear me out."

I told him I was already upset. I was cold, too. "Where's your car?"

"I'll get to that. You want my jacket?" He started to take it off.

I told him I didn't. But I went over and sat at the table. He sat beside me, one knee bouncing. I thought of the principal in sixth grade, coming to get me out of Mr. Pile's class.

"Just tell me." I reached over to still his knee.

"I joined the army."

I removed my hand. It wasn't the kind of joke he would make.

"Yeah." He laughed a little, smoothing back his hair. "I went down on my birthday and signed up. The recruiter was happy to have me." He took in my expression. "Let me explain, okay? I thought about—"

"You can undo that," I said.

"I signed a contract."

"It's just been a day," I said. "You can undo it."

My teeth started to chatter. He took off his jacket and put it over my shoulders. It was cotton, unlined, but it still carried his warmth.

"Listen," he said. "This is the best way for us. And it's the best way for me. Just for me, Nora. I can't tell you how good it felt when I told him I'd done it. The look on his face. We both knew it. He doesn't own me, not anymore."

"That's right," I said. "Now the army does. Leonard, undo it."

"It's three years," he said. "A three-year enlistment, and then I'll be done. Then I can pay for school myself. I won't have to answer to him for anything. But if I go up to school, that's four years without you. And the clock wouldn't even start until next fall. So really that's four and a half. With the army, the clock starts ticking as soon as I'm in basic."

"When's that?"

"Next month."

"Where?"

He reached under the jacket to find my hand. "Kentucky. Fort Knox."

"Undo it."

A gull circled over the dumpster, then landed on the edge of the picnic table. There it stayed, inspecting us as we quarreled. Leonard asked what I had against the army. It would be the same as going off to college, he said. He'd just learn different things. I told him I had nothing against the army, but since I'd known him, he'd been talking about getting into a certain kind of school.

"You told me that," I said. "It wasn't just your father. You, Leonard. You wanted to go."

"Well," he said. "That's not what I want anymore." He shrugged when he said this, like it was just a little change of plans. "I don't want to live like a pool ball. Aimed and pushed by somebody else." He turned and squinted at the gull. "The secret to happiness is freedom," he said. "And the secret to freedom is courage."

I asked if he was quoting someone, and he nodded and said

the name of somebody Greek. That made me turn hard. I told him that for somebody so smart, who'd read so much and remembered so much, he was being awfully foolish. I told him what he'd done made no sense to me. If he waited just five months, he could at least graduate from high school, get his own place, and do whatever he wanted.

"Except see you," he said. "You'll still be living at home, scared of my mother, what she'll say. I might as well be serving my country. I might as well be anywhere. I'm done living under that roof."

The waitress came out with our tray. She started to comment on the weather, then took in our faces and went silent. She set the tray down and gave me a knowing look before she went back in.

"Will you eat something?" he asked.

I shook my head. Even with the jacket, I was cold. Something bad was going to happen to him. I knew it.

"Leonard," I said. "There's no reason to lock yourself into something. A year from now you might decide—"

He stood up so quickly that I stopped talking. He put his hands behind his neck and walked to the palm tree. I could see, under his thin shirt, the tense muscles of his back. But when he turned around, his face was calm.

"That's just it," he said. "I want a lock. You don't want to get married now? Okay. Fine. I accept that. But I'm committing. I'm committing right now. And if you change your mind about me, I won't like it, but you won't have to feel bad because I'm making this decision for me. I want something I can't undo. That's what I need right now. I'm so sick of him telling me how grateful I'll be, how he thinks he knows me, knows everything. He doesn't."

Intractable, I thought. That was another thing his mother said.

"What did your mother say?"

He didn't answer.

"What did she say?"

"That I've changed. She said you changed me. She didn't mean it in a good way. But it is in a good way, Nora. I needed to change."

"Did she cry?"

His mouth tightened. I could see he didn't like to think of it. But I made myself picture Mrs. Lifton in tears, standing in her bright, pretty kitchen as her husband and son threatened and yelled.

"Where's your car?"

He sat beside me again. "He took the keys back. I don't care."

"How'd you get here?"

"Walked." He turned back to the tray. "Why don't you eat something?"

"How will you get to Kentucky?"

"The bus."

"I'm not hungry." I stood and started to take off the jacket. He shook his head, refusing it. I was glad. I wanted to keep of him what I could.

"Nora . . ."

"Good luck." I just started walking. I didn't even turn around. I didn't kiss him goodbye or tell him that I loved him. I believed, incorrectly, my hardness might still change his mind.

7.

My history book had a map of the United States in the back, and though it did not note the location of Fort Knox, I knew it was close to Louisville. Every morning, I opened my book to the map and moved my fingertip around that part of Kentucky, sending good wishes. I'd written to Leonard that I regretted how mean I'd been to him on that cold day at Triplett's. But I had no idea if my letters reached him. After a month, and then two, no letter came back for me.

My friends did their best to cheer me up, and I did my best to be cheered. Irene had joined the girls' basketball team, and Roberta and I went to her games. As the weather warmed and the days grew longer, I found I could finish my shift at the library and get to Spa Beach before sunset. Or a big group of us would meet out on the pier, eating salty fries and watching the waterskiing teams race by in pyramids, sometimes three rows high. Through all of this, the ache in my chest remained.

Mae liked my friends, and if I had them over, she did her best to keep Janet busy and out of the bedroom we shared. Usually, it was just Irene and Roberta who came over, but one rainy Sunday in March, our friend Marjorie came, too, and she brought along a *Seventeen* magazine to show us a quiz she'd taken: "Do You Know the Score for the Job of an Airline Hostess?" Marjorie had gotten eleven out of eleven, and she told us we could each take the quiz if we wanted, or she could save us some time and just tell us the job qualifications, which she then counted off on one hand: between five foot two and five foot seven; single; with good health and eyesight; and attractive in appearance and personality.

We were all sitting on the floor between my bed and Janet's. Each of us looked at the other three.

"I'm not single," Irene said.

Marjorie waved this off. "They just mean you can't be married. And if you're a high school graduate, you can make two hundred dollars a month." She bobbed her eyebrows. "While meeting pilots."

Roberta crawled past me to the record player so she could reset the needle. She'd bought an album of flamenco music that afternoon, and it was all she wanted to hear. "No thank you," she said. "My cousin's friend was an airline hostess, and she said a baby once threw up on her, and once a month, she had to kneel so her supervisor could check her roots. It's a rule you can't dye your hair."

Marjorie pointed out that none of us dyed our hair, and Roberta said it was the kneeling she found offensive. But I asked to see the magazine. I'd never been on an airplane, and I cleared five foot two by a hair. Part of me thought it would be exciting to fly all around the world, not to mention making so much money. But even when I was taking the quiz, and doing okay on it, I knew that even if I never heard from Leonard again, I didn't want to be an air hostess. I wanted to stay close to my family. It wasn't that I was fearful of new people or new places. I think that because I'd lost my mother so suddenly, I was always aware that another loss like that was possible. And even if nobody died, if I were far away, I'd miss everyone.

Also, I didn't care about meeting any pilots. I missed Leonard. I lowered my head and tried to focus on the flamenco record. It was then that I heard the stutter and glide of roller skates out in the hall. I looked up as the door opened a few inches. One of Janet's eyes peeked in.

"You've grown, sweetie," Roberta teased, as the skates made Janet look taller. "What are you, seven now? And already taller than Nora."

"Ha ha," I said, and motioned for Janet to roll in. She was supposed to stay out of the room for another hour, but unless we were talking about something private, nobody minded her. To my surprise, she stayed where she was. She opened the door a little wider, blinked at me hard, then did it again.

"Is the music too loud? Did your mom say to turn it down?"

She shook her head. I excused myself and stepped out into the hallway. She motioned for me to lean close, and when I did, she used a hand that smelled of peanut butter to push my chin to the side. She used her other hand to cup my ear, and I felt the heat of her breath on my cheek.

"You got a letter." She rolled back on the skates, but caught herself, and again drew close to whisper. "You got a letter from Leonard."

"Where?" I asked. "Honey. Where's the letter?"

"Mom has it. Don't tell her I told you."

I kissed her forehead and stepped past her to the kitchen, where I found Mae on her knees, scrubbing the inside of the oven.

"Excuse me," I said. "Did the mail come today?"

I'd spoken quietly. My father and Bobby were on the other side of the wall, listening to a ball game. But Mae must have heard the mad in my voice, because the scrubbing inside the oven stopped. She yelled for Janet, and we both heard the skates roll into the bathroom, and then the door slam shut.

"Mae? Could I have my letter please?"

She stood, wiping her hands on her apron. The armpits of her housedress were stained with sweat, and she had a streak of soot on her cheek. I knew my stepmother loved me. She'd been in the kitchen working while I lounged with my friends. But at that moment, I didn't care.

"Settle down," she said. "It just came this morning. I was going to give it to you as soon as your friends left." She climbed the step stool and retrieved an envelope from the top of the refrigerator. "You seemed like you were enjoying yourself. I'd hate for you-know-who to ruin it."

I could see Leonard's writing from where I stood. I reached for the envelope, but Mae held it high above us both.

"I'm going to say something to you first." She kept her eyes on mine. "You were pretty torn up when he ended things. It seems to me you're finally starting to be your old self again. And I just want to say, from experience, that you can't trust anything a man says when he's got a bunk bed and a locker and not much else. They get lonely, Nora. They'll say anything."

"Yes, ma'am." I held out my palm.

She handed me the envelope. "Why did he join the army anyway? Wasn't he going off to college?"

"I guess he changed his mind." I turned and carried the envelope into the hallway, where I could hear the flamenco record coming from my room, and the ball game from the other side of the house.

Dear Nora,

I hope you aren't still too mad to read this. I'll get right to it: I have ten days leave in late April. My parents believe I'll get in on the 23rd, but I'll actually get into Tampa late on the 21st, a Friday. I'm going to spend the weekend in Bradenton, just across the bay. My parents don't know anyone there. They've never even been there, and neither have I.

I understand what you would be risking. But I would very much like you to take the ferry to Bradenton and meet me on Saturday morning. It leaves from Pinellas Point on the half hour. I'll wait by the dock all morning.

Love,
Leonard

When I looked up, I saw Mae leaning on the kitchen doorway, watching me. I put the letter back in the envelope.

"You're right," I said, smooth as soap. "He's just lonely." I managed a rueful smile.

Before I returned to my room, I folded the envelope and pushed it deep in my back pocket. I would not mention it, or our plans, even to my friends.

I told Mae that Roberta had no date that Saturday and wanted me to stay over. I'd carefully chosen the moment—my stepmother was preoccupied with making a grocery list while Bobby and Janet were making unbidden suggestions. When Mae asked them why they couldn't be more like me, meaning not always pestering her to buy every sugary item in the store,

Janet pointed out that I was old enough to have my own job and buy what I wanted myself.

"That's true." Mae looked up at me. "But if they really talk me into getting those dadgum Oreos, I'm giving some to you and Roberta both."

I was amazed. I could apparently lie with real competency, now that I was properly motivated. But I hated having to lie to Mae again. I was also breaking my promise to Leonard's mother, while she'd held up her end of our deal.

But when the big morning finally came, and I got on the ferry, all I felt was impatience. The sky was cloudless, and the water glinted in the sunlight. We were halfway across the bay when someone spotted a dolphin, and then a whole pod of them, racing alongside us. The woman seated next to me yawned and said, "That and a nickel will get you a Coke," but I went out to the deck to get a better look. At school, I'd just learned the word *portent*, and this seemed to me a good one. I did lament forgetting a hairbrush. The night before, I'd slept with my hair in rollers, and by the time we docked, my curls were gone, whipped out by the wind.

We hadn't even docked when I saw Leonard. He was standing in the crowd of people behind a metal chain. He wore a straw fedora I'd never seen and a green-checkered shirt I knew well. When a ferry worker lowered the chain, most of the crowd moved toward the water. Leonard stayed where he was, his hands in his pockets. Under the fedora's brim, his face was serious and still. Even after I waved, he didn't see me. I started to wave again, then stopped. Soon enough, I would be beside him, our time together already slipping away. For now, it was all ahead of us. I wanted to seal these last seconds in my mind: the gasoline-scented breeze on my cheek, and the way he stood so straight, and looked so hopeful, waiting for me.

But once I was off the ferry, I didn't want to wait anymore. I slipped past other passengers and ran up the dock, the strutting gulls in my path taking flight. Leonard saw me just as I reached him, and he moved toward me so quickly that we collided more than embraced, the impact knocking off his fedora. He lifted me and spun me as if we were back in the gym, and I pressed both hands against his head, shorn and smooth. He smelled different, like new soap, and I could feel the drumbeat of his heart. Someone picked up the fedora for him, and he thanked them without letting me go. When he did put me down, he put the fedora back on, then held both my hands in his.

"What's with the hat?" I asked.

He laughed. "The haircut made my ears grow."

I thought the haircut looked good on him, and I told him so. He'd only been away a few months, but he looked older, in a good way. The angles of his face were more pronounced.

"Are you hungry?"

I nodded, still taking him in, the gold of his skin, the hollow of his neck. He reached for my bag, looping it over his shoulder. He took my hand as we walked up to the road, to where the taxicabs waited. Just getting into one felt thrilling. I'd never been in a taxi, or in a town where my family wasn't. The driver asked where we were from, and Leonard said Kentucky. They went on to make easy conversation while I stayed silent, my gaze on the meter, alarmed by how quickly the numbers increased. Leonard seemed relaxed, his arm around me, his hand warm on my shoulder. I looked out the window as we passed little houses and fruit stands. He's with you now, I told myself. Don't think about later.

Bradenton's downtown was smaller than St. Pete's, but we found a diner just opened for lunch. When we walked in, "'A' You're Adorable" was playing on the jukebox. The lone waitress, smoking behind the counter, pointed to a cluster of balloons tied to a chair.

"If you order a banana split," she said, "you get to pop a balloon to find out a price—anywhere from full price to only a nickel."

"What do you think?" Leonard asked. "I'm feeling lucky." He had his hand at my waist, warm and addling my brain. I told him I'd be fine starting with dessert if we could share it. The waitress handed him a sewing needle, and Leonard said I should choose the balloon. When he popped it, we all three jumped, then laughed. The little ticket that fluttered to the floor read FULL PRICE.

"I'll give you extra whip cream," the waitress said. She put out her cigarette and headed to the kitchen. "And you can set anywhere you like."

We chose a high-backed booth by the jukebox, now playing a Glenn Miller song.

"How's school?" he asked.

"The same," I said. "Tell me about Fort Knox."

"Family okay?"

"Everyone's fine," I said. "Tell me."

Under the table, he put his ankles around mine. I closed my eyes, just wanting to feel it, the press of his skin against mine. When I opened my eyes, we were both silent, staring. The waitress yelled something to the cook, maybe wanting to remind us of her presence. I leaned forward.

"You don't have to say if you regret it. I just want to hear how it was."

He nodded. "In hindsight"—he looked at the table—"if I didn't want to be told what to do anymore, the army probably wasn't the best choice."

I felt no satisfaction in this. I told him I wanted details. He said the first week was the hardest, and through most of it, he was sure he'd made a mistake. He'd heard about drill instructors, and thought he knew what to expect, but he'd had no idea. Even in the second week, and the third, and the fourth, he was stunned by fatigue, and the constant screaming, the threats and the insults. He said that was why he didn't write to me. He didn't feel he could complain to me, because I'd tried to stop him.

"You could've complained," I said.

"Well. Now that I'm on the other side of it . . ." He looked at me with trepidation. "I don't want to make you mad again."

"You won't," I said. What was done was done.

He went on to say he really had learned things, just as he'd intended. Mostly to follow orders, and quickly. But he could also disassemble, clean, and reassemble an M1 rifle with his eyes closed. And shoot one well enough. He said a lot of recruits came from the country, and they'd grown up shooting squirrels and deer. He was fumbling at first, getting heat for how clumsy he was with a gun. But he learned. He said he'd also learned to dig a foxhole, which was harder than he'd predicted, especially when the ground was cold.

At this, his face brightened. "It snowed up there. I hadn't seen snow in years. I forgot how beautiful it can look, how it softens everything." He squinted. "Why're you looking at me like that?"

It was for every reason. I wanted to reach across the table, pull the bristly top of his head toward me, and kiss it. The bell on the door chimed, and a woman came in with several young children. They made their way to the balloons.

"I had no idea if you'd come today," he said. "I thought, 'well, if she's still angry, I guess I'll just go back to the hotel and want to die.' But then there you were, on the ferry. You came." He leaned across the table. "What's in the bag?"

I glanced down at its zippered top. "Things," I said. "Things are in it."

"Like overnight things?"

I met his gaze. Someone popped a balloon, and I flinched again. He didn't.

"I don't want to presume," I said.

"You should presume." He kept his eyes on mine. The waitress came over with our water glasses. I felt dizzy, everything in me humming. I didn't trust myself to speak until she left.

"Well," I said. "There's also a present for you in my bag. If you're interested."

He said he was. I unzipped the bag, took out the little velveteen box, and slid it across the table.

"It's not a ring," I said, and tried to laugh, but I was nervous. I'd gone to the Buy-and-Sell downtown, not just to stretch a dollar, but because it was hard to imagine Mr. or Mrs. Lifton ever setting foot in such a place, with its musty smell and shelves full of chipped plates and glasses, and just one tiny window above a framed sign that read A SHIP REALLY IS LIKE A WOMAN—YOU CAN'T LET A GOOD PAINT JOB FOOL YOU! But when the old man behind the counter asked who I was shopping for, I still got scared and said I wanted something for my cousin in the navy.

The man said, "Oh, I have something perfect," and he reached into one of the cases and took out a silver bell the size of his thumbnail. He showed me where *Lucky Little Bell of San Michel* was engraved on the side, and he said this was a reference to the legend of a shepherd boy who got lost from his sheep, and who was full of despair of ever getting home until he heard bells ringing. The shepherd boy followed the ringing to a ravine, and there he saw San Michel, who we would call Saint Michael and who gave the shepherd boy a bell from around his neck, saying it would always lead him home. Which it did. The man at the Buy-and-Sell said that during the war, because of the legend, people on the island of Capri, off the coast of Italy, started selling little bells as good luck charms to American pilots who came to Capri on leave before flying back into danger. The man said good luck eventually brought them home, and that's how, every now and then, one of these little bells ended up at his shop in Florida.

I knew he could have been making all this up, just to sell me a trinket. But I'd decided to believe him. And it was wonderful, watching Leonard open the box, and seeing how pleased he was to lift the bell from the box by its chain. He squinted to read the engraved words, and I told him the story the man told me. If Leonard thought the story might be made up, he didn't show it. He said he liked it more than any gift he'd ever gotten.

"And clearly it works," he said. "I mean, somebody brought this one back."

I nodded, though I was sure he understood, as I did, that there might be plenty of lucky bells burned up or buried all over Europe.

He shook it by his ear. "It really rings." He turned it over. "It's got a little clapper in it."

I sipped my water. "Where are they sending you?"

He brought up his knee so he could loop the bell to the shoelace of one of his high-tops. "I'll switch it to my boots later," he said.

"Leonard." I felt the first flutter of worry. "Tell me where."

He didn't answer. The waitress set down our banana split,

which appeared at least half whipped cream. She made small talk until she saw we didn't want it, and again left us to ourselves. Leonard nudged the banana split toward me, but I shook my head. He picked up his spoon and poked at the whipped cream, then set the spoon back down.

"Japan," he said. "Kyushu."

I will tell you that right at that moment, sitting there in that diner, I knew something bad would happen to him. I felt it as a weight inside me, something hard and sharp in my chest.

"Come on," he said. He moved the banana split out of the way and reached for my arm. "It's not even three years anymore. I've already done fourteen weeks. But I know it's far."

"It's by the Soviet Union," I said. "That's why they're sending you there. Japan's by the Soviet Union."

"It's by a lot of places." He lifted my hand and kissed it. "I'll be fine."

"That could change," I said. "Three years. We could be at war with Russia any minute."

He said if we went to war with Russia, I'd be in as much danger here in Florida as he would be in Japan. Everything was different now, as the Russians had the bomb, too. I knew that was right. Or I'd heard that before. But my foreboding, what I felt, was for him.

"And I'll be on a big American base over there. Missing you, sure, but not in danger. I'll probably be doing some officer's laundry. Mopping floors, that kind of thing."

A fly landed on the whipped cream, already melting. Neither one of us waved it away. The jukebox went silent, then shuffled and clicked through its records.

"Do your parents know?"

"Not yet." He paused, rubbing his temples. "I'll tell them when I see them tomorrow."

They would hate me even more. But that wasn't what was needling me. I still felt it in my chest, that he would die. If he went to Japan, he would die.

"Leonard," I said. "Don't go. Let's just go somewhere together, me and you. We can get married." I hesitated, then made the decision. "I'll marry you right now if you stay."

The mournful eye took me in. "It's too late for that," he said.

"No, it isn't." It would only be too late if he went overseas. For now, he was with me, right in front of me.

"Nora," he said. "It's too late." He explained that at this point, it was Japan or jail. And anyway, he'd taken an oath. And still, I argued. When I started to cry, he handed me a napkin.

"We have right now," he said. "We have tonight." His voice was soothing and certain. "Come on, Nora. Come on. It won't be forever. I'll be fine."

But he wouldn't be. I knew it. And I would never love anyone as much. I knew this as well.

Later, when I was being interviewed, really, interrogated, about why I made the decision I made that night, I would be asked, again and again, how I could have been so foolish. Had I been drinking? No. Did he pressure me? He did not. There was only the headiness of our names on the register, *Mr. and Mrs. Williams*, and the key to the room, the lock on the door, and inside, a queen bed, a bathroom with a shower, and a view of the Manatee River on its way out to the sea. We left the heavy curtains open, and the sheer curtains rose and fell with the breeze for the rest of that day, and into the night.

I didn't say all that to the social worker, of course. I was already mortified. And anyway, she would have had none of it. Everything in her expression, her tone, said she'd heard it all before.

"Why take the risk?" she asked. "You knew he was going to leave."

"Because I loved him," I said. "Because I had a bad feeling, a terrible feeling."

"Nora," she said. "That doesn't make any sense. If you felt you were about to lose him, why would you want to get yourself into this predicament? Why would you shame your family?"

"Because it would be our only chance." I was crying. It didn't matter. She remained unmoved. "Because I wanted that with him."

"And? What else did you want?"

"Nothing," I said, and I told her more truth, or what I believed was the truth: I'd made not a decision, but a mistake. We thought we were being careful. I wanted to die, having to say these words to her, but I made myself. I told her the army sent him home with condoms, but not with clear instructions on how to use one. We didn't know he couldn't linger, I said. Linger. That was the word I managed.

"I don't believe you," she said. "You're a smart girl." She waited. "Maybe too smart."

She was good at her job, the social worker. Because I hadn't yet acknowledged, even to myself, that I remembered holding on to him, my calves wrapped around his, his quickened heartbeat against mine. He was stronger than I was, of course, but maybe not at that moment. Or maybe he really didn't know, or didn't feel, what was happening. I did. But I wasn't afraid, not of that. I feared only never getting to touch him again, never hearing him say my name. I feared him being lost—not just to me but to the world. So I held on.

The other fear would come later, when I was again alone.

8.

In those days, a letter from Japan, even from a military base, took weeks to reach an address in the States. So Leonard was already gone a month before I learned that he had, in fact, been put on laundry detail the day he arrived in Kyushu. He wrote that they were keeping him busy: When he wasn't folding shirts, he was doing drills or scrubbing something. In his next letter, he wrote that he'd been getting a little free time, and he enclosed two swans made of folded paper. He explained that this kind of folding was called origami, and though some Japanese people could make all kinds of things, he'd only learned to make a swan.

I was glad that he'd sent me two of these swans, as I kept one on my dresser, pristine, and every time I saw it, I thought, *Okay, see? He's fine.*

The other swan I unfolded and refolded until I figured out

how to make one myself. On the first day of summer vacation, I showed Janet how to do it, and one afternoon, we tore out the pages of a magazine and made dozens of swans to give to our friends. I was doing all this, making origami swans and working at the library, going to school and acting as if all was fine, even as I began to worry, and even as that worry turned to panic. I've already acknowledged, and will acknowledge again, that a part of me perhaps wanted to get pregnant that night in Bradenton. But once I was back in my regular life, that part of me was gone.

For a while, I was able to convince myself that I was just late, and that the worrying itself was causing the lateness to go on and on. But by early June, I could no longer tolerate the smell of a cooked egg, much less the taste of one. I'd always loved eggs, and when Mae noticed I was holding my breath and declining even my favorite omelet, she asked, "You're not expecting, are you?"

She was joking. As far as she knew, I hadn't been on a date since Leonard and I went to the Harvest Bash dressed as Phyllis and Walter. But when she saw my face, she apologized.

"I tease you because you're a good girl," she whispered. "I didn't mean to offend you. I can be a little crass." She gave me a pleading look. "Don't mention it to your dad, okay?"

I could only nod, dazed and full of dread. Mae could be crass, compared to my mother, and she only went to church on Christmas. But she, too, had standards. She'd once mentioned an unmarried pregnant girl from her hometown, and though there'd been sympathy in her voice when she said the boy who was responsible left town, she still called the forsaken girl trash. I'd asked, "Do you mean she was trash before it happened? Or because of it?" It was a serious question. But Mae had only waved her hand and said, "Oh you know, the whole family, trash."

And my father, of course, would never have mentioned such a girl in the first place.

I could tell no one of my terror. Irene and Roberta were kind girls, but they were truly good girls, smart and ambitious. What I'd done was outside the bounds of what was expected of us and everyone we knew.

The heat of previous summers in Florida had not particularly bothered me. But that summer, as the days grew warmer, I spent most nights awake and sweating, staring into the whirring box fan in the window, and wishing I was Janet, carefree and snoring softly in her bed. More than anything, I wanted to talk to Leonard. And yet I was too afraid to write out my fear in a letter. I knew that army mail was often censored, and it seemed possible that incoming mail might be read as well. I imagined an older man in uniform, mustached and officious, sending my letter back to my parents. This sounds paranoid, but I can say that I felt like a criminal, as if I'd committed an actual crime. I can see why I would feel this way. They still call out-of-wedlock births "illegitimate," and it's not the baby who did anything wrong.

On the first official day of summer, a radio announcer reminded us that the sun would soon start setting a little earlier every day. He meant it to be encouraging, that we were headed for milder temperatures. But I heard only the certainty of time passing, and the inevitability of what would unfold. I got out a sheet of stationery and wrote only eighteen words:

> *Leonard, I think I'm expecting. I'm never this late.*
> *I'm scared, and I don't know what to do.*

It seemed both unnecessary and unwise to sign this letter, or to write my address on the envelope, which I mailed from a postbox near the library. Once it disappeared into the slot, irretrievable, I felt as if I'd set a giant machine in motion. Leonard would have to tell his father, who would have the satisfaction of thinking he'd been right about me all along. Mrs. Lifton would know that the word of her future daughter-in-law meant nothing. She would know I was the kind of girl who promised one thing and did another, the kind of girl who could look right at you and lie.

But Leonard would help me, as soon as he knew. He would do whatever he could. Of this, I was certain.

Two days later, Mae found a pillowcase full of firecrackers under Bobby's bed. It turned out that for weeks, he'd been using his allowance to build a stockpile in preparation for the Fourth, even though we had a firm rule in our house against firecrackers, because, as Bobby put it, exactly one person in Mae's dingaling town had blown his thumb off in 1928. When Bobby came home from the pool to find that Mae had first soaked the entirety of his Texas Busters, Sputtering Devils, and Step-on Torpedoes in the kitchen sink, and then spread them on a towel in the front room, he said a curse word at regular volume, and my father looked at him as if he'd vomited on the rug. My brother had, by then, grown too big to be taken over a knee, but no one was surprised when he was sent to his room without dinner.

The weekend that followed was especially hot and humid, and early Saturday morning, Mae, my father, and Janet left for the beach. I told them I couldn't go because of work, which was true, though I was glad for the excuse. Bobby, still in the doghouse, was given a big pot of potatoes to peel, and our father said if he knew what was good for him, he'd have the task completed before their return.

"Don't you help him," my father told me. "He lied, and he cursed, and he needs to face the consequences. You, on the other hand, should kick back and rest." He looked at me, frowning. "You've been looking a little tired, honey. Are you feeling okay?"

I told him that kicking back and resting sounded nice. And indeed, when I got home from the library, I spent the rest of the afternoon lying in bed in front of the window fan, the shades pulled low to keep out the sun. There was still enough light that I could see the origami swan on my dresser, and I imagined the mailbag with my letter to Leonard in the hold of a ship, maybe already halfway across the ocean. It might be in Leonard's hands by early July. I didn't know if, or when, the army would let him come home.

There was one thing I did know. I wouldn't finish high school. I'd wanted to go to St. Pete's junior college and train to be a teacher. Leonard's father would never believe it, but it was the truth.

When I finally emerged from my room, the light in the kitchen window had softened to dusk, and crickets were singing at full volume. Bobby sat shirtless at the kitchen table, peeling the potatoes. I asked if he'd eaten, and he said he didn't have time to eat. He'd gotten a late start, and he wasn't sure when they'd be back. I almost admonished him, but he looked so downhearted I got out a knife and sat beside him.

"You never had to do this," he muttered. "You never get in trouble. You never do anything wrong."

Just you wait, I thought. But at that moment, I was okay, enjoying the work. One thing I'm good at is peeling potatoes—I'm quick, and I get all the skin. So as sour as Bobby was acting, I knew he was glad I was there beside him. I thought about how when he was little and sweet, a toddler with chubby knees, we'd sing "Swinging on a Star" together. I would sing the melody, and he'd do the *bum ba dee dum* backup. At the part that asked *Or would you rather be a fish?* he would pucker his lips and flap his little arms, and when I sang *Or would you rather be a pig?* he would oink, and doing this had been just about his favorite thing in the world. He was older now, and in a bad mood because of the potatoes. But when I started to sing "Swinging on a Star" as I peeled, he smiled a little, still peeling, and to my surprise, he soon joined in with the *bum ba dee dums*. When I got to the pig question, he oinked with his old gusto. That got us both laughing, and for a good minute, my troubles receded from my mind.

But then he nudged my knee and asked me to sing "Dream a Little Dream."

I hesitated, though I knew why he wanted me to sing it. Our mother loved this song. Most nights, she'd sing it to us as a lullaby. When she was too tired, she'd just say the one line from it before shutting off the light: *Sweet dreams till sunbeams find you.*

Bobby set down his knife. "Nora?"

"Just thinking about her," I said, wiping my cheeks. What I didn't say was that I hoped he'd been wrong that day we saw the manatee, when he said our mother was still with us. I didn't want her seeing me now. She would be so disappointed.

"You don't have to sing it," Bobby said. "I didn't mean to make you cry."

I told him I was fine, though it was clear that I wasn't. After a few moments, he patted my back, as if he was the one who was older.

Maybe a third of the potatoes remained unpeeled when we heard the car in the drive. Bobby kept frantically peeling, even as the screen door creaked open and Janet ran in wearing her sailor swimsuit and matching cap, excited to tell us about the dead fish they'd seen on the beach.

"It was bigger than I was!" She held her sunburned arms high over her head. "All bloated up like a balloon! The birds wouldn't leave it alone, and we could smell it in the air all day." She moved toward the table and stood on tiptoe to peer into the pot of potatoes. "Oh," she whispered, frowning at Bobby. "You were supposed to be done."

He gave her a tortured look. "Where are they?"

"Outside talking to Mr. Vitori." She tugged at her swimsuit strap. "There was an invasion. The communists did an invasion."

The knife stilled in my hand. "What invasion? Where?"

She appeared frightened by the question, or the intensity of my tone. I stood, patted her shoulder, and hurried to the front room. The screen door opened again, and Mae appeared, a towel around her neck.

"There was an invasion?"

"Well, hello to you, too." She wiped her feet and turned to the kitchen. "Janet, come on back to the bathroom now. You're tracking sand all over the house."

"Mae," I said. "Where was the invasion?"

"I forget. Far from here." She looked past me. "Janet! Don't make me tell you again."

I pushed open the screen door just as my father was coming up the steps, his forehead shiny with sweat.

"Where was the invasion?"

"Korea." He hung his keys on the hook and crouched in front of the radio. I held my breath as he turned the knob, dialing through static and piano music. He was breathing heavily, and his beach shirt smelled like sweat. "The North Koreans invaded the free south," he said. "Did it early, while everyone was sleeping. It's still morning there, and they're just steamrolling through."

He made a pummeling motion with his fist, and he didn't notice when I flinched. He wasn't being cruel. My father still believed Leonard had broken my heart the previous fall, and he'd taken to referring to him as "the idiot" if he referred to him at all.

"Will there be a war?" I asked. "Will we be in it?"

"I don't know," he said. "Nobody wants that. But if we let them take this, they'll just take more."

"It's by Japan," I said. I was talking to myself. "Korea is close to Japan."

My father held up his hand. He'd found the news, an announcer breathlessly reporting the NKPA capture of a coastal highway, and terrified South Koreans fleeing a city just forty miles from the fighting. I could hear Bobby still at work in the kitchen, the scrape of the knife, the peelings dropping into the bucket. Even in my panic, I understood he was hurrying to finish the potatoes, scared that my father would go into the kitchen and see that he'd started too late.

But my father and I both stayed by the radio, still and silent even during the commercial breaks. Through the front windows, I watched insects flutter in the glow of the light by the door. In Korea, and in Japan, it was late morning.

After a while, my father noticed my distress and put his hand on my shoulder.

"I know," he said. "God be with that city."

I had to look away, shamed by his assumption that I was thinking of the South Koreans fleeing for their lives. For I was like Bobby, trapped in my own fear, my own heart.

9.

Mae must have told my father that Leonard was stationed in Japan, and that we'd been corresponding. My father, bound by patriotism, stopped calling him "the idiot," and assured me he would be fine. By then, the 24th Infantry Division had been sent to Korea. I knew that meant Leonard.

"It's just a police action," my father said. "And Korea's a little country. They don't have anything to match our army. Trust me, sweetheart. He'll be back in Japan in a week."

I soon received a letter from Leonard, posted from Japan two days before the invasion. He'd written it when he was as oblivious to what lay ahead for him as he was to the content of my last letter, which of course hadn't yet reached him. He wanted to know how I'd done on a chemistry test I'd been studying for, and he told me that he'd joined a baseball team.

All the Japanese teams wanted to play against Americans, he wrote, so there was a game to play, or at least attend, whenever he was free. He'd been studying the Japanese language in a little book he read on the ship over, and when he tried to use it before a game with a Japanese team, the Japanese players had laughed at how bad he sounded. But one of them, the pitcher, did try to converse with him a bit, correcting his pronunciations. Later, this same Japanese pitcher struck him out.

I've been here just six weeks, he wrote. *And it feels like years. I try not to think about it, how long it will be until I see you.*

Mae said of course my letters would still reach him, even in Korea. Everybody knew soldiers liked mail, and the army would make sure he got it. It just might take more time, she said. And of course he might not be able to write back right away, even if he was perfectly fine.

In early July, the radio reported that the first American casualty was from Skin Fork, West Virginia, and nineteen years old.

Mae said if I really wanted to stop worrying, I should just call Leonard's parents, as the army would let them know first if something happened. She was sure that they would appreciate my concern.

I was sure they wouldn't. Instead, I called Dale, or I tried to. His mother answered and said he was spending the summer in Europe before he started at Dartmouth in the fall. She sounded surprised—maybe because I didn't already know Dale was in Europe, or maybe because any girl was calling her son at all.

"May I ask who's calling?" she asked, not unpleasantly. But I was afraid, unsure if she was close with Mrs. Lifton. Without giving my name, I apologized and hung up.

Just before school started, the bodies of forty-one American soldiers were discovered near a hill in Waegwan, Korea. They'd been shot and left in a ditch, their hands still tied behind their backs with communications wire. I read this at our kitchen table, sitting by myself. Mae was doing dishes. I didn't see her turn around.

"Stop looking at that." She snatched the paper away from me, folded it, and put it on the other side of the table. "It's not doing you any good."

I told her I wasn't done reading it. When I reached for it, she picked up the whole paper, carried it to the sink, and pushed it down into the dishwater. "Just call his parents for Pete's sake." She wrung out the whole mess, letting it drop into the garbage with a thud. "I can't take one more minute of you acting like this. It's too hot."

I shook my head. I could see from her face this wouldn't be the end of it, but I did not expect what she would do next, which was to rush over to my chair, grab my arm, and pull me to my feet.

"You need some air," she said. She got one strong arm behind my waist and steered me to the back door. I was wearing just my nightgown, so I crossed my forearms in front of the small but firm mound of my belly. She opened the screen door and pushed me outside. Before I could turn around, I heard the click of the lock. I cupped my hands against the screen and watched her lift the telephone's receiver.

"Mae?" I pounded on the hot siding. There was no shade where I stood. The bottom of my feet burned. "Mae! What are you doing?"

When I tried to push out the window screen, she slammed the glass window down. I pounded on that, helpless as I watched her yank open the drawer where we kept the directory.

"How about that?" Her voice was muffled through the glass. "Maybe I myself want to make sure he's fine. Maybe I've got some sense of how to do that."

I kicked at the door with the ball of my foot, but she walked to the other side of the kitchen, stretching the receiver's cord. I felt my panic, my head going light in the scorching heat. She had her back to me, but I could hear her speaking, her voice softer and more pleasant than before. I would know soon. At least I would know. A bee hovered near my shoulder, and still I did not move.

Please, I thought. *I will never lie again. This time I mean it. Just please let him be alive.* I was praying to God, praying to my mother, praying to any entity who could help. Even as I made this promise, I understood that if Leonard was already dead, neither God nor my mother could change that. And even if they could, neither God nor my mother nor anyone who'd been watching would still believe any promise from me. But I pressed my palms together, picturing Leonard that first day in the courtyard, sitting in front of the bougainvillea.

Only when Mae turned back to the window and gave me the thumbs-up, her smile full of I-told-you-so, did my hands rise and clutch the back of my sweating neck. *Thank you thank you thank you*, I thought, though already, a feeling of falling, a new dread, swallowed my relief.

She unlocked the screen door and swung it open. "Well, guess what? He's just fine. They got a letter from him yesterday, in fact. He's back on base in Japan, just like your daddy said. He was in Korea for just the first couple weeks, but when things got serious they didn't want the rookies there. So they sent his group back."

I needed to sit, to get out of the sun. I moved past her and sank back into my chair. I leaned forward, my nose to my knees.

"Was he injured?"

"Didn't sound like it." She went back to the sink, running water. "They said he was just moving boxes in a warehouse all day. So still helping, but not in danger." She glanced at me over her shoulder. Whatever she saw in my face made her shut off the water and turn around.

"Oh honey," she said.

I've never been good at holding back tears, and I certainly couldn't do it then. But I hated her pitying expression, what she thought she understood.

"Don't write to him again," she said. "If he's forgotten you,

you forget him. You're too lovely to chase after anyone. Okay? Promise me?"

She meant well. I knew that, even then. But a few minutes earlier, when I was locked outside and bargaining for Leonard's life, I swore that if he were alive, I'd never lie again. I didn't know who or what might have heard me, but a deal was a deal. So I had to tell Mae the truth, which was that I couldn't forget Leonard, and would promise her no such thing.

Most girls I knew wore girdles to school, though in the warmer months, I was one of many who opted for a lighter option, what we called a roll-on. But the day after I turned eighteen, I went down to Maas Brothers and spent twelve of the fifteen dollars I'd gotten for my birthday on two Playtex de Luxe Lightweight Girdles, advertised as having extra hold-in power. When I first took one out of its package and tried enclosing it around my hips, I regretted wasting the money, as I did not think I could bear it. But with desperation comes fortitude, and eventually, the considerable sweat of my body made it easier to yank the girdle up and over the mound. Once that girdle was on, I could take only shallow breaths.

I learned to endure it. Every few nights, I would wash one girdle in the tub while I was taking a bath, and then I would wring it out, tuck it under my robe, and hang it way back in my half of the closet. I smuggled in a bowl to catch the drips, and while Janet slept, I heard the dripping through the night.

I was in French class, writing out conjugations, when I felt the first flutter inside me. I kept on as if nothing were happening. No one watching me would have known. I'd grown so used to pretending what was happening to my body wasn't happening, and feigning calm when I wanted to scream.

The next time I felt something, I was alone, so I put my hand to my belly, and this will sound strange, but what came to me was the image of a baby porcupine. I'd seen a picture of one, so small it could easily fit in someone's palm, barely able to open its eyes but already covered in quills. So it could hurt you without meaning to, and likely would. But it also looked so fragile, in need of care and warmth. I whispered, "It'll be okay," and I felt myself understood.

I realized, too late, that I had no way of knowing if this was true. I didn't know what would happen to either one of us. My reassurance, well meant, might be a lie.

I didn't know where Dartmouth College was, but when I told the head librarian I hoped to send a letter to someone there, she found the address in New Hampshire and said if I just wrote the recipient's name and *student* on the envelope, they'd probably get it to him.

"A Dartmouth boy." She smiled at me. "Pretty impressive. I bet he'll be glad to get a letter from you."

I doubted it. I wrote and rewrote that letter to Dale, but

there seemed no way to ask if he'd heard from Leonard without sounding pathetic. Even after I'd done the best I could, I wasn't sure I'd hear back. Dale owed me nothing. In high school, he'd more or less lost his best friend because of me. And now he was far away, doing something impressive, and I was the one Leonard had no time for.

A week later, I received a letter from New Hampshire. Dale apologized for the brevity of his response, and for his handwriting. He said he didn't have much time because his classes were keeping him busy, but he wanted to let me know right away that Leonard was fine. Dale had been in Rome when he heard about the invasion. He'd been worried, too, and he'd written to his mother, who'd called Leonard's mother to see if he was okay. She said he was, and that he'd only been in Korea the first few weeks of fighting. He was now back in Japan, unharmed and out of danger.

Dale hoped that I would be as relieved as he'd been, and that I was doing well.

October afternoons were still warm and sticky, but I started wearing Leonard's green jacket whenever I needed a break from the girdles. I would zip the jacket up over my belly before I even got out of bed, and I wouldn't unzip it until I was back under the covers at night. My sweating father opined that I couldn't be comfortable, and I maintained that the ceiling fans made me cold. Mae disapproved of my wearing the jacket, as she knew it had belonged to Leonard. But she said nothing, only showing her disapproval with her eyes.

On the first cool night of the season, my father kept us at the dinner table and announced he had big news.

"Our family is about to get a little bigger." He smiled bashfully across the table at Mae. "There'll be a new baby here in February."

I worked to compose myself, grateful for the general commotion: Janet got up and said "Oh my goodness! Oh my goodness!," then went over and hugged Mae, who looked as happy as I'd ever seen her. Bobby even seemed pleased with the news, though he said it better be a boy.

"Or what?" my father asked, laughing.

Bobby thought for a bit and said he guessed he would keep having his own room, and we all laughed at that. Part of me really did feel joyful—this was the part of me that had gotten so practiced at pretending. But under the table, I gripped my knees so tightly one of my nails pierced the skin. I'd already calculated that nine months from April was January, but I didn't know if I should be counting from April or May. My stepmother had a curvy, ample figure, and it was hard to compare her profile to mine.

Still, when I was alone in the bathroom, I'd look in the mirror, astounded that no one had guessed. I was six months pregnant. The girdles and the green jacket were no longer hiding it. I think the reason no one guessed was a matter of expectation, no pun intended. What I mean is, it's hard to see what you think is impossible. You get one version of a person in your head, and you don't see anything to the contrary. You just can't.

At least that's how it's often been for me: in being seen, and in my seeing of others, too.

10.

When I started wearing Leonard's jacket to school every day, my friends said nothing. I assume they believed I was trying to hide the weight I'd gained, which showed in my face and arms. Mae, on the other hand, was convinced my attachment to the jacket was the sole reason I hadn't been asked to any dances that fall.

"Honey, you're still beautiful. But you need to wear clothes that fit. And no boy is going to stick out his neck for a girl wearing another boy's jacket. They all probably think you're taken."

I'm ashamed to say that in response, I reminded her she wasn't my mother. She was unfazed.

"I can still care about you," she said. "And I know how much you love to dance."

She knew, as I did, the Harvest Bash was fast approaching, and this, during my senior year, would be the first time I would miss it. Just seeing the flyers around school for the costume contest was painful. The morning of the dance, Mae told me I should go without a date.

"I bet plenty of people would be glad to see you there. And lots of boys will want to take a break from their dates and dance with you." She and Janet were at the kitchen table, shaping a pot of syrupy popcorn into little balls for trick-or-treaters. "I'm sure we could come up with something cute for a costume."

"I'm done with those dances." I said this lightly. I was washing my hands, my back to Mae and Janet. Janet got up to hug me from behind.

"I'd dance with you," she said, and squeezed me with all her strength, pressing her cheek against my lower back. Her hands were still sticky with syrup so she held them out, away from the jacket's zipper. "I love you, Nora. I love you sooooooo much."

"I love you, too," I said, my voice tight with fear. I tried to turn to face her, but she held on, and I could only turn halfway. When I looked up, Mae was staring at the front of the jacket. Her gaze moved up to meet mine just as Bobby walked in, reeking of sweat, and announced that he was starving. He wore only shorts and a baseball glove, palm-down, on top of his head. He moved around me and Janet to the refrigerator.

"Wait," Mae said. "I'm out of cigarettes. Bobby, if you go put on a clean shirt right now and get me a pack, and you take Janet with you, I'll send you each with a dollar extra, and you can both get what you like."

He and Janet exchanged looks.

"A dollar each, ma'am?" Bobby asked.

Mae said yes, that was what she'd said, and she told him to get her purse. I stepped away from the sink so Janet could wash her hands. What I remember is looking down at the jacket's zipper, shiny in the window's sunlight, feeling both terror and relief. What was coming, what I'd known was coming, would finally happen. I went back to the table and sat across from Mae. We were silent as Janet searched for her shoes, as Bobby used the bathroom. The moment we heard the back door shut, Mae asked me to stand and unzip the jacket.

When I did, she leaned forward in her chair and pressed both hands against the front of my skirt, and I actually attempted to suck in my belly. But when she removed her hands and leaned back, I could see in her face that she was not fooled. She reached into the pocket of her apron, pulled out a cigarette, and lit it. The smoke irritated the back of my throat, but I didn't dare cough.

"Have a seat," she said.

I sat.

She tapped out ash in a saucer. "Tell me who. And when."

To me, the question was insulting. I pointed at the collar of the jacket.

She shook her head. "You said he's been gone since January. It's October."

I held up a hand to show I needed time before I could speak. A fly hovered over the bowl of syrupy popcorn. She waved it away, then stood and went to the sink, where she wet the tip of a dish towel. She brought the dish towel back to the table, but for a while she just stood there smoking, holding the dish towel by her shoulder. When the fly landed again on the table, she cracked the towel down like a whip, then leaned over and blew a stream of smoke at the dead fly, blowing it off the table's edge.

"We don't have much time." She sat again. "You're gonna need to start talking."

I leaned forward and used a sleeve of the jacket to wipe my face. Then I sat up again and, without looking at her, told her about our night in Bradenton.

She rested her hand on her own belly. "When was this?"

"April," I said. "I told you I was spending the night at Roberta's."

She stood and went back to the sink, running the faucet over the cigarette, which she then tossed in the trash. Instead of sitting back down, she motioned for me to stand and face her. Mae had never laid a hand on me, but as I stood, I braced myself to be slapped.

"You wrote to him?" she asked. "You told him your condition?"

I nodded.

"When?"

"June. And July." My voice wavered. "And August. And September."

She half smiled, as if in recognition. "And nothing from him?"

I shook my head. She covered her eyes. I wanted to tell her she was wrong to think what she was thinking. Leonard loved me. I was the reason he'd joined the army in the first place. But that wasn't entirely true. He'd said he'd done it for himself as well. Even when he'd asked me to marry him, he'd been mad at his father. He'd wanted out of the house.

Mae lowered her hand, and I could see in her eyes that she was torn between revulsion and sympathy for me. She started to say something, then closed her mouth. I could hardly look at her. What should have been a happy time for her was now compromised, embarrassing. She raised her arm, and I shielded my face. But I felt only her hand on my shoulder, pulling me close, and she kept her arms tight around me, the top of my head tucked under her chin. Her hair smelled of smoke, and she had syrup on her collar.

"I'm not sure how to help you," she said. "But I'll try. I'll do what I can."

The next day, she made an appointment for me with a doctor way over in Clearwater. I understood we'd gone out of town for discretion's sake, but this doctor was unfamiliar to me, and I'd never before had to take off all of my clothes for any kind of exam. He was an older man, and I could tell right away he didn't think much of me. When I had my feet in the stirrups, he said, "You're going to have to unlock your knees, honey," and I was scared, but I did, or I thought I did. He said, "I know you can do better than that." The way he said it, I knew what he meant.

But he was the one to tell me that I would have a baby in January—he guessed around the middle of the month. When Mae came in, he told her this. She crossed her arms over her belly and he said, "And I'd guess February for you."

She nodded, and this doctor smiled and said, "Well, that should be an interesting time at your house," and Mae paid and we left.

She said she would tell my father that night, and she had a plan for how she would do it: When he got home from work, before he even came in the house, she would go out and tell him her friend Sheri couldn't get her car started. Sheri was a real person, single and approved of by my father, and Mae was confident that if she asked him if they could go help Sheri get her car running in time for her to get to her evening shift, my father would say yes, even if he was tired and hungry. Once they were far away from the house, Mae would tell him to pull over, and she would explain that there was nothing wrong with Sheri's car. She would get his keys before she told him anything about me, and she would keep them until he calmed down.

My job would be to supervise dinner for Bobby and Janet. Mae said I was otherwise free to do as I liked, though she suggested that as soon as I hear my father's car out front, I should go back to my room and stay there.

That evening, Bobby and Janet clearly sensed my distress. But rather than showing sympathy, they both poked at me, seeming to want any kind of reaction. Janet wanted to know why I didn't have to have milk with my meal, and I reminded her I was eighteen and could drink or not drink what I wanted.

"Why's your hair wet?" she asked.

"I took a bath."

"Why before dinner?"

I told her I wasn't feeling well. Another truth.

"Fevered?" This from Bobby, watching me from across the table.

I shrugged, which he took as a yes.

"Then maybe you should take off that big jacket," he said. Janet laughed, covering her mouth. I stood and told them they could do the dishes. I needed to go lie down.

Mae had warned that I shouldn't be wearing Leonard's jacket when she and my father returned. She said if she were me, she'd throw it away, or she'd at least keep it far out of sight. Back in my room, I hid the jacket under a blanket, then changed into my nightgown. Already the light from the window was dim enough that I needed to turn on a lamp. My father and Mae had been gone for over an hour.

I was still lying in my bed, eyes open, when I heard the car pull into the drive. The front door whined open, and I heard my father's voice only briefly. Footsteps moved down the hallway, but no one knocked at my door. Mae was still in the front room, talking to Bobby and Janet, when I heard the door across the hall, the door to the room my father shared with Mae, shut with a click. I understood that he, too, had barricaded himself.

When Janet came in and turned on the light, I didn't move or make any sound. She either didn't believe I was sleeping or she didn't care, because she sat on the edge of my bed, reached across me, and pressed her palm to my forehead.

"I'm okay," I said. "Just need to rest."

She nestled in behind me, her nose against the back of my neck. "If I get what you have," she whispered, "we'll both get to stay home."

I told her what I had wasn't contagious, but she said I was wrong. My father had been fine that morning, she said, and now, according to her mother, he was sick as well.

The next morning, he left early for work, backing out of the driveway while the sky was still dark. I took advantage of his absence to use the bathroom, then I got right back in bed, and there I stayed, pretending to sleep even as the room filled with light, and even as Janet tried to convince Mae that she, too, was too ill to go to school. Once she and Bobby left for the bus, Mae came back to my room and told me what I already knew: My father had taken the news hard. She said that they'd been gone so long because at first, he would not, or could not, believe what she was telling him.

"But then he did," she said, tightening the sash of her robe. She'd already put her hair up. "Let's just say it's a good thing for Leonard that he's as far away as Japan."

I spent most of that day doing laundry, partly to show my gratitude to her, and partly to keep myself occupied. We had a washer with a manual wringer, and I wore myself out, using both hands to turn the crank, my arm muscles burning, my forehead sweating. When I came in from hanging the third load out back, Mae told me she'd called Leonard's mother.

"You already told her?" I asked. "She knows?"

Mae looked at me like I was crazy. "Not over the phone. You don't know who shares their line. And I know darn well who shares ours." She glanced in the direction of our worst neighbor's house. "I told her that your father and I have something to discuss with them at their earliest convenience." She paused. "What's she like, his mother?"

"She's nice," I said. I had to steady myself against the wall. I didn't want this meeting to happen. "What'd she say?"

"That she'll check with her husband about his weekend schedule." Mae lifted her nose as she said this, as if to imply Mrs. Lifton had been putting on airs. "She said she'd call me back."

I was in the tub when the phone rang. When I got out, Mae said the meeting would happen the next morning, a Saturday. Mrs. Lifton had said that because it seemed they would likely be discussing a private matter, it would be best, perhaps, if Mae and my father could come to their house. She'd asked Mae if she was familiar with Snell Isle, and when Mae said she was not, Mrs. Lifton gave her directions. She and Mr. Lifton could host as early as ten in the morning, she said, or, if that was too early, any convenient hour after that.

11.

Mae told Bobby and Janet that she and my father were going to a wedding, and that was why they had to dress up. She said the groom was someone my father worked with, and they wouldn't know the bride. She made fun of herself for completely forgetting about the wedding until that morning. They would need to stop in town, she said, for a gift. Bobby was more than happy to stay home, but Janet got upset and said she wanted to go, as she'd had a good time at her mother's wedding to my father. She remembered dancing, and also that there'd been cake.

"This one won't be fun," Mae said. She stood outside our room, waiting for my father to finish dressing. She wore a hat with a mesh veil, white gloves, and a long jacket over her blouse. She did not appear pregnant, and I knew this was as she intended. Earlier, she'd had on rouge, but she'd asked me if it was too much, and I'd thought of Mrs. Lifton, what she would think, and told her yes. Mae had washed off the rouge, and she looked better. But I hated to think of her unease, and how it would only grow as my father drove over the bridge to Snell Isle and saw all the houses with wide, well-trimmed lawns and late-model cars parked in circular drives.

"Will you at least bring me back some cake?" Janet had gotten in bed with me, and she leaned against me, sulking.

Mae said she would try. I heard my father open their bedroom door. He walked past our bedroom doorway, wearing a tie and his gray sports jacket. Early that morning, I'd been coming out of the bathroom when he appeared in the hall, still wearing his pajamas. He'd turned away as if insulted, then waited in silence for me to pass.

Now I heard the jingle of his car keys, and his voice, pleasant in tone, giving some kind of instruction to Bobby. That was especially painful, hearing him speak to my brother in a regular, fatherly way. He called to Mae that he was ready when she was, and with those few words, I heard the dread he was trying to cover, and that was more painful still.

They returned by half past eleven. From my bed, I heard the front door open, and then Mae telling Bobby and Janet that she hadn't been able to bring home any cake.

"But anybody who wants a burger and fries better run get in the car. Your daddy's leaving in two minutes. I'm not hungry."

"What about Nora?" Bobby asked.

Mae reminded him that I'd missed school the day before, and I shouldn't be going out for burgers just yet. Janet came back to the room to get her shoes, and when she saw me in bed, she gave me a guilty look.

"It's okay," I said. "You go have fun."

She tugged on one of her braids. "You look sad."

I told her it wasn't the kind of sad that needed a burger. Our bedroom window was open, and I could hear Bobby's voice out front, and more quietly, my father's, and then Janet's when she joined them. The sound of the engine softened as the car backed out of the drive, and I knew this was something I would remember, the feeling I had as I heard this.

Mae came in and sat on the edge of Janet's bed. I sat up and turned to face her, my back to the wall. She'd already taken off her heels and the jacket, and she held a beer bottle in one hand and an opener in the other. Before she said a word, she set the bottle on the floor between her bare feet and unpinned the hat from her hair. Once the hat was free, she placed it beside her on Janet's bed.

"They think you're lying," she said.

I shook my head. My heart was already pounding.

"They said he was home in April, but he was with them the whole time."

"It was before that." I could hear my voice rising, insistent. "He stayed two nights in Bradenton before he went home." I'd already told her this.

She raised her eyes to meet mine. "Nora. They saw him get off the bus."

"From Tampa. I told you. He took the bus from Bradenton back up to Tampa. Mae! I'm telling the truth."

She picked up Mr. Sweet, the stuffed bear that Janet slept with, and set him upright on the pillow. "They said he never mentioned you. Not when he was home. Not in his letters from Japan. Which they're still receiving, by the way. They're getting letters from him about every other week."

I was too stunned to reply.

"They said they would write to him today, and they would ask him if he saw you in April. They'll tell him what you said about Bradenton. But it'll take a few weeks to get the question to him, and a few more to get his reply." She shook her head. "You don't have that kind of time."

"My word doesn't mean anything?"

Not to Leonard's mother. This I already knew. What alarmed me was Mae's uncertainty. I could see it in her face.

"Nora. They let us know about an incident that happened last October. At their home."

I covered my face with my arms. It was my own shame attacking. She hadn't even raised her voice.

"You can imagine," she said, "what that was like for your father, having to sit there in a stranger's living room and hear that about his daughter. And to know that they'd known this about you for a year, while we ourselves had no idea."

I still had my face hidden, but I heard her open the beer

bottle. I'd never known Mae or my father to drink a beer before five o'clock. By the time I looked up, she'd finished half of it, and she was staring out the window.

"She's in Dutch, too, I think. The mother, I mean." She set the bottle back between her toes. "He said she was supposed to tell us, and he wasn't happy that she hadn't. I almost felt bad for her, sitting there all scrawny and silent while he glared at her. You can tell who's running the show in that marriage. But he's right. She should have told us."

I had difficulty squaring Mae's description of Mrs. Lifton with what I knew of her. She wasn't scrawny. She was tall and slender, with the kind of figure Mae usually admired. I believed my stepmother might be speaking out of anger, or out of loyalty to me. If it was the latter, I didn't deserve it. Mrs. Lifton had tried sticking up for me. And I turned around and stung her. Twice.

Mae leaned forward and rubbed her forehead as if it hurt.

"Do you want your cigarettes?" I asked. "I can get them."

"I've had four in the last hour." She lifted the bottle and took another swig. "The good news is there's a place you can go and have the baby. Those two must've guessed why we were coming over. They'd already made some calls."

"Where?" I was suddenly warm, sweating all over. I pushed the blankets off my legs. "What place?"

"Out of town. Maybe out of state. Wherever there's an opening. It's a home for unwed mothers, which is what you are."

"Can't we wait to hear from Leonard?"

"Do you know what you'll look like in another month?

We're lucky we have this option. Apparently, these places have waiting lists. But he's got somebody he went to school with looking into it."

I pressed my hand against the mound, warm and firm. "Then what happens?"

"They find a home for it. A good home. And nobody here will know, including Bobby and Janet. We'll make something up." She chewed her lip. "I'll come up with something."

"I can't lie," I said. "You know that."

She looked at me. "Clearly, you can."

There was nothing to say to that. When I composed myself, I told her I was sorry. I told her I was grateful for her help, for her saving me. She said nothing. I worried she'd hate me forever, or, at least, never again think of me the same.

"When I say I can't lie," I told her, "I'm not saying I won't try. I'm just saying I'm not good at it."

"Well, you need to get good at it. Fast." She stood up, holding out the beer as if she meant to make a toast. "That's the whole point of sending you away. So you can come back and hold your head up. But you have to toe the line. Do your part. These places aren't cheap. Even just paying for half of it, we'll run through our savings."

The weight of this felt physical, staggering. "I'll pay you back," I said.

She bobbed her eyebrows as if to wish me luck.

"Who's paying the other half?"

"They are."

"But I thought—"

"Because of the shower incident," she said. "Because it happened in their home, and with their son, and because she didn't tell us. But neither one of them believes this baby has anything to do with their precious son. They were both very clear about that."

I felt a good strong kick then, not just a flutter. I didn't move. I didn't even look down.

"Mae. Does my dad think I'm lying?"

I could see she didn't want to answer. I took the blow.

"Do you believe me?"

She was quiet for several seconds, and I could see that she was still making up her mind. But she nodded. My relief was small, and temporary.

"It doesn't really matter," she said. "Practically speaking, I mean."

The following Tuesday, when Mae and I were again alone in the house, I learned that the Liftons had secured a spot for me in a maternity home in Paterson, New Jersey, and that I would be leaving for New Jersey on a sleeper train that very afternoon. I still don't know if the home in Paterson was truly the only place available, or if the Liftons just wanted me that far away.

"It's good that it's so far," Mae said. "You won't know anyone up there, and nobody'll know you."

She said I could use her suitcase, and I should first pack my schoolbooks, and then whatever clothes I could fit around them. She would tell my teachers what she would tell everyone else: Her mother in Arkansas, who lived alone, had taken a bad tumble on the stairs.

"This is actually good timing." She gestured at her own belly. "People will understand why I can't go myself, why I have to send you."

She'd been busy thinking, coming up with plans for correspondence. She'd collect my assignments from my teachers, and I could send them back to her completed. She was sure that Bobby and Janet would want to hear from me, and my friends would expect letters, too. I would have to give everyone her mother's address in Arkansas. Her mother would forward all mail to me in New Jersey. My letters home would also have to go through Mae's mother, so she could send them on with an Arkansas postmark. Mae said I would need to include envelopes already addressed in my handwriting.

"You told your mother?" I asked. "She knows?" I'd only met Mae's mother at the wedding, when I was fourteen. I could hardly bring her face to memory. And now she knew this about me.

"She'll keep it to herself," Mae said. She rolled my toothbrush into a dish towel and tucked it into the suitcase. "Arkansas City is a little town. Probably nobody here will know it. But I'll tell you what you'd need to know, just in case somebody asks."

I knew I shouldn't argue. She was saving me, or she was trying to. But I doubted that anyone, even Bobby and Janet, would believe that after missing three days of school on account of sickness, I'd suddenly been called away to a medical emergency in Arkansas.

"People believe all kinds of things." Mae glanced at the open window, then lowered her voice. "Listen. I'm going to tell you something. Don't tell anyone else. If you do, I'll know. But Janet's father is still very much alive, okay? He's living in Virginia with the German woman he brought back. Okay? We were married when he left, and I was expecting. Janet was just born when I got the letter saying he was so sorry, but he'd gone over there and fallen in love with a German girl, like he'd fallen in a well or something. Whoops, not his fault."

I stared at her, stunned.

"I know," she said. "I thought he was supposed to be over there *fighting* the Germans."

"Does Dad know?"

She looked insulted. "You think I'd tell you if he didn't? My mother knows, too, and people from home. But nobody in Rolla needed to know. And nobody here does, either. People think different about a widow than they do a divorced lady. I don't care whose fault. And he's as good as dead to me, and good as dead to Janet."

"Does she know?"

"No. And don't you tell her." Her eyes turned threatening. "I'll tell her when she's older, when she can understand." She frowned at the coat I was packing. "Is that your only coat?"

I told her it was.

"That's a Florida coat. You'll need a real coat." Her voice wavered. "Do you remember snow? New Jersey is far north. It's going to be even colder than Missouri. You should have a warm hat. And mittens."

My father came home at noon. He put his car keys on the hook and went straight back to their room, and he stayed in there, the door closed. Mae told me she would drive me to the station, and I realized that he'd only come home early so she could have the car. My face must have shown my hurt.

"He'll say hello when you come back," she whispered. "I'll see to it, okay? But right now, just let him alone. He's doing the best he can."

I knew what she meant, what she didn't say: Given the circumstances, my father was showing restraint. He hadn't screamed at me, or called me names, or shamed me in front of my siblings. He'd not reminded me how hard he worked, how hard he'd always worked, so his children could be on solid footing to reach for whatever they wanted, and that I'd thanked him with the humiliation of making him sit in the Liftons' spacious living room and hear what they thought of me, and why. He'd had to take their money because he had no choice, even as they called me a liar, and insinuated worse. I had no grounds to expect that he might show me love, or caring, or even pity, not when he was still reeling.

And yet, even then, I knew I would have preferred my father screaming at me, or calling me names, or almost any outright burst of emotion over the cold repugnance he showed me those awful days before I left. It frightened me more than being sent away, more than the idea of giving birth among strangers. My father had often said I reminded him of my mother, which for him, was the greatest of compliments. I had her general decency, he liked to say. Packing my suitcase for New Jersey, I understood he might not ever say this again.

Mae worried that the suitcase, with four of my schoolbooks inside, would be a strain for me to lift in my condition. But I carried it out to the front room and showed her I could heft it to my shoulders. She handed me a peanut butter and honey sandwich she wanted me to keep in my purse.

"I'm going to check the mail," I said.

I said this casually, like I wasn't really thinking about it, but she looked at me with exhaustion. I could see myself in her eyes, how pathetic I seemed.

"I already got it," she said. "There was nothing that would interest you."

I nodded. I'd gotten better with the disappointment, or more practiced with it, at least. "You'll tell me when you hear from the Liftons?" I asked. "When they hear back from him?"

"Sure."

"Do you promise, Mae? You have to write to me right away. Or if he sends a letter here."

"Promise." She looked at her watch. "We should leave."

I didn't follow. It was just past two o'clock. My train wouldn't leave until four.

"Before the kids get home," she said.

When I protested, saying I wanted to tell them goodbye, she gave me a wary look.

"You're going to tell them you're going to Arkansas? You've got to be convincing, Nora. If you can't manage that yet, we should go before they get home."

I knew she was sick of my crying. I lowered my head as I pulled on my gloves. They were thin and white, dainty things, appropriate for train travel.

"We can go now," I said. "Thank you."

In the car, she said she would tell them I'd wanted to say goodbye, but I'd understood her mother was in urgent need, being so injured and all alone. Bobby and Janet would be upset of course, and perhaps bewildered. But she would tell them they could write to me in Arkansas whenever they wanted; and that she was just so grateful to me for agreeing to go help her mother get through these next few months. If it weren't for me, she would tell them, she didn't know what she would do.

TWO

12.

The home in New Jersey was called Shaded Acres, a name that didn't match the property. I doubt it covered even one full acre, and though I imagine the trees in front of the house gave shade in warmer weather, when I arrived, most branches were bare. In any case, *Shaded Acres* was what it said on the stationery, and it's how they answered the phone. The house itself was a big Victorian with a turret and a curved front porch, and it was one of several similar houses sharing the same street. There wasn't a sign out front, and if you were to put me on that same street today, I probably wouldn't be able to pick out the house where I lived for ten weeks. I'd recognize it from the back, though, as I remember that an extension of low-ceilinged offices had been built on to the back of the house.

I remember more about the home's interior. The common room was on the second floor, with a stained-glass window that made drifting dust motes turn gold in the afternoons. The living room had a brick fireplace, and so did many of the bedrooms, but above each was a framed sign that read NO CHIMNEY ACCESS! NO BURNING!! DO NOT REMOVE THIS SIGN!! As if one of us girls might waddle outside with a tree saw, wave to the neighbors, and try to bring in kindling. The furnace was always running, pushing out dry heat that made my cuticles crack and my nose itch. You couldn't open the windows because they'd been sealed for the winter. The other girls regularly complained that they were too hot, especially at night. Not me. Even under a blanket, even wearing a wool sweater stretched over the porcupine, that whole winter, I was cold.

They had sixteen of us staying there at a time. Around once a week, someone would leave for the hospital, and the next day, a new girl would arrive to take the empty bed. The youngest girl that I saw there was thirteen. The oldest, who came in just as I was leaving, looked at least thirty. We slept in twin beds, two or three to a room. The night I arrived, the admitting nurse, after checking my head for lice, told me my room was on the second floor, and that I'd have just one roommate, Lucy.

"She's a colored girl," the nurse added. "Is that a problem for you? I see you came in from Florida."

"No ma'am," I said. This admitting nurse and I had already gotten off to a bad start. When she first introduced herself, she said *nurse* like *noyce*, or that's how it sounded to me. I'd asked her what a noyce was, and she thought I was making fun of her.

"No ma'am what?" she asked. "No you're not from Florida, or no you don't have a problem?"

"It's not a problem," I said. It wasn't. I understood the North was, in some ways, a different country, and that as a visitor, I would need to adjust to its customs. But I don't want to pretend that I was able to simply rise above my upbringing. It was more the state of mind I was in. On the long train ride up from Florida, when I'd been trying to sleep and also trying not to cry in front of the other passengers, I thought about a story Leonard had told me he'd read about a regular man waking up one morning to find he'd turned into a giant insect. The man-turned-bug was still himself, Leonard had said, wanting love from his family, but the family was horrified by the scurrying, antennaed sight of him; and because this new form of him could ruin them all, financially and otherwise, his own family locked him away until he died. Now I know this story is Kafka's "Metamorphosis," and I've read it myself, but when Leonard was telling me about it, I only thought it was a strange story that could never really happen. And yet on the train to New Jersey, that story was very much in my head.

I was humbled in spirit, is what I mean.

Lucy was never rude to me, but she wasn't particularly friendly. At first, I worried that she somehow sensed I was from a Jim Crow state, and that I'd never before shared close quarters—or really, anything—with someone who wasn't white. But after a few days, I understood she likely hadn't given me that much thought. Her bed was just a few feet from mine, and I guessed she was around my age because she had the same *Modern Calculus* textbook that I did. But she seemed mostly unaware of, or unconcerned with, my presence. If I asked her a question about the chore list, or what day we could do laundry, she would look at me and blink slowly before answering, as if first needing to come all the way out of a dream. Once that happened, she'd answer in as few words as possible, then go right back to being quiet. She did her schoolwork sitting up in her bed. If she finished before lights out, she'd scooch down under the covers and just lie there, belly up, staring at the ceiling.

It wasn't just Lucy who stayed quiet. We ate meals in shifts, eight girls at a time, and if the nurse charged with making sure we ate our vegetables tried to get a conversation going, she eventually gave up. I myself spoke only when spoken to. If you would have seen me up there that winter, pale and teary and blowing on my hands, hardly talking to anyone, you wouldn't have known that my whole life, I'd always been one to strike up conversations with people, and the first to smile and say hello. But the best way I can describe the feeling of that place is that it felt as if we girls were naked, and everyone else was fully dressed—the social workers especially; but also the nurses; the neighbors we could see from our windows as they shoveled snow and sometimes looked up and saw us watching; the doctors who came to examine us in the offices at the back; and even the loved ones writing to us, or not writing to us, from home. It was that humiliating, being there. I didn't really look at the other girls, partly to spare their embarrassment, and more because I didn't want any of them, or anyone, looking back at me.

Mae wrote to tell me my English teacher from home had assigned Voltaire's *Candide*, and one of the nurses lent me her copy. I had no trouble appreciating that the story on the whole was satire, and Pangloss's cheerful interpretations were not to be trusted unless your goal was to roll your eyes. But the nurse had underlined *"Let us work without reasoning," said Martin; "it is the only way to make life endurable,"* and I think she and I agreed that here, Martin had a point.

I took the advice and stayed busy. A chalkboard in the kitchen listed our assigned chores for the week: cleaning the bathrooms, emptying garbage pails, sweeping and mopping, that kind of thing. If I heard a girl say she was too tired or nauseated to do her chores, I went ahead and did hers as well as mine—not to be nice, but to keep myself occupied, and to try to wear myself out. In the evenings, after I finished my schoolwork, I wrote letters home via Arkansas, cheerfully reporting to Janet and Bobby, and to Irene and Roberta, that Mae's mother was slowly getting better, and that this part of Arkansas was quite pretty.

I napped a lot. That was another reason, besides staying warm, that I followed Lucy's example, doing my schoolwork and writing letters in bed. Sometimes, I'd nod off while still holding my pen. And yet at night, as soon as my head hit the pillow, I would suddenly feel wide awake, my thoughts inevitably turning to Leonard. I'd imagine him bursting in the home's front door, still in uniform and full of apologies, desperate to explain, begging my forgiveness. Maybe even happy about the porcupine. He'd bring my hand up to his lips the way he used to, looking at me like I'd hung the moon. Everything would make sense again. I'd tell him there was no need for forgiveness, if it was just a misunderstanding.

My case manager at the home, Mrs. Kilgore, said my having these imaginings made it clear that I was still living in fantasy land, which is what had landed me in the home in the first place.

I've previously referred to the sessions with the home's social worker as interrogations, which was indeed how my appointments with her felt. Twice a week, I had to walk down the hallway of the first floor's extension and knock on her office door. Mrs. Kilgore was a vital-looking woman who let me know, in the first meeting, that she'd already brought up four children within the sanctity of marriage before she went back to school to get her degree. She wore heavy wool cardigans buttoned to her throat. On my first visit, she explained that she had to keep her office window at least a little open because if we girls got too warm and comfortable, we invariably got so sleepy we didn't hear a word she said.

I could certainly believe that. Her office had a big, soft chair for me to sit in, and a needlepoint pillow that said *Seek to Improve Each Day* that I had to either squash behind me or keep in my lap. The view from her office window was mostly blocked by the branches of a pine tree, so while the air coming in the window was freezing, it at least smelled nice. Still, halfway through my second session, I pointed out that I could actually see my breath. She took mercy on me and closed the window. Within twenty minutes, my eyelids turned heavy. She didn't like that at all.

"Nora, wake up!" She clapped her hands in my face, then stood to crack open the window. "We have work to do, you and I."

This work, according to Mrs. Kilgore, was her helping me better understand myself and my true motives, so I wouldn't have the baby, go home, and then end up in the same predicament once again. She wanted me to know most maternity homes didn't take second offenders. I told her I most definitely would not be a second offender, but Mrs. Kilgore, wise and all-knowing, was not convinced. She said something in me had made me reckless in the first place, and until that thing was addressed and corrected, I could very well put myself and my family through the expense and embarrassment of an illegitimate birth once again.

"I've seen it happen," she said. "More than once. More than twice."

She had theories about girls in my situation, and theories specific to me. As I've acknowledged before, and will acknowledge now, not all of her theories were wrong. Or not completely wrong. That night in Bradenton, I do think, in the back of my mind, getting pregnant didn't seem like the worst thing that could happen, because the worst thing would be Leonard dying and me not having anything left of him. I didn't take into account that Leonard might live, and still leave me to fend for myself.

Mrs. Kilgore told me she was glad I could admit that my situation was something I'd willed, and that this admission was proof I was making progress. But she felt I was still being dishonest, with her and with myself. I had no idea what she meant, and when I told her this, she specified: She didn't believe for a minute my worry that I'd made such a poor decision because I worried Leonard would die.

"Well, no," I said. "It wasn't the only reason."

She leaned forward. "What was it, then?"

I almost laughed. I mean, she wasn't so old. But she saw it in my face, what I was thinking, and she shook her head.

"No," she said. "It wasn't just carnal desire that brought you here. Not really. In fact, the real reason had nothing to do with this boy at all."

I thought she was going to make me guess, and I was stumped, so good thing she went ahead and told me. It turns out Mrs. Kilgore was sure I'd done such a foolish, selfish thing because I missed my mother. That's how I learned that she had a file on me, full of information from Mae, or Mrs. Lifton, or both. Even before I said a full sentence, she knew the very year my mother had died.

"Nora," she told me, with some sympathy, "you are, and remain, a child in search of the mother you lost. That's why you did this."

I told her this theory didn't sound right to me at all. I missed my mother. I hated that she'd died—the time she didn't get, and the time I didn't get with her, and the time that my father and Bobby lost, too. But that night in Bradenton, I wasn't thinking about her at all.

"Not consciously," Mrs. Kilgore said. "Your subconscious, is what I mean."

That was a big subject with Mrs. Kilgore: my subconscious. She said it made decisions for me, and those decisions were irrational because of my immaturity. Specifically, I had immature fantasies of motherhood, and I was immature for my age in general. This immaturity should be expected because I'd lost my mother at a crucial age, and it was common knowledge among those who studied psychology that a present mother was essential for the appropriate maturation of the child.

I told her I appreciated that she'd gone to college, but I was pretty sure what was going on in my head that night very much had to do with Leonard and how I felt about him. And how my body felt. That was as honest and as explicit as I felt I could get with Mrs. Kilgore, but she shook her head.

"If you would be more cooperative with me, Nora, and more honest, I could help you find emotional maturity. There's a saying, you know. 'The social worker succeeds where the mother has failed.'"

I told her my mother hadn't failed at anything. She just died.

"Do you see how upset you're getting? Clearly, I've touched a nerve. I'm not saying it was your mother's fault. But she left you when you needed her the most. Are you honestly going to sit here and tell me that loss hasn't shaped you in every way?"

Here, she glanced down at my belly, and just that glance drained me of fight. It was like having a serious argument with someone, standing up for what you're sure is true, and then having the other person smile patiently and tell you that you have lettuce in your teeth. Only I couldn't pick out the lettuce and resume fighting. The porcupine was always with me, not just a big scarlet *A* for *Adultery*, but another *A* for *Abandoned*, and a big scarlet *D* for *Dumb*. Throughout every session in that cold little office, the porcupine sat heavy on my bladder, sometimes shifting, sometimes still, and always proof of my poor judgment.

Those sessions with Mrs. Kilgore lasted only fifty minutes at a time, but they uniformly wore me out. By the time she said I could be excused, I'd usually go straight upstairs to my bed and lie there with my arms over my head. Once, just once, Lucy looked up from her homework and said I'd only have to have a few more sessions with Mrs. Kilgore, especially if I didn't argue with her.

"Just act like you agree," she said, her voice almost a whisper, though we were the only two people in the room. "Once she gives you the go-ahead, you get to start going to Miss Berry." She was in her bed, writing a letter to someone, and wearing one of her pretty maternity dresses. I'd had to wear whatever the home had to lend out, including a baby-blue nightmare with a print of yellow ducks all over it. Lucy had come in with maternity clothes of her own.

"Who's Miss Berry?" I asked.

"The other social worker. She's got an office downtown, and it isn't freezing like Kilgore's. And she's nicer. You'll get there. Just don't argue."

I thanked Lucy for the advice. I also told her how much I liked her dress, which was made out of burgundy velvet that looked both soft and warm. In response, she did her slow-blinking thing, nodded once, then looked back down at her book. I got the message: conversation over. I didn't take it personally. It wasn't like I ever saw Lucy chatting away with any other girl in the home. Maybe it's that all the other girls were white, or maybe that's just how she was, or how she was that winter. She might have been like me, different from how she was at home, wherever that was for her. But one of the nurses was a black woman, older, and when she was done with her shifts, she sometimes took Lucy out for drives, just the two of them. I once saw them from our window, talking in the parked car. Watching them, I felt my loneliness, raw as hunger.

What I most remember about Lucy is that the day she was packing for the hospital, she left out that velvet dress. I stayed quiet in my bed, writing a paper on the League of Nations. When another round of contractions came on, she sat down suddenly, and I asked her if she wanted me to get anyone or anything. She shook her head, so I went back to my writing.

But I was aware that her suitcase was already buckled, and the dress was still on her bed, folded neatly. She waited until she was walking out the door, suitcase in hand, to tell me I could have it. I thanked her profusely, but she kept walking, and she only called back that she was glad I could use it, as she wouldn't need it anymore.

Every few afternoons, Shaded Acres had a visiting volunteer, meaning a woman from the board or the Ladies' Auxiliary who came to give us a lesson on something. Before the volunteer showed up, we'd help the nurses push the table in the dining room against the wall, and we'd bring in extra folding chairs from the kitchen. Attendance at these lessons was mandatory for everyone except one girl, Carol, who was blind, and well out of high school. Carol would usually come downstairs with the rest of us, one hand on the railing, her other hand on another girl's shoulder. She had a white-tipped cane that one of us would carry down, and once she was off the stairs, she could get around with just the cane. Whenever there was a volunteer, she would come in and sit in the dining room for the first few minutes and decide if she wanted to stay. If she didn't, she'd have one of the nurses help her back up the stairs, or, if the weather was warm enough, she'd go out back and smoke.

I felt bad for Carol, being blind and all, and as pregnant as the rest of us. But I envied her freedom of choice regarding the lessons. One volunteer gave tips on personal hygiene that I found insulting. A few days after that, I sat through an hour of another volunteer explaining grammar rules that I was sure I'd learned in sixth grade. But some of the lessons were on things I didn't know much about, like classical music and Impressionist paintings, and I liked that I was at least learning something. Another volunteer was a former ballerina. She was old, maybe in her seventies, but you could tell she'd been a dancer by the way she held herself, and she had us all stand up and put our shoulders back. She said to pretend we were holding butterfly wings we didn't want to tear between our thumbs and fingers, and she said nothing about our situations, our swollen bellies and faces. She moved around us, pulling back some of our shoulders, and she said we were all naturally graceful, and that whenever a person wasn't feeling confident and wanted to slump was exactly when she had to stand tall.

But I think everyone's favorite volunteer, at least while I was there, was this big woman with two chins and a deep voice who knew how to do all kinds of things with makeup. She started out telling us we didn't need much, or any at all, as we were all pretty young things. She put a little blush on this new girl, and you could barely see any difference. This volunteer said that was the point. "Just a bit of color," she told us, "and maybe a dash of mascara in the evening. You don't want to overdo it." But she kept looking at a girl named Beth who had a long, thin scar on her cheek, and when it was time for this volunteer to go she instead got out a bigger makeup case and told Beth that she could come on up and get her whole face done if she wanted.

Beth went right up, and she kept her back to us while this volunteer went to work, layering on the foundation and powder, drawing back to squint before smudging skin with her thumb. When the volunteer said Beth could turn around, we saw that both of her cheeks had turned pale and smooth, at least from a few feet away. It was so impressive we applauded. By then we'd seen all the bright lipsticks and eyeshadows in the volunteer's bigger case, and I guess she felt bad for us, because she stayed there almost until dinner and made each of us up with whatever colors we asked for. One of the nurses said that the last thing we girls needed was to learn how to look like painted harlots, but another nurse asked if she could have a turn. The volunteer put red lipstick on her and gave her smoky eyes, and it made her look like a starlet.

I still think about that, how happy that volunteer made us that day. And really, whenever someone would come in and treat us like we were still worth anything, and talk to us about something aside from what we'd done wrong or what we were in for, it lifted all of us up in a way that didn't feel bad when we came back down. Or that's how it was for me.

The same was true of the nicer nurses, and one of the doctors, too. He was an old man, and he would make small talk with me during exams—he'd ask me if I thought it was going to snow soon, and if I'd ever been sledding, that kind of thing, and I knew, even then, he was doing this because he understood that putting my feet in the stirrups felt to me like punishment, so by the time any doctor came in I was usually trembling with cold and fear. I imagine it was the same for a lot of the girls there, because none of the doctors who came in seemed surprised to find me crying, or trying not to. But the one doctor, the old one, was kind to me, and though that didn't fix everything or even anything, I do remember it, even now.

13.

Shaded Acres had a radio in the common room, and before November was fully over, it seemed like every station was playing "White Christmas" at least once an hour. Each time I heard it, I'd feel more homesick. For the first time in my life, I would spend Christmas without my family, or anyone who loved me. So there I was, listening to "White Christmas" and looking out the window at snow, wishing I could go back to Florida. But everyone knows that that song isn't really about missing snow.

A lot of girls at Shaded Acres had strong feelings about it. Once, it caused a big fight, because one girl who didn't want to hear it shut the radio off, and that made another girl mad. A nurse came in and scolded us all, reminding us "White Christmas" was written for military men risking their lives and living in all kinds of discomfort, not a bunch of girls who were perfectly safe in a big old comfortable mansion right here in America. We'd all be home soon enough, she said, and so when we heard that song, we shouldn't think of ourselves and our own problems, but of our troops in Korea, who were truly in danger, and much less comfortable than we were. She said nobody was thinking about them anymore, and true patriotism was dead, but her husband was over there, fighting communism for all of us and just trying to stay alive, while she was worried out of her mind and having Christmas with their kids without him. And here we were thinking that song was about us. Every day it was like the whole country had forgotten there was even a war going on at all.

"I didn't forget," I told her. I'd been following the news as best I could. I knew there was still plenty of fighting, and that Leonard might have been called back to Korea.

She gave me a quick, approving nod. "Then quit your crying," she said.

A few days later, another nurse took me aside and asked if I wouldn't mind missing the volunteer lesson so I could read the newspaper to the blind girl, Carol. She said that Carol had specifically asked for me.

This surprised me. I didn't think Carol even knew who I was. I only saw her at lunch, as we were on different shifts for dinner.

The most I'd spoken to her was when she asked for the butter. I'd said, "Here's the butter," and set the dish by her hand.

"She said you're a good reader." The nurse shrugged. "Excellent elocution, she said. She's already out back."

I frowned. "Outside?"

"It's not so bad out. We've got an extra coat you can borrow."

I didn't like the idea of sitting outside, even wearing a borrowed coat. But I said I'd do it, partly because it seemed coldhearted to say no to a blind girl, and partly because I was curious. I couldn't guess how Carol would know I was a good reader. No one had ever said anything to me about my elocution, and I'd never had reason to think there was anything special about it.

The nurse gave me a long navy coat that smelled like mothballs and said sorry, that was the only one she had to lend out, and that I could come get it whenever I wanted. She also gave me the Sunday edition of *The New York Times*. I put on the coat and carried the paper out back, where it was cold enough for me to see my breath. Carol was smoking a cigarette, sitting on one of two lawn chairs pulled up close to the house. She wore a black coat with a fur collar, and she had a little fur hat that matched. I said hello and asked if she still wanted me to read to her.

"Oh yes. Thank you. That would be quite lovely." Her dark glasses obscured her eyes, but she turned her face to me and gestured to the empty chair. I'd noticed earlier that Carol had a strange, staccato way of speaking, emphasizing different syllables than most people did. It was how people in movies sometimes talked, though I'd never met anyone who talked this way in real life.

When I sat, she sniffed the air, then wrinkled her nose.

"It's the coat," I said. "I had to borrow one."

"Poor you." She reached over and moved two fingertips along the coat's sleeve. "Well. You'll be warm enough."

To my surprise, I was. The chairs were wind-sheltered by a tall fence on one side and a cluster of pines on the other. I could still see my breath, but the sun was bright. A three-quarter moon sat high in the blue, so faint it was hard to see. I made my left hand into an L and raised it. Waning.

"Do you want me to read a particular section?" I asked. I worried she expected me to read the whole thing to her.

"Hmm." She lifted her face to the sun. Her nose was long, regal looking. "I'd like to start with the food section. My mother told me there was something about l'Escoffier?"

I'd had enough French that I could figure out how *l'Escoffier* might be spelled, and after a minute of looking, I found the article. It was about a group of people who called themselves the "l'Escoffier Group" and regularly got together at a hotel in New York so the members could discuss what kind of sherry went best with turtle soup, or if a fish soufflé should really be called a mousse. That kind of thing. While I was reading, Carol tapped her cigarette into an ashtray resting on her belly. I worried she'd burn her coat, but she didn't.

When I finished, I asked if she'd like me to read her another article.

"Not just yet, dear. I need to digest that, so to speak." She said *dear* like *de-ah*, the way Franklin Roosevelt would have said it. "Say, Nora, are you familiar with Escoffier?"

"I can tell it's a verb," I said. "Does it mean to scoff?" I really thought that might be it, like this group of food snobs met at the hotel to scoff at what regular people ate. Carol laughed and said Escoffier was the name of a famous French chef.

I decided I didn't like her much. She seemed condescending, and I already felt low enough. I was glad to see she looked like she might be going into labor soon, and therefore leaving any day. That nice coat of hers was a maternity coat, and still, the buttons strained.

"Do you want me to read another food article?"

She took off her hat and scratched above her ear. She wore her hair very short, in what we called a shingle style. I suppose it was easy for her to take care of. "I can't place your accent," she said. "You almost sound . . . Midwestern? You're not from anywhere close."

I stayed quiet. We weren't supposed to say where we'd come from, not even the state. We'd all been warned that if any girl could correctly tell Mrs. Kilgore another girl's last name or hometown, the tattling girl would get a cash reward, and the girl who'd been dumb enough to compromise her own privacy would be reported to whomever was footing her bill.

"I'm allowed to guess." Carol sounded annoyed. "You're just not allowed to tell me. I'm quite skilled at guessing. For example, your new roommate hasn't said two words to me directly, but I'd bet my teeth she's from Long Island."

I had no idea if this was a good guess. I'd never been to Long Island, and my new roommate, Helen, had barely said two words to me, either. She wore her blond hair in a long braid she left in even while sleeping, and she hardly looked pregnant yet. When she first arrived, I tried being friendly, as I could see she was younger than I was, maybe sixteen. But she stared at my belly with revulsion, and that was before she saw that the porcupine had grown big enough to force my belly button out a few inches, and it looked like the stem of a pumpkin. The first time I had to change clothes in front of her, she saw the pumpkin stem, put her hand over her mouth, and literally gagged. That made me feel great, let me tell you. I almost said, *Listen, Helen sweetheart, this is exactly where you yourself are headed, okay?* But of course she knew that already, which was why it probably scared her to look at me.

"I don't care where Helen's from." I folded the newspaper section neatly. "She's rude."

Carol lit another cigarette. She had her own Zippo lighter with a flip top, and she needed no assistance with it. She told me later that she could see shadow and light, and she could of course feel heat.

"Go easy on her," Carol said.

"What do you know about it?" I didn't appreciate this unsolicited advice. I'd put up with all kinds of unkind behavior from Helen, without ever being unkind back. I looked at Carol, which I felt I could do freely, as she couldn't see me looking at her. Sanctimonious, I thought. Sanctimonious and condescending.

She leaned closer to my chair. She smelled like Mae, like cigarettes. "We're alone, correct? No one else is out here?"

I looked around the backyard and told her we were.

"Your last roommate, Lucy. She's an interesting one." She was still leaning close. "You know, her baby's father wanted to marry her. Vernell. That was his name. Vernell."

"Where'd you hear that?" I asked. It seemed like a weird thing for her to make up. But I'd never once seen Lucy talking to Carol, or to anyone, really, besides that one nurse.

Carol waved away the question. "That's what her mother wanted, too. My God, she could really put the heat on, that woman. She went on and on, saying it was her grandchild, that she should have a say. She said Lucy didn't belong here with so much white trash, meaning us! Meaning even yours truly!" Carol leaned back her head and laughed. "I'm from Greenwich, for God's sake. Even our trash isn't trash."

I said nothing to this, though I was of course aware Carol had just told me the name of her town. I didn't want to interrupt her. I had no idea how she would know anything about Lucy's mother.

"But Lucy dug her heels in. Did she ever. She had no intention of marrying Vernell. She was dead set on finishing school.

I'm sure she will. She was a bit of a cactus, I know, but I admire that kind of spine."

"And how exactly do you know all this?"

She shrugged and smiled. The porcupine, maybe feeling the sun even through the mothball coat, shifted inside me. I patted my belly, trying to soothe it. For all I knew, it liked the sun.

"Well," I said, "if you can't tell me how you know so much, I'm going to assume you're making things up."

"Assume what you like, dear." She exhaled a long stream of smoke. "Would you read me an article about Korea?"

It didn't take long to find an article on Korea, but it was all bad news. Just a few months earlier, things had been going well, with the UN troops and the South Koreans pushing the North Koreans way back up. But now China was involved—the article said that Chairman Mao had just sent around half a million seasoned Chinese troops down to Korea, with a million more reinforcements at the ready. The US didn't have anywhere near as many soldiers over there, and President Truman was saying if China kept it up, he might be forced to use the atomic bomb. In six months of fighting, over thirty thousand American soldiers had been killed. The article quoted the exact number, and when I finished reading, I stayed quiet, running my fingertip over that number. All I felt was the smoothness of the page.

"I suppose you're worried about your man," Carol said. "The soldier who stopped writing."

My mind whirred. I stared at her face, at her dark glasses, her twitching grin. Then I knew, or at least I guessed. I turned as best I could and looked over my shoulder, to the left of our chairs. The pine tree closest to the house was the same one I could see through Mrs. Kilgore's office window. Next to it, in the slushy snow, I could still see the imprint of where Carol had carried her chair.

"You listen?" I hissed. "You sit there and listen to our sessions?"

"There's no need to whisper." She exhaled another stream of smoke. "She's only there in the mornings. It's like a scheduled soap opera, only relentlessly sad. I doubt any advertiser would sponsor it." She grimaced and affected a shiver. "All the immorality. All that *immaturity*."

"You should be ashamed. That's an invasion of privacy."

"Oh please. I don't even know your last name. Or if Nora is really your first. And even I can't guess where you're from. My God. It's driving me batty. Ohio? Is that it? I've got this theory that Ohio is the miniature of the entire country, with everything pressed in together."

"I'm not telling you where I'm from," I said. "I'm not telling you anything. It's wrong, what you've been doing. You better stop. You're lucky I don't go in and tell on you right now."

"Not luck, dear. I'm an excellent judge of character. And you're not the tattling kind." She lifted her chin and smiled. "At least you've got some fire in you. At least you speak your mind. And even if Matron Kilgore doesn't believe you, please know that I, for one, am entirely convinced that it was lust for young Leonard, and not grief for your mother, that brought you here."

I dropped the paper by her boots and stood, waving away her smoke. "Is that why you asked for me? So you could laugh at what you know about me? Are you going to ask each of us out here, one by one?"

She shook her head, no longer smiling. "No. I only asked for you."

"Why?" I clenched my teeth to keep them from chattering. I couldn't believe she knew Leonard's name, and that she thought the whole thing was funny. Or any of her business. I wanted to haul back and slap her. Add that to my list of wrongs, I thought: slapping a blind pregnant girl who was sitting down.

"Because I like you." She shrugged. "I'm not due for another three weeks. I thought your company might make it more bearable. I know you all pretty well." She shrugged again. "You're my favorite."

It seemed like the truth, or like it might be. I couldn't think of any other reason why she would have asked for me in particular. And I couldn't remember the last time anyone had said one good thing about me. I pushed my hands in the pockets of the coat.

"You don't look like you have three weeks left," I said. "You look like you're about to pop."

She used the toe of her boot to nudge the newspaper toward me. "Once I do, you'll never see me again. So sit down and read me the obituaries. Please?"

I looked back at the house. It was too late to go into the lesson. The volunteer would be getting ready to leave. "Why do you want me to read the obituaries?"

"Oh, I love them," she said. "My mother and I have a game. We read all the nice things someone said about the deceased, then try to guess what they were really like."

I almost told her that sounded mean, but I made my own argument against that opinion. Those dead people had been loved enough, and respected enough, to get an obituary in *The New York Times.* And now they weren't feeling any pain. Meanwhile, Carol and I were stuck at Shaded Acres, our due dates looming. Somebody dead would have to be petty to begrudge us a little fun.

I sat down and found the obituaries. Carol's guesses about departed souls being braggarts, shoplifters, or habitual arsonists soon got me laughing. I eventually made my own attempts, and to my satisfaction, I got her to laugh, too.

14.

I got permission to skip any lesson with a volunteer if Carol needed me to read as she smoked. She was always outside first, and within a week, she told me that I needn't announce my arrival, as she could smell my approach in the mothball coat. I told her the smell was worse from inside the coat, though really, I didn't mind. I couldn't quite button it up over my belly, but I liked that the pockets were lined.

I soon learned that Carol did plenty of reading on her own. Every week, her mother mailed her a novel in Braille, and Carol would burn right through it. She'd already read all of Dickens, she said, but what she really liked were mysteries by Agatha Christie or James M. Cain. I asked her if she'd read *The Sun Also Rises*. She said that she had, and that she'd liked it. I told her that I'd tried to check it out from the school library, only to be told that it was vulgar, and inappropriate reading for a young lady.

"Hmm." She seemed amused. "You're either from the South or the Midwest. But I already guessed that much." She was quiet for a while, then said, "There's nothing graphic in the book, not that I remember. The problem, I imagine, is Lady Brett. That's the main female character. She's beautiful and sophisticated. She does as she likes. Sexually, I mean. And almost everyone in the book is in love with her."

She went on to explain that Lady Brett was also in love with the narrator, but he was made impotent by a war injury, so Lady Brett wouldn't marry him.

"And it's not that she wants children." Carol paused to take a drag, but I could see she was still thinking. "She comes out and says she doesn't want them. So this is a woman character who likes sex for its own sake, and has it, and won't settle for a life without it, even for love. But nothing terrible happens to her. She isn't murdered. She isn't pregnant and abandoned, or left impoverished, or even disrespected. She's unhappy and drunk most of the time, but that's true of the men in the book, too. So she gets away with it, more or less. The freedom with herself, I mean. That's why the schoolmarm called it vulgar."

I thought of Leonard's mother, reading this same book. When I'd told her the shower with Leonard was my idea, she'd looked horrified. I suppose it's one thing to read about Lady Brett, and another to have someone with the same proclivities spending time with your son. But both Mrs. Lifton and her husband had been right about one thing. They'd been worried I'd end up pregnant.

I'd already told Carol that the next time she was listening in on my sessions with Mrs. Kilgore, she shouldn't expect any fire and argument from me. I'd taken Lucy's advice to heart. I was determined to graduate to the nicer social worker, Miss Berry, no matter what Mrs. Kilgore said about me or my true motives. It wouldn't kill me to sit there and listen quietly, only talking back in my mind.

I'd also told Carol that I didn't want to hear personal details about other girls in the home. It didn't seem right, not when we all already had the naked and exposed feeling of being at Shaded Acres.

Carol said fine—she would stick to telling me what she knew about girls who'd been here but were already long gone. She told me that her first roommate, Judy, had not only been married when she arrived, but the mother of a two-year-old who was being cared for by her mother-in-law back home. According to Carol, Judy wanted to give this new baby up for adoption because the two-year-old was showing signs of locked-in syndrome, and her pediatrician back in Chicago said Judy's coldness was likely the cause.

"I assume it was Chicago," Carol said. "That accent is hard to miss."

"What's locked-in syndrome?" I shifted in my chair, my arms around my belly. The day was overcast, colder than before. It was a nice feeling, knowing the porcupine was safe and warm.

"He's not talking, apparently," Carol said. "The child, I mean. And he won't look at her, or anyone. Judy said she didn't know what she did wrong, but she didn't want to do it to another one. Her husband wanted her to come home, but her mind was made up."

"She told all this to you, or to Mrs. Kilgore?"

Carol nodded back in the direction of Mrs. Kilgore's window.

"What did Mrs. Kilgore say?"

"She was sympathetic. Surprisingly so." Carol adjusted her glasses. "But she agreed that if Judy couldn't figure it out, what she'd done wrong, the new baby would be better off with someone else."

I blew on my hands, then put them back in the coat pockets. I hadn't seen much of Judy—she'd left a week after I arrived. I remembered she'd worn a wedding ring, and I'd thought it was a little pathetic that she felt the need to pretend in front of the rest of us. She'd been seated across from me the night we had liver for dinner, and I know she saw me stuff my entire serving into my napkin and up my sleeve when the nurse wasn't looking. She'd smiled a little, and looked away, not saying anything. It was hard to imagine she'd been so cold to her child that he wouldn't even look at her.

"Don't tell me anything else you heard," I said. "Even about girls who are gone. It's not my business."

"Such a goody-goody." Carol leaned back her head and blew smoke straight up. She exclusively smoked Lucky Strikes, which her mother mailed to her every two weeks in an eight-pack carton. "It's not gossip. You'll never see Judy again. You don't know anyone she knows."

I told her that it didn't matter. All I had to do was imagine her telling people I'd never meet about Leonard not writing back, and his parents thinking I was lying about Bradenton. I wouldn't like it.

Carol said fine, no more overheard stories. But she would tell me something she'd heard directly from her first roommate, a girl named Florence who told Carol that a week before she came to Shaded Acres, she'd tried swallowing two full bottles of castor oil over the course of an hour, and got so sick she had to go to the emergency room, where she'd hallucinated that she was tied to the blade of a windmill for hours, and truly felt that was happening to her, though obviously, the castor oil did nothing to change her situation as she'd still had to come to Shaded Acres and tell all this to Carol. Carol said what Florence should have tried was giving herself salmonella, which could have killed her just as easily, or maybe more easily, but at least that had a better chance of working as intended.

"How do you know that?" I asked.

"I told you," Carol said. "Florence told me herself."

"No. I mean about the salmonella."

"Oh. My mother knew someone who died that way. But she knew another girl who tried it, and she allegedly survived."

I had trouble imagining Carol's mother, this Connecticut woman who bought Lucky Strikes by the carton, and who apparently told her daughter things even Mae didn't know or wouldn't say. Carol told me that her father knew Frank Sinatra because of the business that he was in, and that she'd actually met him once, at one of her father's parties, and when Frank Sinatra took her hand, just briefly, she'd felt warmth moving up her arm, and whatever caused it was mutual. She could hear in his voice, and feel in his grasp, that he, too, was struck by whatever passed between them. She said her great-great-great-grandfather had lost his head, literally, in the French Revolution, and that her great-great-great-grandmother had seen it happen. She said she lost her vision when she was fourteen, after what she called "a tumble" from her favorite horse, Fleetfoot.

"He's fine, by the way," she added. "Right now, I imagine he's grazing happily outside of New Haven. My mother wanted him shot, but he was worth too much." She gestured at her belly. "Of course, she'd like to see this one's father shot, too."

"Did you love him?" I asked.

"The horse? Oh, yes."

I clicked my tongue. "Carol. The baby's father."

She tilted her head from side to side, as if letting a little weight roll back and forth. "Say, did you hear that? That's a hawk."

"Did he propose?" I asked.

"The hawk? I don't think they're so formal about it."

That's how it was, talking to her. She'd tell you anything in the world about somebody else, but if you wanted to know about her, you had to dig. It was hard to imagine Carol being dumb about a boy, or about anything, but clearly, something had gone wrong. I wanted to know what it was.

"It wouldn't have mattered," she said finally. "He was already married."

I gasped. Even with the dark glasses covering her eyes, I could see that she was irritated.

"Sorry," I said.

"I'm fine, thank you. Say, Nora, do you ever listen to Brahms?"

"The composer?"

"Yes, the composer."

I tried to think. "I know the lullaby. Brahms's 'Lullaby.'"

"Well. You should listen to more of him. I tell you, the three intermezzi of 117, they destroy me. But he has jaunty pieces, too. Earthy and folky. You'd like him."

I had no idea why she thought I'd like classical music that was earthy and folky. I liked the Andrews Sisters. I liked Frankie Laine. And she was just changing the subject again.

"Carol. Are you going to tell me more about how you ended up here?" I didn't feel bad for pressing her. She knew so much about me. About everyone.

She shook her head. We sat without talking, listening to the hawk. It's a lonesome sound, that cry.

"I got a proposal," I said. I didn't know if she cared.

She turned to me. "You think he meant it?"

I told her the truth, which was that I was sure Leonard

meant the proposal at the time, but there was a chance that all he'd really wanted was a way to get out from under his parents. Now that the army had given him that, he might have no more use for me. I tried to sound accepting, and matter-of-fact. But the whole time I was talking, I was hoping Carol would tell me that it sounded to her as if he'd truly loved me, and it didn't make sense that he would just stop.

Instead, she said, "I'm sorry." As if that was the end of that, too bad for me.

"But he wasn't like that," I said. "If you knew him, you'd understand. I still can't believe it, that he's just not writing back at all, when he knows I'm up here about to have a baby. His baby. Carol, honestly, he just wasn't that kind of person."

She exhaled a stream of smoke. "But Nora, you're naive."

I flinched at the pain of it, how that hit me.

"I'm just telling you, that's how you strike me. Old Kilgore may be wrong about your motivation, but she's right that you'd believe just about anything. It's sort of endearing. Actually, it's quite endearing. You're such a straight shooter, you assume everyone else is, too. But you wouldn't be the first girl to be promised the moon and then let down."

"I know that," I said. But I was thinking she didn't know Leonard. She didn't know him as I did.

"Well," she said. "Maybe he truly felt love for you at the time, but these things happen. He probably met somebody over there." She shook her cigarette until the burning tip went dark. "My brother had a friend stationed in Japan, and he said Japanese women were the most beautiful women in the world. And generally more sophisticated."

"Okay." I held up my palm, a worthless shield.

"Or they might still have USO girls, or what-have-you." She laughed a little. "You said he was nineteen?"

"My God, Carol. Shut up." I surprised myself, saying that. I never said *shut up* to anyone, even Bobby. But my already-tormented head did not need the suggestion of Leonard staring dreamily at the beautiful Japanese woman who taught him to make paper swans, or some USO girl, lithe and laughing, cute in her uniform and right there in front of him, not eight months pregnant with a runny nose, wearing a stinky coat in New Jersey.

"Sometimes a girl needs to hear the truth," she said. "I tend to say what other people are thinking. At least to people I like. I think it's kinder, in the end."

I closed the coat around me and heaved myself up from the bench. "Then you've done your good deed for the day. You can get a nurse to help you up the stairs."

"Nora. Don't go."

"Too late," I said. "I'm going."

"I'll tell you a secret."

I told her I didn't want any more of her secrets. I was tired of her blabbing about other girls. I realized I'd believed every story she'd told me about them. Hook, line, and sinker. I really was naive. Dumb as a rock.

"This secret is about me. About my plans."

"I won't believe you anyway," I said. "I've wised up." I

wasn't about to sit down again. It was a lot of work to get myself up out of a chair, and I didn't want to have to do it all over again. "It's cold out," I said. "What is it?"

"We're alone?"

"Of course we're alone. I wouldn't do that."

"No," she agreed. "You wouldn't." She beckoned for me to lean down, then cupped my ear to her smoky breath. "I'm keeping my baby," she whispered.

I almost laughed. I should have felt free to. Tit for tat. I didn't think she could possibly mean it. Then I wondered if she was testing me, to see if I'd believe anything.

"How are you going to work that out?" I asked. I would have asked this of any girl who wasn't married, but Carol keeping her baby seemed the most unimaginable of all. I couldn't guess how she would change a diaper. I pictured her pushing a stroller with one hand, tapping her cane with the other.

"I'll figure it out," she said.

"You said he was married."

"He is."

"You'll marry someone else?"

"Maybe. Maybe not."

Then I did laugh. I couldn't help it, though I could see from Carol's face, the set of her jaw, she wasn't kidding.

"You're just going to go home with a baby, and not be married? I don't know, Carol. Maybe things are different where you're from. But they can't be that different."

"Money makes things different. And I came into mine two months ago."

Came into mine. I'd never heard this phrase. I pictured Carol walking into a room knee-deep in cash. She'd spoken as if this were something that would happen to everyone eventually, if they could just find the right room.

"What are you talking about?"

"On my birthday. I turned twenty-one. My grandmother left a trust." She lifted the ashtray and gestured to her belly. "You tell me who better to be a mother to this child, if it's anything like me? Assuming it inherits my heart? Or my mind? It'd be a crime to leave it with some milquetoast simpleton who won't understand it." She paused to take another drag. "If it's a boy, I'll name him David, and there won't be any of this Davey business. David. If it's a girl, Brenda."

She said these names with confidence, the way she said everything. For all I knew, she really could keep her baby. If she grew up riding horses and living in a place where even the trash wasn't trash, she could probably afford help. If anyone helping her said anything about her low morals, I suppose she could just fire them.

"Don't tell anyone," she said. She didn't seem particularly concerned that I would. "They can't make me do what I don't want to do, but they'll put up a fight. I'd rather put it off."

"Who?" I asked. "You mean the nurses will put up a fight? Or your parents?"

"All of them. And Miss Berry, that busy bee. You'll see when you meet her. She seems quite *invested*, to say the least."

"Lucy liked her," I said.

"Everyone likes Miss Berry. I myself find her perfectly pleasant. She just doesn't know what I know." Carol smiled again, tapping out ash. "You understand? I know best. It's me."

In early December, the nurses put up Christmas stockings for us in the common room. I thought that was nice of them, though we could tell they'd used the same stockings in previous years, as each girl's name was just written on a piece of paper fastened to the top with a safety pin. One girl peeked in hers, and then all of them, and let us know we were each getting a hairbrush and a pocket-size New Testament. The general feeling was disappointment. But the head nurse's jolly husband helped her carry in a real tree, which we got to decorate with donated ornaments and strung popcorn. A nativity scene sat at the center of the dining room table. The manger and the figurines were made of a silvery metal that reflected the chandelier's light, and somebody surrounded the whole thing with fluffed sewing batting, meant to look like a heavenly cloud.

Mae sent Santa-themed gift tags for me to fill out and return so she could attach them to the presents she'd already purchased and wrapped on my behalf. *You got both Bobby and Janet water guns*, she wrote. *I worried Bobby was too old, but he'll be glad to have it once Janet's armed. And I can tell you now, I'll love what you got me. But my goodness, Nora! You shouldn't have spent all that money!* She made no mention of my father except to tell me I'd gotten him a gift certificate to the bowling alley he liked. On his gift tag, I only wrote, *Merry Christmas, Dad*, and then my own name, printed small.

Every time I wrote to Mae, I asked if she'd heard from the Liftons. Every time she wrote back, she didn't mention Leonard or his parents at all.

Mrs. Kilgore congratulated me for my growing maturity. "You're no longer talking about that young man coming to rescue you," she said. "That's good. Because he isn't. He's made his priorities clear."

I didn't argue with her, mostly because of Lucy's advice.

15.

The day of my first appointment with Miss Berry, the nurse who drove me to her office parked, left the engine running, and pointed through the windshield to a double-door entrance. "You go in there. Take the elevator to the third floor, first door on the right. I'll be back to pick you up in an hour."

I hesitated. It was cold out, and snow was coming down in small, fast-moving pellets. But my real concern was that there were a lot of people bundled up and walking on the sidewalk. I hadn't left Shaded Acres at all since I'd arrived.

"You need help?" the nurse asked. I could tell she meant I should get a move on.

It turned out I was fine. Out on the sidewalk, no one paid me any attention. But when I walked in through the double doors and saw a little huddle of people waiting for the elevator,

I turned around and took the stairs. It seemed likely that some of the people waiting for the elevator worked in the building, and given my condition, they'd be able to guess who I was going to see, and why. I didn't exactly hop up the steps, though. Not at eight months pregnant, and wearing a heavy coat. When I knocked on the door that read *Miss G. Berry, Licensed Social Worker, Adoption Services*, I was still out of breath.

But the pretty woman who opened the door looked at me like she couldn't believe her good fortune.

"Nora?" She put her hand to her chest. Manicured nails, clear polish. "Is it really you?"

I nodded. I'd picked up from the nurses that in this part of the country, younger women didn't always like being called ma'am. And honestly, the woman before me didn't look much older than Carol. She had high, rounded eyebrows that gave her a cheerful look, and apricot-colored hair that fell in smooth waves to her shoulders. She wore a teal jacket that matched her skirt, and pink lipstick. So nothing like Mrs. Kilgore, which seemed a promising sign. But I did not relish being gazed upon by such a put-together person with my nose running and shoulders heaving from the stairs, not to mention I was wearing the mothball coat that I could barely button.

"Come in, come in, you poor thing. I'm Miss Berry, and pleased as punch to meet you. It's dreadful out today, positively. I'm counting the days until spring."

Her office was spacious, with two floor-to-ceiling windows, both shrouded in steam from the radiator. She had a typewriter and her own telephone. A crystal vase at the edge of her desk held roses, red and long-stemmed.

"Have a seat, sweetie. Either one is fine." She moved behind her desk, gesturing to the two soft chairs that faced it. "Would you like a cookie? I made them just yesterday. They're oatmeal. Some with raisins, some without. That's me all over, anyone will tell you." She smoothed the lapels of her jacket. "I just want everyone to be happy. Oh, sorry. Where is my head? Let me take your coat."

I was glad to relieve myself of the coat. But once I did, I felt even more self-conscious. I was wearing a purple wool cardigan over the dress Lucy had given me, along with a pair of knee-high wool socks that Mae sent in the mail.

"I bet you can't wait to get home to sunny Florida." She hung the coat on a hook by the door. Her gaze moved to my belly, then back to my face. "Won't be long now!"

I let myself drop into one of the soft chairs. She asked again which kind of cookie I'd prefer. Carol had told me about these cookies—warning me they'd be dry. But I told Miss Berry I liked raisins, thank you, and she opened one of the drawers of her desk.

"I've heard such good things about you." She was prying off the lid of the cookie tin. "The nurses tell me that you're a lovely young lady, with excellent manners. And your grades from home are impressive. Are you thinking about college?"

I found myself unable to answer. I felt generally addled, unable to focus. I just wanted to go home.

"Oh goodness!" Her eyes widened. "I'm not at all implying you won't get married. I of course attended college, and I certainly plan to marry before I'm twenty-five." She leaned across her desk. "I'll be a little older than the average bride, but I know I'll be a better wife and mother for my schooling and work experience. I tell every girl who comes in here: forget all that bluestocking nonsense. If you get a degree in something practical, you'll certainly use that knowledge as a wife. And believe me"—she glanced at the roses—"a better class of man knows it."

I was close enough to the roses that it seemed like I should be able to smell them, especially as there were so many. But even when I leaned forward, breathing in the room's steamy air, I smelled nothing. From this new angle, I could see that the top folder had my initials written on the tab.

"In the meantime . . ." She leaned back into her chair. "I don't mind making my own money for a few years. I'm able to buy pretty things when I want them." She smiled, and a dimple appeared in her right cheek. "But the real reason I'm here, of course, is that I love helping people. Especially girls like you. Oh goodness. The cookies. Honestly! Where is my head?"

She put two cookies on a tissue and slid the tissue toward me. I thanked her, and she said I was most absolutely welcome, then lifted my folder from the stack.

"By girls like you, I mean that you're not just smart, you're obviously caring and mature, doing what's best for the baby."

I was silent, mostly because I'd bitten into a cookie. Carol was right. Even with the raisins, it was like having to swallow flour. Miss Berry waited politely. I covered my mouth with my hand.

"Do some girls decide to keep them?" I asked. "Excuse me. Girls from the home?" I was only thinking of Carol, trying to ask without giving her away. Miss Berry's rounded brows moved low.

"Goodness. Why do you ask?"

I could see by her face I shouldn't have. I worried she somehow knew I meant Carol, though I'd never said her name. "I was just wondering. Some of the other girls are older, and I just thought . . ."

"Even if they're older, what kind of life could they offer a child?"

She stared as if waiting for an answer. I used my tongue to dislodge a raisin from my back molar.

"You know . . ." She laced her fingers over my folder. "I like to remind you girls that Joan Crawford adopted her children. Think about that. Those children might have grown up in poverty, scraping by and humiliated, teased at school. But the girls who birthed them put them first. Now I'm not saying this baby"—she gestured across the desk to the porcupine—"will be adopted by a movie star. But I promise you we'll place it with a couple with the resources and stability a child needs."

I nodded, encouraged. I'd seen a picture of Joan Crawford and two of her children in a magazine. Both were towheaded, and looked nothing like Joan, but they appeared happy enough, sitting with her on a beach. The little boy wore a sailor suit, and the little girl had flowers in her hair.

"But she wasn't married," I said. "Joan Crawford."

Miss Berry continued smiling, but she tilted her head. "I'm sure it was a very particular circumstance. Nora, I have to ask. You're still committed to letting this baby get adopted to a stable and loving home, correct? Mrs. Kilgore assured me that you were."

"Yes," I said. On that subject, Mrs. Kilgore and I agreed from the start. "I mean, I don't see how I'd keep it."

She nodded, but she didn't say anything. The porcupine shifted, and I shifted, too, relieving the pressure on my tailbone. I could hear a police car's siren, or an ambulance's, getting louder. I thought that was why Miss Berry had stopped talking. I thought that she was waiting to let the siren pass. But even after it did, she stayed quiet. She seemed to want me to say something.

"Excuse me," I said. "I really was just asking. I didn't mean anything by it."

She put her hand to her chest. "That's a relief. I'm thinking of all you have ahead of you, all you can have. I would love to see you go home with your past behind you, and an untainted future ahead of you. That's my job. We can talk about college, or beauty school, or secretarial school, or finding a nice young man, or whatever it is you want." She again leaned across her desk. "So tell me. What is it you truly want? More than anything?"

I considered the question. No one else had asked me any such thing, not even Mae.

"I want to hear from Leonard," I said. "I want to hear for myself that he knows this is happening."

The friendliness drained from her face. She straightened, gazing down at my folder as if a small, poorly behaved version of Leonard were hiding inside.

"He does know." She looked back up at me. "Your stepmother said his parents confirmed they were still receiving his letters. He's choosing not to write back to you." She slid the tissue box to the edge of the desk. "Ask yourself. What excuse could he possibly have?"

"Somebody else might not be telling the truth," I said.

"Who?" she asked. "Who might not be?"

"Maybe my stepmother." I grabbed a tissue. "I don't know. I want to hear it from him."

She tilted her head again. "You think your stepmother might be lying?"

I shrugged. I sometimes felt suspicious of Mae. If not for Janet, she might have thrown Leonard's letter from Kentucky away without even telling me, thinking she knew what was good for me.

"Nora. May I be honest with you?"

She waited for me to nod.

"I find it interesting," she said, "that you feel comfortable accusing other people of lying, even your stepmother, who clearly loves you. But you refuse to believe that this Leonard is capable of anything except walking on water."

I didn't say anything. I was glad we were downtown, far from the home, and that Carol couldn't be outside listening to how naive I sounded.

"You break my heart," Miss Berry said, and indeed, she did seem truly unhappy, her eyes growing shiny, her pert little nose turning pink. "You girls. You break my heart."

Before I could say anything else, she shook her head and flipped open my file.

"Obviously, I can't call Japan," she said. "But I have the number for his parents right here. If you want to hear it from them, I can call them now." She checked her watch. "It's day-time charges, so I'm going to limit you to three minutes. I'll have to pay the charges myself."

My heart pounded. The Liftons weren't on my approved call list. No one was. Even Mae had said the rates were too high, and we'd need to stick to letters. Miss Berry reached for her phone.

"We'll just get it over with." She was already dialing. "I hope they don't complain that I let you call. Your parents won't like it either, if they hear about it. But maybe it'll bring you some clarity."

I worried that meant she could lose her job. Still, I didn't stop her. I kept my gaze on the porcupine, rising and falling. She was really making the call. Even with the receiver pressed to her ear, I could hear the ringing. It was daytime, a weekday. Mr. Lifton wouldn't be home. There was that, at least.

I heard the line pick up, then Mrs. Lifton's voice: "Good afternoon, Lifton residence." It seemed impossible that all along she could be reached so quickly, and so easily. I held my breath as Miss Berry introduced herself, apologizing for the interruption.

"I have Nora here with me," she said. "She wishes to speak with you briefly. I hope you don't mind?"

Mrs. Lifton said something else, and Miss Berry, her eyes lowered, held the receiver out to me. With a trembling hand, I took it.

"Mrs. Lifton?" I used a finger to close my free ear. Across the desk, Miss Berry looked at her folded hands.

"It's Mr. Lifton, Nora. How are you?"

I couldn't speak. It wasn't yet two in the afternoon. He shouldn't have been at home. "Oh," I said. "I thought Mrs. Lifton answered. I heard her answer."

"Yes. We're getting ready to leave town. For the holiday. What is it that you need?"

The way he asked this, as if he couldn't guess what I might want to know, made me again suspicious of Mae. I straightened my shoulders.

"I'd like to know what you've heard from Leonard."

"No one told you?" He sounded surprised.

"No," I said. "No one told me anything."

"Oh. Well. We let your stepmother know, what Leonard wrote. We assumed she would tell you."

Mae, I thought. Oh, Mae. I closed my eyes.

"He wishes you the best. Leonard wishes you the best."

Miss Berry leaned back in her chair. Her gaze was still averted, but I knew she'd heard him.

"His best," I repeated, steely now. "Anything else?"

The line stayed quiet. I was aware of the seconds passing, my three minutes slipping away.

"Mr. Lifton? Are you still there?"

"He was sorry for your predicament."

I rested my hand on the porcupine, looking at the windows. The sky was overcast enough that when the stoplight changed from yellow to red, the steam took on the same tint.

"We're sorry, too." His voice quieted. He sounded embarrassed. "Mrs. Lifton and I are both glad you'll be able to move forward with your life. We heard you were doing well up there, considering. I'm sure it hasn't been easy."

I nodded. I'd never taken to Leonard's father. But he'd at least always been his true self with me, not feigning warmth he didn't feel. For all I knew, it wasn't Leonard's future he'd been worried about, but mine. He knew his son. He'd known him for longer.

"What did he say about Bradenton?"

Miss Berry looked up with a pained expression, two fingers pressed to her lips.

Mr. Lifton sighed. "He . . . contradicted your claim. He wrote that he never saw you when he was on leave. He said you must be mistaken."

I blinked. Mistaken.

"We talked it over, Mrs. Lifton and I. We admit we can't know for certain who's telling the truth."

"I'm telling the truth." I kept my voice even. "We were together in April. In Bradenton. This is his child, sir."

"Well," he said. "You understand. We can't know."

Miss Berry leaned across her desk, one arm extended, offering to take my hand. I couldn't move. Mr. Lifton cleared his throat.

"We're paying half your bill, Nora. I'm not sure if you knew that. But we are, because of what occurred in our home last year. And that's the most you or your family can ask of us. Given our . . . uncertainty about the current situation."

"I'm telling the truth," I said again.

"Well. The fact is, Leonard is unable to do as you hoped."

"You mean unwilling." I clutched the receiver. Leonard's mother had tried to protect me. I'd thought her a fool, but I was the fool. She'd been alive for longer, and knew a boy's heart could change. She knew her son, as Mr. Lifton did. I was the one who didn't know him.

"I want you to listen closely," he said, his voice surprisingly gentle. "We acknowledge that on at least one occasion, our son conducted himself poorly regarding your welfare. But Nora, you have to acknowledge that you yourself made poor decisions. You promised Leonard's mother that you would stay away. And now you're telling us you broke that promise. So you can understand. We don't know who to believe."

They believed Leonard. I could hear it in his voice.

"We've done all we can to help you get your life back on track. But this mess has all been painful and draining for us as well." He paused. "It was my understanding, I mean with your parents, that you wouldn't contact us. That our business with you would be concluded."

"I'm sorry," I said. I didn't want him to call my father. "I won't call again."

"Then I'll let it go. Provided that you mean that. I don't mean to be harsh. I know you're young. And my wife was always fond of you. But this has been terribly hard on her, especially. Please know that we'll be sending you good wishes. In the next few weeks, and after that. Our hope is that we can all, finally, put this behind us. And you can go on to live whatever kind of life you want."

"Thank you, sir." I truly appreciated his frankness. I wished Mae had shown as much. I lifted my chin. "You won't hear from me again. Goodbye."

I handed the receiver to Miss Berry, and she put it back in its cradle. I looked at her with dread. She had every right to gloat.

"Nora," she said. "Are you familiar with Mary Wollstonecraft?"

I shook my head. I didn't care about Mary Wollstonecraft. I wanted to die.

"Well, over a hundred fifty years ago, she wrote a book called *A Vindication of the Rights of Women.* And one thing she says in it is that she didn't wish for women to have power over men, because what they needed most was power over themselves. And in my opinion, you showed that just now." She put her hand to her heart. "True power. Because you kept yourself together. That couldn't have been easy, hearing that. I'm sure you wanted to scream. But you didn't. You stayed polite and got off the call. That bodes so well for your future. You might not believe me now. But it does."

I believed she was trying to be kind. I was crying full-on by then, my face in my hands. She came around her desk and tried to kneel beside me, but she couldn't because her skirt was narrow. She crouched as much as she could, squeezing my shoulder. She smelled like a perfume I didn't know.

"Listen to me," she said. "I know you feel positively awful right now. But you just took your first step in the direction of dignity. Do you hear me?" She gave my shoulder a little shake. "For goodness' sake. Keep going."

16.

Carol started having contractions just before dawn on Christmas Eve. Within half an hour, the nurses had her packed up and ready to leave. Bad weather was on its way, and it was decided that as soon as the nurses on day shift arrived, the night nurse would take her to the hospital. Better safe than sorry. By the time I made it downstairs, Carol already had on her fur-collar coat and the matching hat, and the night nurse held her suitcase. I asked if I could run upstairs and get dressed and come along to the hospital, and the nurse looked at me like I'd asked to borrow a thousand dollars.

"I'll be fine, dear," Carol said. The way she said it, it was like she could have been talking to anyone. I knew she had other things on her mind, to say the least, but still, her coldness hurt my feelings. We'd spent so many hours outside talking, and those hours had been the only parts of my time in New Jersey that didn't feel lonely. Once she left, those times would be over. I'd never see her again.

"I'll miss you," I said, my voice wobbly. She smiled like what I'd said was funny. She turned to me, though, holding out her arms. Because we were both so pregnant, I had to come in on one side of her. I held on to her a little too long. I'd forgotten how it felt, having another person put their arms around me. The last person I'd hugged was Mae.

"Now, now." She patted my shoulder. "We'll always have Paterson." She was about to say something else when her breath caught, and she stepped away quickly. The nurse looked at her watch and told her to keep breathing. We helped her over to the bench by the door, and she leaned forward, squeezing our arms, until the contraction was over. I'd never seen Carol look scared or even upset about anything, but I could tell she was frightened, and I was glad to be at her side. But almost as soon as the contraction ended, a day nurse came in, all bundled up, kicking snow off her boots, and said the roads were still okay but they wouldn't stay that way for long.

And then both nurses were helping Carol down the front steps to the night nurse's car. I didn't have on shoes, just socks, so all I could do was call out good luck, and hope that she would hear me.

The rest of Christmas Eve was probably my hardest day that winter. Even if Carol hadn't left that morning, I think it still would have felt especially long and gray. The nurses seemed gloomy, too, probably wishing they could be home with their families instead of trapped in a big house with a bunch of sad, pregnant girls. They got some of us to bake and ice cookies, and I helped with a jigsaw puzzle. But most of us, myself included, wanted to try to nap the day away. Sleet tapped on the windows, and we could hear the wind, and the trees creaking. At dinner, the lights of the chandelier flickered more than once. The whole time, I kept wondering how Carol was doing. The nurses said the hospital had a generator, and that they were sure she was fine.

I knew they'd never tell us if something went wrong. Or if Carol really did keep her baby.

I was surprised by how low I felt. I'd only known Carol for a few weeks. But the feeling I had made me think of when my mother took both Bobby and me to the county fair and bought us each a red helium-filled balloon tied to a string. This was an unusual expenditure for her—Bobby and I were used to being told we couldn't have everything that caught our eye. But neither of us had ever seen helium balloons before, and we were so taken by the wonder of them that she made an exception. She tied the strings to our respective wrists, but Bobby's hands were still small, and I don't think he understood how quickly the balloon would leave him behind if it got the chance. Within ten seconds, up it went. My mother tried to console him, telling him the balloon was just trying to get to heaven where it would be happier. He didn't buy that at all, or he didn't care. He was crying, begging my mother to get it back. I felt so bad for him I tugged the string of my balloon off my wrist, but I let go before he had a good hold of it. So up my balloon went as well. What a sorry sight we must have been, the three of us standing there together, looking up, watching those balloons get smaller, until we couldn't see them at all.

I made myself wait until Christmas morning to open the three cards I received by way of Arkansas. Irene and Roberta had each sent a card wishing Mae's mother and me a Merry Christmas, and Irene enclosed a little candy cane, smashed to pieces on the journey north. The third card was from Mae, and when I opened it, a five-dollar bill slipped out. In the card, she wished me a Merry Christmas from everyone, and apologized for just sending cash. She'd been so tired all winter, she wrote, which made sense, as she, too, was pregnant, and getting close to the homestretch. I wrote her a thank-you note so it could go in the post the next day, then went to the common room, where I shook my New Testament and hairbrush out of my stocking. I went down to the office to thank the nurses.

One nurse said that I was most welcome and wished me a Merry Christmas. But the other nurse asked if I knew anything about the Baby Jesus missing from the nativity set in the dining room. I told her I didn't, and she gave me an earful anyway, letting me know whoever did take the Jesus might think she was pretty funny, but that set had been in her family for generations, brought over from France by her great-grandmother. She said she'd brought it to the home trying to be nice to us girls, and this was how we thanked her for the trouble.

I almost got smart with her, as I didn't like being accused, but then I saw this nurse was trying not to cry, and I understood: That little silver Jesus was her red helium balloon. The other nurse tried to change the subject by looking out the window and saying how surprisingly warm it was outside, and didn't the ice look pretty, like so much glitter?

I asked if I could borrow the coat. On my way out of the office, another girl came in, and that same mad nurse started in on her about the missing Baby Jesus, so at least I knew not to take it personally. And as soon as I got outside, I saw that the other nurse had been right about how pretty the ice on the trees looked now that the sun had come out, everything catching the light, even the melting ice dripping from the trees and the house's eaves. It sounded like I was out in the rain, but I was dry, the sun warm on my face.

"Can you hear that?" I whispered, and waited, though the porcupine was never active at that time of day. I still felt my words would reach it. "It's not all so terrible out here." I put a hand on either side of my belly, swaying a little, and thought about the porcupine swaying with me, content. It didn't know it was going to end up with somebody else. "They'll be better for you," I said, as if I knew them, or anything about them. I only knew they'd be married.

After a while, my hands got cold enough that I pushed them both into the coat's pockets, and I felt something hard in the right pocket. I pulled it out and found myself looking down at the metal Baby Jesus, partly wrapped in a torn envelope. The envelope had a stamp and a postmark from Greenwich, Connecticut. The return address was in Greenwich as well.

Later that day, when no one else was in the dining room, I tucked the Jesus back into its crib. As Carol knew very well that I would.

My roommate Helen was gone all day on Christmas. Her mother had picked her up that morning, and she returned in the evening, humming "Silver Bells," her long hair not just freed from its braid, but curled at the ends and shiny. She carried in a portable record player, along with several records she hadn't even opened yet. She plugged the player in by her bed, then asked if it would bother me if she listened to a few records before lights out.

Her politeness startled me. I'd remembered Carol saying that I should go easy on Helen, and I'd done my best to do just that. But I didn't think she even knew my name.

"Sure," I said. "That'd be nice."

"Okay, great." She fanned four different records out on her bed. "Which one do you want to hear first?"

I thought, huh, maybe a certain someone was visited by the ghost of Jacob Marley in chains, and was forced to see her past, present, and the future if she didn't change her rude ways. But really, I guessed Helen was just in a good mood after spending a happy day with her family. One of her records was an Ella Fitzgerald, the one where she sings Cole Porter songs. I chose that one, and soon enough, Helen and I weren't alone. As I said, we mostly kept to ourselves in that house, but let me tell you: If you want to get a bunch of lonely pregnant girls in a home for unwed mothers to shamble into your room on a winter evening and make themselves comfortable, or as comfortable as possible, start playing "But Not for Me" at an even moderate volume. You won't have to wait long. By the time that song was over, I was sitting on my pillow, my knees pulled up to my belly, so two other girls who wanted to listen could sit on the edge of the bed.

Helen took more requests. She had the soundtrack for *South Pacific*, so of course somebody wanted to hear "I'm Gonna Wash That Man Right Outa My Hair." As soon as it was over, someone else asked if we could hear it again. Still, I was enjoying myself, singing along, and all of us pretending to scrub out our hair whenever the chorus came on. But then that song ended and somebody saw Helen's Mel Tormé record and asked to hear "Blue Moon." I almost got up and left. I had no interest in thinking back to that night on the beach when Leonard first said he loved me, and I first said I loved him. The memory now carried a searing pain, and a longing for what wasn't coming back. Still, I stayed where I was, half nestled under my blankets. Just hearing the title of "Blue Moon" already had me thinking of that night. If I got up and went downstairs, I'd be thinking of it while cold.

Another girl, Wanda, appeared in our doorway. She said we had to turn the song off immediately, unless we all wanted bad luck.

"It's not bad luck," Helen said, but she turned off the record. I didn't wonder why. Wanda had arrived at Shaded Acres the week before, looking like someone tried to cut off all her hair with a knife. It had grown back a little, and one of the nurses trimmed the ends. But Wanda was hard to be around without feeling uneasy, as she was always picking her fingernails down to the quick, and I'd twice seen her slap her own face.

"Yes, it is," Wanda said. She scratched at one of her arms, hard enough to make me wince. "A blue moon means you'll be betrayed. And just hearing that song might make it happen."

"What's a blue moon?" Helen asked. "I thought it was just how the moon looks when you're sad."

I didn't know. I only knew the expression, "once in a blue moon," meaning not very often. But the girl with the scar on her face, Beth, said a blue moon was the second full moon of the month, which didn't happen very often, and never in February.

"I always heard it was a good thing," Beth added. She was up next, due any day. She sat on my desk with her knees splayed, fanning her face with a magazine. "Seeing a blue moon. And maybe hearing the song. It means you get a second chance."

"It means betrayal," Wanda said. I'll say this for Wanda: She'd clearly been given an unfair share of troubles in life, but she had beautiful eyes, large and almost sea green. She scanned our faces, one at a time. "A blue moon means you'll be betrayed. And hearing the song might do it, too."

"Too late," Beth said, and I laughed, as did another girl on my bed. I think we were all a little surprised to find out, so late in the game, that we could joke around like this, and find some comfort in one another. For me, that feeling didn't last, as Wanda's gaze fell on me and stayed there.

"It means you'll be betrayed in the future," she said. "The moon where I lived turned blue last fall. I was soon betrayed."

She really talked liked that, Wanda. You half expected her to drop the act and laugh at herself. She never did.

"You mean from the fires in Canada?" Beth asked. "It was all the smoke from it. Where I lived, the moon turned more of a lavender."

Another girl acted like she knew exactly what Beth was talking about, adding that the moon had turned brown where she lived, and that her mother thought an atom bomb had gone off, and was sure the end was nigh. Then Helen piped up and said the moon where she was looked pink from the fire. I seriously wondered if they'd all gotten together to play a joke on me. I didn't remember the moon over St. Pete ever turning any crazy color.

Years later, when I was again working at a library, I looked up news for Canada in the summer of 1950. Everything those girls told me that night was true. The fire started in June, in a forest in British Columbia, growing and blowing east, burning through the summer and into the fall, when a six-hundred-mile stretch of its smoke drifted across the Great Lakes, darkening skies as far south as Georgia. Farmers reported having to milk cows at odd hours. Birds sang as if greeting the dawn at two in the afternoon. All over, people were calling the police and radio stations, asking what to do, as they truly thought that the world was ending.

I didn't know any of this, that night at the home, and so I stayed silent, half listening as the other girls discussed how the moon looked from their respective homes. The only other girl who didn't join in was Wanda. She stayed in the doorway scratching her arms, showing no interest in the conversation as it moved on. When she did talk, it was only to maintain that she'd seen a blue moon in the fall, and that she was sure, still, of what it meant.

17.

My last memory from before I gave birth was biting my own knuckles while lying on a moving gurney, with daylight in the high windows and a nurse running alongside, telling me that I needed to breathe or the baby wouldn't have enough air. I'd been holding my breath because the contractions felt like the porcupine was truly a porcupine, its quills undulating into my flesh. Everyone knows about some women screaming bloody murder through labor, and here's the reason: It hurts so much you think something's gone wrong, that what you're feeling is worse than any normal labor has ever felt, and that you must be dying. When I could speak again, I asked the nurse how long it would take until I went into twilight. I wanted out before the next contraction.

"Hold my hand," she said. "We'll count down from ten together."

I don't think we got to five.

I woke up alone in a hospital room, the window dark, the blinds down. The only light came from a yellow lamp at the head of my bed, and my throat felt like I'd swallowed sand. I wore a gray-checkered hospital gown and a cotton diaper, the crotch soaked with blood. Mae's suitcase stood in a corner, buckles still buckled, handle-up.

I tried to call out for someone, and found that I could only make a high-pitched, whispery sound. I didn't trust myself to stand, so I waited.

"You're still here," I whispered. "It's over, and you're still alive." I was talking to myself now. The porcupine was no longer a porcupine, but a baby in another room, gone from me. "You should be happy," I added. Good try, but telling yourself to be happy when you aren't is like telling your skin it shouldn't itch. Still, if someone would have come into that room and asked why I was crying, I wouldn't have been able to say.

What did help was thinking that Carol had maybe been in this same room, and before her, Lucy, and before her, all the girls from the home who were already gone before I arrived. And they'd all woken up with bloody diapers, too, and probably alone. And they were likely fine now, back in their worlds, their regular lives. Except Carol might have her baby with her.

I'd long finished crying when a nurse came in and gave me a friendly hello. I said hello back, and she said she could hear in my voice that I needed water. She went out and came back with a full cup, which she told me to drink. I drank half and then stopped.

"Is the baby okay?"

She smiled and nodded. She was checking my pulse.

"Boy or girl?"

She met my gaze. "Little girl," she said. "Seven pounds, one ounce. Just fine."

I smiled at this. I would have done the same for a boy. I just liked knowing. *Daughter*, I thought. Not a porcupine, but a little girl, separate from me. Breathing her own air, as I did.

The nurse helped me to the little bathroom, which was right in my room, and she brought in a new cotton diaper she helped me step into. My mouth felt strange, my lips rubbery. After the nurse helped me back to my bed, I thanked her.

She patted my shoulder and said, "You are most welcome, sweetheart."

That gave me confidence. "Could I see her, please?"

She looked down at her watch. I didn't know if she knew what I did: Miss Berry and I had decided that it would be better, easier, if I didn't see the baby, if I trusted it was in good hands and drinking top-of-the-line formula so I could just focus on my future. Miss Berry had said that was the smart option, and what most girls wanted. Sitting in her office, eating one of her sawdust cookies, I agreed this would be the best plan.

But now I was curious. I wanted to see her face. I wanted to see and touch the feet I'd felt kicking inside me for months.

"It's the middle of the night," the nurse said. "You're not in the maternity ward, you know. You're on a different floor. Miss Berry asks that we put you girls somewhere else."

I pushed my hair back and felt something crusty. I tugged out what I could with my nails, examining the flakes. Dried blood. "Why?"

"Because it's quieter." She looked at me like I was a little slow, and then I understood: Because of the babies. Because they would cry, and we would hear them.

She showed me where the call button was, but she told me not to use it to ask for the baby, as the nurses on my floor wouldn't have time to go up to the nursery.

"I'm almost off shift," she said. "I'll tell someone from maternity to check on you in the morning. You can ask then."

The nurse who came in the morning said she couldn't bring the baby down because she was sleeping. The next time this nurse came in, I asked again, and the answer was the same.

"Can't you just bring her in asleep? I won't disturb her." *She's my baby*, I thought, though I knew not to say as much. But she was mine. I hadn't signed anything yet. "I just want to make sure she's okay."

"She's fine." The nurse had me sit up so she could fluff my pillows. "I just saw her. And we don't want to disturb her. Babies need their sleep."

That's when I got scared. For all I knew, the baby might not even be alive. I worried that the nurses might think it a kindness not to tell me. But it wouldn't be a kindness. I wanted to know. When this nurse turned away from me, I reached out fast and took hold of her arm. I wasn't squeezing it or anything, but I had a good hold.

"I just want to see her," I said. "I want to see that she's okay for myself. That's all."

She glanced at my hand and then looked back at my face in a way that encouraged me to let go.

"I told you. She's just fine. You can talk to Miss Berry about seeing her tomorrow." She said this in a soft way, like she felt bad for me. But she turned around and walked out.

The rest of the day, I drifted in and out of sleep. I ate the chicken salad they brought in for lunch. Sometime that afternoon, a girl around my age wheeled in a cart full of books and magazines and asked if I'd like to check anything out. She wore a red-white-striped pinafore over a white dress, and she had a little Red Cross pin on her collar. I thanked her and took a battered copy of *Jane Eyre*, though my head still hurt, and I didn't think I could keep my eyes open for long.

"One of my favorites," the girl said. She had a wide smile, all teeth. Her shoes were patent leather. "I'm a senior in high school, and it was assigned just last fall."

I felt a little better, having her in there with me. We had a friendly conversation about books, though I'm sure my side of it wasn't exactly sparkling. This girl had read a lot of things I hadn't. All the Jane Austens. *Moby Dick*. After a while, she asked where I was from. I said, "Different places," and she let it go at that.

"Do you go by the maternity ward?" I asked. "Have you seen the babies?"

She told me she usually went by maternity at the end of her

shift. She said every volunteer wanted the maternity ward. You had to work your way up.

"My baby's there," I said. "I just had a baby."

She put her palm to her chest, looking worried. "And you have cancer?"

"No," I said. "They just put me here. Maybe you could take me to the maternity floor, to the nursery? I haven't seen her yet."

She fidgeted with the pinafore. "I'd have to get a wheelchair. I'm not supposed to leave the books."

"Wouldn't take long," I said.

I almost had her, I think. But her gaze shifted to my left hand, and I could see in her eyes she was putting things together. Click click click. Before I could say anything else, she'd already wheeled her cart into the hall. She called out that she'd get a nurse for me.

"It's not contagious," I yelled. I don't know if she heard me.

Once she was gone, I wasn't embarrassed. That surprised me. I'd gotten so used to feeling ashamed of myself, but this time, I thought this other girl was the one who should feel ashamed. She'd seemed pretty impressed with herself, standing there in her striped pinafore and rattling off the names of all the books she'd read. As if they'd taught her anything that mattered, or done her heart any good.

I read *Jane Eyre* to pass the time. I liked it okay. But it made sense to me that the volunteer in the pinafore had liked it so much, as Jane also thought she was a little better than people who weren't as morally upright as she was. Still, the early part of the book helped me not to feel so sorry for myself, especially when Jane got to Lowood and the girls there started actually dying because the conditions were so bad. Those poor English girls were half-starved and half-frozen, getting typhus and tuberculosis, but the people in charge were more interested in making them listen to sermons about heaven and hell than they were in truly helping them out in this world. Jane's best friend got sick and died in her arms. Reading all this, I told myself I should feel lucky to be warm in a hospital bed. I had to admit the nurses all seemed pretty obsessed with making sure I was drinking enough water and eating something at every meal.

But the worry for the baby didn't go away. It seemed like the nurses were keeping something from me. And then I started thinking about Leonard, and how he probably didn't even know his child had been born, and if he did, he might not care. It still seemed unbelievable to me that he could have turned so cold and uncaring. I'd start to think there must be a misunderstanding, then I would realize I was being stupid and naive. It felt like I was making myself stand up just so I could knock myself down again, and I hit the ground hard every time. I'd always thought of myself as having a sense about things, a way of knowing in my heart what I couldn't know in my mind. But in the hospital, especially, I only knew I didn't understand anything.

I made myself try to read, if only to remind myself of Jane Eyre and all those girls starving and dying in Lowood, and that things could always be worse.

Later, I would remember this—how even when I was so unhappy and angry and worried, I kept reminding myself that my anguish and confusion couldn't compete with hunger and cold, and the terror of death all around. I was just trying to put my own problems in perspective.

But given what I know now, I wonder if, deep down, some part of me sensed the truth after all.

I woke the next morning to find Miss Berry sitting in a folding chair by my bed, reading the newspaper. She wore a maroon skirt and jacket, and she had a brooch shaped like a snowflake pinned to the jacket's collar. A leather briefcase, the kind a man would carry, leaned against the wall beside her.

When she looked up and saw me watching her, she startled a little, then smiled. "Well, good morning to you!" she said. "How are you feeling?"

I told her that I was achy and sore, and also worried about the baby. She looked at me like she didn't know what baby I was talking about. She really did. I had to calm myself before I clarified. I could smell her perfume, that light pretty scent she always wore, and I knew that if I was about to learn the porcupine was dead or even gravely injured, I would hate this smell for the rest of my life.

"Oh, Nora, she's fine." She reached out and touched my arm. "I saw her myself just now. Perfectly healthy. Just resting. You don't have to worry."

"Thank you," I said. "But I want to see her. I want to see her myself."

I could see she was hurt. She'd just told me the baby was fine, that she herself had just seen her. She took a breath and straightened her shoulders.

"Well, as your advocate, and someone who cares about you, I have to remind you that we talked about this. You and I made a plan. You knew then, when you were thinking clearly, what would be best for you."

"I didn't know I'd be so worried," I said. "If you let me see her, I'll know she's okay, and I won't worry anymore. I'll just see her that one time. That's all I want."

She looked at me for several seconds. I tried to look trustworthy. I believed I was, though my file likely suggested otherwise.

"It's up to you," she said. "It's always been up to you, whether you see the baby or not. I'll go by maternity on my way out, and I'll tell them to bring her down." She glanced at her watch. "But first I need to go over what's next. There are a few things we need to discuss, and I've only got so much time."

Her smile returned as she talked. She said it used to be that she'd have to take a girl to the courthouse to sign the adoption papers, but now she had someone from the courthouse who would bring the papers right to my room. He'd arrive with the papers the following morning, at nine o'clock. She would be there, too, to answer any questions, and she'd come early and help me get presentable.

"You don't need to worry about your hair or anything like that," she said. "He does this all the time. We'll just make sure you're decent."

She said that after I signed the papers, I could stay in the hospital for another week, and have nurses at my beck and call. The hospital would call her to schedule my discharge, and she'd pick me up and take me to the train station. She'd give me money to spend in the dining car, and she'd be happy to take me out to a restaurant if there was time.

"I've already gotten you a ticket to Florida," she said. "But of course you don't want to go home just yet. Most girls need at least a few weeks to get their figures back, and to feel ready to go home. So this is the part I think you'll like." She leaned back in her chair, and the dimple appeared. "I worked out a place for you to recover in private near Cocoa Beach. A widow there manages a thrift store, and she sometimes offers a room and meals in her home to girls who need temporary lodging. It won't cost your family anything. You just need to help her in the store. She knows you have your schoolwork to do, and she said you could do that in the mornings, and then work at the store in the afternoon. I've spent a lot of time corresponding with her, and she is an absolute dear."

"Okay." I wondered how long I'd be wearing the diaper. Miss Berry looked so refined and contained in her skirt and jacket. I still felt swollen and unsightly, like a different species entirely.

"She said you'll stay in the back room of the store, you know, sorting through donations and getting things presentable for customers. I imagine you could hold back some cute things for yourself. Think how good it will feel to be slender again, and to try on a pretty dress with a real waist. Your stepmother said you don't know anyone in Cocoa Beach. That's correct?"

I told her I didn't.

"Then it's perfect. I mean, you'll still want to keep a low profile. You won't see anyone in the store's back room, but Mrs. Clark, that's the widow, said she'd be happy to take you to the beach on weekends. If you do happen to bump into someone you know, it wouldn't be a catastrophe. You could just say you're on a vacation, maybe with your stepmother's mother, the one people think you're caring for."

I understood that this planning was all for my benefit. But I felt a heaviness move over me, as if my very blood were weighted. I thought of that old fairy tale about the girl who chose to dance a few steps in red shoes, and then couldn't stop dancing, even after she grew so exhausted she had somebody chop off her feet just so she could rest. But even amputation didn't work: The chopped-off feet kept dancing around in the red shoes. That would be me, replacing dancing with lying. I'd told one lie, and then another, and now I'd have to lie to nearly everyone until I died.

Miss Berry reached over and gave my elbow a squeeze. "As soon as you feel like your old self again, you'll go home. In the meantime, I'm pretty envious." She looked out the window, at the silvery sky. "You'll be down at the beach with the Florida sun. And I'll be up here freezing."

She waited, not saying anything else. I realized she was waiting for me to thank her.

"Thank you," I said. "I appreciate it." I didn't know if I should remind her to ask if I could see the baby. She didn't seem to be thinking about it.

"You're welcome." She carried her chair back over to the wall. "That's something I really like about you, Nora, how you appreciate the help you're getting. Not every girl does. But you've been such a pleasure to work with." She appeared almost bashful, telling me this. "I want to help every girl, but many of them are . . . well, they tend to focus on themselves. I hear a lot of woe-is-me in this job, let me tell you. But not from you."

"Oh," I said, surprised to hear that she saw me this way. Since I'd arrived in New Jersey, and long before then, there'd been plenty of woe-is-me in my head.

She glanced at the door, still open to the hallway, and closed it. A maroon winter coat hung from a hook at the top. The maroon was the exact shade as her jacket and skirt, and I knew she must have purchased it as a set.

"I definitely shouldn't tell you this." She came close again, lowering her voice to a whisper. "But I want you to know that I found the best people for your baby. I had to work my tail off, but I found the dream couple. I really did. He makes an impressive salary, but he isn't arrogant at all, and she was a music teacher before they married. She can play Bach and Beethoven and all of that, but also things you hear on the radio. They have a piano in their living room, and during my home visits, she played and he sang along. It was so much fun, watching them. They both have warm, outgoing personalities."

I nodded, encouraged. I wanted her to keep talking, to tell me everything about them.

"And they're sweet to each other. So sweet." She touched her hand to her chest. "You can tell how much love they have to give, how excited they are. They've been ready to adopt for a while now, but I managed to convince them to wait for this baby. Your baby, Nora. I mean, I did that for them as well. I told them of your sweetness and your intelligence, and they agree that if she inherits your character, she'll fit right in with them. They have extended family on both sides, all living close by. You're not going to believe this, but the woman's sister just had a baby two weeks ago, and they're one block over. So she'll have a built-in playmate. They're just ideal, Nora. I'm positively thrilled."

"Thank you," I said. I imagined the woman at the piano, the man standing with his hand on her shoulder, and the baby in a bassinet, looking like me and Leonard. My heart felt full, thinking of that. I don't mean I was happy. My heart felt full in my chest the way my eyes felt full before I cried.

"It was my pleasure," she said. "I worked hard for this placement because I know you're a special girl."

I didn't think I was so special. I'd been compliant at Shaded Acres, and generally good-natured. But that was true of a lot of girls there.

"Leonard's smart," I said. "I mean, you can tell them that. Like crazy smart. He took college courses when he was in high school. He kept testing out."

Miss Berry didn't quite roll her eyes, though I could see she didn't believe Leonard was smart, or she didn't care. Then she seemed to reconsider.

"I'll tell them that," she said. "I agree. They'll be glad to know it. These are highly educated people. They'll want the same for her, I'm sure." She looked at her watch. "Goodness," she said. "I'll see you tomorrow, okay? I'll try to get here by eight."

"You'll remember to ask them to bring her in?" I wanted her to know I meant today, not tomorrow. "On your way out?"

Miss Berry tilted her head. "I said I would, didn't I?"

I nodded.

"Well." She took her coat off the hook and slipped it on. "I keep my promises."

I guessed the point she was making.

"I always say"—she rested her hand on the door frame—"doing what you'll say you'll do is the definition of integrity."

There wasn't much I could say to that. So I only nodded to show I understood, and she nodded back, pleased.

18.

I know it's common for people to say that when they first hold their newborn child, they feel overwhelmed with love. I've heard a lot of people say they count the fingers and toes, though I've personally never met anyone born with fewer than the expected numbers. In any case, I didn't do that. I just cried. Because even though she was wrapped in a pink blanket, with most of her tiny head covered in a white knit cap, I could see where the forceps had grabbed her—the curved, red line of the wound started just to the side of her right eye, arced by her little ear, and ended at one corner of her mouth. I didn't touch it for fear of hurting her, but I could see the interior of the curve was slightly lower than the rest of her head.

"That won't even scar," the nurse told me. This was an older nurse, gray haired. She put her hand on my back. "I know it looks bad, but trust me. That isn't permanent damage. They mostly got hold of her cheek, not up above the ears. And it missed her eye completely."

That only made me cry harder, to think she might have lost an eye just trying to take her first breath. She was so light in my arms.

"It really is common," the nurse said. "If you're under twilight, you can't push."

She meant well, but that made me feel worse, to think I'd let her down, this little baby. When she was the porcupine, I'd assured her that she would be fine, that everything would be okay. And when she needed me, the one time I had a job that only I could do, I wasn't there. Asleep at the wheel.

"I'm sorry," I told her. "I'm so sorry. I understand now. I do."

Both eyes popped open. Blue. It was as if she comprehended my words, and knew exactly what I meant: I now understood I was her mother. She was my responsibility. I couldn't check out on her again.

"She knows your voice." The nurse gently rubbed my back. "If she could talk, she'd tell you she's glad to be here. She'd tell you there's nothing for you to feel bad about at all. She'd tell you she's going to be just fine. It's okay, sweetie. Come on, now. You yourself have been through a lot."

I wanted to believe it. The blue eyes were still open, searching. I thought, wow, blue eyes or not, if Leonard's parents saw this baby's face even for a second, they'd know that I wasn't lying. She had the same eyebrows that he did, exactly. I peeked under the white cap and saw a tuft of hair, dark as his.

Her hand emerged from the top of the blanket. I brushed the tip of my pinkie against her palm, and she grabbed hold of it. That was something, feeling that. She was here on this earth, her own person. And she knew I'd made her a promise, even just in my head.

"See? She's shaking hands." The nurse laughed. "She's saying 'Good job. You got me out!'"

After a while, the nurse pulled the chair over to the window and sat in it. Maybe she wasn't sure if she could leave me alone with the baby, or maybe there was a rule against it. But she stayed quiet, watching the window, or just thinking. I lowered my nose close to the baby's mouth and breathed in her soft exhale. She made a little sighing sound, and she shifted in her blanket, then started to bleat like a lamb.

"Due for a bottle," the nurse said. She stood and moved to my side, arms outstretched.

"Can't I feed her?"

"You'll have a hard enough time when your milk comes in. Do your breasts hurt yet?"

I shook my head.

"Well. They will. And if you nurse her, even once, they'll hurt more."

"I don't care about that."

"You say that now," she said. "I'm telling you."

"Can I just give her the bottle?"

She nodded, but she asked me if I was sure. I understood, as I understand now, that she was trying to protect me. She didn't want me to get attached. But I didn't care about my attachment, and I wouldn't have described what I felt for the baby, my daughter, that way.

I kept her with me the rest of the day. I got to change her diaper and see her whole, squirming body, head to toe, and I got to cup my hands around her feet. Even with that terrible mark on her cheek, I couldn't stop staring at her, and I loved, just loved, the feeling of swaying her side to side in my arms. That older nurse—Anne was her name—kept coming down to check on us, and she'd hold her so I could use the bathroom. I remember this nurse's name because I asked her what it was, and because I am still so grateful for her kindness. I think maybe she'd been a nurse so long that she wasn't afraid of breaking rules, or she wasn't afraid of Miss Berry.

Anne's shift ended at six, and the nurse who came down after her said the baby would need to be back up in maternity for the night. I had to say good night, and kiss her little forehead, and let the nurse take her.

The feeling I had, once she was gone—that's when I knew for certain that I didn't want to sign the papers. I had no trust fund, no money to come into. But I got ready for bed, thinking, thinking. I was sure I could figure out a way.

It was on this evening that my breasts turned tender and hot, just as Anne said they would. I wouldn't have called the pain agonizing, not compared to contractions. But I couldn't get comfortable, no matter what position I tried to lie in. A nurse said that after a couple of weeks, my body would figure out that the milk wasn't needed, and so the pressure would go away. In the meantime, there was aspirin. She gave me two, and ice packs to put in my bra. For most of that night, I was awake.

At the first light of dawn, I got up and opened the suitcase. The two blouses I'd brought from Florida still didn't fit. But the skirt I'd worn on the train did, as did my old friend the purple cardigan, which I put on and buttoned high. While I was tying my shoes, a woman in a smock brought in my breakfast tray and told me I looked nice. I understood she didn't mean pretty. The little bathroom mirror showed me my face looked as doughy and pale as it had looked all winter, and the ice packs in my bra made it look like I was trying to smuggle something. I didn't care about any of that. What I wanted was to look competent. Mature.

But when the morning nurse came in, she said I'd have to change back into my gown. "No street clothes until the day you're discharged. Sorry. That's the rule."

I didn't argue. This wasn't Anne, but a young, round-faced nurse I hadn't met yet. She gave me more aspirin and new ice packs. She said because I was up anyway, she'd have someone come in and change my bedding.

"Thank you," I said. "Would you also please bring me my baby?" I'd thought about saying it just this way, planned it out in my head.

The nurse said, "I'll check and see if she's awake."

I knew what that meant. She was already headed for the door.

"I saw her yesterday," I called out. "Miss Berry had Anne bring her to me. She was with me all afternoon."

But the nurse kept walking. "Miss Berry's coming to see you soon, isn't she? You can take it up with her then."

I suppose I could have hit the call button, and made her, or someone, hear me out. Theoretically, I could've stayed dressed, figured out what floor maternity was on, and tried to get there myself. But I never really considered doing that. The only person who seemed to think I had any claim on my baby, aside from me, was Anne, and she'd gone home. I was scared that if I tried to leave my room on my own, someone would call security.

It seemed wiser to stay polite and patient. I was good at being agreeable. I saw this agreeableness not as a trait, but as a skill—one that had served me my entire life.

Miss Berry arrived at eight o'clock sharp, her cheeks flushed from the cold. She wore a mustard-colored dress with buttons that sparkled and a clip-on hat with a little feather on it. The hat looked dry, but the ends of her hair hung damp and flat at her shoulders. I could smell the wet wool of her coat as she hung it on the hook.

"Oh my goodness!" She made big eyes at me. "It's positively cats and dogs out there! The rain is blowing sideways. I'm afraid my umbrella didn't do much good."

She got a washcloth from the bathroom and sat down to dry her briefcase. She told me it was important not to rub leather when it was wet, but to pat gently, slowly working the moisture inward. She was still patting the briefcase when she looked up at me.

"Lucky you. Snug as a bug up here. So nice that the clerk comes to us and not the other way around. I'd hate for you to have to go out."

I'd gotten back in bed because my breasts hurt more when I was upright. The younger nurse had helped me wash my hair and change into a fresh hospital gown, and she told me she thought I was ready to matriculate from cotton diapers to regular underwear and a pad. But I wouldn't have said I felt snug as a bug, or even comfortable. I sensed a small but sharp pain behind my eyes, like a tiny, embedded razor. Still, I'd combed my hair, and I felt clean.

"Ugh. These gray days. I can't stand them." Miss Berry walked around my bed to the window, her heeled shoes clicking on the floor. The blinds were already up, but she raised them a few inches more. "I was thinking, Nora, you must be getting tired of hospital food. There's a bakery down the street that has eclairs to die for. I could run out after your appointment and get us some." She clicked back past my bed and retrieved a shopping bag from behind the briefcase. "I got you a little present." She came close and held out the bag.

I knew I shouldn't open it.

"Miss Berry . . ."

She shook her head. "Don't you worry. I'm a working woman. If I want to buy a present for one of the sweetest girls I've ever met, I'm allowed." She opened the bag, reached in through the tissue, and pulled out a pale pink robe with white flowers on it. She held it up under her own neck and then leaned down so I could feel it. The material was smooth like a ribbon. Not silk, though. Rayon. I knew the difference because of Mrs. Lifton.

"I was thinking you could wear it now? The clerk they send is an older man, always respectful, and he won't be here long. But you might feel more comfortable? And I thought it would look so pretty on you." She held a sleeve open so I could slide my arm in. "You can take it back to Florida with you if you like it. That's the great thing about a robe. It'll still fit as you get your waistline back."

I got one arm into the robe okay. But I had to sit up so she could get the rest of it behind me. She saw me wince and clicked her tongue.

"Oh Nora." She gestured at her own breasts, though hers were regular size, nothing leaking beneath the mustard-colored dress. "They're tender? Did they tell you you need to keep them dry? That's important."

I told her they did tell me. She saw I had something else to say, and she waited, looking worried. I had just one arm in the robe, but I eased myself back on the pillow.

"Miss Berry. I can't sign the papers. That's my daughter. I can't let her go."

She stopped smiling. She looked at me for several seconds, then walked back over to the chair by the wall. She sat in it lightly, her back straight, her ankles crossed and tucked. This new angle made her harder to look at. I tried lifting just my head, but that hurt my neck, so I pressed my hands on the mattress and fully propped myself up.

"Please know how much I appreciate all the work you've done on my behalf."

Her eyes dulled. I understood I was going back on our agreement. But she might have been staring at a wall, not a person, certainly not one of the sweetest girls she'd ever met. I told her that when I'd said I only wanted to see the baby one time, I'd meant it, but now my heart had changed. I told her I'd hated that the baby was hurt by forceps because I'd been too afraid to stay awake and help her get born, and now I knew I needed to stay near her, aware and watching. I wouldn't be able to bear not knowing if she was hurt again in the future, or if she was unhappy or scared.

"But you would know, Nora." Miss Berry closed her eyes. "You'd know because I've spent months picking out the best placement possible." She opened her eyes and pointed at me. "Just for you." She let her hand fall into her lap. "This couple I've selected, they're the best applicants I've ever seen. And they're terribly excited. They've been waiting, counting down the days."

She said all this as if it would change my mind. But I'd already thought about them, this couple with the piano. I felt sorry for them. I bore them no ill will. "They can adopt a different baby," I said.

"Obviously. Obviously they can adopt a different baby. But I wanted them to have this baby, yours, as a favor to you. That's why I put in so many extra hours, and told them to just be patient, even when I worried they would throw up their hands and go to another agency. Because I wanted your baby to have the best placement." She pressed her hand against the collar of her dress. "Don't you see? All of this for you. Nora. I've grown to care for you so much."

I didn't know what to say to this. I admired Miss Berry for her beauty and her nice clothes, for her good posture and her office with her name on the door. I appreciated that she was so much nicer than Mrs. Kilgore. But that was the extent of my caring. Hearing the quiver in her voice, I felt coldhearted. She didn't really matter to me. Not in comparison to the baby.

"Do you know who I really care about?" she asked. "This baby. I thought you and I had that in common. Where is it you plan to take her? Do you think you can take her back home? Tell your father that you're sorry about them blowing through their savings trying to help you, as you've decided to bring home your illegitimate child?"

I shook my head. I knew I couldn't take her home. Even Mae would say no. "There must be some way." I folded my arms under the ice packs to ease the pressure. "Someone who could help?"

"When you figure out who that is, let me know. Nora, come

on. You've got to think responsibly. This isn't a doll. This isn't a game."

I felt cold liquid on my arms, melting ice seeping down. I knew the baby wasn't a doll.

"Could I bring her to Cocoa Beach?" As soon as the words left my mouth, I realized this was the very thing a little girl might ask about a doll. "Could you ask the woman there, the widow? I could keep her with me at the store when I worked. We could stay in that little room together. Just until I figure out where to go?"

Miss Berry reached up to smooth the damp ends of her hair. "Let me ask you something," she said. "Do you really think there's anything loving or truly maternal about taking a baby to stay in the back room of a charity store just so you can have what you want? Think with your head. It's not fair to try to get what you need from a helpless baby. Nora, I believe you have the capacity to be a mother someday. And you have plenty of time to have children. When you're married, when you're truly mature, you'll be able to take and not give."

"I don't care about other children," I said. "I want her. She's already born."

"You don't know what you want. You don't even know where you'd take her. You say you care about her. Do you really want her to grow up without a father, everybody knowing she was born out of wedlock? Think about when she's older and the kids at school are shunning her and teasing her. Think about what you're throwing away on her behalf. Stability. Not to mention a father who loves her, who'll provide for her, not some blow-about who's long gone." She looked hard at me. "Listen to me. This is the one day, the one day of your life that you can't be selfish. You have to put her first."

I couldn't argue with any of this. But I thought of Rochester telling Jane Eyre about the cord he felt between them, a cord knotted under his rib cage. He knew that if it were severed, he'd bleed internally for the rest of his life.

"Did Carol keep her baby?"

She looked so surprised that for a moment, I felt I'd gained something.

"Just to be clear," she said. "This is blind Carol you're asking about? You think she's caring for her illegitimate baby?"

My confidence ebbed. "I know that was her plan."

"I see. Well. I can't violate client confidentiality. I will say that it was my experience, and perhaps yours, that Carol said a lot of things. I will also say it's my observation that you believe people easily. Mrs. Kilgore thought she'd made headway with your psychology, your immaturity, your gullibility. Apparently not."

With that she stood, holding her briefcase by its handle. I thought at first she would come toward me. But she turned and retrieved her coat.

"You're leaving?"

She nodded. "I want to catch the clerk before he heads over here. I don't want to waste his time. I hate wasting people's time."

"Then you'll come back?"

She shook her head. "I'm afraid my day just got more complicated. After I go to the courthouse, I've got to knock on the door of the people who think today is the day they're finally getting a baby, and I've got to tell them that you've changed your mind. They're going to be devastated. Absolutely devastated. And very angry with me. But I should tell them in person, and right away. I owe them that, at least."

She put on her coat. It was a different coat than from the day before, and it was beautiful, dark gray with wide lapels. Even in my panic, I noticed it.

"I wish you the best," she said. I don't know if she remembered this was what Mr. Lifton had told me. That Leonard wished me the best.

"You're not coming back at all?"

She kept buttoning. "I can't help you anymore. I work in adoptions. It sounds like you'll need to speak with someone who works in public assistance, aid programs, that sort of thing. I don't know about all that."

My breathing quickened. I sat all the way up, scooting back against my pillows. My breasts, cradled in my arms, felt scorched from within. "What do I do now?"

"You mean when you get discharged and you have nowhere to go, and you have a baby with you? I have no idea." She took her umbrella off the hook and started to walk out.

"Wait," I said. "Miss Berry!"

She stopped.

To this day, I have trouble watching game shows. Now that most of those shows are televised, the camera loves to zero in on the faces of people having to make all-or-nothing decisions under the pressure of a ticking clock. Some contestants laugh about it, but you can tell when people really need the money, or they have people they love who need it. Those people don't laugh. They look sick to their stomachs, like they already know they'll regret what they're about to say for the rest of their lives. And with those game shows, that's just money on the line.

"Can I have a day to think?" It took everything I had not to claw at my breasts in front of her. "I don't know that I'm thinking straight. I didn't sleep last night." I heard the whininess in my voice and lowered it. "This couple. Could you ask them to wait just one more day? If they're nice as you say, I'll think about it. I will."

"No." She stayed in the doorway. "I'm sorry. But I won't make them dance on your string. You'll just draw out their pain, and I don't want any part of that. They deserve better, these people."

"But there are other couples, right? These aren't the only people in the world who want a baby. Other people will want her, even if I wait?"

"Sure. You'll need to find another social worker to help you, though. I won't trust you with another couple's hopes and dreams. Or with my reputation. Once burned, twice shy. That's me."

"How do I find another agency?"

She shrugged. "The telephone directory? Call some doctors maybe. Or a minister. One of them might know of an interested couple. But you'll need to be careful." She checked her watch. "You can't expect the kind of background check I did—all the interviews and home visits. You'll be taking a risk. I'm sorry, Nora. I really do have to go."

She was actually out of the room when I called to her again. She turned and held the door open. She kept one foot in the hall.

"Would they let me see her every now and then? And maybe send pictures? Just so I know . . ."

"It doesn't work like that." She spoke quietly. "They don't want to share the baby. No one normal is going to want that. They want her to be their baby, and lovingly care for her as their own. Come on now. What you're suggesting might make you feel better, but it would be so confusing for the child. You're only thinking of what you want. Not what she needs. I'm just so surprised at you, Nora. So surprised."

I looked at the far corner of the room, where Mae's suitcase stood. It was made of sturdy cardboard, blue with white stitching. I'd been careful with it, but one of the silver buckles was already broken. Inside were the two cardigans, the Florida coat, the maternity dress I'd worn to the hospital, some underwear, and a few shirts and skirts that might fit me again, or might not.

"They should have her," I said. I was still looking at the suitcase. "Don't call it off. I'm sorry, Miss Berry. I'm truly sorry. You can take her. I'm not thinking straight. I'll sign."

She stayed where she was. She told me she didn't believe me. She was uncomfortable, she said, with my ambivalence. For all she knew, I would change my mind again. And I needed to be sure. Once the papers were signed, they were signed.

"My girls give me their babies," she said. "Gladly. Gratefully. I don't take them, Nora. I don't like how you're framing this. And I won't risk the clerk getting all the way up here so you can change your mind again. If you even seem unsure, he'll get the wrong idea. I've got a reputation to think about."

I could see why she wouldn't believe me, why no one would. But I did mean to stop thinking of myself. I felt I couldn't think at all.

"I'm sorry," I said. "Please?"

She shook her head. "I won't dance on your string either. I like to try with you girls, and to be kind. But I won't be made a fool twice."

It took several minutes for me to convince her to come back in. I had to beg her to take off her coat and sit down. I didn't hold any of this against her. I was thinking she was smarter than I was, for she understood that a person could lie while looking right at you, or change their minds, whatever they promised or said they felt.

When she did say she'd give me another chance, I was so grateful. I thanked her more than once. I put the pink-and-white robe on over my ice-soaked gown and thanked her again. When the clerk showed up, I looked him in the eye and answered his questions, ignoring the itch of my breasts and the ache in my head and the worry for all the worry to come, a lifetime of worry, the cord severed, the helium balloon already rising high without me.

Even when Miss Berry left the room and said she wanted to give us privacy, I signed where the clerk told me to sign. When he said it was permanent, that I couldn't take it back, I said I understood. And when he asked me again, I told him yes sir, I was absolutely, positively sure.

THREE

19.

The moment I stepped off the bus, my father called out my name with such jubilance that strangers turned to look, and he slid past Bobby and Janet to reach me first, his arms spread wide. It was just past six, still daylight, but his cheeks were rough with stubble, and his neck smelled of sweat and cigars. Before he let me go, I guessed—correctly—the reason for his good cheer.

"You've got a brand-new sister, honey." He clapped between my shoulders, and the vibration moved down my spine. "Born last night, seven pounds, four ounces. Healthy as a carrot."

I heard myself congratulate him. I was aware of the corners of my mouth lifting into a smile. He stepped back to make room for Janet, who sang out my name, attached herself to my side and told me the baby's name was Shirley Ann, born with red hair the same shade as her own, the same shade as their mother's. Bobby hung back, his hands in the pockets of dark slacks too warm for the day. He appeared to study my face.

"Let me get that, honey." My father took Mae's suitcase. "How was your trip?" He looked right at me, his expression pleasant. It was as if we'd gone back in time.

"Fine." My heart drummed. I avoided Bobby's gaze. "Good to be home, though. How's Mae?"

"Doing great." He turned toward the parking lot, swinging my suitcase by the handle. He was light on his feet, boyish in his movements. "These two have already seen her and the baby. We'll take Bobby to work, and then I'll take you and Janet back to the hospital so you can introduce yourself to Shirley." He looked over his shoulder at me and grinned. "Mae can't wait to see you. We've all missed you, honey."

Palm trees lined the pebbled path. Janet was still attached to my left hip, her arms wrapped around my waist. Bobby fell in step on my right.

"What's Arkansas like?" He made no move to hug me.

"A lot like Missouri." I squeezed Janet's shoulder, but I turned my head to look at him. He'd grown at least an inch. "Where do you work? You look spiffy."

"Florida Theatre. I take tickets." He waited. "I wrote that to you. I wrote that to you in a letter."

I told him I'd forgotten. I told him that he looked taller. "You should sit up front," I said. "You need the leg room more than I do." I managed a laugh, but I couldn't look at him. He knew. I was almost sure of it.

My father had already put my suitcase in the trunk, and he opened the back door for me and Janet. The inside of the car smelled the way it always had, like the polish he used on the seats. It seemed impossible that just a few months earlier, I rode to the train station in the passenger seat, where Bobby was sitting now. My father would have only changed the oil once since I'd last looked out the front windshield, terrified of what lay in wait, the porcupine still with me, still growing. Now it was over, and the porcupine was gone, a baby in someone else's house. Janet snuggled up against me and thanked me for taking care of her grandma.

"She said she's all better because of you." She rubbed the soft end of one of her braids against the inside of my elbow. "She said you were as nice as I said you'd be. I like your hair like that. Did you make that skirt? I like the little poodle on it."

I shook my head. I'd pulled the skirt from the donation bin in Cocoa Beach. The widow had pointed out that my hair looked thin in places, and she suggested a shorter cut. She'd been a kind woman, soft spoken. Most evenings, she sat in her car, eating pistachios, while I walked on the beach.

"Did you like my grandma?" Janet whispered. "You can tell me the truth now. I know you couldn't in your letters."

I told her yes, I really did like her grandma. My father slowed for a stoplight, humming to himself. Beside him, Bobby stared straight ahead.

Janet traced the outline of my skirt's poodle. "Does she still have that little pond with ducks? That's all I remember about her house."

I told her I felt warm and turned away to roll down my window. When she asked again, I put my hand under the skirt, where the poodle's mouth was, and made like it was trying to nibble at her knee. She squealed and had me do it again, then laughed with her head thrown back. I thought of her missing father, not dead at all, living happily in Virginia with his German bride. I would not cross Mae and tell Janet anything—this I already knew. But now I wondered about this man who'd abandoned this sweet, laughing girl beside me. Did he have new, half-German children he would not abandon? Was he a good father to them? When he was bouncing one of them on his knee and telling him he loved them, did he think of his older, red-haired daughter at all? Did he know she lived in Florida? Or even that her name was Janet? When Mae first told me the truth, I'd thought of him as coldhearted, a snake shedding his skin.

One might call that moving forward. Or slithering away.

When we arrived at the theater, Bobby got out, and Janet asked if I would stay in the back with her for the drive to the hospital. I was glad to tell her yes, as I still felt uncertain of my father. I would only know when he and I were alone if his friendliness was a performance. And I sensed in Janet a true need for my attention in her mother's absence. She rode with her head in my lap, telling me about the three badges she'd earned for her junior Scout sash, and about a classmate who'd been gravely injured after walking in front of a swing set, and about the two songs she'd learned to play on her recorder. I glanced out the window as we moved past Mirror Lake, and my gaze found the pink roof of the library rising above the trees.

"Are you tired of me?" Janet asked. "Do you want me to be quiet?"

I told her I wasn't, and that I'd missed her. When I looked up, my father caught my eye in the rearview and smiled.

Upon our arrival at the hospital's main entrance, Janet said she had to go to the bathroom, and she found one the size of a closet with just one toilet. She closed the door behind her, and I heard the click of the inside lock. I stood next to my father, my gaze trained on the door. Ten full seconds of silence passed. Okay, I thought. He wasn't angry anymore, but things between us wouldn't be the same. I clenched my teeth, accepting it.

"Seven pounds, four ounces," he said. "I remember you were seven pounds even." When I looked up at him, he smiled at me with what appeared true affection. I understood he was making me an offer. The terms were clear.

"That's great," I said. "I can't wait to meet her."

When Janet came out of the bathroom, she took my hand, and the three of us proceeded down the corridor with no sign of discord between us. There was plenty of discord within me. I can't say what my father felt.

"The baby might be in the nursery," he said. "But we'll check with Mae first." I focused on the smoothness of the linoleum, the steady rhythm of my steps. Janet told me she was working on her first aid badge. She'd made a kit, and she wanted to show it to me when we got home. Home, I thought. Home. But I smelled the same hospital disinfectant smell I'd smelled in Paterson. We turned a corner, and a nurse behind a desk greeted my father by name.

"Back already?" she teased. "Don't you need to sleep?" My father laughed and introduced me. The nurse said that she'd heard that I'd been helping a relative in Arkansas. Wasn't that good of me, she asked, especially as no one wanted to leave Florida in the winter.

"It's good to be home." I kept my gaze on her low hairline.

"I bet." She came around to the front of the desk. "And I know someone's excited to see you."

She opened a door to a long room with beds curtained off on each side. As we walked, I heard the high-pitched cries of one infant and then another. I was amazed that my feet kept moving, at what I could will them to do. We were almost at the last set of curtains when the nurse held up her hand for us to wait.

"Mrs. Chesnow? Knock knock. You have visitors. Are you decent?"

The softness of Mae's reply prepared me: She would have the baby with her. Yet when the nurse pulled back the curtain, I flinched at the screech of hooks. It was good that I did this, as it gave me cover, a moment to press my hand to my pounding chest. My father and Janet laughed. Mae lay in bed, cradling her baby in a blanket.

"Oh Nora! Oh hello!" Her voice was an excited whisper. She didn't have her eyebrows drawn on, but her cheeks were flushed, her smile wide. She glanced down into the blanket, then up at me. I thought of something Mrs. Lifton once told me about acting. The secret, she said, was to actually believe, in your own mind, that you were the character you were playing. You had to forget yourself, and forget the audience, and become the person you were playing. You had to feel what they were feeling. That was the way, she said, to make real laughter come when laughter was called for, and real tears as well.

So this is what I attempted. Before I crossed the room to take Mae's hand, I told myself, even in my mind, that I'd really just gotten back from helping her mother in Arkansas, and that I was eager, only eager, to meet my new half sister, because I was still a regular girl. This mindset, I know, was what allowed me to lean over and kiss Mae's cheek before peering down at Shirley's tiny face, which bore no mark or injury. Her mouth was the size of an almond. A feathery line of lashes laced each closed eye. When I said she was beautiful, I meant it.

"Stay right there."

My father pointed a camera at us. The shutter clicked. Janet complained that she wasn't in it, so Mae and I beckoned her over. The shutter clicked again.

I saw these photographs later. I'm wearing the poodle skirt I pulled from the bin in Cocoa Beach, and a white blouse I found there as well. In both pictures, I'm smiling, my arm around Mae in the first picture, around Janet in the second. I think anyone who looked closely could see my smile was strained. For me, Mrs. Lifton's trick of pretending was like walking in high heels—I could do it, but awkwardly, and not for long.

"You should hold her," Janet said. "You just have to wash your hands. There's a sink out in the hall." She was already tugging me by the arm to the door. I pulled back, but she didn't let go.

"Janet, stop." Mae's voice was firm. "Nora's tired. Can't you see how tired she is? She's been traveling all day. And you both have school in the morning." She looked up at my father. "Monte, I'm sorry. Thanks for coming by. I'm actually pretty tired myself."

My stepmother and I glanced at each other. That was all I got, just a glance. But I caught the sympathy in it. Mae wouldn't make a habit of that kind of thing; I suppose she was afraid, perhaps rightly, that such a blatant acknowledgment of the truth would have been my undoing. But that look from her is what stopped me, I think, from losing my mind completely. Though for a long while, I would feel as if I had.

On my first day back at school, Roberta and Irene were waiting by my locker, where they gave me a card and a bag of watermelon Jolly Ranchers. Roberta told me she liked my shorter hairstyle and asked how Mae's mother was doing. I said thank you and fine, relieved that I didn't have to say more, as there was much they wanted to tell me: One of Irene's poems had been selected for the opening page of the yearbook, and Roberta was head of the planning committee for the senior prom.

Irene rolled her eyes. "She's not telling you the big news."

Roberta lifted her hand shyly. The diamond was small, but it caught the light from the arched window behind us.

"Stan proposed?" I asked. "When? You didn't write anything about that."

She said that he proposed just the week before, on Valentine's Day. The wedding would be in October. Her sister, good old Becky, would be her maid of honor, and she wanted me and Irene for her bridesmaids. Irene would already be up at Gainesville, but she'd come back for the wedding.

"You'll be in town, right?" Roberta asked. "You'll be at the junior college?"

I congratulated her and told her yes, absolutely, she could count me in.

My first class was Algebra II. Walking in, I was nervous, but no one stared or smirked. Mr. Fray acknowledged my return, calling me "Miss Diligence" and pointing out that even though I'd been busy helping in a family emergency, I'd still turned in every assignment, done neatly and correctly, which was more than he could say for some people. There were groans all around, aimed at him, not at me. Then he turned the conversation to algebra, everything was the same, back to normal.

It seemed that Mae was right. People mostly believed what you told them. I did my best to focus on what Mr. Fray was saying, but for the rest of class, I kept looking at the backs of my classmates' heads, at the buzz cuts and pin curls and sprayed-stiff chignons, wondering what secrets they might hold. What I might never guess.

On my way to my next class, I had to walk by the junior courtyard. The wall of bougainvillea was again in bloom, and two girls were sitting on the bench where Leonard and I first talked. I was only grateful that as a senior I had rights to the better courtyard with the fishpond, where I'd never once talked with Leonard. In three months, I would graduate. I only had to keep moving forward.

At lunch, Roberta and Irene saved me a seat on the fishpond's retaining wall. A sign forbade us from feeding the fish, but an unwrapped Twinkie floated near the middle of the pond, and Irene, a respecter of rules and of all living creatures, insisted on retrieving it. Her first attempt was unsuccessful, and I was charged with grasping her non-reaching arm so she could try to get hold of the Twinkie without falling in. When she finally lifted it from the water, I recoiled, as did Roberta. The nearest trash can was a good ten feet away, but Irene got up on the retaining wall and made the shot. More than a few people saw the Twinkie sail into the trash, so Irene and I were not alone in cheering. My laughter was sincere. For a full minute, maybe more, I was nearly the girl I'd been.

Someone tapped my shoulder, and I turned to see the freckled face of Hazel Morgan. I didn't know Hazel well—in tenth grade, we'd both been in choir. And she'd been in my first class that morning with Mr. Fray. The back of her head, with its neat pageboy, was one of many I'd studied.

"Aren't you good, Nora Chesnow, taking care of a relative all winter?"

She was smiling, but there was a meanness to her voice. To her right were two other girls I knew by sight, though not by name. They both wore the excited, vigilant expressions of people who'd paid good money to see a magician, but still wanted to catch the sleight of hand.

"Who was the relative?" Hazel asked. Her singsongy tone showed off her soprano range. Heads turned. Other conversations grew silent. I couldn't answer. I couldn't speak at all. For several seconds, I heard only the birds in the branches above. It seemed that Hazel and the girls beside her already knew everything, even about the marks the forceps left, the injuries to that tiny head.

Irene hopped down from the retaining wall, wiping her fingertips on her skirt. "Her grandmother fell. You know that, Hazel."

Hazel's gaze didn't leave my face. "Must have been a bad fall. Where exactly in Arkansas were you?" She gestured to one of the watchers beside her. "Donna here is from Jonesboro. But she's been all over the state."

I knew the name of the town, the one I was supposed to say. Mae had drilled me on the details. If I'd been able to repeat them with any conviction, it might have made a difference. But I had no faith in that possibility. I'd been kidding myself, thinking I'd fooled everyone. People, even my friends, were just being polite. I was as bad a liar as ever.

"Tell them, Nora." This from Roberta, now beside me as well. She touched my arm, and when I turned, her eyes were desperate, imploring.

"Arkansas City," Irene said. "I got letters from her all winter. So did Bertie."

Hazel's freckled brow furrowed. She looked only at me. "Cat got your tongue, Nora?"

This got one of her friends laughing, though the other girl looked away.

"Well," Hazel said. "Whatever you did up there, it did wonders for your figure."

Someone outside my field of vision laughed. Someone else shushed them, then laughed as well.

"Nice talking to you," Hazel said, though she stayed where she was, looking at me. She knew I'd be the one to flee. And she was right. I turned and walked out of the courtyard. I didn't cry. I kept my head up. I was surprised I managed that much.

I'll never know what motivated Hazel to corner me like that. There hadn't been any previous trouble between us. It's possible that she was rankled when Mr. Fray praised me in class. Or maybe she just didn't like lying, or the idea that I was getting away with something. Some people feel consequence is important, not something to be evaded.

A lot of people feel that way.

All afternoon, I grew increasingly aware, given the stares and silences, that news of my conversation with Hazel had traveled. I marched on from class to class, telling myself I could tough it out.

My last class of the day was gym. Because it was raining, we were inside shooting baskets, girls on one side, boys on the other. I heard laughter, turned, and there was Robbie Delvers with a basketball under his gym shirt, his friends laughing. When they saw me looking, they hid their faces, but they laughed even harder. Plenty of girls were smiling, too.

That was it for me. Three more months in that school would have felt like twenty years. I said nothing to the teacher, just headed for the locker room to change.

I came home to an empty house. A neighbor had given us a cherry pie to help us through Mae's hospital stay, and I ate a full slice without sitting down. Even my chewing was angry. Maybe Mae could've convinced everyone I'd been in Arkansas. Maybe anyone but me could've done it, and not stood frozen in the courtyard, terrified and mute. In six years, the only lies I'd told successfully had gotten me on the ferry to Bradenton. I should have learned my lesson, once and for all.

The next day, I went to the library. My supervisor was happy but surprised to see me, as I wasn't due for the first shift of my return until the weekend. I told her that due to unforeseen circumstances, I needed to quit school and obtain full-time work as soon as possible.

"Oh, Nora." She gave my arm a gentle pat. "I'm sorry to hear it. I'll see what I can do."

She was a nice woman, my supervisor. For all I knew, she never believed the lie about Arkansas either, and she expected all along that I'd be too humiliated to return to school. But I'd chosen my words with care, and she might have assumed what I hoped she would: that my family had fallen on hard times financially, and it was because of my embarrassment, for my father, and for all of us, that even as I thanked her, I couldn't look her in the eye.

I didn't tell anyone about dropping out until my stepmother was back from the hospital. Bobby and Janet had already left for school, and my father had left for work. Mae listened with Shirley at her breast, her robe half open, her hair uncombed, her eyebrows still naked of pencil. She didn't ask why I'd dropped out, but I could tell by the slump of her shoulders that she guessed. I told her I was sorry, and she shrugged. All winter, she'd picked up my school assignments, mailed them to Arkansas, and delivered my completed assignments back to my teachers. So all of that work for nothing.

"Well, you're eighteen," she said. She glanced down at Shirley, who stared into the distance with dreamy eyes. "It's your choice."

She said she'd tell my father for me, and we both knew that would be the end of it. Regardless of how he felt about my leaving school, he would guess my reason, and he wouldn't want to discuss it.

Mae used her pinkie to tug her nipple back from Shirley, who already looked different than she had at the hospital—her head rounder, her pruney cheeks turned round and smooth.

"I have to pee," Mae said.

I didn't offer to hold Shirley. I'd done dishes the night before, and in the morning, while Mae slept, I'd made breakfast and packed lunches. But I would not touch Shirley, not even for a minute. Mae seemed to grasp this rule without my announcing it. She stood and carried Shirley to the hall.

"I got more hours at the library," I called out. "So I can start paying you back. Sooner, I mean."

She'd already shuffled out of sight, but I heard her open the bathroom door. "When you can," she said, and closed it.

20.

Every time I clocked in at the library, I both worried and hoped that once I was out with the books, I'd catch sight of Leonard's mother. The Liftons were listed in the newest city directory, their address on Coffee Pot Boulevard unchanged. But week after week, I didn't see her. I suspected that she was avoiding the library because she didn't want to see me.

I still took my lunch breaks sitting on the bench out front, reading while I ate. I'd found a copy of *The Sun Also Rises* in the donation bin at the thrift store in Cocoa Beach. I put a dime in the till, made a cloth wrapper to hide the cover, and brought it home. Most of the story was people being drunk, and watching bullfights, and getting in fights, and sometimes going fishing. But I thought Carol was right about Lady Brett. And I liked the part when Lady Brett tells Jake that another man they knew behaved badly, and Jake says well, everyone behaves badly when given the proper chance.

It was my own book, so I underlined that, and thought about it for a while. It could be a cynical way of looking at human beings, or it could be an understanding way. Take your pick. I wondered if Leonard's mother had noticed that line when she came to it. And if, later, she ever thought of it when thinking of me.

One afternoon, just after I'd finished my lunch, someone sat on the bench beside me. Out of the corner of my eye I saw work boots and denim jeans.

"Shouldn't you be in school, young lady?"

It sounded like the voice of authority. I turned to see that it was just Russ Crandle, my lab partner from ninth-grade biology. I'd done all the work, as Russ lacked aptitude as well as motivation. Still, I wasn't unhappy to see him. I hadn't talked to anyone my age in weeks.

"I could ask the same of you," I said.

"You calling me a young lady?" He laughed his high-pitched laugh, which always surprised me, as even back in ninth grade, his speaking voice was deep. "I was doing some work over there on the shuffleboard flooring." He nodded in the direction of the courts. "I came out here, and who do I see sitting by herself but Miss Nora Chesnow, looking lovely as ever."

I told him I was working at the library, full time, and he gave me a long, thoughtful look. I should note here that since ninth grade, and probably before that, girls in school had called Russ Crandle "Bambi" because of his enormous light brown eyes, lined with dark lashes that I coveted for myself. Back when he was my lab partner, before I'd met Leonard, I, too, had seen the appeal of those eyes. But now I didn't like him sitting on the bench and looking at me, Bambi eyes or not. I could only guess what he'd heard.

"Good for you," he said. "I dropped out last year. Got read the whole sermon about how I'd regret it, throwing my life away and all that. But I'm already making more money than the teacher who said it, I bet. Started a business. Florida Flooring." He got out his wallet and gave me his card, which looked professional, the company name and number printed in red. *Flooring Done Right* was printed in black beneath.

"Wow," I said. "You're doing great." I really was impressed. In school, Russ had a reputation for starting, and finishing, fights. And he'd once come to biology tipsy, humming "Sioux City Sue" and making jokes while I worked. I wouldn't have guessed he'd be handing out business cards one day.

"You should keep this." I tried to give the card back. "I'm not in the market for flooring."

"How bout you write down your number?" he asked. "Fair trade."

I told him I wasn't interested in going out with anyone, and that it was nothing personal. He made a face like he didn't believe it.

"You're still mad?" he asked. "About the eggs?"

I didn't know what he was talking about.

"It was Buddy that hit you," he said. "If it makes any difference, I was only aiming for Leonard. We'd been egging people all night, just having fun, and then I saw that car he drove." He winced. "I know that's no excuse. But I had the biggest crush on you, and before I could even work up the nerve to ask you on a date, you were going around with him. In that car his daddy bought him. I don't feel bad about egging that car. Still don't." The Bambi eyes blinked. "But I didn't want to hurt you, Nora. You've always been sweet to me. To everyone. I'm really sorry."

"I had no idea," I said. I was talking about the eggs. I had guessed, even in ninth grade, about the crush.

"Jesus." He slapped his own knee, hard enough to hurt. "I'm an idiot."

"It's fine," I said. I meant it. Things might have turned out the same, even if not for that night.

Russ scooted to the middle of the bench. "Let me take you out somewhere nice. Try and make up for it."

I told him there was no need. He said okay, well, he wanted to take me somewhere nice. I told him that I wasn't a good investment of his time.

"That's for me to decide," he said.

I declined again. The next day he came into the library, this time wearing a collared shirt and so much cologne that when he approached me, my eyes watered. I told him I was working and didn't want to get in trouble. He said that was fine, as he was there to get a book, though he didn't know the name of it, and he didn't have a card. I passed him off to a librarian and went back to shelving. When I went outside for my break, there he was, waiting by the library's statue of Apollo, which was tall and alabaster white. This Apollo was mostly unclothed, and his muscular physique rose up from a square of boxwood that didn't quite reach his knees. When Russ saw me, he turned his head in profile and raised one arm to mimic Apollo's stance. It was hard not to notice their similar builds. Russ held the pose, flexing.

"Don't you need to work?" I asked.

"That's the beauty of being my own boss." He lowered his arm and smiled. "I work when I want. Stop when I want."

I said that sounded nice and started walking. I didn't want to be rude, but I had just enough time in my break to walk once around the lake. Russ asked if he could join me, and I said he was free to walk as he liked on a public path.

"That's my truck in the parking lot." He pointed. "The blue one. Bought it myself." He smiled. "Nobody handed it to me."

I appreciated the jab against Leonard. I told him it was a nice-looking truck, which it was. Even my father would have said so.

"I'll probably get the newer model next year," he said. "We're about to sell our property. We'll make a lot of money on the sale."

I didn't ask for more information, but before we'd made it halfway around the lake, he made sure I got it. He said that a new highway was going in along Thirty-Fourth Street, and an out-of-town buyer had plans to build a shopping center over what was now Goose Pond and the surrounding properties. Most of their neighbors had already sold. Russ's mother was holding out, and the buying price kept getting higher.

"Everybody thought it was funny we lived in the swamp," he said. "Who's laughing now?"

I knew what Mae would have said: *You need some dip to go with that chip on your shoulder?* Still, most of me was glad for the company. Neither Irene nor Roberta had called me or come by since that day I walked out of the courtyard. I didn't hold that against them. They'd both tried to save me, at risk to themselves, while I didn't try at all. Or couldn't. We'd all taken water safety together. One thing you learn is that when somebody is drowning, you shouldn't think you can save them on your own. It's not like in the movies. Most people can't pull a drowning person to safety. It's far more likely that, without even meaning to, they'll pull you down as well.

A few days later, Russ again found me outside the library, and he updated me on the increasing price being offered for his family's land. The number he quoted seemed unlikely to me, but I didn't question him, as I didn't care. He was convinced I did. If you asked him today, he'd likely say his telling me this number helped change my mind about him.

What really happened is that right around the time Russ

started hanging around the library, Bobby came home from the swimming pool with a bleeding lip and an eye so swollen he couldn't open it for almost a week. I was startled when I saw him, though I knew my brother wasn't exactly a model citizen. Mae had told me that when I was away, Bobby drove some stranger's Studebaker around town for ten minutes—with no license, as he was just fifteen—before an officer pulled him over. But he generally got along with people, and hadn't been in a fight since he was in third grade.

When I asked him what happened, he told me to mind my own business.

Mae said to leave him alone about it. I noticed he didn't get in trouble, not with her, and not with my father. Still, I might never have put things together if not for Janet, who waited until we were alone in our room, the light already off, to tell me what she wasn't supposed to.

"It was about you," she whispered. "The fight."

I lay there in the dark, sweating. I told her to please elaborate. I had to explain what *elaborate* meant, but then she was happy to do so. She'd been at the pool, too, she said. She'd seen the whole thing. Her mother had told her, sternly, not to say anything about it to me or anyone else.

"When we walked by," she whispered, "one of those boys said something, and they all laughed."

Janet said that she couldn't hear most of it, but she heard "sister," and at first she thought they meant her. She couldn't guess what she might have done to cause them to laugh at her, so she asked Bobby, and that's when he turned around and started back to the boys. They were my age, she said, all of them bigger than Bobby.

"But he hit the one who said 'sister' right in the belly. Mom said he should have kept walking."

"That's right," I said, glad for the dark that obscured me. Again, I felt like a cockroach, a creature that should crawl on the floor.

"The lifeguards broke it up. They made Bobby leave because he started it, and they made the other boy leave because he kept hitting after they blew their whistles. Bobby can't go back to the pool for a week, but Mom said he shouldn't go back at all, because the other boy probably only got kicked out for a week, too, and even if not, he could be waiting by the fence. She told Bobby to stick to the beach, and he said fine. But he told me he won't."

I nodded. My brother had long preferred the swimming pool over the ocean. But I knew his pride, what was left of it, was also likely involved. I asked Janet to describe the other boy, the one who'd said something about me. She said he had hair so blond it was almost white, and that after the lifeguard threw him out, he'd gotten into a station wagon with wood on the sides. I knew exactly who that was. Jerry Pinter had been on the swim team with Leonard. Even when school was out, he went to the pool so often that his pale hair sometimes had a tint of green. And he was good friends with Robbie of the basketball-under-the-gym-shirt hilarity. I'd seen them riding together in Jerry's Woody Ford.

The next day, when I came home from work, Bobby was mowing the front yard. I could have waited in the shade of the house, but I wanted some distance from any window where Janet might be lurking. So I stood on the driveway, in the sun. My thinking was that I would summon my courage and apologize to him, for the lying and for the embarrassment.

When Bobby saw me, he gave me a quick nod and kept going with the mower. I waved and pointed for him to turn it off. He did. But I saw in his still-battered face such unmitigated fury that I looked back at him with the same, even as I knew that I was the one who'd made things difficult for everyone. My brother, my younger brother, had been hurt trying to defend me. And yet I wanted to take off one of my sandals and throw it at him.

He leaned on the mower's push bar. "What?"

"Just act like you don't know me," I said.

"No problem," he said. "Because I don't."

With that, he started the mower back up, and I went into the house. I headed directly to his room and found his swim trunks, which I hid under my mattress. A few days later, I heard him looking for them, slamming drawers and asking Mae if she'd seen them, then finally accusing her of taking them, which got him sent to his room. If he suspected I was the real thief, he didn't say.

The next time Russ came to the library, I asked him if he'd like to go swimming. He suggested the beach, but I told him I preferred the pool. He told me the pool was fine with him, and that he could do all kinds of dives off the high board. I said I probably wouldn't swim, but I'd be glad to sit and watch him from a reclining chair. I still had stretch marks, and I didn't want to wear a suit. So I wore shorts and a blouse, and I read while Russ was in line. Whenever he was climbing up the high dive's ladder, I'd put my book down to watch. After he got out of the water, I'd clap or give him the thumbs-up.

Russ truly was a good diver. He could tuck his legs and do a full rotation off the high dive. He could do a backflip, too. And I could tell he liked that I was watching. He'd strut out to the end of the board with his chest puffed out, then look down at me and wave. I was happy to watch and wave back. In his swim trunks, his resemblance to Apollo was even more apparent. I didn't have that ecstatic giddiness I'd had with Leonard, but I appreciated Russ's beauty, the power and vigor of his body, the smooth skin over his muscled back. I didn't like that I noticed.

I thought, my God, even after everything, I haven't changed a bit.

The next time Russ and I went to the pool, I was again disappointed. But on our third visit, I spotted a Woody Ford in the parking lot. It wasn't an uncommon model at the time, but I was hopeful as Russ paid our admission. Once we were inside the fence, I spotted Jerry's white-blond hair. He was with one of the boys who'd laughed when Robbie put the basketball under his shirt. Jerry and this other boy were in line for the low dive, talking to each other. When I walked by with Russ, they both looked down at the wet concrete like it was the most fascinating thing they'd ever seen.

I set our things by a reclining chair. Russ jumped right into the water, wanting to cool off before he got in line for the diving board. I was hot and miserable, wishing I could get in. But I smiled as I made my way back over to the low dive. Jerry and the other boy were still in line. They pretended not to notice my approach.

"You two have anything you want to say to me?"

I knew they'd heard me, though I was facing the pool, watching Russ thread his way across. Leonard had been able to glide a quarter of the way across the pool without coming up for air, not even upsetting the surface. Russ was a splashier swimmer, chopping his way down a lane. But he was almost as fast. I could see I wouldn't have much time.

"Excuse me," I said. I had on dark glasses, my eyes obscured. "I asked you a question. If you've got something to say, say it to me, not my brother. You're three years older than he is. You bother him again, or even look at him, and I'll have to find someone I know to take up for him. You understand, I'm sure."

Jerry's friend took a careful step away from him, though that meant he was barefoot on dry concrete. He hopped from one foot to the other as Jerry stared straight ahead. I cleared my throat, and Jerry nodded.

"You're sure?" I looked back out at the pool. Russ had reached the end of the lane and was now chopping his way back. I didn't know if he'd do another lap. "'Cause if you wait until later, it won't make a difference. I'll still let Russ know. You might as well get it out now."

"I'm sure," Jerry said. He sounded enraged, which I found satisfying. I heard the spring bounce of the board, and then a splash. The line moved forward. I wished both boys a good afternoon and went back to my chair. Before Russ was even out of the pool, Jerry and his friend abandoned the line, opting to instead put on their shoes, grab their towels, and leave.

I returned my brother's swim trunks that evening. He was in his room, and I tossed them on his bed without saying anything. He didn't say anything to me. Nor did he even say hello when he saw me at the pool the next day, or the day after that, or any time that summer, though Russ and I were there almost every evening.

By June, I was taking off my cover-up and getting in the water. I got sick of being hot. If Russ noticed the stretch marks, he didn't say anything, and no one else did either. By August, I had a pretty good suntan, and the stretch marks were harder to notice. I'd heard Mae telling a friend she was rubbing olive oil on her belly and her legs, so I got a bottle for myself, and it helped.

21.

Russ and I had been seeing each other for only four months when he took me to a seafood restaurant with a view of the water, a wine list, and a roving accordion player who'd just started to play "Embraceable You" when Russ reached across the table for my hand and asked me to marry him. I told him no as gently as I could, wishing I hadn't just ordered the crab and asparagus pappardelle. Not cheap. But Russ didn't get upset. What he did was shoo away the accordion player and list the reasons I should reconsider.

For one, he said, he'd wanted to marry me since ninth grade. Apparently, he'd made up his mind about this while I dissected a frog as he watched and squirmed, or while I labeled a diagram for him to copy. At first, he said, he just thought I was so little and cute, but he'd come to admire my personality, like how serious I seemed with my schoolwork, and how I was a nice girl but not a snob, and friendly to everyone. He said he'd also long appreciated that I, unlike other girls he'd dated, didn't curse or dress like a slut. Even his mother liked me, he said.

When that set of declarations didn't change my mind, he moved on to an economic argument. The sale was going through, he said, and his mother was giving him a good percentage of it to put into his flooring business. He already knew how he would invest the money. He could assure me that any wife of his was going to be more than comfortable.

When this failed to persuade me as well, he moved to his final argument, which was that he'd heard I'd gone away to have a baby, and everyone knew it, though nobody could guess who the father was. And yet he still wanted to marry me. He was that crazy about me.

I glanced at the accordion player, now two tables away. "If you don't start speaking more quietly," I said. "I'll leave."

I wasn't bluffing. I would have gotten up and started walking, though it was already dark out, and I would have nowhere to go but home, where even Janet was preoccupied with the ever-increasing charms of Shirley. St. Pete still didn't have a television station, but that was no problem for my family, as every evening they gathered in the front room to watch Shirley on her blanket, delighting in her new ability to gum both her hands and feet. The night before, she rolled over for the first time, and though my bedroom door was closed, I heard the applause, loud and clear.

So I was relieved when Russ lowered his voice.

"Not trying to be mean," he said. "You know what I'm saying. Most men would only see you as an easy mark. Not wife material."

He said this with regret, as if he were sorry to be the one to break the news. I told him that he wasn't telling me anything I didn't already know. But I'm sure he could see I was reeling. All that money spent on New Jersey, all that lying, and apparently, the only person who believed I'd been in Arkansas was Janet.

"I'll probably leave town," I said. "I can leave anytime. I'm eighteen. I can go anywhere."

I was talking more to myself than to Russ, considering the possibility. I'd almost paid Mae and my father back. And there was no need to stick around for Roberta's wedding. In August, she'd called to let me know her mother had decided to cut back on the number of bridesmaids, meaning from me and Irene to just Irene. She said she hoped I would still come as a guest. I wasn't sure that was true.

Russ leaned forward, Bambi eyes merry. "I notice you haven't left yet."

"I don't want to live far from my family," I said. It was true. Even with the isn't-Shirley-so-cute party always going on at home, I didn't want to go so far away that I'd hardly ever see them. For me, that seemed even more lonely than staying.

"I understand," he said. "I think that's sweet, that you want to stay close to home. I don't want to leave town either."

"Sounds like I might have to," I snapped. "Given what you

and everyone knows." I could do it, I thought. I could go just far away enough where no one would know about New Jersey. Atlanta, maybe. I could go make a new life, new friends, and move forward, just as Miss Berry said.

The accordion player drew close, smiling at us. Russ rolled his eyes and made a "go away" motion with his hand.

"Honey." He sighed, looking at me with what appeared real sympathy. "Even if you leave town, even if you go somewhere where nobody knows, you won't be able to hide what's happened from a husband." He lowered his gaze. "You understand what I'm saying? A man can tell."

I felt I would be sick. My only comfort was that Russ wasn't speaking from experience, at least not experience with me. All this time, I'd refused his more ardent advances, trying to portray myself as virginal, a wait-until-marriage girl, stalling for time. Stupid. He'd probably known about the baby from the beginning, when he first asked me for a date.

"You marry somebody else," he continued, "someone who doesn't already know, and you'll have to take your chances. You could try lying, but you're no good at that. Even if you just say nothing, if you wait until after the wedding, he'll know on the wedding night that you weren't truthful. Damaged goods." He shrugged. "With me, I already know. And I still love you. So you wouldn't have to worry."

I told him he sure knew how to sweep a girl off her feet. But I did feel unsteady, even sitting down. When I tried to take a sip of water, the ice rattled in my glass.

"I tried romance." He gestured at our surroundings, the waiters in tuxedoes, the candlelit tables. But the accordion player, no longer his friend, had moved on to a bouncy polka.

"For your information," I said, "I don't care if I'm wife material. I don't want to be a wife."

He pulled his head back. From the look on his face, I might have told him I planned to move to Russia. I might have told him I was from Mars.

"Don't you want kids?"

I shook my head. Just her. I wanted no more after her.

"Why not?"

"I just don't." I didn't owe him more than that, crab pappardelle or not. If he wanted to cancel the order or eat it for himself, fine. I could give him the phone number for Shaded Acres, and he could call up Mrs. Kilgore or Miss Berry and they could all talk about how crazy I was, thinking one little baby couldn't be replaced like a pair of shoes.

"You'd be such a good mom," he said. "Seems like it to me."

I shook my head. Obviously not. I didn't even know my daughter's name. I didn't know if she was dead or alive. Or suffering. I had no idea.

"Okay," he said. "But you still need someone to care for you. And someone you can care for." He shrugged. "I don't really like kids anyway."

I didn't say anything to this, but I made note of it. I wasn't sure I had it in me to live my whole life alone. Aside from Janet,

Russ was the only person who seemed to still want to be around me at all. I put my hand back on top of the table, and he reached around the candle to take it.

"Tell me who it was." He ran his thumb, rough with a callus, over the skin of my knuckles. "You should at least tell me that."

I tried to pull away my hand, but he held tight. I told him it didn't matter.

"It does to me. I'd like to have a talk with him."

"He's not around," I said.

Russ squeezed my hand once, then twice. "The only guy I ever saw you with was Leonard Lifton, and he was off in the army by the time in question. You can't give me a name?"

I shook my head. "I won't."

He kept at me about it until our food came. But I was never tempted. At the pool, I'd been relieved that Jerry Pinter got the message to keep his mouth shut well before Russ got out of the water. And it seemed likely that Leonard would eventually come back to St. Pete, if only to visit his parents. I didn't want anyone seriously hurt, not even Leonard. At least I usually felt that way.

The Wednesday before that Christmas, which was Christmas of 1951, I dressed for work then went out to the kitchen, where I found Mae still in her bathrobe, blowing on a plate of mashed carrots while Shirley shouted *babababa* from her high chair and pounded her spoon on her tray. Her two top front teeth had just come in, and she grinned at me as if wanting to show them off. Mae didn't seem as happy.

"I shouldn't have made these." She glared at me, then at the carrots. "I can't give them to her until they cool, and"—she cupped a hand around her mouth and lowered her voice—"she takes forever to eat them." She put her hand down, her voice returning to regular volume. "I'm supposed to drop off the muffins by ten, and I haven't had a minute to soap myself down."

I checked my watch. The muffins were for Janet's classroom, and Mae had made them the night before. It seemed to me Janet could have just taken them with her on the school bus. But she'd insisted her mother should bring them at the appointed time as all the mothers of her classmates had done. Janet had specifically asked Mae to comb her hair and put on a clean dress so as not to embarrass her in front of her teacher.

"Just give Shirley something else," I said. "Why's she having carrots for breakfast anyway?"

"Because I'm her fool." Mae opened her robe and sniffed one of her armpits. "You know she loves carrots. I switch it up now, she won't eat at all, and she'll be fussy when we get there."

"Can't she just eat a muffin with the kids?"

Mae gave me a haunted look. "I made exactly the right number." Her voice was low, simmering. "What the teacher asked for. And anyway, she wants the carrots. You look nice, by the way. You look all ready for work."

"Thank you." I poured my coffee. I knew what her compliment really meant. In her mind, I'd carried on with my rules about Shirley for too long. I was being dramatic. Enough was enough. We both knew I didn't have to be at the library until eleven.

"I'll feed her," I said. "Go take a bath."

She kissed me on the cheek and said she'd be quick. As soon as she was out of the room, Shirley let out a howl of sorrow.

"Now now." I closed my eyes, trying to get in character. I hated the sound of Shirley's crying, the helplessness of it, the persistence. I hated hearing it even when I was back in my bed, the covers pulled over my head. Some people just shrug off a baby crying because that's what babies do, but if you look at them, you see their pain, their frustration. Their worry and sadness—it's all real to them, and frightening.

Still, as Shirley pounded and cried, part of me thought, *Oh, you're upset because your mother left you for ten minutes? Try a lifetime. Think how that feels.* I told myself that my own daughter was probably just fine, getting love and everything she needed from the nice people with the piano. When I picked up the bowl of carrots and tapped the spoon against the bowl's edge, Shirley went quiet, staring at the bowl. I sat at the table beside her.

"I like carrots, too," I said. "Which makes sense. You and I are sisters." I was pushing myself, trying. I knew if I kept not looking at Shirley, and never holding her, my list of regrets might grow even longer. But I rarely got this close to her. From where I sat, I could pick up the sweet, milky scent of her breath.

"I'm sorry," I said, still stirring. "It's not your fault. Never said it was."

She glowered at me with teary eyes. Behind me, water for Mae's bath whistled through the pipes. Shirley resumed crying, banging her spoon on her tray.

"She's coming back." I blew on the carrots. "I promise." I turned on Mae's little radio for distraction. What I got was the opening strains of "White Christmas," hardly a surprise in December, but I started to laugh in a giving-up kind of way. I thought of the nurse at Shaded Acres who'd yelled at us for feeling sorry for ourselves. I wondered if her husband was still in Korea, and if that nurse was yelling at a whole new crop of crying pregnant girls, and pointing out that "White Christmas" wasn't written for them.

Shirley reached for the carrots. When I told her no, they were still too warm, her screaming grew louder. I got a piece of ice out of the freezer and stirred that in, then tasted a spoonful on my tongue. "Okay," I said. "Problem solved. Thank you for your patience."

She really was crazy about carrots. As soon as I nudged the bowl in front of her, she used the spoon she'd been banging to dig right in. I knew Mae meant for me to watch her, so I stayed where I was, listening to "White Christmas," and wondering about Wanda, again living in whatever town she'd come from, scared of blue moons and more betrayal; Lucy might be in college, getting ready for final exams, maybe still at war with her mother, but free forever from marrying Vernell. I wondered about the unknown girls who were at the home now, sleeping in the beds we'd slept in, scared out of their minds, and going downstairs to listen to the same crew of volunteers: the makeup artist, the ballet instructor, the woman who'd had us make collages. I wondered if Miss Berry was still working in her office, or if she'd married the man who sent the roses.

And I of course wondered about Carol. When I first got back to St. Pete, I still had her address memorized, and I wrote it on a scrap of paper, then taped the scrap to the ceiling of the closet I shared with Janet. But I hadn't written to her, and I had no plans to. When she gave me her address, she thought she was keeping her baby, or she was pulling my leg.

Shirley had only eaten maybe a third of the carrots when "White Christmas" ended and the news came on. The North Koreans and Chinese, as part of cease-fire negotiations, had released their list of UN prisoners, and the list included the names of over three thousand American soldiers currently held captive in North Korea. President Truman said that this list was unverified and should be treated with skepticism, but *The New York Times* had gone ahead and published the list in its entirety, printing each man's name, rank, and service number. The reporter moved on to news of a Thai prince getting married in Paris, then said he had to break for another commercial.

Shirley swayed her head to the Pepsodent jingle, which made her spoon miss her mouth by an inch. She thought that was pretty funny. I laughed with her, but I had the feeling of walking in high heels. When I heard the bathwater turn off, I was glad.

I gave Shirley the thumbs-up. "She's almost done," I said.

When she finished eating. I cleaned her face and arms and got the message that she needed a new diaper, so I carried her back to the room she still shared with my father and Mae. Almost every day, Janet wanted to know when Shirley's crib would move into our room. Mae kept putting her off, and I understood she was continuing to give up both spaciousness and privacy out of kindness to me. But that couldn't go on forever.

When Mae came out, dressed and refreshed, I handed Shirley over, packed my lunch, and left for the library on my bike. It was a pretty winter day—the breeze pleasant, the sun bright. I didn't pedal with any particular urgency, but I arrived early enough for my shift that I had time to walk around the lake before I went in. Instead, I went right up the steps and inside, where I said hello to the librarian at the front desk before making a beeline to the newspapers. The library had its own subscription to *The New York Times.*

The front page noted the prisoner list, along with a forecast of more icy weather and a report of Russia executing two American spies. I set the paper on a nearby table, and turned one page, and then another, my gaze moving over smaller news items and advertisements for Christmas gifts. *Give her what she'll love! Ho ho Hoover.* The list of prisoners started on page 14, the names printed so small I had to lean over and squint.

I found Leonard's name on page 15, between *Lieb, Thomas,*

and *Liles, Paul.* I still had his service number memorized, from writing it on so many envelopes.

I folded the paper, and I put it back in its place. I walked back over to the librarian I'd just said hello to and told her I was sorry I couldn't stay for my shift. She asked if I was okay, and I told her the truth. Before she could ask me anything else, I was already out the door.

22.

I let my bike fall onto the Liftons' front yard, the front wheel still spinning as I ran for the door. Her yellow car was the only one in the drive, but if I'd seen her husband's, that wouldn't have stopped me. I pushed aside their Christmas wreath to knock, my fingers stiff from gripping the handlebars. I could hear music through the open windows, something with violins, some symphony she'd know the name of that I didn't.

I counted to five, then knocked again. I thought, my God. My God. He's a prisoner. So not in Japan. What did I feel? Confusion. And something like hope, rising up, only to be knocked down by what I knew was likely. He'd been sent back to Korea, then caught. He might be in danger, and that was serious. But he didn't love me, and he didn't care about the baby. Nothing regarding me had changed.

When I cupped my eyes to the screen of one of the front windows, I could see past the living room into the dining room, where a mug and a plate sat on the table. I decided to go home and telephone. That would be the right thing to do. But as I was getting on my bike, I felt the breeze lift my hair, and I threw down my bike again. She had a sprinkler going in the side yard. I ran right through its mist to the back.

And there she was, on the little patio off her bedroom, wearing dungarees and an untucked shirt that was too big for her, the sleeves rolled up to her elbows. They still had all that nice patio furniture, exactly as it had been, but she stood by the sliding glass door with her back to me, her hands on her hips. When I said her name, she spun around.

"Oh my goodness! Nora! I can't believe it. My goodness. How are you?"

I was still working to catch my breath. I was surprised by how much older she looked, even in the shade of the overhang. I hadn't seen her in two years. I likely looked older as well.

"Did you know Leonard's a prisoner in Korea?" I asked. "His name's on the list, in the paper."

When she stopped smiling, she looked even older. She was thinner than I remembered, and it showed in her face. I could see, for the first time, what she would look like as an old woman, in twenty, thirty years.

She put her hand to her chest. "Oh you saw the list. Of course. I heard it was out today. We've known for some time, though. Leonard was captured in July." She stepped into the sunlight, shielding her eyes. What she saw in my eyes must have worried her.

"This last July," she added. A honeybee emerged from a white flower on one of the climbing vines. She reached over to shoo it from my face.

"I thought he was in Japan."

"He was, Nora. They sent him back to Korea in the spring. Sweetheart. Do you want to sit down?" She gestured at the love seat. "You look like you need to sit down."

"No ma'am. Thank you." Her lemon tree was taller than it had been. They had a cover over their swimming pool. Beyond their lawn and the retaining wall, the water in the bayou glinted.

"That was in March," she said, "that he was sent to the fighting. After . . . after you were in New Jersey. When we learned he'd been captured, we were actually relieved. I mean, it's better than the front. You know? He's not having fun, but he's safe."

I told her that I did need to sit down after all. She took me by the arm and guided me to the love seat, then she told me she'd be right back with some water. She went inside, locking the screen door behind her. Even in my distress, I wondered if she was calling my parents, or the police. Her husband had told me to stay away. They'd paid half the fee. The baby was gone. Our entanglement was concluded.

She came back out with a glass of water and sat beside me. She was barefoot, her toenails unpainted.

"He's not hurt?"

"No." She closed her eyes and put her hand to her chest. "He's fine."

"You're lying," I said. "You're lying to me."

She opened her eyes. We stared at each other. She had to be lying. I wanted her to be lying. On the ride over, I pedaled as hard as I could, weaving through traffic, terrified but also elated because finally, finally, something made sense: Leonard never wrote because he couldn't.

"Oh Nora," she said. "I'm so sorry. I see that you got your hopes up. But he's really okay. He was in Japan, on base, before you left for New Jersey, and he was still there, in Japan, when you came back." She reached for my arm. "Sweetheart. You've got to move on."

I pulled my arm out of reach. "How do you know he's okay? He's a prisoner. How do you know?"

"Well, he writes to us," she said. "I'm sure his letters go through their censors, but it's his handwriting. He says he's fine. He sounds like himself."

"Meaning?" Bitterness curdled inside me. "What does sounding like himself mean?"

She caught the edge in my voice and hesitated.

"Really," I said. "I want to know."

"Okay." She threw up her hands. "He wrote that he misses my lasagna. He said the food was adequate, but only that. And he wishes he had a book or two, as there isn't a lot to do. But he knows how lucky he is, riding out so much of the fighting in Japan, and now as a captive. He said other men there, you know, other prisoners, came in injured in battle. But he wasn't. Thank goodness. He was just caught."

"Huh," I said. I was thinking how unfair that was, all those men getting hurt. Decent men, probably. And he was fine. "Does he ever ask how I'm doing?"

She bit her lip. I saw the pity in her eyes. I didn't care.

"Mrs. Lifton, did he meet somebody over there? Is that what happened?"

She winced, then nodded.

Okay, I thought. Okay. At least I knew. I told myself it shouldn't hurt so much. He was no prize. If some other girl didn't care about character, she could have him. But a sob rose in my throat. He'd fallen in love, was what had happened. He really had moved on.

"This girl. She's still in Japan, waiting for him?"

She nodded again. "I'm so sorry, Nora."

I didn't want her apology. We both knew she'd tried to warn me. I'd just been the first girl brave enough to talk to him, to see he didn't have the confidence he should. Perhaps I'd given him confidence, and he'd taken it to Japan. I didn't know if this girl he loved now was a USO girl or Japanese, or anything about her. And I didn't want to know. He had the right to fall out of love with me, and to fall in it with someone else. But he'd had no right to leave my letters, my pleas for help, unanswered. Or to say I was lying about Bradenton.

"Let me ask you something, Mrs. Lifton. Did he ever ask if his child was a boy or a girl? Was he curious at all?"

I knew I was making her uncomfortable. That was okay with me. I wasn't going to sit there and act like her son was a decent person. As if I were the liar and he wasn't. How tragic that he missed her lasagna. How devastating that he didn't have a book to read, and he had to just sit and stare at whatever walls were keeping him safe.

"Just to be clear," I said. "He knows about the baby?"

She nodded. "He was sorry about it. He was glad you could get a fresh start."

I stomped my foot so hard she flinched.

"There's no fresh start! Mrs. Lifton, I've got a little baby out in the world, and I didn't know her name, or if she's even alive. And for what? Nothing would have made it worth it, giving her away. But I'm still disgraced. My family's disgraced."

"Oh Nora. Oh. I'm so sorry."

Heat rose in my throat. "That was Leonard's child. Okay? I know I broke a promise to you when I met him in Bradenton. But I did meet him in Bradenton. In April, when he was on leave. If he told you I'm lying about that, he's lying. I want you to know that. I've never been with anyone but him." I wiped my face with the hem of my skirt. "I get it now. I was a passing thing for him, but he wasn't that for me."

She reached across my lap and took both of my hands. Her fingers were cool, her hold on me gentle. "Of course you're hurt. Of course. Oh I wish I could undo all of it." Even her arms looked thin, the skin around her elbows sagging. I leaned back to look at her.

"Mrs. Lifton? Are you okay?"

The question appeared to confuse her. I tried to think of the right words.

"I mean. Are you . . . ill?"

She blinked and touched her hand to her face. I worried she thought that I'd meant to be mean. But I had no spite for her. Out of the three of them, she'd been the kindest.

She laughed a little. "I'm afraid you caught me without my face on. A little paint can do wonders for a woman my age."

"I didn't mean . . . Mrs. Lifton, you're so beautiful, still."

I said it because I believed it. But she turned away like I'd embarrassed her again. When she turned back, she looked at me with frankness.

"I should be honest with you. These last few years have taken a toll on me. First there was all the fighting between Leonard and his father. Leonard joining the army, throwing away his plans. When I knew he was in Korea again, maybe on the front lines, I could hardly eat or sleep I was so worried. I'm feeling better now, knowing where he is, and that he's more or less safe. But I just want him home."

Now I had to look away. Everything she'd just listed, everything she'd gone through, could be traced back to me. It seemed a wonder she didn't hate me. But even as I was thinking this, she reached over and tucked a strand of hair behind my ear.

"What are you up to these days?" she asked. "You must have graduated in May."

I didn't want to tell her that I'd dropped out. "I'm just working at the library. Living at home."

"Well. There are libraries all over, Nora. Have you thought you might have an easier time in another place? You said you were disgraced. But that's just here. That's just in this one little town. What's holding you here?"

"My family," I said. It was true. I was trying with Shirley, and hoped I could start to love her. Bobby still felt distant to me, but that might change with time. If I went away again, it might not. And even if I could somehow get a high school diploma, I didn't want to go be an airline hostess, smiling at the general public, assisting with crying babies. I didn't want to meet a handsome pilot or any other man that I'd eventually have to either lie to or horrify. I didn't want to do anything.

"You could always come back to visit them. When you were in New Jersey, did you get a chance to go into the city?"

I knew she didn't mean Paterson. "Just in passing," I said. I didn't know how she imagined Shaded Acres, or how things were there. It wasn't like they took us on field trips.

"Well," she said. "I can tell you I loved living in New York as a young woman. A single woman. People are less judgmental there, not so caught up in everyone else's business."

"I hated the cold," I said.

"I see. What about California then?"

I almost laughed. The other side of the country.

"I could even help you get started. Maybe give you a little seed money? I have friends out there. I could make some phone calls, help you find a situation. You're still young, Nora. A lot of people go out there to start over. People change their names. They change everything."

I was silent, watching her. She hadn't realized that she'd tipped her hand. Maybe her husband thought I was lying about Bradenton, but if she felt guilty enough to want to give me seed money, even on top of the money they'd already spent for Shaded Acres, she must believe I was telling the truth. I was glad that she believed me, but I wouldn't take another penny from her. I didn't want her to be able to write to Leonard that she'd purchased a clean conscience for him. I didn't want her to tell him I was a charity case, either.

"I might get married," I said. "Someone's asked me."

She straightened her shoulders. "I'm not surprised," she said. "What do you think of him?"

I didn't know what to say to this. For the last half year, what I'd mostly thought of Russ was that he wasn't Leonard. Now I saw the differences between them to Russ's advantage. Russ wasn't a coward. He wasn't some little boy needing me as ammunition in his war with Daddy. And Russ loved me, even as I was.

"I think highly of him," I said. I liked the way she was looking at me now, with more respect. "I'll likely say yes."

"Oh Nora. That's wonderful! Where do you think you two might settle?"

"Here," I said. "He's from here. He's got a flooring business."

"Well. He could put in flooring anywhere."

"He's established here," I said. "Quite established." Tell your husband that, I thought. And see you at the country club. But she only looked happy for me.

"Everywhere needs flooring." She paused. "I'm still thinking it might be good for you, even as a married woman, to get away from St. Pete. To not have . . . so much old baggage. You'll likely have children with this man, and you wouldn't want them to hear. What would this fellow think about—"

"I'm not having more children." I wanted her to understand. "That broke me, Mrs. Lifton. That broke me, giving away my daughter. That was my daughter. I had to give her away."

She looked as if I'd slapped her. I could only hope she now understood, in a way she hadn't before.

"You still might be happier, with a fresh—" She paused and started again. "Someplace new. Without the memories."

"My family's here," I said. "Why do you want me to leave town?"

For the first time, for as long as I'd known her, she slouched.

"It's for you," she said quietly. "I want you to leave for you. Before he comes back."

I felt panic rising. "When's that?"

"I don't know. The negotiations have started again. That's

why China released the list. Leonard wrote to us that when it's over, they'll likely come to St. Pete." She glanced at me, nervous. "Of course we want him to come back here. And she's curious about Florida."

With one breath, I took this in. My face didn't change. The sky could have cracked in half, and you wouldn't have known it to look at me.

"Well, well," I said. "I see why you thought I should leave."

She nodded. "Might be easier."

"For me or for him?" I cleared my throat. "Excuse me. For them?"

"Oh Nora. For you. He's my son, but I've always cared about you. Whatever you want to believe, I'm thinking of you. It won't do you any good to have to worry about bumping into them every time you leave the house."

"Maybe he should worry," I said. "Maybe he should worry about bumping into me."

She didn't say anything to this.

"What's this girl like?" I asked, hating myself for it.

"It doesn't matter. Don't worry about her. You have so much potential. You could go anywhere."

A new suspicion came to me. "Did he ask you to suggest I leave town? I bet he'd love that. I'm sure he doesn't want me to meet her. Boy, would I have a story for her."

"She already knows," she said. "Apparently they already discussed the matter."

"The matter?"

"I'm just quoting him, Nora. I'm sorry."

I hated this girl, this girl who might be Japanese or German or a USO girl from Toledo, this idiot girl I knew nothing about, who knew the most shameful thing about me. I didn't envy her, though. If Leonard did bring her back to St. Pete, and I saw the happy couple in passing, I'd just feel sorry for the girl, with her lying coward of a husband. Even if no one believed me, I would know the truth.

I stood up. "Thank you for your concern," I said. "But I won't burst into tears if I see them, I assure you. I'll be fine."

This wasn't a lie. This was a promise to myself. One I was determined to keep.

"Okay." She stood as well. "You're the captain of your ship, Nora. But I'm rooting for you. I hope you know that."

"I do," I said. Leonard was her son, and of course she still loved him, right or wrong. But I could tell she cared for me, still. I could see it in her face, and hear it in her voice. She just didn't understand that a new town wouldn't change things for me. St. Pete was my home. If Leonard and his new girlfriend, or wife, didn't like seeing me, they could be the ones to leave.

I stepped out of the shade of the overhang, then turned back, shielding my eyes. "Are you going to tell your husband I came by? He told me I shouldn't bother you." I waited. "I won't do it again."

"Okay," she said. "I understand. I won't tell him."

Here she was, once again keeping something from her husband for me. I thought of that French saying, *the more things change, the more they stay the same.* I knew how to say it in French. But my accent was still terrible, and it wasn't as if she and I would have a good laugh over it. I took one last look at her, then turned and walked in the direction of dignity, step by shaky step until I reached my bike.

23.

Russ's mother wanted us to have what she herself had only dreamed of: an autumn wedding at Sunken Gardens, with guests invited to sit under shade trees and watch us take our vows beside a waterfall with flowers blooming all around. She paid for the service, along with the reception at the Yacht Club, where every table had an orchid for a centerpiece. By then, she'd sold their land to the developers, and she had no trouble thinking up the names of almost a hundred old enemies and new friends she wanted to see the kind of celebration she could now afford. That was fortunate, because aside from my family, my only guests were three of my coworkers from the library. Irene and Roberta had both sent congratulations and regrets through the post.

But Janet was thrilled to serve as maid of honor, and Shirley, carried by Mae, was an only somewhat fussy flower girl. My father, looking as proud and happy as I'd ever seen him, walked me down the aisle.

Bobby merely attended. I doubt Mae gave him a choice.

As newlyweds, Russ and I started out staying with his mother while looking at houses for sale in town. But then a contractor tipped him off about lots for sale on a soon-to-be-created island by the Gulf-side beaches to the west of town. This new island, called Paradise Island, would be a twenty-minute drive from downtown, which in those days was far. Russ had always wanted his own dock, and the contractor said the island would be shaped like a tree, the dredged sediment packed and shaped in thin branches so every lot would have direct water access. Russ immediately grabbed a half acre on Dolphin Drive, one of the island's cul-de-sacs that jutted out into the intercoastal waterway.

It turned out he was smart to do it. By the time our house was built and we moved in, every lot on Paradise Island was spoken for, and we had new houses going up on either side of us. You could see by the frames they would be like ours, wide ranches with attached garages. From dusk to dawn, I heard the buzz of saws and the pounding of hammers.

Dolphin Drive, being so new and not yet fully populated, wasn't on the paper route yet, but I listened to the news on the radio. I knew the war in Korea was still going on, and that Mrs. Lifton had been too optimistic about the negotiations. I assumed Leonard was still in the prison camp, missing his mother's lasagna while his true love waited patiently in Japan. I still hoped we wouldn't resort to an atomic bomb on North Korea, as I didn't actually want Leonard and his new love vaporized, let alone all the innocent people who'd die along with them. But that was the extent of my caring.

The house on Dolphin Drive was the first place I'd ever lived with air-conditioning. The fifth day of March 1953 might be widely recognized as the day Stalin died, but for me, it will always be the day Russ installed a window unit in the bedroom, and another in the dining room. Hail to thee, great AC. Russ bought a third unit to give to Mae and my father, an early Christmas present. Mae called Russ a prince, and said she'd never slept so well in her life. I still did better in the heat and humidity than most people, but there were long stretches of summer when I was glad to have December at the turn of the dial. Russ also bought me an automatic washing machine, no wringing required, and an electric dryer as well. So I had plenty of time between chores and cooking where I could just crank up the cold, lie on the couch, and read.

The library, like every place that hired females, reserved jobs for the unmarried. They were right that I no longer needed the paycheck, and really, I didn't even need to go to the library at all anymore. If I wanted any specific title, I could just tell Russ how much I wanted to read it, and the next time he was downtown, he'd stop and buy it. I read some of the big novels I'd always wanted time for: *Anna Karenina*, *Middlemarch*, *Les Misérables*. One day Russ dropped me off at Haslam's while he went to play pool, and I found a hardback copy of *Black Boy* by Richard Wright. I purchased it, along with a magazine, and had the cashier put both in a bag.

The next afternoon, while Russ was at work, I started in on *Black Boy*, and I learned that Mr. Wright had been born in Mississippi—not so long ago, not so far away. It was an uneasy feeling to read about, and then to understand, his dread of white people, as I knew that would include me and everyone I loved. One thing I underlined was *Whenever my environment had failed to support or nourish me, I had clutched at books. . . . Reading was like a drug, a dope.* I got that Richard Wright didn't mean an environment like being a married white lady sitting in electrically chilled air on a couch all afternoon, but when I looked up from his book and out our windows, at the skeleton house frames and bare soil of our yard, all I wanted to do was lower my gaze and turn another page.

Richard Wright's mother had a paralytic stroke when he was ten years old, and she had more strokes after that. He wrote that watching her suffer when he was young set the tone for the rest of his life, both shutting his heart and forever opening it to others, making him both tender and violent, both caring and hard.

My mother hadn't suffered before she died, or if she did, I didn't see it. But I understood what Richard Wright said about the pain you feel when someone you love suffers, and how that can change you into a different person. Because when I imagined my daughter suffering somewhere, alone and helpless, it was like the hammering and sawing from next door and across the street were coming from inside my head. I'd tell myself she was happy and safe with the piano people, and that I'd done the right thing, giving her up to them so she could have a good life. Or I'd try to focus on the words of a book. Usually, none of that worked. I just had to wait for the spike of worry to pass.

I couldn't talk to Russ about her. Once, when I'd had too much to drink, I'd made the mistake of bringing her up, and all that did was get him started on who the father was, and why wouldn't I give him a name, and how he'd like to kill whoever it was, et cetera. He got pretty worked up when I wouldn't say who—he'd knocked back a few beers himself—and then I had the added problem of trying to calm him down while still feeling as bad as I did in the first place. Lesson learned.

Mostly I was fine, content with our life, the two of us sharing a home and seeing my family on Sundays. That was enough, what I wanted. So all was well, in some ways. But I remained sure there was something unnatural about me, something cold. Having done what I'd done.

The following summer, the war in Korea really did end, and I heard on the news that all the UN prisoners, including the Americans, were being released. I assumed Leonard and his girlfriend would get married before they came back to St. Pete, which was still small enough that our paths might eventually cross. So it was another good reason to stay home as much as possible.

By then, St. Pete had finally joined the twentieth century and gotten a television station, WSUN. (*Why Stay Up North?* the jingle asked.) Russ had to go all the way to Tampa to get a television set, just in time to watch the World Series. I'm sorry to say that once he did that, I felt I'd found the real drug, the real dope. I still read, but it didn't take me long to figure out that when Russ was at work, I could carry the ironing board out into the living room during my favorite shows.

I particularly loved Betty White's show. She had visiting guests and a live band, but most of all I liked Betty, always so cheerful and put together. She'd come out at the beginning to tell riddles like *What's the difference between a kiss and a sewing machine? One seems so nice, and the other sews seams nice.*

Once, when Russ was sick, he stayed home from work and watched Betty White with me. He thought she was okay, but he said if he was going to watch a woman on television, he wanted her to look like Marilyn Monroe. We'd gone to see *Niagara* earlier that year, and he immediately started begging me to bleach my hair and to wear it short with big curls like Marilyn's. I did it, and I ended up really liking it. Having my hair that way didn't make me look like Marilyn, but I did look like a different person. When I went to show Mae, Shirley started crying—she thought I was a stranger. And it was an easy enough hairstyle to manage. I'd put it up in rollers under a kerchief when Russ was at work, and I'd take them out before he got home. The big curls around my face really did look pretty, and because I stayed inside with the AC, they typically held.

One afternoon, Betty White had a blind woman on her show. This woman, Elena was her name, had been born with sight in Mexico, and she could still see fine when she came to the United States as a child. She grew up in the States, got married, and got to be such a good cook that she and her husband started selling Mexican and Spanish dishes right out of their house in California. When everybody went crazy for the food they served, Elena and her husband opened a restaurant, and it took off. She'd been running the restaurant and expecting their second child when she started to lose her vision. She told Betty White that she got pretty down about it for a while, and the restaurant closed. But she taught herself to cook without her sight, and then she started teaching cooking classes, and because she was so good at that, everybody said she should write a cookbook. She went ahead and wrote a cookbook, hoping she'd make enough money to get herself a guide dog. But everyone went completely crazy for this cookbook, and she made enough money for a guide dog and also a few extra houses, and then somebody decided she should have her own television show, though only people in California could watch it. She told Betty White that when she was on set, she had strings tied to her ankles, and stagehands would tug on one ankle or the other so she would know which camera to face.

And she talked about raising her kids, how she'd taught them to cook as well. All after losing her vision.

Of course this made me think of Carol. Miss Berry had made it seem like I was a fool for even half believing a blind girl could take care of a baby, but here was a blind lady with two kids, a bestselling cookbook, and her own television show. So Carol had been right to think she could do it.

This is an ugly thing to admit, but I felt a little better, knowing that Carol's blindness wasn't what kept her from keeping her baby. That meant she was the same as I was, no better, no worse. I still had her address in Greenwich, and I started thinking about writing to her, to see how she'd done with moving forward. I sort of felt I'd done it. Some days more than others. I wondered if Carol felt the same guilt, the same worry.

I kept my letter to her short, and vague enough so whoever read it to her might think I was just some girl she'd met on vacation or at summer camp. But I wrote out my phone number, along with the hours I'd be available, meaning the hours Russ wouldn't be home. Those hours mostly fell when long distance rates were most expensive, but I remembered she had a typewriter with Braille keys, so I also wrote out my address, not just on the envelope but in the letter as well. I got it out to the mailbox that very day, just before the mailman came.

A week later, I was watching *Betty White* when the phone rang.

"Is it really you, dear?" I couldn't believe it, that I was hearing her voice. She sounded exactly the same. "Mrs. R. Crandle of Dolphin Drive?"

I jumped up and down, holding the cord. I told her I was sorry she had to call when the rates were so high. "If you want to call back before nine tomorrow, I'll be here."

She said that she would, but she at least wanted to say hello while she finally had me on the line.

"Cruel Nora, waiting so long to write. And why did I never guess Florida? Of course it was Florida. I'm in New York, by the way. I got my own place last year, better for everyone. But Mother was good and forwarded your letter. She's not always a brute."

"You're in the city?" I hoped to sound sophisticated, asking it the way Mrs. Lifton would have.

"Yes. Listen, what's become of you, dear? How are things?"

I told her I'd gotten married, and I was living in a nice house right on the water.

"The cad returned from Korea? Or some new lucky egg?"

"Someone new," I said. "Better." I reached up to smooth my hair and felt one of the rollers. "Are you married?"

"Not married, no. But a certain young man keeps me entertained."

"Oh!" I said. "Tell me more." The conversation wasn't going the way I'd imagined it, with both of us talking of guilt and worry, or of the strangeness of what we'd done. But this was nice, too, talking about happy things, talking as friends. "I bet he's madly in love with you," I said.

"Correct." She laughed. "The obsession is mutual, I'm afraid.

I find his taste in music offensive, but I hear he's terribly handsome." A woman in the background, maybe speaking to Carol, said something I couldn't discern. Carol sighed into the phone. "Ah, speak of the angel. Here he is now. David? David. There's a dear. Come say hello to Mommy's friend."

I went right down to the carpet, my legs folded beneath me, the receiver pressed to my chest. Still, I heard the high-pitched "Heyyo?" and then Carol's laughing praise. Through the sliding glass door, I could see Russ's new motorboat, waiting at the dock. He'd applied vinyl letters to spell out *The Last Laugh* on both sides of the hull.

Carol said my name, then said it again. I put the receiver back to my ear.

"I'm here," I said. Faintly, I heard the woman who'd spoken to Carol before say something else.

"It's fine, Birdie. I'll ring if I need you to take him. Nora. You won't believe this, but my son is strong-willed."

"You kept him?" My voice rose up as if asking a question.

"Of course." She sounded offended. "I told you I would, though I admit it wasn't easy. What a gadfly that Berry was at the end. She kept going on about how selfish I was being, and the adoptive mother I was devastating. Apparently a soft-spoken angel who played the piano. With perfect vision, of course. And a husband who loved to sing. A built-in cousin down the street, born just a week before. Berry was perplexed that I could be so heartless. If I loved my child, how could I rob him of all that, just thinking of myself?"

I reached up for the phone's cradle, my finger hovering over the button. It was my own fault. I'd believed Carol had been weak as well. I'd let that ease my conscience.

She laughed. "As if calling me selfish would have ever worked. I said, 'Yes, thank you, dear. It's a trait I hope my child inherits. If he doesn't, I'll have to teach him the value of it. Selfishness I mean.' Oh, I could smell her smoldering. But she didn't give up. She'd go home and come back the next morning, freshly perfumed and ready to do battle again."

The child, David, said something, and Carol paused to tell him he would need to either wait in her lap or go back to Birdie. I heard the whine of a buzz saw from across the street, then Carol's voice again.

"On the third morning I just started screaming that someone had to let me telephone my mother, and finally a nurse let me. Once Mother arrived, it was all over. She saw that I wasn't giving in. We hired one of the nurses to come back with us, and that was the—"

"I signed," I said. "I signed away my baby."

She was silent. I felt myself falling, though I was already on the floor, my forehead pressed to the carpet.

"Well, I assumed so, Nora. That was your plan all along—"

David's voice broke in, high and insistent. Shirley showed the same impatience whenever Mae was on the phone.

"We'll go soon, darling. Nora? Are you still there?"

I sat up. "I have to go," I said. "My husband and I, we're having another couple over tonight."

This was true. Peg and Buddy would arrive at six. But I was just making a salmon casserole, and I'd already sautéed the celery and whisked the cornstarch into the milk. I could have done the rest while on the phone.

"I'll call back. Tomorrow, you said? Maybe earlier?"

I touched my hand to my hair, to the rollers. "No," I said. "Please don't call here again."

She thought she'd misheard. She made me say it again.

"But you wrote to me."

"I didn't know," I whispered. And then she understood.

"Now hold on, Nora. I wasn't trying to be cruel. I didn't know that—"

"I don't want you to call back." My voice was calm, certain. "Okay, Carol? I don't. I shouldn't have given you my number. Will you promise?"

She was quiet. The buzz saw went quiet as well. For what seemed a long time, maybe half a minute, there was only the sound of David's crying. I felt cold to it, unmoved.

"All right," she said. "I promise. But Nora—"

I shook my head. Nothing she could say would console me. And for all I knew, with Carol being Carol, consolation wasn't what she had in mind. I felt as if I were hanging from a cliff, my fingernails dug into the earth. Any added weight would do me in. She might not understand that. So I pressed the button, ending the call.

24.

Russ came home a few hours later. When he saw me, he took a step back, jingling his keys.

"Whoa," he said. "Why'd you do that?"

I told him I'd just felt like it. By this, I meant that after I got off the phone with Carol, I decided I wanted the rollers out of my hair. But instead of unrolling them, I got the kitchen scissors and cut them out. My hair was still wrapped around them when they went in the trash.

"Jesus." He put his free hand on my shoulder and turned me around. "It's just that . . . Jesus. Can somebody fix it?"

I shook my head. That had been the point. It had never occurred to me, not once, that Miss Berry might be lying about the couple with the piano. I wondered how many girls she'd told this lie to, and how many had believed her. Carol hadn't. Not for a minute.

"I'm not trying to be mean," Russ said.

"I know," I said. I could tell when he was trying.

He put his hand in my hair and tugged on a few strands like he was hoping that would make them longer. "I don't think we can cancel," he said. "They got his mom to watch Buddy Jr."

I told him we didn't need to cancel. "I'll put a ribbon in it or something. I made a salmon casserole. It's all ready. Go ahead and shower."

With that, I went back to the kitchen. I didn't want to cancel. Buddy was hardly my favorite of Russ's friends, but his wife, Peg, was always nice to me.

Russ was still getting dressed when they arrived. I opened the front door, and they both gasped. Peg recovered more quickly.

"You're like Audrey Hepburn!" She stepped closer to where I stood in the entry. "Wow. I could never be that brave."

"Glad to hear it," Buddy said, and laughed until Peg hit him. He wore a bright red shirt with an embroidered parrot on the pocket. "I'll hide the scissors, just in case."

"He only means I don't have the face for it." Peg stepped inside and started to take off her shoes. When I told her she needn't bother, she shook her head. "They're killing me. My feet got bigger with the baby, like my butt."

Buddy strode past me and hollered for Russ, who emerged from the hallway in clean clothes, his hair still wet from the shower. He didn't smile, and I understood that he was embarrassed of me. The ribbon didn't really help.

"What's buzzin', cousin?" Buddy twirled his hat on one finger, then handed it to me.

"Let's take the boat out, catch the sunset," Russ said. "We've got all night to eat."

That was fine with me. My casserole would lose its little soufflé top, but Russ knew, as I did, that going out on *The Last Laugh* calmed him like nothing else could. When he came home angry about a lazy employee, or an unpaid bill, or the streets clogged with tourists who couldn't drive, he'd often head directly to the boat and stay out on the water until he felt better. Sometimes he went by himself. Sometimes he liked to have me with him, sitting beside him and not saying anything even when he stepped on the gas and turned an arc so tight I was sure we'd tip. For me, a few moments of terror seemed a fair exchange for a smoother evening to follow.

This evening as well, getting behind the wheel of the boat did wonders for his mood. Peg had tied a kerchief around her hair, but we were going so fast the wind snatched it into the water, and soon enough, her hair looked pretty crazy, too. We stayed out for almost an hour. By the time we sat down for drinks on the patio, the clouds were pink with the setting sun. The construction workers had all gone home, and our limb of the island was quiet. Buddy and Russ reminisced about youthful antics, and I sipped my drink, trying to focus on how good the breeze felt against my neck and ears without so much hair in the way. But I was mostly thinking of Miss Berry, how she lied about the people with the piano. She might never have even met the people who adopted my daughter. She'd just wanted me to sign, to get her away from me.

"Okay," Buddy said. "I see we're boring your poor wife to death. Time for a change in subject." He smiled at Peg. "You want to tell them the big news?"

I looked across the table in time to see Peg shake her head. I knew what Buddy would say next. I had time to get into character.

"Buddy Jr. will soon be a big brother." He popped an olive into his mouth. "This one's due in June."

How wonderful, my character thought. I reached across the table to squeeze Peg's hand. I said congratulations. Russ jumped up and ran around the table so he could slap Buddy on the back. I'd set out a fresh pitcher of vodka lemonade, and before Russ sat back down, he topped off everyone's glass and made an earnest toast that included the word *shazam*.

"Thank you, friend." Buddy looked at me, and then at Russ. "So when are you two gonna have an ankle biter?"

Before either one of us could answer, Buddy whipped his head toward Peg.

"What was that for?" He leaned down to rub his leg.

"Rude question," she whispered. I sipped my drink, the lemonade tart on my tongue. The ribbon in what was left of my hair felt tight, so I tugged it out. From the corner of my vision, I could see Russ leaning back in his chair. He smiled at me in a wistful sort of way. I looked at my watch, then out at the water.

“It’s not rude.” Buddy took another swig. “It’s a good question! We’re not getting any younger.”

“I’m going to check on the casserole,” I said. I didn’t look at Russ, and he didn’t look at me.

Peg jumped up and said she’d come in with me. I told her she should just sit down and relax, but she shook her head, glared at Buddy, and pushed her chair in.

In the kitchen, she told me that she was so embarrassed, and that Buddy was drunk, and that he just didn’t think sometimes. Peg had gone to high school in Clearwater, and because she’d always been so friendly to me, I’d convinced myself that she’d heard nothing of my going away my senior year. But that evening in my kitchen, she looked at me with so much sympathy that I was sure she knew about the baby. Looking back at her, I felt the pressure of tears, and not from sadness. For a moment, I felt understood.

“Have you and Russ ever thought of adopting?”

I was holding the casserole dish, a pot holder on each hand. I shook my head. Behind her, the window over the sink let in the last amber light of the sun.

She stepped toward me. “My cousin in Pensacola adopted a little boy last year. I saw him at Christmas, and oh my goodness, this child.” She raised her palms as if in surrender. “He’s just beautiful. And they brought him home when he was just two weeks old. My cousin is the only mama he knows.”

Even with the pot holders, I could feel the heat of the dish, my fingertips starting to tingle. I could have set the dish on the counter, but I didn't.

"It did cost quite a bit, I think. They had to save for years." She looked around the kitchen. "It looks like that wouldn't be such a problem for you and Russ. And you know, they've got all those orphans coming over from Korea. But there's white babies, too, maybe orphans, or their parents didn't want them. It breaks my heart. All these little babies that need homes."

"Why does it cost money?" I asked. "If the babies need homes, why does it cost?"

She tilted her head, thinking. "I guess I don't know," she said. "There's the hospital. But my cousin and her husband paid a lot more than we did to have Buddy Junior. I guess they have to pay the agency."

Again, Miss Berry appeared in my mind. Her pretty clothes. How I'd admired them.

"Why are you laughing?" Peg asked. When I didn't answer, she told me to set down the casserole dish so I wouldn't burn my fingers.

"This is my house," I said. "Don't tell me what to do."

Poor Peg. Here she was on her big night out, trying to be nice. I'm sure she wanted to go home right then. But there was nothing for her to do but follow me back out, where Buddy and Russ were talking football, specifically the NFL draft. The conversation didn't pause as she took her place at the table. When I served her some of the casserole, she thanked me, and said nothing else, turning away to gaze out at the water. It was almost dark, a full moon rising, ghostly and close to the horizon.

Russ said he liked the casserole. His eyes were glazed, his cheeks red. He smiled at me as if my haircut no longer offended him. I imagined telling him I had to go visit an out-of-town friend for a few days. I could take the train up to New York, and then a taxi to Shaded Acres. I could pound on the front door, and as soon as it opened, I'd run inside and tell any girl who would listen not to believe the story about the couple with the piano, and not to believe anything Miss Berry said, and to instead ask her how much she got paid every time a girl signed the papers. But even with my head buzzing from the vodka, I knew that the girls there now would just think I was some crazy woman with crazy hair. News of my visit would get back to Miss Berry, who could just think up a different story, maybe adoptive parents with a pony ranch, adoptive parents who'd already put up a swing set made of gold, adoptive parents who ran their own summer camp in Maine.

Another problem with the plan was that Russ would never believe me. I was as bad at lying as I'd ever been. And he knew I didn't have any friends.

I offered everyone seconds. Only Peg, still silent, declined. I poured drinks and looked at the fading light on the water. I told myself that the people who adopted my daughter might be good people, piano or not. It seemed like someone who took the trouble to adopt a baby might cherish one more than someone who'd just had one by accident. On the other hand, Mae had recently called to tell me how the man who'd moved in next door kept his sweet dog in the backyard where it had no shade, and where it had nothing to do but lie there and be lonely and miserable. If the neighbor ever came out to pet or play with the dog, Mae hadn't seen him do it, not even once, and she said that Janet spent more time than anyone feeling bad for the poor thing, and scratching his nose as best she could through the chain-link fence.

"Why get a dog if you're going to treat it like that?" Mae asked me, as if I would know, which I didn't. I only knew that most people who got dogs wanted to be good to them. But something made that neighbor think he needed a dog, or wanted one. And now that dog was suffering.

Buddy snapped his fingers. "Hey. Here's something that might be of interest to Nora." He grinned at me from across the table. "Her old boyfriend is back from Korea. I saw him downtown last week."

I took this information in, holding it like a breath. I braced for what would come next: A report of Leonard's new girlfriend, or wife. How pretty she was. How in love they seemed. I was in no mood to hear it.

"Oh yeah?" Russ said. "I heard he got captured over there. How's he look?"

"Like Nora made a trade up." Buddy flexed his brows. "He was a block away, just crossing the street. But, you know, I was surprised to see that he could still walk, after . . ." He made a low whistle.

"After what?" I asked. I was surprised. Leonard's mother said he wasn't injured.

"Well, you know . . ."

Buddy appeared uncharacteristically somber. I turned to Russ, who looked back at me and shrugged.

"We don't know what you mean," Peg said. She seemed generally annoyed. "So spill it."

Buddy pushed back his chair and stood. "I mean, it's got to be hard to walk upright . . ." He got behind his chair and leaned over it, his belly flat against the table's surface. ". . . after bending over for the enemy for soooooo long!"

Russ clapped and laughed his hyena laugh. Peg put her face in her hands. Buddy remained bent over the back of his chair, one fist pounding the edge of the table. "I'll sign your petition, Mr. Mao! Please! Please! For you, my love, I'll do anything!"

I had no idea what he was talking about. I understood that he was insulting Leonard, and I didn't mind that. But I worried he would tip the table.

Peg looked at her watch. "May I remind you there are ladies present?"

"Ladies? Where?" Buddy stood and made a visor of his hand. Peg told him to take a seat.

"What petition?" I asked.

Buddy looked at me. "You don't know?"

Russ set down his drink. "Nora doesn't pay attention to the news." He gave me a woozy, affectionate smile. "She likes her books, her made-up stories. With the television, she likes to watch people talk. Or sing and dance."

That embarrassed me. "I used to pay attention," I said.

Russ reached over and cupped the back of my neck. "It's okay, honey. You're still the sweetest."

He was drunk. I could hear it in his voice and see it in his eyes. No good would come from giving him a hard look, or even pushing his hand away. I turned to Buddy. "What petitions?"

Buddy explained that the Chinese had gotten American prisoners to sign petitions against our government. Now that the war was over and the prisoners were coming home, most everyone who signed was saying they didn't mean it.

"But they knew what they were signing," he said. "Traitors, every one of them. They were weak. They caved in."

"He says sitting here in the US," Peg said. "His belly full, drinking spiked lemonade."

Buddy held his ground. He said that compared to Americans who'd been held in Germany and Japan, the prisoners in Korea had been on easy street. Peg said she didn't see how he could know that, and Buddy said he'd seen pictures of a big inter-camp Olympics that the Chinese organized for the prisoners.

"Looked like a good time," he said. "Volleyball and baseball. Track and field. None of them appeared to be skin and bones. Maybe they got extra treats or what-have-you for turning traitor, trick ponies for the Chinese." He lifted his napkin to dab at a wet spot by the embroidered parrot.

"I heard their biggest problem was boredom," I said. I said this partly so I wouldn't look so ignorant about the news. But it was exactly what Mrs. Lifton had said.

Russ looked at me, amused. "Where? Where did you hear that?"

I sipped my drink, wishing I'd stayed silent. I'd never told Russ about biking over to the Liftons' that day, or seeing Leonard's name on the list of prisoners. I never mentioned Leonard to him at all.

"Everybody knows it," Buddy said. "I guess technically they were prisoners, in that the Chinese didn't let them leave. But it looked like a far better deal than being a prisoner in Leavenworth, which some of them are about to find out."

Peg grimaced. "Let's stop this. It's disrespectful, talking about any soldier like this."

"They disrespected us, honey. They disrespected the country."

"All of them?" I asked. "All the prisoners over there signed?" I felt slow from the vodka, thick of skull. But I was trying hard to keep up. Obviously, Leonard wasn't on his way to Leavenworth, if Buddy had just seen him crossing the street in St. Pete.

"Not all," Buddy allowed. "Some stood strong. But they were the exception, not the rule."

"I'm sure you would have held strong," Peg said. "Given you suffer so much as a cold and you're the biggest baby I ever met. And your sister told me that when you tried to go out for football, you fainted at the first practice. Right out on the field."

She was truly irritated, not joking at all, but both Russ and Buddy howled with laughter.

"In his defense," Russ said, "I recall it was a very warm afternoon." He turned serious. "I wouldn't have let myself get captured in the first place. I would have died fighting." He shrugged. "That's just how I am."

"But you think Leonard signed?" I asked. I tried to make the question casual, as if I had only a passing interest. But I clutched to the idea of Leonard having a general lack of integrity.

Buddy said he didn't know for sure if Leonard Lifton had signed a petition.

"Talking through your hat all around," Peg said.

Russ nudged my arm. "You're probably the one who can make the best guess on that, Nora. You went steady with him. What's his character like?"

I hesitated. I didn't know what Leonard had signed over there, or what he got in exchange. But that wasn't what Russ was asking.

"Weak," I said. "He had everything handed to him, his whole life. And he doesn't really think about the consequences of his actions. Not in my opinion."

Russ and Buddy were both pleased with this answer. Only Peg looked at me with disapproval. I held her gaze, no problem, no regret. I was sure I'd spoken the truth.

25.

Before Russ and I were married, I'd told him again that I didn't want more children, and I'd told him I wouldn't change my mind. Once we were married, I could get a prescription for a diaphragm, but the doctor warned me that even using a diaphragm, every time, it would be possible for me to conceive. I told Russ he'd either have to pull out or use a condom to increase our safety. He said no way to condoms, but when we were first married, he was pretty good about pulling out in time. Whenever he wasn't, he swore it was an accident. In any case, for the first year we were married, my luck held.

But it seemed like after that evening that Buddy and Peg came over, Russ's accidents started to happen more frequently. I'd get mad, and he'd get mad back, saying he didn't like that I was accusing him of doing it on purpose. But then he'd say that if I really loved him, I'd have a baby with him, and that I must have loved Mr. Nameless more.

It was during these kinds of arguments that he would sometimes get rough with me physically, especially if he'd been drinking. He'd grip my arm while he enunciated his points, squeezing enough that I would cry. He would tell me I was dramatic, and that I didn't know how lucky I was. He'd say that he'd shown me so much more understanding than another man would have, and that if he'd really wanted to hurt me, he could have.

Soon enough, though sometimes not until morning, he'd be sorry, telling me how much he loved me, that I was all he'd ever wanted, and that he didn't want to hurt me for anything. But that would usually lead to him telling me how our troubles would end if only I would agree to have a baby with him. It bothered him, he said, that I'd done that for someone else.

I pointed out that I'd always been clear, from the very beginning, that I wouldn't have a child. I never said "another child," because even when Russ was being sweet, he could flip back to anger pretty quickly. But I did tell him, over and over, that I did not love the unnamed man. And that, in fact, I despised him.

"Then just give me a name," he said.

I said I didn't want that name in my mouth. I said I didn't want it in our marriage. And I could tell him, in all honesty, that I felt fortunate to be his wife. I knew very well most men would never have agreed to marry someone with my history in the first place, and he was right that he worked hard, and his hard work was why I lived in such a beautiful home, close enough to my family but far out of town and out of sight of all the people in St. Pete I didn't want to see. This included not just Leonard and his new girlfriend or wife, but his parents, and most of the people I went to school with, and also toddlers coming into the library with smiling mothers for story time, and even my sophomore-year English teacher who once cornered me while I was in the waiting room for the dentist. She wanted me to know how surprised she was that I never graduated, as she always thought I had so much potential.

If you gave me a choice between any of that and sitting on the couch with a beer and a good book on Dolphin Drive, I'd pick the second option, every time. I only went into town on Sundays to have dinner with my family. On the way home, we'd stop to do the shopping, and Russ would come in with me. Even if he was in a bad mood, or tired, or smiling at the checkout girl while flashing his Bambi eyes, I felt better having him with me. People saw him, and either watched what they said, or stayed away. Both options were fine with me.

That Christmas, Russ got me a pair of diamond earrings, and also the present I'd asked for: a copy of *Meditations* by Marcus Aurelius. I'd recalled a substitute teacher advising us to read it when life became difficult, or when we anticipated difficulty. I anticipated that January, particularly the 16th, would again be a struggle to get through. My daughter would turn three.

I still have that copy of *Meditations*, the same one that Russ gave me. I see that I underlined *Choose not to be harmed, and you won't feel harmed. Don't feel harmed and you haven't been.* I took the advice to heart. That whole winter, and into that spring, I worked at that choosing, every day.

One thing Russ loved to do was go to the exhibition games between the teams who came down to St. Pete for spring training. He usually didn't care if I stayed home, but that spring, when the Braves were playing the Yankees, he and his friends all got tickets, and tickets for the wives as well.

"Everyone's going but Peg," he said. "And she's got a good reason."

I understood that meant I was going, too. I was trying to get along with him, choosing my battles, as they say. He'd gotten mad about my wanting to bring a book, so I didn't.

The day of the game turned out to be a nice one, sunny but not too hot. There were three of us couples plus Buddy, and we were up in the high, shaded section by the perimeter fence. Just beyond the field, Tampa Bay alternately sparkled and darkened in the shifting sunlight, and while Russ watched the game, I sipped my beer and tried to think of every shade of blue I'd ever heard of: azure, indigo, denim, cornflower, sapphire. I'd just come up with cerulean when everyone around me got to their feet, so I did, too, though I still couldn't see the field. Russ said that one of the Milwaukee players had been injured and was on the ground by second base, and that he seemed hurt enough that the game was paused.

Buddy announced, to no one in particular, that he was going to take a leak. When he stood, something outside the perimeter fence caught his eye. He moved close to the fence, looking down.

"Get a load of this!" he called out. "Is that our returned captive down there? Making friends?"

Russ got up and made his way over to the fence. I didn't move, but my heart pounded as if I'd been running. I guessed who Buddy had seen.

Russ peered down through the fence. "Well, well," he said. "Looks like the Reds taught him a new attitude toward race relations." He turned to Buddy and bowed. "We all workers, all the same. Repeat after me, good student."

Buddy yipped and bowed as well. I turned back to the field. In my panic, this is what I thought: They were looking at Leonard and his Japanese fiancée, or wife. I imagined she and Leonard were holding hands, smiling at each other on the way to the parking lot, maybe leaving the game early so they could go park at the beach. I sipped my beer, then started to chug it, concentrating on its cold slide down my throat.

"Nora," Russ said. "It's Leonard. Come look."

"I don't want to get up," I said. One of the other couples went over to the fence and looked down. The wife, Lois, only said, "Hmm," before she and her husband sat down again. Buddy announced he was about to pee himself and started down the steps, still holding his drink. Russ came back over and sat beside me.

"Whoa," he said, "slow down." He took my empty can and set it by his feet. "I would think you'd at least be curious."

I shook my head, still watching the field. "I'm scared," I said. I hoped Russ would think I meant I was scared for the injured player, who was now on his feet, or rather, on one foot. A medic on each side of the player braced him by the elbows.

"Oh honey." Russ put his arm around me, patting my shoulder. "Sweet girl. He'll be okay. They'll get him fixed up."

The injured player stopped to lift his hat to the crowd. I joined the standing ovation, clapping until my palms were stinging, promising myself that whatever happened, I'd keep my head up. If I came face-to-face with Leonard, I'd either nod or say a curt hello. There was no point in trying to make Leonard feel ashamed, no point in trying to make him feel anything. He already knew what he'd done. If he didn't feel his conscience by now, he never would.

The game resumed, and Buddy hurried back up the aisle, taking the steps two at a time. He was already in his seat when I saw Leonard, alone, walking up the aisle steps. He had sunglasses on, but I recognized his long body, even his gait. He carried two cups. Buddy noticed him as well.

"Aw, look!" Buddy's voice wasn't particularly deep like Russ's, but he could make himself heard. "Leonard's friend had to go sit in the colored section. I bet he's sad. I bet he wishes we could all go to North Korea and get our brains washed clean, too."

Leonard was too far away to hear any of this. I watched him make his careful way to an empty seat beside a girl with light blond hair cut just beneath her ears. He handed her one of the cups and took the empty seat.

I put on my own sunglasses and closed my eyes. *That cucumber is bitter, so toss it out! There are thorns on the path, then keep away!* Thank you, I thought. Good advice. I knew that Marcus Aurelius, being a Roman emperor, had had bigger problems than seeing Leonard Lifton at a ball game, but his words helped me all the same. *Enough said. Why ponder the existence of a nuisance?* Why indeed. Apparently because I needed further torment: I opened my eyes to study the blonde. She wore a turquoise sleeveless dress that showed off her slender arms.

I looked down at my hands, clutching my empty cup. *To love only what happens, what was destined. No greater harmony.* The crowd quieted, waiting as the pitcher paused to stretch. Out of the corner of my eye, I saw Buddy lean forward, his hands bracketing his mouth.

"Hey Leonard! Hey! Lifton! Why you being so cold?"

Leonard's head turned slightly. But he only adjusted his sunglasses, then again looked back at the field. The blond girl said something to him, and he put his arm around her, leaning close to better hear her. I forgot all about Marcus Aurelius, staring at the tanned back of Leonard's neck with so much burning contempt it seemed impossible he wouldn't feel it.

"Come on, Lenny!" Buddy stood. "Hey! You rooting for the Braves? I'm guessing you can relate. They got a little red on their uniform, too."

Other people started to turn around. Some of them were frowning, but it was hard to tell if they didn't like what Buddy was saying, or if they were just annoyed because he sounded drunk and they were there to watch the game. An older bald man, maybe five rows down, turned around and said, "Son, that's enough of that."

"You talking to my friend?" Russ asked. His voice was so deep he didn't have to shout. The bald man turned a little more, looked at Russ, then turned back again to face the field.

"Good decision," Russ said, and he and Buddy laughed. I think what happened then was that Leonard recognized Russ's laugh. He and Russ had never been friends, but Russ's laugh, so unexpectedly high-pitched, was something a person might have to hear just once to remember. In any case, when Leonard turned around, the girl beside him turned as well. They were far away, but I saw enough of her to see she was indeed very pretty. That's not why I hated her. I hated her because she'd believed Leonard's lie about me, and because if they weren't married yet, they would be. She'd be able to keep her child. No New Jersey for her. She tucked her blond hair behind her ear, said something to Leonard, but he kept looking up at us. He took his sunglasses off. Buddy or Russ were both waving, delighted they'd finally gotten his attention.

But Leonard looked only at me.

I took off my sunglasses and smiled. It wasn't a nice smile. If I could have cursed him to hell with just my eyes, I would have done it, and I did my best.

I was so focused on Leonard, conveying my rage to him, letting him feel it and know it and maybe even fear it, that I didn't notice that Russ had stopped waving and laughing. I felt his gaze on me before I saw it, the hair on my arms rising even before I turned to face him.

"Well, well," he said, and nearly smiled. "Mystery solved."

For the rest of the game, Russ said nothing to me and nothing more to Leonard. The game ended without further incident, and Leonard and the blond girl stood and made their way to the aisle. Russ remained seated, talking to his friends about the mistakes of the losing team. After our group made our way down the steps, I stopped to use the ladies'—not just to pee but to splash water on my face and try to calm myself. When I came out, Russ was still talking to Buddy about the game. He asked if I was ready to leave, with no anger in his voice or expression.

I let myself hope that would be the end of it. Now he knew what he'd always wanted to know, and maybe he'd be satisfied.

But as soon as he and I were in the car, alone, he turned silent, and wouldn't look at me at all. Because of the game traffic, it took twenty minutes just to get out of the parking lot, and that whole time, neither one of us said a word.

When we finally pulled out onto the street, he said, "I'm just curious how he managed it. He'd been gone almost a year before you went away."

I didn't answer at first. I got it in my head that I still didn't have to tell him, one way or the other. But he flew through a red light, and the car coming on my side had to slam on their brakes.

"He came home for a visit." I said all the words in one exhale.

Russ didn't say anything to that. By then I'd learned, the hard way, that when he was in a mood, the smart thing was to stay quiet. So that's what I did, the whole ride back through town and out to Dolphin Drive. When we got home, he walked in the house ahead of me, jingling his keys, and left the front door open. I was hoping that he'd go right back out to his boat. And that he wouldn't want me with him.

But when I walked in, he was there in the entry. He pulled me close, one hand on the back of my head. "You're my wife," he whispered, nuzzling my neck. "You're my wife, you're my wife, you're my wife." This surprised me, though not in a bad way. I'd take Russ amorous over Russ angry any day of the week, and though his kisses were sloppy from drinking, the same was likely true of me. Things started to get pretty escalated right there in the entry, on the hard linoleum, so I suggested we go back to the bedroom, and he said he didn't want to. I suggested the couch, and he said that was fine. But when I said I needed to go get my diaphragm, he acted like he didn't hear me. I said it again, and he shook his head and carried me to the couch in a bear hug, like we were slow dancing, but without my feet touching the ground. I squirmed, then thrashed. I raised my voice. He didn't let go.

Things got ugly quickly. I fought, probably longer than was smart. We were both still a little drunk, but it seemed only I was the worse for it. All I got for my trouble was a good smack across the face that hurt enough, and scared me enough, that I went quiet and still, and stayed that way until it was over. As soon as he rolled off me, I got up and ran to the bathroom, locked the door, and washed off and out what I could.

I stayed in the bathroom for a long time. Eventually, he got on the other side of the door and said he was sorry. He said I needed to try to understand how it felt for him, as a husband, to be denied fatherhood by the woman he loved while looking at the good-for-nothing who'd abandoned me, who'd treated me like I was nothing, and knowing what I'd allowed with someone else. He kept on, banging on the bathroom door, crying and telling me how he loved me so much that he couldn't stand the thought of me ever being with someone else, even in the past. But I couldn't leave him, he said. I just couldn't. He knew I wanted to.

He was right. At the time, I didn't think of what he'd done as rape. I'm certain he didn't think of it that way, either. What I felt, sitting on the bathroom floor, was obliterated.

There was only one place I could go, and Shirley now slept in my old bed, sharing the room with Janet. I would have had to sleep on the couch. And more than that: If I left my marriage and returned home, I would embarrass my family further. All that together sounded even less appealing than just sticking things out with Russ.

Eventually I got hungry, and I knew if I made something for myself, I'd need to make something for both of us. So I came out of the bathroom, and he and I had dinner.

But before that, when I was still in the bathroom and he was crying and pounding, I stood and turned my back to the door, looking at myself in the mirror. My jaw was slack, my eyes dull. I remember I did something strange. I lifted my hand and waved at myself in the mirror, and I saw myself wave back, and my reflection smiled the small, sad smile of a consoling friend. And I felt better, even as I knew it was just me waving.

It's strange to remember this moment now, when I'm so much older. I was the wretched girl in the mirror, but I was also who I am now, the one who waved.

By the next morning, I had a plan. I didn't want to wait and see if I'd been lucky or unlucky. I couldn't bear the wait. And I remembered Carol saying that if a girl was serious about not wanting to be pregnant anymore, salmonella was her best bet.

I'm not saying it was a good plan. It wasn't. But I already had some chicken in the fridge.

That Monday, as soon as Russ left for work, I sliced off a thick piece of raw chicken, put it on a plate, and carried it out to the table on the back patio. There I left it, right in the sun. After some consideration, I went back in and got a mesh strainer to keep off the bugs, then came back in to do my chores. When I finished, instead of having lunch, I sat at the dining room table and drank three beers, one after the other, until I felt ready.

But I got pretty scared when I went outside and actually looked down at what the chicken had become. In just those few hours, the whole thing had grown a thin coat of slime around it. Under the slime, the meat had turned from pink to gray, and the fat from white to beige. When I bent down for a closer look, it was like smelling death itself.

I took the chicken back inside, cut it into little pieces, and managed to get down almost a third of it. I was crying the whole time, partly because I knew I might be killing myself, and partly because the feel and smell of the chicken was so disgusting, even with every swallow washed down with more beer. All that misery was for nothing, though—as soon as I stood, I had to rush to the sink to throw up. I couldn't bear to eat any more, so I went out to the dock and tossed the remaining pieces in the water. Almost immediately, a pelican cruised down and swallowed them.

The next morning, I repeated the whole process, and though again I couldn't eat much, what I got down stayed down. Once I sobered up, I just felt a little queasy. I still made dinner, and I ate with Russ. We watched *The Perry Como Show* and stayed up for *What's My Line*? I went to sleep fine, but in the middle of the night, I woke up feeling as if I had a live animal in my bowels. I barely made it to the bathroom, where both ends of my digestive tract committed fully to getting not just the chicken, but everything, everything, out of me. Our second bathroom came in handy, as I told Russ I wasn't coming out, even to sleep. I rolled up the bathroom rug, and I used that for a pillow.

In the morning, as soon as he left for work, I went out and got my real pillow, and also a blanket, the portable radio, and a cup. I brought all that into the bathroom, and that was where I stayed for almost a week. Russ called his mother at one point, asking her if he should take me to the hospital, though I'd already told him that he shouldn't. His mother said she'd heard there was a bug going around, and that I just needed rest and water. Through the door I told him, "Oh, okay, that's good to know. Thank her for me, please," though by then, I thought I was dying. I don't mean that as a figure of speech. I mean there were several nights that week when I lay on the bathroom floor truly believing I would die there, and that I wouldn't reach my twenty-second birthday, or get to tell anyone but Russ goodbye.

Even when I felt well enough to go back to living in the rest of the house, I went on feeling shaky and nauseated for weeks. But I did get my period on time. Now I understand I was probably never pregnant to begin with. I have a friend who's a nurse, and she told me that if I had been pregnant, I likely would have stayed that way, and the salmonella would have only increased the chance of problems with the baby's spine and brain. So, all in all, not great advice from Carol.

But I also know that if I had been pregnant, I never would have actually given birth. If there'd been no other way, I would have taken Russ's bowling ball, tied it into the skirt of my dress or apron, and jumped off the dock. I'm certain of this. I recall my state of mind. My resolve was absolute.

When I felt healthy again, physically I mean, I told Russ what I'd done, and why. I described exactly what the chicken looked like before I ate it, and how it felt sliding down my throat. He thought I was kidding at first. When he understood I wasn't, he got scared.

"And I'll do it again," I said. "I'll always be able to find something. I'll go out to the water myself and get scallops. I'll leave them out in the sun for a week."

He told me I was crazy. He told me I should be in a mental hospital, doing something like that.

"Sounds great," I said. "You find one I can go to, I'll start packing."

It soon became clear which one of us was making empty threats: not me. He told me okay, he was sorry he'd gotten pushy, but the words had barely left his mouth before he moved on to talking about how he'd been drunk, and how he wanted to be a father, and how unfair it was about Leonard, et cetera. I didn't want to hear it.

"I told you," I said. "If you changed your mind and want children, okay. Go find somebody else."

He started crying, telling me I didn't realize how much he loved me, how I'd always been the girl for him.

We went on like that, married, for the rest of that spring.

26.

On a rainy day in April, I went out to get the mail and found, along with a bill and a few advertisements, an envelope with my name and address handwritten on it. The envelope had no return address, but when I saw *NYC* on the postmark, I guessed it was from Carol. I actually rolled my eyes, so put-upon did I feel. But I'd only told her she shouldn't call again. I'd never said she couldn't write.

Inside was a sheet of office paper with the following quote, typed:

> "*. . . you really must try hard to keep your melancholy within bounds and see that it does not last too long. Life is precious and such moods as the one you are in consume us body and soul. Do not imagine that life has little more in store for you. It is not true . . .*"

Beneath the quote was *Love, Carol*, also typed. That was it, the whole letter, but it made me mad enough to ball up the paper and throw it in the garbage, then turn around and slap the refrigerator. She had no right to tell me to keep my sadness in check. Maybe life felt precious to her, living with her child, knowing she hadn't failed him. I stood there in the kitchen, my palm stinging. I got the letter out of the trash, unballed it, and read it again.

The words stayed in my head for the rest of the day, and for some time after. Especially the last two sentences, as I'd very much been imagining that life had little more in store for me. And I think I knew, even then, that extraordinary luck had landed me in the same maternity home as Carol DeWitt. Because it's extraordinary luck, in any circumstance, to make a friend who doesn't just distract you, or get you to laugh in hard times, but who also cares about you enough to hold out a hand to help you out of your muck, even when you don't deserve it.

It turns out that quote she sent to me was from Brahms. I guess he wrote more than just music. The words Carol sent to me were from a letter he'd written to Clara Schumann after her husband had been dead for a year, which was about a hundred years before Carol decided I also needed to hear them. I remembered her talking about Brahms, about his intermezzi that she liked so much, and how she thought I'd like his earthy and jaunty pieces. But I didn't know that quote was from him until later, when Carol and I spoke again.

In May, Bobby graduated from high school. Russ drove me into town for the ceremony, and in the family pictures taken on that day, I'm standing next to Russ with his arm around me, and I'm smiling, my hair grown down past my ears. Bobby remained cool to me that day, even though I got him a card and told him how proud of him I was, and Russ gave him an envelope with twenty dollars in it. The following week, Bobby left for the Naval Training Center in Maryland. I bought another copy of the Marcus Aurelius book and gave it to him as a going-away present. Hurt as I was, I was glad he was leaving. I told myself that, at least.

The rest of my family remained in St. Pete, and they always seemed pleased to see us. Janet turned twelve that June, and my father suggested Russ and I arrive early for her birthday dinner so he and his favorite son-in-law, ha ha, could listen to a ball game while I helped Mae with the food.

Russ agreed to this plan, even though we had a nicer television at our house, where he could have watched the game in greater comfort, as we had two air-conditioning units, and Mae and my father had just the one. It was my sense that Russ was trying to get back in my good graces, and he seemed truly sorry about what had happened after we got home from the stadium in March. I appreciated his remorse, and his efforts to make me happy. My mind did, at least. My body was a different story.

He was still good-looking, objectively speaking. I could see that. But my desire for him left me. Even when he was being nice, it didn't come back.

When we arrived at the house for Janet's party, my father came out front to greet us, and though he embraced me first and kissed my cheek, he was clearly distracted by the sight of Russ's new truck, a tamale-red, bull-nosed Chevrolet 3100 Deluxe, purchased just the week before. My father declared the truck a beauty, admiring its shining grille and the lockbox bolted across the bed. Russ pointed out the custom gauges and air-conditioning vents as my father peered in the windows, nodding with approval. He still drove the Ford he'd bought when we were in Missouri, but he said, often, that he respected Russ for his industry and work ethic. If he felt any resentment, he didn't show it.

"Well done," he told Russ. "An excellent choice." Russ thanked him and said the compliment meant a lot, coming from him. My father smiled and looked at me. "Same for you," he said, and laughed.

It took me a second to understand he meant I'd chosen well with Russ. Something in my expression made him pat my shoulder.

"I'm glad you're here, honey. Mae could use some pleasant company. I'll leave it to her to explain."

The front room, where the television was already tuned to the game, was at least cooler than outside. Russ and my father each took a seat, and I followed the scent of vanilla to the kitchen. When Mae saw me, she nodded, but she didn't turn off the mixer.

"I'm way behind schedule," she said. "Shirley will be up from her nap any minute, and Janet and her friends will be here in half an hour. I sent them to the movies. And I still need to ice this cake." She glanced back at the screen door. "Sorry. I've had a bad afternoon."

I went to the sink to wash my hands. A picture of Bobby in his sailor whites was held to the fridge by a magnet that read *Best MOM in the WORLD.* When Mae turned off the mixer, I asked why her afternoon was bad. She looked over her shoulder and whispered that just an hour earlier, she and my father both had an unpleasant exchange with their neighbor, who was still leaving his dog out all day, no shade, in the terrible heat.

"I can't stand it." She used the tip of her pinkie to sample the frosting. "I've been thinking about a solution, thinking and thinking, and I finally convinced your father this morning."

Mae's solution had been to see if the neighbor might consider letting them take the dog, which they would then give to Janet as a birthday present. Once she got the go-ahead from my father, she waited until Janet left for the movies, then went over to the neighbor's front door, bearing a plate of cookies and the friendliest of smiles. The neighbor heard her out, then said he'd sell her the dog for thirty dollars.

"I should have just dropped it." She stirred more sugar into the frosting. She had her hair tucked under a kerchief, and sweat trickled down the back of her neck. "But I had to be stupid and contrary, pointing out that he didn't seem to enjoy the dog much. Next thing you know, he's yelling that it's his dog, and he can treat it however he wants, and now he won't even sell it to me. Your father had to come out and ask him to settle down, and this man, he was even rude to your father." She bulged her eyes in disbelief. "We finally got him to agree that Janet could still feed him scraps through the fence and pet him. That was it. So all that talk with a lunatic, and we're back to where we started."

I went over to the window. The fence was the neighbor's, chain-link and taller than I was. The dog stood on the other side of it, panting and staring in my direction, likely watching for Janet. Or maybe just dreaming of shade. It was a skinny, knee-high mutt, tan with a mark like a white star between its ears. I turned back to Mae and told her I was sorry, and that at least she tried.

She pulled the beaters from the mixer and tossed them in the sink. "Trying doesn't do diddly."

"I'll set the table," I said.

She said she could do that. What she really needed was for me to run to Nolan's and pick up some birthday candles. "I can't believe I forgot," she said. "It's a little thing, but she'll miss them. Especially as we had candles for Shirley."

"That's no problem." I started to walk to the front room to get Russ. "Need anything else?"

"Just take our car, honey." Mae opened the oven and shrank

back from its heat. "Let Russ watch the game. The keys are under the seat."

I told her Russ wouldn't mind taking me.

"You know how to drive." She put on pot holders and eased out the cake. "Just drive yourself."

In the front room, Russ said something, and my father laughed.

"It's like riding a bike." She shut the oven door with her hip. "You used to do that, too."

We looked at each other. She'd been short-tempered before I even walked in, because of the neighbor, because of the heat. She just wanted to poke at someone.

"Let me know if you need anything else," I said.

"I keep thinking you'll get better." She muttered the words to my back. "But you keep getting worse."

I turned around. "What's that supposed to mean?" Of course I already knew. I wanted to say *Get your own damn candles*, and walk out. But I'd been looking forward to the party. I wanted to give Janet her presents. I wanted to sing "Happy Birthday" with everyone else.

She walked around the table and stood close, peering at me.

"We sent you to that place in New Jersey because we thought that was the best thing for you. We really did. And I don't know what else we could have done. But my God, Nora. You never came back." She grabbed hold of my hand. "You were bold when I met you. Bright and bold. Tell me. Where did that girl go?"

I had nothing to say to that. It seemed to me that she'd already put it together. I took my hand back, told her I'd get the candles, and went out to the front room to get Russ. He asked me if I'd been out in the sun, and I told him the kitchen was hot.

Before we left, Mae called out for me to please pick up some milk, too, and I said fine, I would.

In the truck, Russ fiddled with the tuner, searching for the game. Fine with me, as I was still needled by what Mae had said. It wasn't any business of hers if I wanted Russ to drive me to the store, and to go in with me. She didn't know what it was like for me to come into town, with all the people I didn't want to see. We hit a pothole, and the tools in the lockbox rattled so loud that I cried out, my hand on my heart. Russ laughed, then saw my face and apologized. I turned back to my window, felt the pressure of tears, and pinched the bridge of my nose to stop them. I thought of the dog waiting by the fence.

"Nolan's is right up ahead," I said, pointing at the turn. Russ drove past it, saying he'd been meaning to check out Central Plaza. He wanted to know what they'd done with the place.

I got the joke. Central Plaza was the shopping center built over the land that had included the site of Russ's childhood home. I'd heard on radio advertisements that this new shopping center had over two thousand parking spaces, and the Publix there was air-conditioned. I was curious about it myself. But when we arrived, I saw we were hardly alone in our interest. We circled the massive lot twice without finding a space.

"The whole town is here," Russ said. "Let's just go back to Nolan's."

I looked at my sideview mirror. Where did that girl go? She was here. I was still her. I could go into a store by myself to pick up some candles and milk. I turned to Russ.

"You can drop me off. I'll run in."

He looked at me, surprised.

"It's fine," I said. "You can just listen to the game. I'll be right out."

He dropped me off in front of the Publix and said he'd circle the lot until I came out.

"Ten minutes," I said, and slid down onto the hot blacktop. I wouldn't tell Mae that I'd gone into the Publix by myself. For one, I didn't want her to know she'd gotten under my skin. For another, she wouldn't be so impressed. And so far, I was fine. I didn't recognize any of the shoppers streaming past me, pushing carts and carrying bags, fanning themselves with free hands. The automatic doors parted before me, and the air-conditioning hit me like a wave.

It was the nicest grocery store I'd ever seen, the interior cool-toned and gleaming. There were at least ten checkout lines, every one of them busy. I walked fast but with my chin up, just another shopper, and found the milk without trouble. By the time I walked past the meat department, I felt calm enough to go up to the counter to ask if they had any giveaway meat for a dog. The man behind the counter wrapped up some old turkey for me, free of charge. He said he didn't know where they kept birthday candles, so I walked up one aisle and down another, weaving past other shoppers until I saw a stock boy on his knees, loading up a bottom shelf with cans of soup.

"Excuse me," I said. "Could you please tell me where I might find some birthday candles?"

The stock boy turned around. He wasn't a boy. He was Leonard, wearing a pale gray apron, and a matching bow tie. I stood there, not even breathing, holding tight to the turkey and the milk.

"Nora." He got to his feet. I turned on my toes and started walking, sirens going off in my head. He wanted to talk? No. I didn't want a polite conversation with him, pretending bygones were bygones. I had plenty of things I wanted to say to him, but I didn't want to say them in a crowded grocery store, with Russ circling the parking lot. All I wanted was to escape.

I got in the shortest line for checkout, my heart pounding, sweat cooling on my hairline. The woman in front of me turned to me and smiled. Maybe she saw I didn't have a lot to buy, or maybe she saw my face and worried that I was ill. For whatever reason, she said I could go in front of her. I might have thanked her. I hope I did. When it was my turn, I dropped the turkey, picked it up, and explained that it was just free scraps for the dog. The cashier nodded, and I paid for the milk. I had trouble even counting out the change, my mind whirling. Leonard had looked different. Older? But that made sense. He was older.

He'd wanted to say something to me. But there was nothing he could say. Nothing worth hearing. He'd had his chance to explain. He'd had chance after chance after chance.

"Have a nice day," the cashier said. I could tell from her tone she'd maybe said it to me before, and I didn't hear her. She nodded to the bag boy, my grocery bag already nestled in his arms. "Jimmy here will walk you out."

I managed to smile at Jimmy, grateful for him, for his strength and stability, though he was just a kid, and not much taller than I was. And then Leonard was beside him, towering over us both.

"I got this one, Jimmy," he said. He lifted the bag and looked at me. "Ready, ma'am?"

If I'd been able to speak, I would have said that I'd carry my own groceries. If I'd been able to control my voice, I'd have kept it icy and quiet and calm. But I was sure that if I opened my mouth, I would start shrieking right there in front of the cashier and the bag boy and the nice lady who'd let me go in front of her. I looked at Leonard's gray apron and thought, *He wants to be my bag boy? Okay. Fine with me. That's all he is to me now.* I pulled my sunglasses down, picked up my purse, and started walking to the automatic doors. I hadn't quite reached them when he caught up to me.

"You cut your hair," he said.

I stopped and looked up at him. I liked that he couldn't see my eyes, that they were hidden by my sunglasses. But I could stare up at him, seeing clearly. He wasn't as handsome as he had been. His right eyebrow was mostly gone, the skin beneath it smooth and shiny. He had a blister near the tip of his nose, and his hair had thinned considerably. Ugly on the inside, I thought, coming out. It was then I caught sight of his left hand, the one that clutched the paper bag. It would only occur to me later that he wore no wedding ring. At that moment, all I noticed was that his hand was missing two fingers—there was a little nub where his pinkie had been. The ring finger was cut off at the knuckle.

Someone said, "Excuse me," and I turned to see a woman with a cart. Leonard put his hand on my shoulder to guide me out of her way.

"Don't touch me." I knocked his hand off my shoulder. I didn't know what to make of the missing fingers. I couldn't think. The automatic doors slid open for the woman, and the heat of the day blew in.

He shifted the bag. "Guess your hair isn't all that's changed."

He said this in an accusing way, a disappointed way. I took off my sunglasses so he would see my disgust, so he would know I didn't care about his disappointment. I didn't even care what happened to his fingers. I wanted to grab his bow tie and twist it until he couldn't breathe. I wanted to press my thumbnails into each of his eyes, to not let up even after he yelped for mercy. He was disappointed because I wasn't being a good sport? He had no idea. I wanted not just to hurt him, but to wound him as I was wounded, to scar him as I'd been scarred.

Instead, I crooked my finger and beckoned him to lean close. He looked nervous, but he did.

"You think I'm just going to smile nicely at you, play catch-up?" My voice was quiet, but I articulated each word. "Thank you for carrying my damn groceries? Just give me the bag and go back to stocking soup. You're a pathetic excuse for a man."

He handed over the bag. I looked again at his hand, at the nub and half knuckle. He deserved it, I thought. Whatever had happened to him, to his fingers, it wasn't enough.

"Nora." He spoke quietly, through clenched teeth. "I was just trying to tell you hello. And to say congratulations. I heard you got married."

My anger flamed. I could barely breathe. If he thought I was going to now congratulate him on his marriage to the blond girl, their vows already taken or imminent, he was wrong.

I made my voice syrupy. "Step outside with me, will you?"

I didn't wait for an answer, just turned and started walking. The doors again slid open, the heat and humidity engulfing me. I scanned the lot for Russ's truck, didn't see it, and moved behind a column at the store's entrance. I didn't know if Leonard would follow, but when I turned, there he was, looking down at me, his face incredulous. As if my anger surprised him. Get ready, I thought. You have no idea.

"On second thought," I said. "I'll take your congratulations.

Because that's the right word. I married a man with integrity. I married a man who isn't a coward."

His head snapped back. It was like I'd hit him. I was glad for this.

"You don't know what you're talking about." He said this sadly, like he was up on the cross. *Father, forgive her, for she knows not what she's talking about.* I wanted to kill him. I held tight to the groceries, worried I'd drop them. At the bottom of my vision, the edge of the paper bag trembled.

"I know better than anyone." I moved closer. Even in the shade, I was already sweating. "You're a coward, Leonard. Not a man at all. You should be ashamed."

He pressed his hand against the column like he needed to. "You weren't there," he said.

It was then I realized: He thought we were talking about Korea, about the petitions. I was so outraged that I laughed, even as I felt a sob rising. He wasn't thinking about her at all, this child I gave birth to. His child.

"You weren't there," he said again.

I stepped toward him, and he stepped back. He looked afraid, seeing my face. He was right to be afraid. "I don't care about the petitions, Leonard. I'm talking about the baby." The sob escaped my throat, my words garbled. But I wasn't done. I had more to say. For me. For her. I would keep my dignity later.

He started to say something. I shook my head. There was no excuse he could make.

"I don't love you anymore, either," I said. "Believe that." I imagined fire shooting at my eyes, burning his face, and what was left of his hair. "If you fell in love with someone else, that's your prerogative. That's fine. But you lied to your parents about me. Or tried to. Your mother knows I wasn't lying. She knows that was your child. She knows you left me to face everything, everything alone."

He stepped away from me, his face very still. He looked more afraid than before. I stepped closer.

"That girl can think whatever she wants about you, about me, whatever you tell her. But I know the truth."

He had nothing to say to that. A bead of sweat rolled down his forehead, catching at the shiny patch on his brow.

"So you're damn right I'm different, because she's still with me. My daughter." I slapped my hand against my chest. "And I'll never get over it. Never. So you can take your congratulations and go straight to hell. And I hope your fingers rotted off because of the rot inside you, in your cold heart." I stepped away from him, breathing hard. "Are we clear? Anything else you want to congratulate me on?"

He tugged at his bow tie and raised his hand, a plea for mercy. No, I thought. No. He would get none.

"Nora. Hold on." He blinked at the grocery bag, then again raised his eyes to mine. "What are you talking about? What child?"

I shook my head. It was beneath him, even him. I was stunned that he would attempt such a lie. "Don't turn my stomach. Your mother told me you knew. She wouldn't lie. You've known for years."

"Nora." He'd freed himself of the bow tie, but he appeared to be struggling to breathe. "Listen to me. This is the first I'm hearing about any baby. What are you saying? This is my child, you're saying? Ours?"

I believe, to this day, this moment subtracted years from my life. I felt my heart contract in my chest.

"Where is she now? Nora? Where is she? What are you saying?"

I couldn't speak. I could barely breathe. Behind him, Russ's truck rolled slowly toward the entrance. I could see him through the windshield, scanning the store windows. I looked back up at Leonard.

"Please step forward," I whispered. "Please. Get behind the column. Please."

I had a lot of nerve, asking him for that, asking him for anything at that moment. But my tone had changed. Leonard seemed dazed, but his eyes moved in the direction of the parking lot, and he seemed to understand. He stepped toward me, behind the column. He pressed both hands to the top of his head as if needing to hold it in place.

"Stay where you are," I whispered. "I'm going to walk away now, and please just stay where you are until I'm gone. Will you do that for me? Please."

He nodded. I almost apologized. But even then, so early, I

understood how meager any apology would seem in comparison to the offense, the offenses. I looked at his hand, the one with the missing fingers, then back up at his stricken face.

“Thank you,” I whispered. I turned and walked out toward the parking lot, my arm raised in a wave. Russ saw me and braked. I climbed in, staring straight ahead. I didn’t know if Leonard would stay behind the column. I couldn’t bear to look. The truck’s radio was still tuned to the game, and the play-in-progress kept Russ’s attention as we rolled forward, braking for shoppers with carts. I thought of Leonard’s mother on her back patio, holding my hand, telling me I ought to move away. She’d suggested California. She’d suggested New York. She’d offered me money. She’d wanted me gone.

An ad came on the radio. Russ lowered the volume and asked me how it went. I told him I didn’t find the candles.

He made a face. “In that big place?”

I said we could just drive over to Nolan’s, if he didn’t mind. He said that was fine, but he gave me a sidelong glance.

“You look like you’re about to faint, honey.”

I wiped my hand across my forehead. “Well,” I said. “It’s hot.”

“Yeah.” He turned a corner, sharp. The tools in the lockbox slid and clinked. “Want to know what I think?”

I waited, holding my breath. We were almost at a stop sign. I could jump out if I had to. Where I’d go after that, I couldn’t guess.

“I think the Publix probably had candles. I think you just

got flustered, going in by yourself." He reached over and squeezed my shoulder. "It's okay, sweetie. You tried."

I didn't say anything. He started to laugh.

"You're adorable." He shook his head, still laughing. "You can't lie to save your life."

It turns out he was wrong about that. I'll get to that as it comes.

27.

I managed to keep myself together through Janet's party, smiling as necessary through dinner, through candles and cake and the opening of presents. But the image of Leonard's hand, the nub and knuckle of those missing fingers, kept appearing in my mind's eye. His mother said he hadn't been injured in the fighting, but his mother was a liar. It seemed unlikely he'd lost those fingers playing volleyball or missing her lasagna.

"Earth to Nora," Janet said, using the Martian voice from *Bugs Bunny*. She waved a forkful of cake in front of my face. "Are you at my party or not?"

I didn't snap at her. I could see she was having a hard time, not enjoying her own party. Everyone, even Janet's friends, kept looking at Shirley and talking about how cute she was with icing all over her face.

"Sorry, honey," I said. "I was just thinking of how much you've grown up."

It could have been true. Janet was already as tall as I was, and wearing a bra. But she gave me a skeptical look, and I could see I'd hurt her feelings.

I tried to make it up to her. After her friends went home, I told her about the turkey scraps I'd gotten, which seemed to lift her spirits. I followed her out back, where the dog was still waiting by the fence. I'd been warned by Mae not to say anything about the fight with the neighbor. She felt it was best if Janet never learned the transfer of the dog had been a possibility.

Russ came out and pronounced the dog a mutt, and tragically ugly. He added that he once had a much better-looking dog that was so well trained he could put a piece of sausage on its nose and the dog wouldn't eat it until Russ, and only Russ, gave it the okay.

"Five minutes, ten minutes, whatever," he said, touching the tip of his own nose. "Bug would wait. His whole body would tremble, because the scent would be driving him nuts. But he wouldn't dare till I said."

"Neat," I said, again unconvincing.

Russ eyed the neighbor's dog, who wagged its scraggly tail at Janet. "This one doesn't look as smart," he said. "But you should at least make it sit and shake first."

Janet ignored the advice, slipping another piece of turkey through the fence. "The owner's mean," she whispered. "It never gets to go anywhere but this hot yard."

Russ allowed the dog's lot was a shame. He said that when he was growing up, a good dog just stayed with you, no fence required. If it ran away, you had to shoot it.

Janet looked at him, then at me. She twisted her mouth to the side, as her mother often did. "Don't get a dog," she said.

I told her we wouldn't. The fence was too tall for me to reach over, so I stretched my fingers between the metal links, scratching the dog's hot fur. The dog immediately made a sighing sound, staring up at me in a hopeful way, as if I could somehow help him.

"Sorry," I said. "I can't." Not a lie. There was nothing I could do for him. Russ said he was hot and went back inside. As soon as the door shut behind him, Janet turned to me.

"What's the matter?" she asked. "What is it?"

"I'm okay," I said. "Just tired."

She narrowed her eyes, waiting. I forced a smile, and she shook her head. She told the dog she'd see it later, and went inside, letting the door slam behind her.

"You know who could have pulled that off?" I whispered. The dog had turned its head so I could scratch the white star between its ears. "Leonard's mother. She's a far better liar than I'll ever be."

Of course she was. She was a trained professional. When she was young, she'd been a good enough actress to get paid for it. I might have considered that, that day on her patio. But I hadn't.

The dog thumped its tail against the fence. I crouched low, our faces level. The dog's stare changed, turning plaintive. I again told it that I was sorry, and I stayed with it, in the heat, until Russ stuck his head out and said he had work in the morning, and that we should get on the road.

She called the next morning, when Russ was at work. I was mopping when I heard the phone. As soon as she spoke, I recognized her voice, though it sounded hoarse from crying.

"Is this a good time to talk?"

How nice, I thought, for her to be so considerate of my time. What a thoughtful person. But I was curious as to what she wanted to say to me. I told her to go ahead.

"I'm almost relieved." Her voice was flat. "I've had the Sword of Damocles above me for so long. I don't have to worry anymore."

I could have laughed. I wanted to crack the receiver against the countertop. "That's what you have to say to me?"

"No," she said. "I want to try to explain. You probably think I'm a monster."

I didn't correct her. I stayed silent, waiting. She took a deep breath and began.

The first thing she told me: Leonard was reported MIA long before I went to New Jersey. They received the telegram on July 10, 1950, just two weeks into the fighting. She said that as soon as she read that telegram, she went out of her mind. Both she and Leonard's father knew people who'd lost sons and brothers in the previous war. They knew what MIA usually meant. But it was exhausting, she said, the not knowing. Worse than grief. They suspected he was probably dead. From the beginning, Leonard's father was more convinced of that than she was. She worried he was dying, suffering. The worst part, she said, was the hope.

They didn't tell anyone he was missing except for family in New York. That was her idea, keeping it quiet. She didn't want to have someone from the newspaper calling her house, or some well-meaning acquaintance coming up to her in the supermarket and giving an opinion on whether or not her son was alive. Her husband felt the same. He kept going to work, but they stayed in mostly, just trying to get through every day, waiting for a letter, or another telegram, for any news at all. But day after day, week after week, there was nothing.

"When your stepmother called," she told me, "the first time I mean, when she just called to see if he was okay, I told her what I'd been telling everyone. That he was fine, back in Japan. Safe. It was the easiest way to get people to stop asking."

This whole time, she and her husband were reading the same news articles I'd been seeing, about UN forces coming across dead Americans, their hands tied behind their backs. She said she stopped sleeping. Her hair started falling out. She'd lie awake at night, imagining Leonard, her beautiful boy, dead in a ditch, or dying.

"I don't want to make excuses," she said. "But you can't imagine what that's like. Your child out there, and you don't know where, and you don't know if he's okay, or if he's getting hurt."

"Excuse me," I said. "I know exactly what that's like."

She was quiet. I stretched the phone cord so I could walk to the back window. One of our patio chairs had been blown sideways out into our yard, the new grass yellowed from heat.

"I know sorry isn't enough," she said. "But I'm sorry, Nora. You don't know how sorry I am."

She said they'd guessed, as soon as Mae called again and said they needed to talk, that I was expecting. Leonard's father was certain that my predicament had nothing to do with Leonard. He believed some other boy had disappointed me, and in my desperation, I was trying to make the most of Leonard's inability to defend himself. He imagined I'd tried writing to Leonard, and received the same MIA red stamp on my returned mail that they'd gotten on theirs. He didn't know that I'd been too scared to write my address on the envelopes, and that none of my letters, stating I was pregnant, could be returned. He was all but certain I knew very well that Leonard was missing, and was using that to my advantage.

"And what did you think?" I asked. I was rubbing my bare shoulders, my knees pulled up to my chin. I reached over and switched off the AC.

"I wasn't sure. You'd promised me you wouldn't see him

again. John was so angry with me for not telling your father about the shower. He said I'd let you manipulate me. He said you'd either broken your promise to me, or you were lying about Bradenton. Either way, we couldn't trust you." She sighed. "I wasn't myself, Nora. I couldn't think."

I shook my head. She was right that I'd broken my promise to her. She was right that night I was so scared in her car, I'd cried and convinced her to lie to her husband for me. But it wasn't the same as what they'd done to me. And what they'd done to Leonard.

"You let me think he was just ignoring my letters." I gripped the receiver so tightly my hand hurt. "You made me think I was alone, that he knew and didn't care. Mrs. Lifton, you let me go up there and give my child away."

Another long silence. I was wasting my breath. Everything I'd just told her, she already knew.

"I'll say this," she said finally. "That day you called from New Jersey . . . I was the one who answered. When the social worker was about to put you on, it made sense for John to take the phone. It made sense to him, and it made sense to me. He thought you'd been able to manipulate me once, and that you'd do it again. I didn't argue. I handed him the receiver. Oh Nora. I wasn't sleeping. I was hardly eating. I never went out. But I knew it was wrong for him to tell you Leonard knew about the baby. That was going too far. But once the words left his mouth, once you'd already heard them, there was no going back. You see? If I'd have contradicted him, even in that moment, if I'd wrested the receiver from his hand and told you the truth, nothing could ever be fixed. I knew that if Leonard was alive and came home, you'd tell him what his father told you, that he'd known about the baby and didn't care. And Leonard would never forgive him. Never."

"Who would?" I asked. "Who would forgive a thing like that?"

She didn't answer. I tried to picture where she was in her house. They had the telephone in her sunny kitchen, and an extension back in their room. She might have taken the phone out to the patio where she'd held my hand and told me I should move away.

"You make it seem," I said, "like it was just your husband lying. But you're worse than he is. You lied to my face."

She told me she'd hated lying to me, and that she'd tried to make it so she wouldn't have to. She told me that the day I found her on her back patio, she'd been hiding from me. She'd seen me roll up on my bike, and she had just enough time to drop to her hands and knees and crawl down the hallway to her bedroom.

"We'd just learned ourselves he was alive," she said. "The night before the list came out. Someone from the State Department called and said he was on it. We were ecstatic. It was going to be another Christmas without any news, and then all at once, we knew he was alive. I didn't even think of you. Then

John left for work, and there you were, running up to the door. I hid from you because I didn't want to lie to you. But you came and found me out back. I had no choice."

"You had a choice," I said.

"Yes," she said. "You're right. It was either lie to you, tell this terrible lie that might make you finally go away, or let my family explode. For years, the only thing I had to hang on to was that he would come home alive, and the three of us would be a family again. When we saw his name on the list, the damage to you was already done. So yes. You're right. I had a decision to make, and I made it. I looked you in the eye and lied. With everything I had."

A pontoon boat rolled slowly down the intercoastal. Its wake caused *The Last Laugh* to rise and fall by the dock.

"You lied to Leonard as well," I said. "Your own son."

She said not at first, not exactly. She hadn't needed to. They first heard from him in late 1952. He was still in the camp, but the Chinese were starting to let the prisoners write home. When they got Leonard's first letter, they could tell he'd sent others, letters that never reached them. He told them he still wanted news, any news at all, about me.

"We read that"—she paused to let out a shaky breath—"and even John knew you were probably telling the truth. About Bradenton, I mean. But you were married by then. I'd seen the announcement in the paper. So I wrote Leonard to tell him that. That you'd gotten married."

I closed my eyes. He must have tried to write to me directly.

He would have sent the letter to my parents' house. Mae, I thought. My anger swelled. But when I spoke this theory into the receiver, Leonard's mother disagreed.

"I wouldn't blame your stepmother. His letters to you might never have left the camp. When he came home, he said that prisoners collecting firewood had found sacks of outgoing mail, addressed to the States, rotting out in the woods. I didn't know if one of his letters reached you or not. I was sick about it, worrying."

"You got lucky," I said. "Lucky you."

She said she didn't feel lucky. Lucky he was alive, yes. Lucky he was coming home. But she hated hurting him, letting him think I'd just forgotten about him, or changed my mind, when he was still over there, alone. And when he was finally home and safe, she couldn't tell him about the baby. What good would it have done? They couldn't get the baby back. And I was already married.

"We'd just gotten him back. You have to understand."

My eyebrows shot up. I didn't have to do anything. "That was your grandchild," I said.

She made an ugly, wheezing sound. I was unmoved. More lying? More fakery from her? I couldn't know. When I was a girl, dazzled by her, she once told me I'd see the world differently after I'd seen more of it. She'd been right about that.

"I'll have to live with that," she said. "I'll have to live with that for the rest of my life."

Good, I thought. Because so would I.

“Nora?” she asked. Her voice sounded tinny and far away. “Are you there?”

I sure was. I looked around the kitchen, at the mop waiting in the corner. I didn’t think she deserved an answer. I hung up without giving her one.

28.

I didn't go to sleep that night. I stared into the darkness, listening to Russ snore and thinking of that day in the ballpark, the hateful way I'd smiled at Leonard. Outside the Publix, I'd looked right into his eyes and told him I'd hoped his fingers rotted off because of the rot inside him.

I didn't know if he and the blond girl were engaged or already married. They'd looked happy at the ball game, his arm around her. And she'd stood by him through the insults from Russ and Buddy. I imagined this girl putting her slender arms around Leonard now, consoling him. It didn't make me unhappy. I wanted him to be consoled.

There would be no such consoling for me. I could talk to Mae, eventually, if I could catch her alone when she wasn't trying to do a million things. For now, I could guess what she'd say. She'd be even more disgusted by Leonard's parents than she already was, which was saying something. She'd probably feel terrible for Leonard, and guilty for judging him so harshly. I'd have company in that, at least. But Mae wouldn't be able to change anything. She couldn't undo every hurtful thing I'd said and done. She couldn't go back in time to that day in New Jersey, and tell me to un-sign the papers. Mrs. Lifton had been right about one thing: Knowing the truth wouldn't fix anything. What was done was done.

I thought of my daughter, how light she'd felt in my arms. Even on her first day in the world, even with the injury from the forceps, she'd looked like Leonard. Now she was three and a half years old, and I didn't know what she looked like, or what her name was. If she was alive, she was likely sleeping, and I thought of her waking to light coming in some window, familiar to her, that I'd never see. *Sweet dreams*, I thought. *Sweet dreams till sunbeams find you.* That was the most I could give her, that wish.

I was still awake when Russ's alarm clock buzzed. In the warmer months, he rose before dawn so he could meet his crew early enough to get their workday done before the punishing heat of the afternoons. He turned on the light only briefly, then turned it off before he whispered my name. I feigned sleep in the darkness.

I wasn't angry with him. He'd had nothing to do with what happened with the Liftons, or with the baby. I just couldn't bear to pretend I felt anything aside from desolate. I heard him go out the front door. The engine of his truck turned over, then growled alive, then faded as he drove away. The edges of the bedroom windows lightened to gray, then lavender. The drilling and hammering started up. And still, I didn't move. My limbs felt like concrete.

I was still lying there when the phone rang. Right away, I knew. I don't think it was any kind of magic telepathy, just a process of elimination. Russ was busy working. Mrs. Lifton had already called. A salesman wouldn't call so early. Even Mae rarely called before eight. This sounds like a lot to consider while a phone is ringing. I suppose I was expecting him to call.

I jumped up and hurried to the kitchen, all my lethargy gone. But once I was close enough to grab the receiver, I just stood there. If you would have seen me then, staring at that ringing phone, you might have thought it was a coiled viper that God himself had commanded me to reach out and pet. I was scared of what he had every right to say to me. I had no hope of forgiveness, or of the mercy I hadn't shown him.

But the phone kept ringing, and I knew what I owed him. Finally, I made myself pick up.

Much later, not on this phone call, Leonard told me that day at the Publix, after he watched me get in Russ's truck, he went back inside with his bow tie still dangling, clocked out, and drove home still wearing the apron. His parents were both home, happy to see him until they saw his face. The first thing he said was that he didn't want to hear any more lies, not one.

His mother sank to the floor, her back against the refrigerator. His father came up with the idea that they should all go into the living room and try to talk things through like civilized human beings. Leonard said he wasn't sure that's what they were. He went back to his room, wedged the back of a chair against it, and started packing.

Five minutes later, he came out with his army duffel bag on his shoulder, blowing past his father, who followed him to the front door and told him he was again hurting his mother, hurting her terribly, and that she'd already suffered so much, for years, because he acted without thinking, without trying to stay calm, and here he was doing it again. Leonard didn't respond, just threw his bag into the car they'd given him as a homecoming present. It was a nice car, even nicer than his old Plymouth: a brand-new Chevrolet Bel Air with power steering, royal blue. His father, still standing in the shade of the house, reminded Leonard he was the one who'd purchased the car, and Leonard, conceding the point, turned around and pitched the keys like a fastball. His father jumped out of the way, and good thing for him, as the keys hit the terra-cotta bowl by the door with enough force that the bowl shattered. Leonard took the duffel bag out of the car, turned back to the street, and started walking.

It was a Sunday evening, and nothing was open downtown. But he had cash from his last paycheck at Publix, and he used it to get a room at a hotel charging off-season rates. The nightstand in this room held both a Bible and a city directory. He used the latter to find the phone number and the address listed under *Crandle, R.* He found Dolphin Drive in the directory's map.

In the morning, he walked to the bank where he'd recently deposited the three years' worth of hardship pay the military had finally decided to send to him. He withdrew all of it and took a cab to a used car dealership, where he got an exceptionally good deal on a nine-year-old Buick with a dent in the passenger door. The salesman, also a veteran, noticed the missing fingers and asked what happened. Leonard told him, and the salesman asked to see his military ID, then went inside and talked with the dealership owner, another veteran, who cut the car's total price by a third.

This salesman also asked Leonard if he was okay, and mentioned that he looked distressed.

"I'm fine," Leonard told him. "But thank you, sir." He made himself convincing. In the last few years, he said, he'd grown particularly adept at appearing one way when he was feeling something else.

The salesman believed him, or at least didn't press the matter. He asked if he could take a picture of Leonard by the Buick, as they liked to show off all their satisfied customers with pictures on a board inside the dealership. Leonard said yes, posed beside the Buick's good side, then got in and drove twenty minutes west to the Gulf-side beaches. On the main strip of Treasure Island, he found a diner where he ate a hamburger while staring out the window. Then he put his shoes in the car and walked down to the shore, not realizing he was talking to himself until sunburned strangers and little kids building sandcastles started giving him looks. He thought that his sunglasses hid that he was sometimes crying. If they didn't, he didn't care.

When night fell, he drove to Dolphin Drive, located our address, and saw Russ's truck parked in the driveway. He turned around and drove back over the causeway to Treasure Island, where he checked into a hotel, took a shower, and tried to sleep. At four in the morning, he drove back to Dolphin Drive, parking far enough away that Russ wouldn't notice his car, and there he waited. When I was lying in bed, listening to Russ drive away in the dark, Leonard was still parked on our street, watching. When the truck's taillights faded, he drove back over the causeway to the diner, which had a pay phone. He'd already gotten change.

I'd like to talk to you in person," he told me. "I'm staying on Treasure Island, at the Starlight Motel. There's a diner across the street, but I could meet you anywhere."

For what, I thought. Maybe to berate me, as I'd berated him. Maybe to ask questions I couldn't answer: *Where is she now? Do you know anything about the people who have her? How could you have believed them? What the hell is the matter with you?* But he didn't sound angry. I stood there in my nightgown, squinting at the rising sun. I couldn't guess why he was on Treasure Island, so close, but too far for me to walk to. I told him I didn't have a car.

"I could come pick you up," he said. "I'm sorry for the rush, but I'm leaving town, probably tomorrow. I just want to talk with you first. I could wait around a few days if you need time. I don't mean to be sneaky, Nora. If you want to wait and talk with . . . with Russ, or if you think he should be there, that's okay. I'll wait."

I almost laughed at that, the idea of my telling Russ that I needed to talk with Leonard, and Russ being okay with it.

"Don't come to the house," I said. I thought of the construction workers across the street. Russ was friendly with some of them. "I'll walk down to Paradise Boulevard and meet you there. You know where that is? When you come off the Treasure Island Causeway, it's on the right." Of course it would be on the right, I thought. If he turned left he'd drive into the water. "I could be there, at Paradise and Treasure, in half an hour."

"Paradise and Treasure," Leonard said, and he laughed a little. I got that he was laughing at the words, how happy they sounded, how wrong for the occasion. I couldn't laugh, but I told him yes—Paradise and Treasure, that was where I'd be.

It seemed foolish to put on makeup, especially when it was so hot and sticky out, with a hundred percent chance that I'd cry. My hair had grown out a little, but not enough that I could pull it back into anything but a little knob. I told myself it didn't matter what I looked like. This wasn't exactly a date.

But when I slid into the front seat of the dented Buick,

Leonard smiled at me as if I were Venus rising up on the half shell. I think he might have reached over to embrace me right then if the car behind us hadn't honked. He put the car in gear, and we lurched forward, both of us silent as he accelerated. Humid air rushed in the windows, and gulls sailed low over the causeway. I was both tired from not sleeping and wide awake, hardly able to believe that this really was Leonard sitting beside me. Leonard who was not cold, not heartless, and not the snake I'd told myself he'd become, but the same as he'd been when I'd known him. When I loved him. Even with the thinned hair and the patchy eyebrow, it was still him, watching the road with eyes I still could have drawn from memory.

On the other side of the causeway, he made a hard right, and I caught sight of his injured hand, the pink nub and the half finger. My good feeling drained out.

"Sorry," he said. "Almost missed the turn." He parked in the shade of a pink stucco diner. "I ate here last night. They said they'd be open for breakfast."

I said that sounded good, though I was shaky by then, getting nervous. I didn't know if Russ knew anyone on Treasure Island. And I kept looking at Leonard's hand, at the missing fingers. It was fortunate he'd parked in the shade, because by the time he turned off the ignition, I was in no condition to go inside.

"Hold on." He got out, went into the diner, and came out with several paper napkins. He got back in and handed them to me. "I'm sorry," he said. "Oh, Nora. I'm so sorry. I had no idea. I hope you know that."

That made me cry harder. He was right in front of me, saying the very words I'd so wanted to hear that winter in New Jersey. But it was like finding tickets for the circus that had just left town. His words, his sorrow, they weren't worthless to me. But they were too late to do any good.

I asked him what happened to his fingers.

"Frostbite." He winced as he said this, either because it hurt him to think of it, or because he knew it would hurt me to hear.

"What happened to your eyebrow?"

"Napalm. Our own. I was lucky compared to . . ." He shook his head, not wanting to continue.

"Oh, Leonard," I said. I'd been so convinced he wasn't suffering.

"Did you ever see her?" he asked. "Did they let you?"

No one had ever asked me this. But of course, if anyone in the world would understand the loss of her, and what my short time with her meant, it would be him. I told him I'd spent almost a whole day with her, and I told her that she had his eyebrows, and that I'd loved her right away, and I still did. I told him how her cheek had been injured by the forceps, and though the nurse told me she would heal completely, I could only hope that was true.

"I bet she's okay," he said, like he really believed it. But he didn't know. He couldn't.

I told him I was the one who should be apologizing. I'd given our child away. I was crying so hard I could barely talk, but I tried to describe it—what was going through my head when I signed the papers. I told him about Miss Berry, and how she'd told me not to be selfish, and how I'd been so tired, and so unsure of what would happen if I'd refused to sign. Because I'd given up on him completely. I'd believed every lie.

By the time I stopped to catch my breath, I felt like his mother, not wanting to make excuses for myself, and going on to do exactly that.

"Nora." He started to reach for my shoulder, then changed his mind. He put both hands back on the wheel. "Listen to me. You don't have to apologize for that. I understand. Really. More than you know."

We stayed in the car, in the shade, and he told me what he meant, and what those years had been like, for him.

He'd been captured in Osan, forty miles south of Seoul. It was July, hot, and he was wearing his summer-issue uniform. Their dog tags were confiscated at gunpoint. They all knew what that meant. They could be killed without any consequence, without any record, without even a grave. In the daytime, they were locked in houses or schools, or watched over in open fields. Thirst was always with them, as was hunger. They would see UN planes overhead and hear the whistles of falling bombs. Artillery fire often sounded close, just a few miles to the south. Night after night, the guards marched them north, using bayonets and rifle butts to encourage speed.

In early November, when I was on the train to New Jersey, feeling like a shunned cockroach and still hoping he would write, Leonard and over eight hundred other prisoners were staggering through the mountains of North Korea in the last and deadliest stretch of the march. Leonard was still wearing his summer uniform, now ragged and filthy, and too big, the belt tightened, then tightened again. The steep terrain turned slick with ice and frozen urine and shit and blood from the prisoners ahead of him, most sick with dysentery, some injured in battle. Men slipped, got back up, or didn't. You helped someone if you could, if you could do it without stopping, without holding up the line. Every mile or so, a prisoner wouldn't get up, couldn't, and the rest of them would keep moving, then hear a gunshot from the back. If a Good Samaritan got involved—or a pleading friend, a defiant officer–they'd hear two shots. You either kept up or you didn't.

Leonard had the lucky bell I'd given him pinned to the laces of his right boot, and it glinted in the moonlight as he stepped double time. Even as men dropped around him, even as he heard more shots from behind, he told himself he could make it just a little farther, then a little farther, then a little farther after that.

Their destination, a prison camp near Pyoktong, North Korea, was where most of them would die. The camp was just south of the Yalu River, and on the other side of this river was

China. Leonard's group arrived nine days into November, just after China entered the war. The Yalu was already frozen solid, and every day, Leonard and the other prisoners watched Chinese tanks roll south across the ice, one after the other, with so many Chinese soldiers marching behind them, their uniforms clean, their guns ready. Leonard understood, with everyone else, they wouldn't be going home anytime soon.

When he told me this, he wanted to make one thing clear: The prisoners who would die in the camp that winter, and there were a lot of them, didn't die from giving up, from giving-up-itis, whatever people who weren't there wanted to call it. Those men froze to death, or succumbed to illness or starvation, or any combination of the above. Despairing or not, Leonard said, they did their best, and worst, to survive. When a man in Leonard's tent died in the night, they told the guard he was just sick so the rest of them could split up his daily ration, a bean ball the size of a fist. They kept that up for over a week, Leonard said, sleeping next to the man's frozen body.

Most prisoners had dysentery, and were too weak to even stagger through the snow to the latrines. The ones who could were put to work. Leonard was assigned to the crew that dragged the bodies of deceased prisoners to a cove where they were stacked like wood in a cord, every one of them naked. They had no shovels to dig into the snow and the frozen ground, and the clothes couldn't be wasted. Leonard said for months, he wore somebody's shirt over his head, just his eyes showing through the collar. He used the leg of somebody's trousers for a scarf. But he'd never forget the sound, he said, of the back of a man's head getting dragged across ice. These were the bodies of their friends, their commanding officers, or men who'd helped them stay upright on the way to the camp.

He said that when his fingers froze off, it didn't hurt. His pinkie turned black first, and one day, when he gave it a little tug, off it came, easy as a petal from a flower. A few weeks later, the same thing happened with the end of his ring finger. Hunger was a scream inside him, unrelenting. He ate his own scabs, and half a bean ball tugged from a dead man's pocket. He ate lice, mostly for vengeance. Apparently, lice do just fine even in freezing temperatures, drawing warmth from human skin. Pretty soon, he figured out if a man stopped picking at lice, he was on his way out.

He wasn't the only one who put this together. If a man stopped picking at lice, everyone would start eyeing the doomed man's socks, feeling bad for him, saying prayers for him, but still. Leonard didn't realize he'd stopped picking until an army captain on his work crew, a man named Zimmerman, grabbed his shoulder and said, "Come on, now. Kid. Hey. Come on," like he was trying to talk Leonard out of something. This army captain, Zimmerman, started asking Leonard questions about where he was from and what he planned to do when he got home. Leonard told him about Florida, and about his parents, and how guilty he felt for what he was putting them through.

But mostly, he said, he talked about me.

He'd lost the lucky bell by then—he couldn't remember how.

The army captain said that didn't mean anything, and there was no such thing as a bad omen except if he made one in his head. He said Leonard should try to imagine me there beside him, and what I would say if I could see him.

"I got good at it," he told me. We were still in his dented car, in the shade of the diner, the upholstery beneath my shorts soaked with sweat. "It was crazy. You were there, Nora. You were in the camp, right in front of me like you are now. You were wearing that blue shirt you wore in Bradenton, short sleeved, your skin suntanned. Your hair stayed dry in the snow. You wanted me to go up and talk to people." He laughed, scratching his head, his thinned hair. "You kept telling me I should try."

More often than not, he took my advice. He'd never been so socially outgoing in his life.

"I couldn't always do it," he said. "When I had dysentery, no. And even when I was okay, more or less, I was never as good at it as you were. But when I did manage to get other guys talking, I'd feel better. It helped some of them, too, I think." He shook his head. "I know it did."

Because of the vitamin deficiency, the general starvation, they all started going night blind, which was as terrifying as anything, he said. Starting at dusk, ending at dawn, he could have his hand right in front of his face and not see it. A full moon would make no difference, even on a cloudless night. But even in those long black-out hours, he said, he could hear my voice. On those nights, imaginary-me didn't suggest he go try to make conversation with anyone. I just told him, again and again, that I loved him, and wanted him to come home.

"You saved me," he said.

I wiped my eyes, shaking my head. I didn't want to argue about it. But he was talking about the imaginary-me, the me that lived in his head. The real me had been in New Jersey, falling for lies and full of spite.

"You did," he said. "No question. Well, you and my big feet. A lot of the guards, they didn't have good boots. But nobody wanted mine. That made a difference for me, I know."

The following April, when our child was three months old, when I was back in St. Pete and getting run out of high school by the likes of Hazel Morgan and some idiot boy putting a basketball under his gym shirt, the Chinese took over management of the camp. The new guards, Chinese guards, all spoke English, and generally had a softer touch. They allowed the prisoners to build a fire and run the burning edge of a stick along the inner seams of their clothes to kill the lice. Rations increased, slowly at first. When the river melted, the prisoners were allowed to bathe in it, and for the first time in months, Leonard got a look at his concave chest and stick arms and jutting-out hip bones. The other men around him were all the same. They stared at one another, quiet. Of the eight hundred Leonard came in with, maybe three hundred were still alive.

Not long after that, the prisoners were called out to the main field, organized into lines, and asked for their name, rank, and service number. This encouraged everyone. And then a Chinese officer, bright medals on his jacket, climbed up on the back of a jeep with a megaphone. This officer was silver-haired but quick in his movements. He spoke English well, and with a British accent. He started off by saying they would all have to work together to improve the conditions of the camp, but it might take a while, given imperialist bombings were not only killing scores of civilians but putting food and medicine in short supply. Meanwhile, he said, they shouldn't think of themselves as prisoners, but as students. From now on, they'd be students of truth.

Conditions continued to improve. They started getting rice, then rice with no maggots in it, then sometimes there was even fish. Doctors were brought in. Some of these doctors asked for volunteer assistants, and because Leonard's crew wasn't dragging as many bodies to the river every day, he was free to volunteer. They assigned him to a Dr. Wang, a middle-aged woman who spoke three languages, none of them English. One thing she did, right away, was diagnose the prisoners suffering from beriberi, and she was able to get hold of thiamine supplements that helped most of them. Antibiotics were harder to come by, but sometimes she could get those, too.

Dr. Wang showed Leonard how to give injections, and clean wounds and instruments. She was a serious person, he said. But when she saw that someone was improving, she would smile and give him the thumbs-up.

So there was plenty that was good about the Chinese taking over. The bad part, the political classes, started that May. Ten hours a day. Attendance mandatory, no exceptions. Classes were organized by rank and race, so Leonard was in a group of around a hundred white enlisted Americans who were marched every dawn to a barn about a mile away from camp. They sat on the ground of this barn—all together in the mornings, in small groups in the afternoons. The instructors, all Chinese, sat on the ground as well, and they were young and friendly. They knew American slang, American jokes. One instructor told Leonard he'd been to Florida, and that he'd even surfed at Daytona Beach. Another could quote Shakespeare and the Bible, Dickens, and Whitman. This same instructor once took an apple out of his pocket, small but unbruised, and told Leonard's group he'd been saving it for his lunch, but could see that one of the weaker prisoners in the group needed it more.

"I'm going to give him my apple," the instructor said. "Because I'm a communist." He handed the apple to the sick man. Leonard and the others watched this man eat it in maybe five bites, core and all.

They had study groups. Literate prisoners read writings by Mao, by Marx. They were quizzed on articles in *The Daily Worker.* Illiterate prisoners were read summaries, and expected to listen closely. Regular guards, armed with batons or rifles, were always watching from the back. If a prisoner didn't want to interact with those guards, he had to be a good student. That meant listening to lessons without eyes glazed over, and also being an active participant—you couldn't just mouth the words to a chant while thinking about how tired you were or whether there'd be any fish at dinner. You had to chant with your voice, and chant like you meant it. You could pick at lice, but your eyes had to be open and attentive, focused on the instructor, and you really had to be paying attention, ready to be called on with a question, and to give the right answer: What was the only true democracy? *Communism.* Who started the war? *Wall Street warlords.* What leaders truly cared about their people? *Chairman Mao, Stalin, Kim Il Sung.* What was the purpose of these classes? *Mental liberation.*

When the instructors noticed bad behavior—someone refusing to give up imperialist thinking, someone failing to come up with examples from his own life to support that day's lesson, someone capsizing on the barn floor and falling asleep—that someone might first get a friendly warning that he needed to adopt a better attitude toward learning. If the behavior persisted, the instructor would eventually signal to the guards, who would hurry over to help the bad student to his feet and out of the barn. Some disappeared for good. The ones who came back, weeks later, appeared deeply shaken, and did not require further warnings.

Leonard said the whole time he was in the barn, even with his brain addled by hunger and thirst and boredom, he worked hard to think his own thoughts. But sometimes the instructors said things he couldn't argue against, even in his head. The Chinese knew all about Jim Crow laws, for example. They had pictures of Hoovervilles and half-naked and hungry-looking American children standing in front of shacks, and they had pictures of J. D. Rockefeller's mansion. They knew things Leonard had never heard about that turned out to be true, like American vets having to protest in DC to get their wartime bonuses, and none other than General MacArthur ordering troops to throw tear gas at the vets and their families. Our own vets. All kinds of things hard to defend, mixed in with a lot of lies and threats, day in and day out, with the lice still biting, and his hunger ferocious. Sometimes thinking he'd never get home.

But he wasn't brainwashed, he said. Nobody was, not that he saw. Some prisoners were more open to what the instructors were telling them. Not many of them, but a few. There was one guy he came in with, from Louisiana, who'd never had a decent pair of shoes before he joined the army, who'd been hungry his whole life. He was open to the lessons. But not brainwashed. Leonard didn't like that word at all. He said whoever made it up had never set foot in Camp Five, guaranteed. They all knew those petitions they signed were propaganda. He signed because if there was one holdout, everyone suffered. Food withheld. Health wise, not every man was out of the woods. Not at all. The day before Dr. Wang disappeared, she signed her name to an open letter of apology for prioritizing sentiment over revolution—meaning she'd given some sick prisoner medicine even though he refused to write an essay about how well the camp was run. Leonard didn't think for a minute her brain was washed.

"She was like us," he said. "Just wanting to live."

He tapped the fingers of his right hand on the steering wheel. We were still parked in the shade of the diner. But it was midmorning now, or later. The breeze coming in the windows was already hot. I wanted the discomfort, was glad for it. Even as I knew it couldn't compare.

"If you're watching a movie," he said, "if you're watching a Hollywood actor play the tough guy, you think, 'Well if I were in that situation, I'd be like him, the one who doesn't break on anything.' But when I was there, that first winter and spring, the petitions weren't the breaking I worried about."

He said he had bigger temptations to resist. Snatching a bean ball from somebody still alive but too weak to fight back; taking somebody's socks before he was actually dead; ratting on somebody for making a Mao joke so he'd get extra rice for a week. He said he'd be lying if he claimed he was never tempted, and anyone who didn't understand that had never gone hungry for long. His goal, his only goal, was to survive without hurting someone else's chances. Not everyone managed that, he said, but most of them did, and anybody who stayed human in Camp Five had much to be proud of, signed petitions or not. He could only hope the people calling them brainwashed and weak never had to find out what they'd do in similar circumstances.

"I called you a coward," I said.

He shook his head. "My parents made you think that. They

lied to you. Nora, I'm telling you all this so you know I understand. I understand why you signed."

I rested my forehead in my hands. The paper napkins he'd gotten for me were wet with tears and snot, and wadded up in my lap. I told him I appreciated the connection he was trying to make. But what I signed in New Jersey, giving away our daughter, wasn't just a petition, wasn't just propaganda. It meant something. And I wished, so much, that I could take that signature back.

"But the circumstances," he said. "They weren't so different."

I didn't agree with this at all. New Jersey wasn't North Korea. I hadn't lost any fingers to frostbite. Nobody poked me with a bayonet. That day in the hospital, I was tired, but not starving. I could have stood up to Miss Berry. Carol did.

"Did she have somewhere to go?" Leonard asked. "Did she have somewhere to take her baby?"

I nodded, thinking of her trust fund, the room with money she'd come into. Leonard held up his hands like, *well, there you go.*

I'm aware that some people never really come back from wars, even once they're home and safe. But it's also true that others come back completely themselves, and even stronger in some ways. With Leonard, for example—the whole time we were talking in his car, his knee didn't bounce, not once.

I'm not saying his mind was unscathed. But I think now that the very things that held him back when he was young—his shyness, his stubbornness—helped him during the long days in that barn, and helped when he was back in the US and having to face people who thought he was weak, and a traitor. Long before he set foot in Korea, and before I met him, he mostly kept to himself. You could think of that as a bad thing, a lonely thing. But I think a lot of people who keep to themselves also know how to keep their own counsel, whatever is going on around them.

Someone like me, wanting to get along with people, might not have fared as well.

Things got easier, he said, all through 1952. They didn't know the list of prisoner names had been released, or that their captors now had reason to keep every one of them alive, even happy. They only knew that they started getting protein every day, and then larger portions. Political classes became optional, and nearly everyone stopped going. When the weather turned cold again, each prisoner got a padded coat and a hat with earflaps. The dying pretty much stopped. The Chinese put up a basketball hoop and volleyball net in the camp. The prisoners knew what that was about, and sure enough, professional photographers showed up to take pictures. That fall, prisoners were offered a chance to compete in an inter-camp POW Olympics, the games that Buddy had mentioned. For a lot of guys, it was their best chance to see if friends had survived in other camps.

Or to ever go anywhere again. They didn't know how long the fighting would last.

I asked Leonard if he'd competed. I was hoping they'd had a swimming competition, and that even with his missing fingers, he might still be able to butterfly across a pool with speed and grace. I wanted him to say yes. I wanted him to still have that.

He shook his head. "It was mostly new captures who competed. Those of us who came in that first winter were still too weak." He paused. "And I was pretty down at that point."

"Just at that point?" I didn't understand. "When things had gotten better?"

He looked embarrassed, rubbing his chin. He told me that by then, he'd gotten his mother's letter, telling him I'd married Russ.

"You had every right," he said. "I know that. I want you to be happy, Nora. Even if it's not with me."

A man in a Hawaiian shirt came out of the diner, followed by a woman holding a toddler. The woman shielded the boy's face from the sun, and the man hurried ahead to the car on Leonard's side and opened the passenger door for them. Leonard and I were quiet, waiting for them to drive away. Before they did, the woman looked out her window at us and said, "Oh my goodness, it's so hot out here. You two should go inside!"

We nodded and smiled, waiting for them to leave. We couldn't go in, both of us sweat-soaked and teary. Leonard asked if I wanted to get out and walk down to the water, just long enough to cool off.

He had the same long stride he'd always had, but he slowed to keep pace beside me, just as he'd always done before. He told me he'd been swimming almost every evening after he got off work at Publix. He said that when he was in the camp, he'd dreamed of the ocean. It had been there with him, too.

I was thinking I'd take off my sandals and get my legs wet, but the tide, once we stepped into it, felt so cool that we kept walking. Soon, we were in up to our necks. When a wave rolled in, we both rose with it, dog paddling beneath the surface. I took in his face, the angles and shadows of it. He looked older than he should have, his skin weathered, his lips grown thin. But if I'd been seeing him for the first time, if he were some stranger bobbing next to me in the water, it would have been like all those years ago, when I first saw him in the courtyard. I would've felt the same pull.

It's hard to know what a child will inherit, what features and traits get passed along to the next. I'd already wished for our child to be alive and happy, wherever she was. But I now also hoped that she would someday look in the mirror and find his beauty, and have some sense, some knowing, from where it came.

When we were back in his car, our clothes still wet, I asked him about the blond girl. He said her name was Joyce.

She studied literature at Rollins, in Winter Park, and he'd met her when she was home in St. Pete for Christmas break. He'd visited her a few times in Winter Park, he said. She'd come back to St. Pete for spring break, too. That's when I saw her at the ball game.

He saw my expression, and his one eyebrow rose. "Nora, you got married."

I brought my elbow to my nose and breathed in. My skin still smelled of the sea. "You think you'll get married? You and Joyce?" I strained to make my voice chipper, but it just came out high-pitched.

He said no. She'd been clear, from the start, that she wanted to stay in Florida. He didn't. He'd only been sticking around, he said, because he knew his absence had been hard on his parents, and he hadn't been sure what he wanted to do next. Now he had no reason to stay. And he was done, he said, absolutely done, with the South. He said there'd been another prisoner in the camp from St. Pete, a sergeant who'd also fought in France. His name was Ronald Lewis, and he was a black man, so he'd gone to Gibbs, not St. Pete High. He and Leonard didn't have any mutual acquaintances. Not one. But when Sergeant Lewis heard where Leonard was from, he came and found him in the camp, and proposed a deal: If only one of them made it home alive, the other would carry a message to the loved ones of the other. Sergeant Lewis memorized the names of Leonard's parents, and my name as well. Leonard told him he could find me working at the library by Mirror Lake, and Leonard memorized the name of the sergeant's wife, who worked as a nurse at Mercy Hospital, and the names of the sergeant's two daughters, who both attended Gibbs.

In the end, they both made it back to St. Pete. Leonard had been home six months before he bumped into Sergeant Lewis at the ballgame, the same one I'd gone to with Russ. The sergeant told Leonard he barely recognized him, wearing civilian clothes, and clean shaven. Leonard laughed and said the same.

"But you know," Leonard said, "we couldn't go get a beer together. We had to leave the field to even talk. This man fought in two wars for this country, and almost starved in Korea, and he can't sit on a bench downtown, or go in the front door of a restaurant. His girls couldn't go to a swimming pool until just this summer, until someone donated the money for a separate one." He squinted through the windshield at the diner. "He's staying in St. Pete because his father is sick. So he's got a reason. I don't. Not anymore."

"Will you go to New York?" I asked. I was thinking he had an aunt there, and cousins. "Or is Dale still in New Hampshire?"

Leonard said no, not New York, and not New Hampshire. He wouldn't go anywhere with cold weather. He gestured to the blister on his nose, and to a scaly spot on his cheek. "Frostbite. It bothers me more in cold weather," he said. "What's left of my fingers, too. I was thinking about Phoenix."

He reached up to pull down his visor, then reached over to

pull mine down as well. I wanted to take hold of his arm and pull him to me.

"Phoenix," I said. "I heard it's nice."

"Maybe Phoenix," he said. "You know, as soon as I got back, my mom was talking about how I should apply to school in California. I couldn't figure it out, how she seemed like she'd missed me so much, then couldn't wait for me to get so far away."

I told him his mother had suggested California to me as well. "Before I married Russ." I spoke slowly. I wanted him to understand. "She told me you'd fallen in love with a girl in Japan, and that I should take my broken heart to California."

He was silent, taking this in. I thought, okay, at least I have that. At least he understands I didn't just get tired of waiting.

After a while, he sort of laughed and said it would have been funny if we'd both taken his mother's advice, gone to California, and bumped into each other out there. But then he closed his mouth tight, and I could see he was trying not to cry. She'd broken his heart, too.

"Are you happy?" he asked. "Are you happy with him?"

I nodded.

He waited. "Will you look at me and answer?"

I turned to look at him and tried to nod once more. My old failing, failing me again.

"It doesn't matter," I said.

He said it mattered to him. He said I'd saved him twice—the

first time in high school when he was so unsure of himself, and dying of loneliness. Or feeling like he was dying. And then again in Korea, where he really might have died.

"You got me through it," he said. "And it's more than that. You know, Nora. I'll be okay. I want you to know that. I've got life ahead of me, and I'm grateful for it. But if I look back on my life so far, and I think of my happiest moments, most of them are with you."

I closed my eyes, wiped my cheeks again. I would have those words as well. They would have to be enough.

"Are you saying it doesn't matter to you if you're happy?"

I shrugged and looked at my hands, all ten fingers intact. "I don't think I can be," I said. "I don't think that's in the cards for me now."

He slapped the steering wheel. I looked up at him. It was the exact same thing his mother had done that night she drove me home.

"Did your mom ever talk to you over there?" I asked. "Were your parents ever in your head?"

He didn't like that question. I could see it on his face. But after a while, he nodded. "Her especially," he said.

Well, there you go, I thought. We'd all helped to bring him home. And not one of us deserved him.

"I better get back," I said. No part of me wanted that to be true. But the shade from the diner had disappeared. It was already well past noon.

"Can I write to you?" Leonard asked. "Would Russ be upset

if you got a letter from me? I don't mean like pen pals. I just want you to have an address. I want you to be able to reach me if there's ever—"

"They seal the records," I said. "She's lost for good."

He nodded. "I mean if you ever need something. Anything. I don't know where I'll be yet, but when I do, I want you to at least know how to get in touch with me."

I wanted to tell him yes. But it wasn't a good idea. I usually got the mail, but not always. I told him if he needed to reach me, he could write to Mae.

He turned the key in the ignition, but we stayed parked in the sun, the engine humming.

"I just want to make sure," he said. "You're happy with him? Being married to him?"

I told him happiness came from deciding to be happy. From the quality of your thoughts.

He raised the one good eyebrow. "You've been reading Marcus Aurelius."

I laughed, and he did, too.

"You know," he said. "He also said you assemble your life, action by action. You've assembled one, Nora. Is it the one you want? That's what I'm asking."

I took a while to answer, to choose the right words.

"I think I'm living the life I should be living," I said. I meant the life I deserved. But I knew better than to say this. I didn't want him hearing sad violins when he thought of me, wherever he ended up.

He dropped me off where he'd picked me up, where the road from the Treasure Island Causeway intersects with Paradise Boulevard. Again there were cars behind us, honking and impatient. We didn't have time for a long goodbye, or an embrace. I thought maybe that was for the best. I'd given a lot of thought to Miss Berry telling me I'd be smart not to ever hold my baby. She might have been lying about that, too, just trying to get what she wanted. But for all I knew, I'd have been better off taking that advice.

When I was again alone, walking back to the house, I came up with the idea that I could borrow Leonard's trick from Korea, and keep an imaginary version of him in my head. When I turned onto Dolphin Drive, the hot wind was blowing so hard I had to hold tight to my sun hat, and with every step, the sawing and hammering got louder. Still, not exactly a prison camp. And it helped, having imaginary-Leonard telling me I was doing fine, that I just had to keep putting one foot in front of the other.

But when I caught sight of my own front door, my feet felt particularly heavy.

"*Keep going!*" imaginary-Leonard said. "*You can do it!*"

My imaginary-Leonard wasn't better than the real one. The real Leonard would have given me entirely different advice. I made it inside, but after I closed the door behind me, I knew very well I was alone.

29.

That afternoon, I did my usual tasks with a focused intensity, making liberal use of bleach and a scrub brush, and sweeping floors I'd already swept. I got a pasta salad ready for dinner, and grated an entire head of broccoli in under five minutes, putting my back into it, as Mae would say. I took another shower, shampooed my hair twice, and checked the drains and my shoes for sand. When I did my final tour of the house, nothing suggested I'd done anything but spend another day at home. Still, when the dryer buzzed, I jumped like a startled cat.

I felt as if I'd already lied to Russ, as if I were already caught.

By half past three I was hungry. Russ liked us to have dinner as soon as he got home, so I tried to tide myself over with a slice of cheese and a beer, then lay back down on the couch. I didn't think I'd sleep, as even with the AC humming, I could still hear the sawing and hammering outside. But I closed my eyes, and when I opened them again, I knew that I'd slept. The light coming through the sliding glass door had the softness of early evening, and the construction sounds had quieted enough that I could hear gulls out back.

It wasn't until I turned my head that I noticed Russ sitting in his armchair. Usually, he showered as soon as he came home, but he was still wearing his work clothes, including his boots. I could smell his dried sweat from where I sat.

"Goodness." I smiled, trying to read his face. "How long you been sitting there?"

"Not long." He only half smiled back. "This idiot contractor doesn't know what he wants." He crossed a thick arm across his chest, rubbing his opposite shoulder. "Sorry if you were waiting. I grabbed dinner on my way home."

"I'm okay." I blew on my hands, cold from the AC. I was still hungry. I thought of the pasta salad I had waiting in the fridge. But I could sense his irritation. "Can I get you anything?" I asked. "A drink? Dessert?"

He looked at me for a long moment, Bambi eyes steady. He'd been drinking. A particular sentence formed in my head, so clearly I could see it before me. *Happiness in marriage is entirely a matter of chance.* I couldn't remember where I'd read it.

"Let's take the boat out." He stood and walked over to the couch, squeezing my toes as he passed.

By the time we pulled out from the dock, the sky to the east was already cobalt blue, and the low, wispy clouds to the west were edged in fuchsia and gold. We passed under the causeway, and then, picking up speed, passed the north side of Treasure Island. I didn't look at it, but I thought of Leonard, back in his hotel, maybe less than a mile away. In the morning, he'd be gone.

"Hand me a drink?" Russ nodded at the cooler. "Get one for yourself."

I got the beers. I alternated sipping and breathing in the muggy air, and soon we were out into the open water. Russ gave the boat enough gas that I could only hear the *thump thump thump* of the cresting waves as we moved past other vessels, all heading into shore for the night. We alone headed out toward the half-sunk sun on the horizon, as if to chase the sky's remaining light.

This life, I thought, this life I had, it was already assembled. I'd assembled it, action by action, choice by choice. And if the quality of my thoughts determined the quality of my life, it followed that if I felt myself to be fortunate in my marriage, I would be fortunate. But riding in that expensive boat, going fast enough that neither the bugs nor the heat could catch us, I couldn't make myself feel fortunate. My thoughts remained low quality, wanting what was too late to want. I guessed the beer wasn't helping. When Russ wasn't looking, I extended my arm and drained what was left in the can into the water.

We continued to head west, out into the Gulf. Russ asked for another beer, and I got it for him. The water smoothed out beneath us, and when I turned around, the lights from shore were far away. I thought about Leonard having night-blindness, unable to see his own hand in the dark. He'd said it was terrifying, the night blindness, even after all he'd already been through. I wondered what Carol would think of that. She might laugh or disagree, but maybe not. She herself could see shadows and shapes.

When Russ finally cut the engine, he did so without explanation, pushing the ignition key into the front pocket of his shorts. I could tell by the set of his jaw he was still in a mood, so I, too, stayed silent, watching the inky water as we continued to drift. He made no motion to drop the anchor.

"How was your day?" he asked.

It was his tone, strangely pleasant, that alarmed me. When I turned to him, he smiled, and my breath stilled in my lungs. His smile was so false that I realized, at that very moment, the story about the contractor was false as well. He'd come home angry because he knew I'd spent the day with Leonard. This was also why he'd taken me so far out on the boat. He already knew. I pressed my palms, slick with sweat, against my knees. I had a decision to make. If I was wrong, if he had no idea I'd spent the morning with Leonard, my confession would borrow trouble I didn't need. But if I was right, if he already knew, denying it would only anger him more.

"It was quite eventful, actually." I looked back at him, meeting his gaze. "You're not going to believe who called me up."

"Try me." He was still smiling. Fear tightened my throat. I thought of my mother, holding me as a baby, smiling down at me. She must have wanted me to have a good life. Even now, even though I'd disappointed her, she would want me to live.

"Leonard," I said. "Leonard Lifton."

Russ didn't bother acting surprised. I saw a shift, a hardening, in his eyes.

"Go on," he said.

My mind was a rabbit, racing and frantic, searching the ground for cover. Even a skilled liar, even an adequate liar, wouldn't know what to say next. But I didn't have to look back over my shoulder to know how far we were from shore. If I screamed, no one would hear me. If I stood and waved for help, no one but Russ would see.

Do not think what is hard is impossible. I pressed down harder on my knees. The boat rose and fell, rose and fell.

"Get this," I said. My rabbit-mind pivoted, racing for a hole. "He's hoping you could give him a job, or at least advice. He said he was too scared to go to you directly. Or too intimidated rather. As he should be."

Russ narrowed his eyes. Of course he did. It made no sense, what I was saying.

"He heard how well you're doing." I held his gaze, straining for logic. "He's fallen out with his parents, so he's broke. He's got no prospects. He was hoping you'd meet with him. Had no shame about coming to me."

Russ leaned toward me, over the throttle, his arm resting along the back of my seat. I could smell his beery breath, and the soap we both used. Water slapped against the hull.

"Let me get this straight." His voice was quiet, calm. "You're saying Leonard Lifton wants me to give him a job? And he thought the best way to do this was to meet with my wife while I was working? My wife who he once made pregnant and then abandoned?"

I thought of Mrs. Lifton, the words she'd said on the phone. *I had a decision to make and I made it.* I nodded at Russ, my eyes wide, in perfect agreement. The story I was telling was ludicrous. I could hardly believe it myself. That was fine. I was in character.

"Tell me about it," I said. "But he wasn't thinking of that. He's plenty book smart, okay. But with people . . ." I reached up and knocked on my head, making a clicking sound with my tongue. "It really didn't seem to occur to him that you might not want to help him. Or that he might disgust me. Which he did."

Russ's hand moved from the back of the seat to my neck. He didn't squeeze, or apply any pressure, but his thumb was on one side, his fingers on the other.

"That makes no sense." He said these words slowly, watching my eyes.

"It's the truth," I said. I imagined Leonard, slouched and desperate, asking me to talk to Russ about a job. I saw myself scornful, telling him that I'd do my best, adding that I could make no guarantees.

Russ's fingers drummed against my neck. "He asked you all this on the phone?"

"No. We went to a diner on Treasure Island. That's a busy place over there."

"So I hear. How'd you get there?"

"He picked me up." I braced myself. His left hand was a loose fist, resting in his lap. "In a car with a dented door. Embarrassing. Surprised that thing even drives."

He cocked his head as if listening for some distant sound, even as he studied me. But there was just the slap and slosh of the water. I looked up, searching the sky. The moon was a waning crescent, faint.

"Did it occur to you that you're a married woman?" He was still leaning toward me. "That you're married to me? That married women don't go on rides with old boyfriends while their husbands are working?"

Save yourself, Mae said. *Honey. Come on.*

I should say here that I never actually saw Mae in the boat with us that night. I wouldn't even say that I heard her voice, not the way Leonard had described hearing mine in Korea. It would be more accurate to say that I felt my stepmother telling me to get my act together, to at least put up a fight.

"I guess I don't think of him as a man," I said. The character, the girl I was playing, laughed and shook her head. "I mean, he's pathetic. Weak-natured. I told you that, that night with Buddy and Peg. My opinion hasn't changed."

That's fine, Leonard said. *Keep going.*

"And now he's broke, no more access to his daddy's money. Driving that sorry excuse for a car."

My voice was steady, my gaze direct. I thought of myself as a child, the yellow bow in my hair, staring down Mr. Pile. But this story for Russ was so much stranger, so much harder to believe. I had the strained feeling of walking too long in heels. I leaned close, nuzzling his neck, his stubble sharp against my nose.

"Did he come into the house?" Russ's neck moved against my cheek as he spoke.

I leaned back to look at him. "No," I said. "Of course not."

He watched me for several seconds, then tugged, gently, on the ends of my hair. "But you got in his car with him."

"I felt sorry for him. He was pitiful."

I could see it then, that he didn't believe me. His staring eyes turned teary.

"I could always tell you didn't really love me," he said. "You say you do, but you don't. It doesn't matter what I do."

Before I could speak, he stood up on the seat and stepped over the windshield, stumbling toward the prow. I cried out, sure he'd slide into the water. But he caught himself.

"Russ." I spoke through chattering teeth. "Please come back. Please."

"Like you care." He pointed at me, and almost lost his balance again. "You'd just get all my money."

I told him I didn't care about his money. I told him I didn't want him to fall into the sea and drown. All of that was true. But I was also thinking of myself, my own pounding heart. The ignition key was in his pocket. We had no radio, no water, and we were miles and miles into the Gulf. If he went in, the key was going with him. I could drop anchor, but aside from that, I'd just have to wait, and hope.

"Russ. Please, come back and sit by me. I do love you. I do."

He looked at me, bleary-eyed, and took another step toward the prow. I thought, well, maybe we'll just die out here, him and then me. Who would care? It wouldn't make any difference to the world, and neither one of us was happy. But then Janet appeared, sort of hovering beside him, teary and plaintive. She held Shirley, silent and staring, on her hip. My sisters.

I stood, holding the windshield for balance. "Russ. Listen to me." I pressed my free hand to my heart. "You are the love of my life."

He stumbled again, then righted himself, his arms spread wide. He looked at me, and I saw his wariness. It was wrong what I was doing. He knew it, and so did I.

You give up too easy. This from Mae, shaking her head.

I opened my mouth, desperate to say something, the right thing. "Russ," I started. "Listen to me. I love only you," I said. "I'm never going to love anyone else the way I love you. Never."

He blinked, his face as open as a child's. It felt like lying to Bambi. It really did. I could see how much he wanted to believe what I was saying. And I would only hurt him again.

Don't be daft, Carol said. *He'll be fine.*

He made his way over and crouched in front of the windshield. He reached for my hand, but instead of letting me pull him down, he started to pull me up.

"Come up here and sit by me," he said. "We'll just sit. Nora. I promise."

I told him no, absolutely not. I tried to wrest back my arm, and I felt my body lift from the seat.

Commit, Mrs. Lifton said. *You have to commit.* I nodded. Okay, I thought. I still hated her. But for all her cruelty, all her lies, she was in the boat as well. She wanted me to be okay.

"I have to tell you something," I shouted. "Just listen, Russ. Just wait!"

He let me fall back to the seat, though his hand stayed on my arm. "What?"

"You really want a baby?" I was fully in character. My smile was shy but bright. It was so mean, what I was doing. I was as bad as Mrs. Lifton.

No. This from Leonard. *You're not.*

"You know I do." His grip again tightened on my arm. "God, Nora. You already know that. Why would you ask me that?"

"Maybe we can talk about it." I heard the softness in my voice, the sweetness in it. "I haven't been fair to you. I know that." I kept my eyes on his. "And just being around Leonard today . . . Well. It really showed me the difference. Things would be different with you."

I couldn't guess what he was thinking. He was still holding my arm.

"Come back in and sit beside me," I said. There was nothing frantic in my voice. "We can just talk about it."

"You're not just saying that." He let go of my arm to rub his nose. "You wouldn't do that."

"No," I said. "I wouldn't."

"You don't lie," he said. "I've always loved that about you. You can't lie. You don't."

"That's right," I said. "I don't."

He climbed back over the windshield, falling hard into his seat. He leaned forward to kiss me, and I kissed him back, though my teeth were chattering, still. I wondered how long we would stay out. It had to be his idea to go home.

I still don't know if I had to take things that far, telling him we could have a baby. But when he finally fished the key from his pocket and started the boat's motor, I felt guilt, but not regret. For even when we were back on our dock, walking hand in hand back up to the house, I was afraid of him. Once inside, I went straight to the bathroom, saying I needed to pee, and I at least got my diaphragm in. I was grateful for that, and, above all, I was grateful to be back on land, still breathing. I was grateful, too, for the dark of our bedroom, as I'd walked on tiptoe all I could that night. I couldn't tell one more lie, even with my expression, even with just my eyes.

But what came to my mind in the darkness, unbidden as Russ labored above me, was that miserable dog Mae tried to save, still pressed up against the fence. I didn't think it was ugly. And I doubted it was dumb. I had no doubt that if it ever got a chance—if a hole in the fence appeared—it wouldn't sit around thinking what it deserved and what it didn't.

It would run.

30.

I waited until he was snoring to slip out of bed and grab my clothes from the floor. In the bathroom, I took out my diaphragm, ran a wet washcloth over my thighs, and dressed. Out in the entry, even after my eyes adjusted to the darkness, I couldn't find the keys to the truck. I started to panic, then thought to feel my way to the living room, where I ran my hand along the cushion of the armchair. My fingers fell on the leather key chain. I lifted them in a fist so they wouldn't jingle.

I left the front door open behind me and ran barefoot across the lawn, a pair of sandals tucked under my arm. Once I'd climbed into the truck, I waited, too scared to even close the door. Dolphin Drive was quiet. No traffic. No cicadas. I was alone. It wasn't like on the boat—nobody was cheering me on or giving me advice. And I hadn't driven in years.

I scooched to the edge of the seat to reach the pedals, then tilted the rearview so I could see myself. I nodded once, then said aloud, "Okay."

As soon as I turned the key, the radio came on playing "Shake, Rattle and Roll" at top volume. It didn't matter, as the engine was louder. I slammed the door shut and backed out while looking over my shoulder, too afraid to even glance at the house. When I shifted into drive and hit the gas, the tires screeched, and the smell of burnt rubber filled the cab. I still have no idea if Russ heard me, or if any light in the house came on. I clutched the steering wheel like I meant to kill it, and when I made the hard left onto Paradise Drive, the tools in the lockbox sounded like loose change poured into a glass.

Treasure Island had only one main drag, coming right off the causeway, so it wasn't hard to find the pink diner, already closed for the night. From the parking lot, I saw the neon-orange sign for the Starlight Motel, which turned out to be a U-shaped one-story. Fifteen orange doors opened to a courtyard with a pool, lit up but quiet. Leonard's dented car was in the parking lot.

I parked the truck beside it, put on my sandals, and got out. The breeze, warm and humid, carried the scent of chlorine, and more faintly, of the gardenia tree next to one of the motel's floodlights. I picked a door next to a window with the light still on, and I knocked twice. A shirtless man who was definitely not Leonard flung open the printed curtain.

"I'm sorry, sir! Sorry! I'm looking for . . ."

The man glared.

"Never mind. I'm sorry."

I turned around, and a door on the other side of the U opened. Leonard leaned out, just his head and one bare shoulder visible.

"Nora?" He was squinting because of the floodlight.

I stood there, taking him in. When I'd seen him at the Publix, when I was still full of venom, I'd told myself he no longer held any physical appeal for me. Sour grapes. If he turned me down now, if he didn't feel the same, I wouldn't let myself be sour. I'd at least be honest with myself.

His room smelled like greasy food, and he apologized for this, pointing to a paper bag from the diner on the nightstand. He said it was dinner he hadn't been able to eat, a burger and fries. I asked if I could have it.

"Sure," he said. When I first came in, he'd put on a shirt backward, and now he was turning it around. "But it has pickles."

I had to laugh. He'd been gone for years, scared and starved and frozen, then thinking I'd forgotten him. And the whole time, he'd kept in his brain that I hated pickles. He took them off the burger before handing it to me. It was the closest we'd been since I'd walked into the room, and we looked at each other for a moment. He gestured for me to take the room's one chair, and he sat on the edge of his bed, looking uneasy. He didn't yet understand what I was doing there.

"I need to eat this first," I said. "Then I'll explain."

He said that was fine, to take my time. But I was nervous, worried about Russ's truck. He might have already reported it stolen. I talked between bites, and explained that I was driving a stolen vehicle, and that Russ somehow knew we'd gone to the diner that morning. I spoke in general terms about his anger, but Leonard looked alarmed.

"Are you okay?"

I nodded. I was. Or I would be. "I'm hoping I can leave his truck here, in the parking lot. And get a ride with you out of town."

"Of course," he said. No hesitation. "Where do you want to go?"

A reasonable question, but I was almost as scared as I'd been on the boat. I wanted to be honest. I had to be. I knew Leonard still cared about me. He'd made that clear. But it wasn't just charity I wanted.

"I want to reassemble my life," I said. "Action by action."

This was some of the truth. He stayed quiet, waiting for me to say more. I folded the burger's wrapper and put it on the nightstand. When I first saw him in the courtyard. I'd walked right up to him to say hello, not knowing if he'd be nice or not. What had Mae called me? Bold and bright. I'd grown dull, fearful, unsure of myself. And I could see why. But I was the same person. My mother named me Eleanor because she admired Mrs. Roosevelt's courage.

"I want to be where you are." I waited, watching his face. He grimaced and didn't say anything. I told myself I'd be okay. I'd wanted to know. It was good that I'd asked, that I'd tried.

He raised his gaze to me, and the pained look left his face.

"I want that, too," he said.

Exuberance. Oxygen in my lungs, in my brain. I stood without effort, a jack-in-the-box sprung, and glided over the bed. I sat next to him. He turned to me and put his hand against my cheek, and it was as if my skin and blood remembered him, everything in me stirring. But I took his hand and shook my head.

"Not just yet," I said. "It's what I want, but not yet."

I didn't want anyone touching me yet. I was still wearing the clothes that I'd grabbed from the bedroom floor, the clothes I'd been wearing on the boat. Not even an hour before, I'd been under Russ, enduring him. And just thinking of Russ made me think of his truck, bright red, in the motel's parking lot.

"Would it be okay if we left soon? Like as soon as possible?" I was still holding his hand. "If you're tired, I could drive."

He said he could be ready in ten minutes.

He was actually ready in five, even using the bathroom, and he was the one who had the good idea of leaving the keys to the truck at the desk. I felt ecstatic and alive, hardly able to believe what was happening. What I'd made happen. And it occurred to me that our leaving town meant I had an opportunity to make something else happen. Something I very much wanted to do. Yet I had no plan, no means of liberation.

I looked around the room, trying to think, and my gaze fell

on the nightstand. I'd eaten all of the burger, but most of the fries were left.

"I should take the keys to the desk by myself." Leonard held out his good hand. "I'll say I found them by the pool."

I looked down at Russ's keys, still in my hand. One key on the chain was tiny, a third of the size of all the others. The key to the lockbox. It felt like a sign, like a nudge.

Leonard put his hand down and asked if I was okay.

I nodded. The lockbox was as wide as the truck bed. I didn't know what was in there, but I could take a look.

"Can we make a quick stop in town?" I asked. I didn't want him mixed up in it. He could wait in the car.

"Okay." He looked at his watch. "But nothing's open."

"I know."

"Oh," he said, as if he now understood. "Your family. You need to tell them goodbye?"

I shook my head, though I already felt the ache of the loss, of all I would miss in the years to come. They would be asleep—Mae and my father, Janet and Shirley. They wouldn't know how close I'd be to them tonight, and I didn't know when I would see them, or Bobby, again. But I didn't want to worry about what my father would think of what I was doing, if I would embarrass and disappoint him again. Mae might understand my leaving was really my way of coming back, or the beginning of it. If she didn't, I'd write to tell her.

"I need something from the truck." I jingled the keys and walked to the door. "Be right back."

Leonard insisted on coming out to the truck with me. And good thing, because once he understood what I was aiming to do, he had a better sense of what tools we might need. I say "we" because even though he was at first unsure of my plan's wisdom, he could tell I had my mind made up.

A half hour later, when he saw the situation for himself, our minds were one and the same.

FOUR

31.

We'd been in Los Angeles for five years before my family came out to visit. By then, my father and Mae had the added incentive of Bobby being stationed in Ream Field, outside San Diego. Two birds, one stone, my father said, and too much time had passed already. I understood the delay. The year after Leonard and I left Florida, Mae had a little boy they named Charles and called Skip. She said if they were going to drive three kids all the way to California, she wanted everyone to be old enough to use the bathroom by themselves, and old enough to appreciate the trip. It would be the biggest vacation they'd ever taken, and by far the most expensive.

They planned to arrive at our apartment on a Sunday morning, and I said I'd serve brunch. Leonard and I woke early to sweep the tumbleweeds of dog fur from the floor and get everything ready. I was feeling so many things—nervous and proud but mostly excited. Whenever I got a letter from Mae or Janet, it was like a car going by playing a song I loved, and by the time I recognized it, the music was already quieting, the car driving away.

"You look nice," Leonard said, likely because I'd changed clothes twice and kept messing with my hair. But he said it again, and then he put on our Bobby Darin record and twirled me around to "Mack the Knife," which really was the best thing he could have done for my nerves, though the lady downstairs thumped her broom at the ceiling, which meant we had to turn down the volume. When we heard a bunch of footsteps trooping up the stairs, Leonard got hold of Phoenix's collar. I opened the door, and there they were—Mae and Janet jostling in the hallway to get to me first, my father behind them, waving and laughing, and Shirley and Skip both wearing Mickey Mouse hats I'd soon learn had been purchased just inside the state line. I ran out into the hall, where Mae and I alone made such a whooping, jumping commotion that the lady downstairs thumped her broom again. Shirley and Skip hung back, wide-eyed, but Janet, Mae, and even my father hugged Leonard almost as tightly as they hugged me.

It soon became clear, however, that they were just as excited to see the dog. Janet got right down on the floor to look into his eyes, asking if he remembered her. That seemed unlikely to me, as she was seventeen now, a junior in high school, and half a foot taller than the last time I'd seen her. She wore her eyeliner winged, done just right. Her embrace smelled of the Chanel No. 5 I'd sent her for Christmas.

"Good Lord," my father said. "That looks like an entirely different animal." He leaned down to scratch the white star between Phoenix's ears. "They fatten you up, good boy? Nora still feeding you fries?"

I sneaked a wink at Leonard. Mae had written, more than once, that this was my father's favorite part of the story—that I'd doled out fries, one at a time, to keep the dog close and quiet while Leonard used Russ's wire cutters on the neighbor's fence. The next morning, when my father went out back to turn on the sprinkler, the neighbor came out, yelling and pointing at the hole in the fence, wanting to know if my father knew anything about it or the whereabouts of his dog. My father told him no, and said he was honestly just as baffled until they got my first letter. Even now, he seemed surprised to see the dog was truly with us.

"Ahem," Mae said. Even frowning, she still looked younger than she was. Her hair had faded to a copper color, no longer as bright as Janet's. But her nails and lips were painted the same tomato red as her dress. "That is a very nice dog . . ." she said, bulging her eyes at my father, and then at Janet, ". . . that they got in California."

We all took the warning. She'd been clear that neither Shirley nor Skip could know that our dog once belonged to their difficult neighbor, who remained in the house next door, and was someone Mae wanted no trouble with.

"It's just love at first sight," Janet said. She was still on the floor, nuzzling Phoenix's neck. "I've never seen this dog before in my life."

If either child sensed a cover-up, they didn't show it. They remained by the door, looking uneasy. I gave them both a little wave, though I knew Shirley wouldn't remember me, and that I was just a name to Skip. Skip raised his chin and scowled at me, looking so much like Bobby my breath caught.

But Shirley waved back, and said, "Hello. I'm Shirley. I'm eight."

Laughter all around, even as I felt the old claw at my heart. I didn't look at Leonard. I knew he felt it, too. In the fall, she'd be starting third grade.

"Who's hungry?" I asked, my voice too loud, too chipper. I was set on the visit being a happy one. My father looked considerably older, with new sunspots on his forehead and hands. Mae had warned me that he'd chipped a front tooth but wouldn't get it fixed—he'd told her that he didn't want to spend the money, but it was her opinion that he was afraid. When he raised his hand in answer to my question, he smiled, caught me looking at the tooth, and put his hand over his mouth.

I explained that our kitchen table was small, so we'd eat in the living room on trays. Skip asked if that meant we could watch television while we ate.

"Absolutely not," Mae said. "We are here to visit your sister and her husband. We're going to talk to each other like civilized people."

In the kitchen, I served Skip the biggest cinnamon roll, dripping with icing, and he seemed to warm to me a little. Leonard whispered to Mae that we'd gotten a Slinky for each child, if that would help to keep them occupied.

"Thank you," Mae said, and took a long swallow of her mimosa. "Glad you got them two. They've been bickering nonstop since Nebraska. They can have them after they eat." She pulled me to her side and kissed my cheek. "Oh, Nora. It's so good to see you. And you've put out a nice spread for us here."

"Leonard helped," I said.

She lifted her glass to Leonard, pulling me close. "Look at you," she whispered. "Landed a doctor who helps in the kitchen."

"Still in training." Leonard held a spatula in one hand, a plate in the other. "On both fronts."

It wasn't true—he cooked all the time, but Mae laughed. Phoenix stood close beside him. Of the two of us, I was far more likely to feed that dog from my plate, but I'd long accepted that I'd always be a close second in his canine heart. I wasn't jealous. I'd told them both, more than once, that I could understand.

Out in the living room, my father stood by the window as he ate, looking down at the cars parked behind our building. "The air is nice and dry out here," he said. "I can see why you like it."

"That's true," Janet said. "My hair's better out here, that's for sure." She sat on the couch's armrest in her cute capri pants, one wedge sandal dangling. "But it's not what I expected of Hollywood."

"We're closer to Larchmont." I walked to the window, checking the sky. The morning's smog had lifted, as I'd hoped. "But if you go just one block over, you can see the Hollywood Sign. We can go look at it later if you like."

Janet said she would like that very much. "I want to get my picture with it behind me." She shimmied her shoulders, exactly the way I'd seen her mother do it a hundred times. "Do you ever have celebrities come into the library?"

I nodded. "June Lockhart came in last March."

Janet frowned. "I don't even know who that is."

"Yes, you do." Mae sat on the couch and poked Janet's arm with the handle of her fork. "That's the mom on *Lassie*, sweetheart. Nora, that's really exciting. Do you remember what she checked out?"

I told her no. Even if I'd remembered, I wouldn't have said. I'd earned a degree in library science, starting at the city college and then moving on to USC, where we'd had respect for patron privacy drilled into our heads. On the other side of the couch, Shirley and Skip shared one cushion. Skip had already finished his cinnamon roll, and he made one hand into an anteater that walked across Shirley's tray to her plate. She shook her head and swatted away his hand.

"I will say I'm a little surprised by the neighborhood." Mae had a bit of egg on her chin, but before I could gesture to her, she turned to Leonard. "It doesn't bother you?"

Leonard pointed discreetly to his chin. "No, ma'am."

He didn't seem offended by the question, though I was sure he knew what she meant. Our apartment was just north of Koreatown. We'd been lucky to find any place we could afford, especially with a dog, but I, too, had worried that hearing the Korean language so often would bring up hard memories for Leonard. He said he'd be fine, and he was right. And it was our Korean landlord, born in Pusan, who introduced Leonard to Ji-ho, who'd served in the US Army. He'd also been held in a North Korean camp, though not the same one as Leonard. Ji-ho was how Leonard heard about the POW group that met at the VA, and sometimes he and Leonard would get a drink after a meeting. They were the only two in the group who'd been held in Korea—everyone else had served in the previous war, and had been held in Germany, Italy, or Japan. The facilitator told Leonard it was especially hard to convince POWs who'd been in Korea to come to the VA at all. Because of the petitions, he said, and the brainwashing business. So I was glad that Leonard and Ji-ho had become friends.

"It's a good neighborhood," I said. "But we're saving for a house. We'd like a yard for the dog."

Janet sighed, swinging one sandal. "I was thinking you'd be checking out books to real movie stars. But I guess they're so rich they don't need a library."

"Maybe," I said. "But even if I was rich, I'd still want to go to a library."

It was true. The Hollywood branch wasn't quite as beautiful as the library in St. Pete, but I still loved going to work, as I got to meet all kinds of people, and learn all kinds of things. I told them how the week before, a woman from Haiti had come in wanting to know why people said "mad as a hatter." She'd grown up speaking French, and she was trying to understand English well enough to feel like she could teach it.

Shirley raised her hand like she was in school. "Hatter was in *Alice in Wonderland*. He's not always nice. He got in trouble for murdering time."

"That's right," I said. I hadn't known she was paying attention. "And I always thought that's why people said 'mad as a hatter.' But when this woman and I looked it up, I learned people were saying 'mad as a hatter' long before that story was written." I told them what else we'd learned: that hats used to be made with a substance containing mercury, and if you were around it enough, it affected your brain. And that happened most often to the people making the hats. So mad hatters.

"Well, I'll be," my father said. He never said *I'll be damned.*

Janet clicked her tongue. "That's sad."

"You were already a librarian in Florida," Mae said. "I don't see why they made you go to college for it."

"I was just shelving in St. Pete," I said. "Now I catalog, make purchases. And I make more money."

"They know you're married?" my father asked.

I nodded. "There's no marriage bar here."

"Hmph," he said. "Don't know what I think of that."

I let it go. I wondered if all he was really doing was verifying that Leonard and I were in fact legally wed. We hadn't been at first, and though no one knew that out here, my father knew, and it must have bothered him. But we'd had to wait on Russ. I'd used a PO Box so even his lawyer wouldn't know where we lived. In the end, Russ was glad to be rid of me. All I had to do was agree that I shouldn't get a penny from him, as I'd committed adultery. That sounded like a bargain to me, but I imagine my admission was hard for my father to swallow.

Mae turned to Shirley and Skip. "Either one of you mice want more food? There's fruit salad in the kitchen. Eggs?" Both declined, and Mae told them to go wash their hands. "Your uncle Leonard got you a present."

Leonard was of course their brother-in-law, but I didn't correct her. Shirley stood and headed to the kitchen, but Skip stayed where he was, his gaze on Leonard's hand.

"What happened to your fingers?" he asked.

My father said Skip's name sharply. The reproach, in my mind, was ridiculous. I mean, they could have warned the poor kid. It's not like he wasn't going to notice. And he was four years old. Of course he was going to say something.

"It's okay," Leonard said. He explained how it happened in a general way. He just talked about the cold, not the starving.

"They're still there?" Skip asked. "In Korea?" He pronounced it *Cree-yah*.

"I suppose so," Leonard said. "Just the bones, I suppose. But see?" He wiggled his remaining fingers. "These all made it through."

"Does it hurt?" Shirley asked. She'd come back into the room, her sticky hands held away from her romper. "Does it hurt where they came off?"

"Sometimes," Leonard said. "It hurts where they used to be, like they're still there." The way he looked at her, with such patience, made a heaviness move through me. I could see the father he would have been.

"Can I touch where they came off?" Skip was already up and moving toward Leonard's chair. Again, my father rebuked him, but Leonard nodded and held out his hand. Skip touched the nub and the rounded knuckle, looking thoughtful.

"Why don't you have any kids?" Shirley asked. She was looking at me. I was aware of the sudden coolness of my skin, and of my father, standing beside me.

Janet clicked her tongue. "That's a rude question, Shirley."

I held up my hand. I just needed a second. Plenty of full-grown adults with alleged brains in their heads asked this question. I could certainly excuse it in a child. And I knew how to answer. Had I not been interrupted, I would have told Shirley that not everyone who was married had children, and that Leonard and I had each other, and loved each other, and we were happy that she and Skip could visit.

"It's a good question!" my father said. "When are you two

going to make me a grandpa?" He chuckled. "Bobby's not even married. I'm about to give up on him."

I looked at him, speechless. I could barely take a breath. No, I thought. No. This is our home. You're in our living room. I felt as if I were a gas stove, turned on and ticking. He looked back at me, still grinning, the missing tooth fully exposed.

I turned to Shirley. "We lost our baby," I said. "She was born the same year you were."

I heard Leonard's quick exhale. Mae was silent, but she closed her eyes. Janet, still perched on the armrest, tilted her head.

"It died?" Shirley asked. There was no cruelty in her expression. No sorrow either. Something a lot of adults don't realize, or forget, is that most children have a steeliness to them, even if they've been brought up with softness. Stories of death don't always upset them. Here's my theory: If you're lucky enough to reach adulthood without deep grief, you get lulled into thinking life is fair, and always will be. But children have no reason to think that, no experience on which to base such a belief. If a child is crying because his mother leaves to run to the store, and somebody tells him he's being silly and that she'll right back, the child thinks maybe, maybe not. Sad stories don't really surprise them.

"We hope she's still alive," I said. "And loved. And happy." I was aware of Leonard, where he was sitting. I'd insisted to him, time and again, that this hope was all we had. No betting. No guessing. My father turned away from me, looking out the window.

Shirley adjusted her Mickey Mouse hat. "How'd she get lost?"

I told her the truth: When our daughter was born, Leonard had been in Korea, and I thought I was alone. I was told she'd be better off with other people, another mom and dad. So I let someone take her to them.

My father stepped closer to the window, as if something outside caught his eye.

"Maybe they're being good to her," I said. "But we don't know where she is."

No one spoke. I kept my gaze on Shirley, who appeared satisfied with my answers. I'd heard she was a big reader. Mae said she loved fairy tales, especially.

"She's not in California?" Skip asked. He'd gotten back up on the couch, sitting close to Mae.

"Probably not," I said. "And even if we knew where she was, we couldn't get her back. And she wouldn't know us. But we miss her as much as any parents would miss a child. As much as your parents would miss you."

Mae shook her head, her gaze still on the floor. I didn't know if she was sad for us, or disappointed in me for ruining the good time. Or maybe she was mad that I'd told her children something shameful, something even worse than a stolen dog for them to repeat in front of the neighbors. I didn't care. My father continued to look out the window, showing me only the back of his head.

"I bet she's okay," Shirley said. She leaned back on one foot. "I bet the people who have her are nice. I bet she has a soft bed to sleep in, and they give her candy when she's good, and they never lock her in the basement."

"That's right," Janet said. She was still sitting on the armrest, clutching the upholstery as if she needed to. "I bet she's just fine." She gave me a look I couldn't interpret, then slid her gaze to her mother, who didn't look up, and then to my father, still studying the window. I felt as if I'd smashed something fragile, something made of glass. I knew that if I looked at Leonard, if I turned my head in his direction, I would start to cry.

I didn't wish to do that. So I excused myself, said nothing else, and walked out of the room.

The bedroom, of course, was Leonard's, too, but he knocked and whispered my name. When I told him he could come in, Phoenix came in with him, jumping up on the bed beside me. Leonard shut the door and sat on my other side.

"Good for you," he said, and put his arm around me.

A toilet flushed—maybe in our apartment, maybe not. I pressed my forehead into Leonard's shirtsleeve, extending my bare feet into a square of sunlight on the floor. I wasn't sorry for what I'd said. But we were being rude. My family had come all this way, and we were hiding back here with our dog.

"I've got to go back out," I said. They weren't even staying that long. The plan was for them to drive down to San Diego that very afternoon so they could meet Bobby for dinner. Tomorrow morning, Bobby would go with them to Tijuana and spend just the day with them there, as he had to report back to Ream Field early the next day, when the rest of the family would head to Disneyland. Leonard and I were invited on all these excursions, but Leonard had clinical clerkship and couldn't get weekdays off. I said I'd have to skip the day in Tijuana because I had to work, and this was true. Nothing had warmed between me and Bobby, and so I'd never asked for Monday off. But I planned to drive down to Anaheim early enough on Tuesday to join everyone else at Disney. Wednesday, I'd go with them to Knott's Berry Farm. Thursday, they'd head back to Florida. I couldn't guess when I would see them again.

Leonard set his big feet next to mine. "How can I help?"

I glanced at my watch. "Take the kids somewhere?"

He nodded and stood. I looked up at him.

"I'm scared."

He crouched, our eyes level, resting his arms on my knees. The patchy eyebrow never grew back. But he was still something to see.

"What's the worst thing that could happen?"

I saw by his face, how serious he looked, that he was really asking. Not for him, but for me. It was a good question. Whatever my father said to me, whatever he refused to hear, it couldn't feel worse than his pretending that New Jersey had never happened, and wanting me to pretend the same. Maybe that lie helped him. Maybe he once believed that it would help me as well. But it hadn't, and I was done with it.

"Point taken." I gave Leonard's hand a squeeze, careful, as always, of the nub. "Just not in front of the kids. Soon as they're gone, I'll go talk with him."

Phoenix followed him out. He shut the bedroom door behind him, but the wall was thin enough that I heard him say he was going to walk the dog, and that the dog himself had asked, privately, if Skip and Shirley would please come along.

"We'll go where we can see the Hollywood Sign," he added, and I thought that was smart, a way to get Janet to go along without making her feel like a child.

We had a mirror above the dresser, and I stood and looked in it. I didn't wave this time, just looked at my eyes, tired and tear-burned, my mascara smeared. I was twenty-six years old, a grown woman. I could face my father and say what I thought, what I felt. If he wouldn't love me anymore, I could bear it. And there was a chance that he really would hear me. I worked to guard myself against this hope, even as I gathered courage.

Phoenix's nails clicked against the floor, and I knew he was doing the little dog dance he did whenever Leonard put on his shoes.

I heard my father's voice. "I'll go, too," he said.

I pressed my hand to my heart, as if just that would console it.

"Nora could take you to see it later, Mr. Chesnow." Leonard's voice was friendly, but there was firmness to it. "You all could have a minute to yourselves here. To talk."

"I'll just see it now," my father said.

Mae whispered something, though I could only make out my father's name. If he replied, I didn't hear it. I stayed where I was, listening as the door to the hallway opened. I heard the jingle of Phoenix's collar, and footsteps descending the stairs.

I opened the door to find Mae and Janet on the couch. Janet had moved from the armrest down to the cushion where Skip and Shirley had been sitting. Her arms were crossed, and she was glaring at the floor. My reappearance must have inflamed her further, for she immediately turned to her mother.

"Anything else you've been keeping from me? My God. What else is there that I don't know?"

Mae looked too annoyed to answer. Janet turned to me.

"Did you know about my father, Nora? That he's still alive?"

"I did," I said. "I'm sorry. I'm sorry that I knew before you did."

Mae rolled her eyes. "Don't be mad at Nora. I told her not to tell you. You were in fourth grade when I told her. You couldn't have kept a secret if I'd tied it to your wrist."

"I'm sorry," I said again. Mae gave me a hard look. I imagine she felt judged by me, and I admit she would have been right. But I still loved my stepmother, and I believed I understood her. She was tough and bighearted and shrewd. She had no problem lying to protect herself, and doling out the truth as she saw fit, even to those she loved. But I could also imagine Janet's bewilderment, having learned the truth about her father so late. I knew a woman from work who'd been in Bakersfield during the earthquake in 1952. She wasn't hurt, but she said she'd been anxious ever since. Years had passed and still, she no longer thought of ground as firm.

Janet touched her hand to her forehead. I thought she was still thinking of her not-dead father, but she looked at me and asked, "It was when you left for Arkansas? To help my grandmother?"

I nodded.

She looked at her mother, incredulous. "Grandma was in on it?" She started to laugh, but when she saw my face, she stopped. "I'm sorry, Nora. It's awful. I just had no idea."

"It's okay," I said. "I know you didn't." I went over and sat in the folding chair, where Leonard had been sitting.

Janet squinted. "That old woman at Haslam's, who got so upset with you. She said something about a baby, a grandchild. Was that Leonard's mother?"

I expected Mae to say no. I couldn't imagine Mrs. Lifton being described this way. But Mae said yes, that was right. She'd been avoiding my eyes, but now she looked at me frankly.

"She knew you and Leonard were in California, and that you'd gotten married. She wanted your address so she could write. I wouldn't give it to her."

"Thank you," I said.

Janet shook her head. "You told me she was Nora's old teacher who'd lost her mind. Even then I knew something was fishy. She was crying, right there in the bookstore."

Mae inspected her bright nails. "I had nothing to say to that woman."

I appreciated the loyalty. I didn't tell her that Leonard's mother must have tracked down our address by some other means. Over the years, she'd addressed most of her letters to Leonard, who sent them straight to the trash, unopened.

"Why can't she have your address?" Janet asked. "What did she do?"

I explained as best I could. It was strange, how those years of confusion and anguish could be reduced to a few facts, all conveyed in less than a minute. And still, beneath the winged liner, Janet's eyes grew wide.

"How could they have done such a thing?" she asked. "His own parents? They're awful, both of them."

I nodded. It was true. And also not completely true. Exactly two of the letters Mrs. Lifton mailed to our address here had been addressed to me. A few years back, I'd opened one, just out of curiosity. Inside a card, she'd written,

Dear Nora,

Please know I still think about you, and Leonard, and your child, often. And I'm still so very sorry.

Geneva

On the front of the card was a picture of a painting by Salvador Dalí. The caption said the painting was *The Elephants*, and I looked at it for a while. Two elephants with impossibly long, skinny legs faced each other across an expanse of desert, the sky orange and red behind them. At their feet, a man and an angel, small as mice, held out their arms to each other, and there seemed a great distance between them as well. Maybe Leonard's mother used that card because she had it on hand. But what I felt, looking at it, was her sorrow.

Still, I'd thrown it away.

"I think they moved back to New York," I said. His mother's most recent letters, all unopened, had an NYC postmark.

"Maybe she did," Mae said. "He's still in town. I've seen him. You can bet I don't stop and say hello, but it's him." She took a breath. "You know she divorced him."

I leaned back, too stunned to speak. I myself was a divorced woman, talking to another divorced woman. But still. Mae and I were rarities. You just didn't hear about many people getting divorced. Especially people like the Liftons.

"The notice was in the paper," Mae said. "She's the one who filed. But he fully recovered. Already remarried. That was in the paper, too. Younger than he is. Leonard doesn't know?"

I shook my head. If he did, he would have told me.

"Where did you have the baby?" Janet asked. "In Arkansas?"

I told her I'd been in New Jersey, at a home for unwed mothers.

She still looked a little dazed. "Did Bobby know?"

"He figured it out," I said. "And judged me for it."

Janet didn't seem to think this was possible, and she asked if I was sure. I told her I was most certainly sure. He just wouldn't come out and say it. Like father, like son, I said. It was at this point that Mae jumped in, making excuses for my father. He'd been so excited to see me, she said. I'd just caught him off guard. He'd spoken without thinking.

"He needs to start thinking," I said.

Janet wanted to know if Leonard and I had tried writing to anyone in New Jersey, just to see if they'd give me any information. I told her yes, we'd tried. The social worker who answered my letter was new on the job, and said she'd never met Miss Berry, though she'd seen her name on some of the older files. She couldn't tell us anything else.

"Even if she could have," I said, "our baby would be eight. She wouldn't know us."

Mae gave me a worried look. "Are you still coming down to Anaheim?"

I waited before I answered. I wanted to spend time with Mae and Janet, and get better acquainted with Shirley and Skip. And to be fair, I could see things from my father's perspective. When I'd first come back from New Jersey, he'd made a contract with me, the terms clear. All these years later, I was the one who'd broken the contract. But it was fine with me if it broke.

"I'll still go," I told Mae. "Wouldn't miss it."

I wasn't just trying to make them happy, though it was clear that was the answer they wanted. I knew if I stayed home, I'd regret it. I could be civil to my father, and try to see the good in him, as he perhaps had to try with me. We'd be able to get through a couple of days, with only the facade of love, at Knott's Berry Farm, and at Disney.

Then I'd say goodbye, and come home to my real life with Leonard, and all we'd assembled here.

32.

That evening, after my family left, I told Leonard about his parents' divorce. For a moment, I saw his bewilderment. Then his eyes hardened, and he shrugged.

"Doesn't matter," he said. "They've got nothing to do with us."

I wasn't sure about this. I'd long wondered if some part of him wanted to open his mother's letters, but felt he couldn't because of me. He had reason to be angry on his own behalf. I knew that. But Leonard was even more loyal than Mae. I didn't want him to think he had to choose.

"It was your mother who filed."

He gave me a sharp look. "So?"

Phoenix rested his chin on the sliver of cushion between us. Leonard scratched the white star between his ears, and I rubbed under his collar.

"You think it was because of us?" I asked. "You think she divorced him because of what happened?"

"Does it matter? They're both terrible. They both did it."

I couldn't argue. And yet only his mother had written. Only his mother kept writing.

"I hope you're not shutting her out for me," I said. "On my account, I mean."

"It's on our account." I could see I'd upset him. The one eyebrow shot up. "What? You want to have her out for Christmas? Because she wrote a few times? Forgive and forget?"

Honestly, I was relieved. If Leonard had said that he missed his mother, and wanted her in our lives, I'm not sure what I would have done. I wanted to think I could call upon my higher self, out of love for him, but I didn't want to be in the same room as that woman. I had my own loyalties—to Leonard, to our daughter. And to the broken, believing girl I'd been.

Two weeks later, I came home from the library and found, in our postbox, a white, business-size envelope with a return address for *Lieutenant R. Chesnow*. That Bobby had used his military rank, along with just the first initial of his formal name, seemed a bad sign. I stood alone in our building's little foyer, holding the envelope between my finger and thumb, scared to open it. It seemed likely that either Janet or Mae, when they'd seen Bobby, had repeated what I'd said about him judging me. Perhaps Bobby felt the need to defend his judgment. Perhaps he'd written to tell me what a wonderful time they'd all had together in Tijuana without me. Perhaps he'd heard that I'd upset my father, and he wrote to scold me for it. The envelope felt light, almost weightless, but any of those heavy things could be inside it.

Of course, those guesses were all just attempts to push down the hope rising inside me. Part of me still believed hope, if proved foolish, would only make the hurt worse. I'm no longer sure that's true.

My brother, when he first walked into our apartment, did pause to embrace me, but like the rest of my family, he seemed most excited to see the dog. "They put some weight on you, good boy?" he asked, crouching in front of Phoenix. "You still eating fries?"

These were almost the exact same questions my father had asked of him a few weeks earlier. I was struck by this, especially because Bobby's voice, which had grown deeper since I'd last heard it, sounded so much like our father's. When he stood again, and we had a chance to truly take each other in, I could see that although his face had lost some plumpness, his smile was still like our mother's. He wore denim jeans and a plaid shirt, but his hair was regulation short.

"Leonard won't be home until two," I said. "We should go ahead and have lunch. I made you something really special."

I think because we hadn't seen each other in so long, Bobby

took me at my word, and thanked me with sincerity. But in the kitchen, when I presented him with a serving of mac and cheese mixed with hot dog slices, he knew he could laugh, and did.

"The good old days return!" he said. It turned out that as a grown man, he was still happy to dig into that particular dish. I asked if he had a picture of himself in uniform, and he seemed proud to take one from his wallet to show me. He asked me about living in Los Angeles, and if I liked my job. He complimented our kitchen clock, which was a miniature grandfather clock, small enough to hang on the wall.

"Thanks," I said. "I found it at a thrift store. I have to remember to wind it every week, or it runs a little late. Like me."

He laughed again. He told me he loved California, and hoped he wouldn't be transferred anytime soon, though he said that it felt strange to live so far away from family. I agreed. For a while after that, there was only the clicking pendulum of the clock, for we both knew he and I had lived in the same state, just a few hours away from each other, for years.

"How was Tijuana?" I asked.

He told me they'd had a good time, and he enjoyed showing them around base. He got a real kick out of Skip, and he couldn't believe how much Shirley had grown. "Not to mention Janet. Already in high school." He paused. "She and I spent some time talking."

I sipped my soda, readying myself. In his letter, he'd only written that he'd like to drive up to see me. He'd signed this letter *Love, Bobby*, but I was still uneasy. I mean, my father still wrote *Love, Dad* on Christmas and birthday cards. The word holds different meanings.

Before Bobby spoke again, he took a deep breath. I could see he was nervous. I thought of the year we'd moved to St. Pete, how determined he'd been to jump off the high dive. He'd been so scared, I remembered, and younger than anyone else in line. I could tell that once he got up on the board, he wanted to turn around and go back down the ladder. But he didn't. He tucked his chin and jumped.

"I didn't know you had a baby," he said. "I knew it was something. I knew something had happened. But I didn't know it was that. Not until Janet told me."

I shut my eyes, listening to the *click click click* of the clock's swinging pendulum. I didn't want to feel the regret that was coming, rolling toward me like a wave. I'd been so sure. I'd never once doubted. I thought of that day I'd seen Leonard in the Publix, all the hateful things I'd said. I hadn't learned a thing.

"I knew you weren't in Arkansas with Mae's mother." His voice wavered. "I believed it at first. I mean, that's what Mae said, that's what Dad said. But your letters were strange. You didn't sound like you. I didn't understand why everyone was lying, why you were lying. You never lied. I thought maybe you were sick, and no one wanted to tell me. I worried that . . . I worried . . ."

I opened my eyes to see him squeezing the bridge of his nose between his thumb and fingers. Growing up, everyone had thought of Bobby as ornery. And he was. But I'd known of the softness, the hurt underneath.

"Oh, Bobby." I tried to take his hand, but he shook his head. "I was scared you would die, too."

I put my arm on the table, resting my forehead on it. I'd tried talking to him when he was mowing the lawn. But I hadn't really tried. He'd been fifteen. He was nine when our mother died.

"Then you came back, and I thought maybe you would tell me what was going on. But you were still lying. And you weren't the same. Next thing I know, you're with Russ, and completely different, not at all like you were. And I was mad about it. Sad about it. Mae and Dad were busy with Shirley, Janet was around, but that wasn't the same. We'd always been together, you and me."

I raised my head. "I thought you heard," I said. "You got in that fight, at the pool."

"I just knew they were saying things about you. I heard your name, and picked up on the tone. I knew it wasn't anything good. I didn't like that they knew more than I did. Guess I was thick in the head, but I didn't know."

I let the regret hit me, full force. How confusing that time must have been for him. How lonely. The day he and my father and Janet picked me up at the station, he'd looked gangly in his usher's uniform. He'd snapped at me for forgetting he'd already written that he had a job at the theater. I hadn't thought of what I might mean to him, or the place I'd held in his world.

"Mae told me not to tell you," I said. "She told me I couldn't." It didn't feel right, blaming Mae. She'd meant well. She'd just been wrong.

"You could have," he said.

"I'm sorry."

We sat there with nothing to say for a while. And then that good man, my brother, glanced at the clock, which hadn't yet struck one.

"You could tell me now," he said. "If you want."

33.

Long before Leonard and I got married, even before we were sleeping in the same bed, I told him I wouldn't have another child. He did ask me why, just so he could understand, and I told him that the social workers and nurses and volunteers who told me she could be replaced were wrong. I didn't tell him that I also worried I just wasn't cut out for the job, that I wasn't fierce enough, or smart enough. That I'd already been given a test, and failed. I told him that when I thought about having another child, everything in me said no.

With this, as well, I worried I was making him choose. But when he said he understood, I knew he meant it. And he never once tried to change my mind, not before we were married, and not after. Leonard was the one who told me that a miracle birth control pill would soon be a reality, available to any married woman. He was doing his rotation in obstetrics, and one of the doctors had told him it would be more effective than a diaphragm.

"It'll just be a little pill you take every day," Leonard told me. "And you won't have to worry."

That seemed too good to be true, that just a little pill could be so powerful. When Enovid came out the following year, I got right on it, but I planned to keep using my diaphragm as well. By the time I swallowed the fourth pill, I was sure that both the magic pill and the diaphragm had failed me, as I felt so nauseated that I had to call in sick for work. My doctor assured me I was not pregnant, and that I was just feeling the first side effects of the hormones. Within a month, my clothes were tight. Painful, white-capped pimples grew and ruptured around my mouth. My doctor told me this was all to be expected, but that if I felt chest pains, or any tenderness in my limbs, I should get to an emergency room right away.

"Makes you wonder if you'd be better off just having a baby," he said, and laughed.

Soon enough, I could see for myself that the nausea and weight gain and acne really were all par for the course. A lot of married women worked at the library. Nobody talked about it, but I could tell, just looking around, I wasn't the only one who decided the magic pill was worth the trouble.

I can't say a particular sight or experience made me start to question my resolve. It was more that I just started thinking about it. I'd grown older, and a little wiser. I knew how easily I could settle into certainty, and be completely wrong. I also think I finally felt safe to even consider the question because I had both the diaphragm and the magic pill, and because no one was pressuring me. The decision would be my own. I had that, and felt it, for the first time in my life.

Except by then I was thirty, no spring chicken. I knew I might be out of time. But for almost another year, I thought it over without saying anything to Leonard. I was thinking of his feelings, and how much he'd already lost. I didn't want to bring him into the argument until I knew my own answer, in my own heart.

When I finally asked him for his own thoughts on another baby, he was caught off guard, to say the least. Phoenix had died of old age the year before, and Leonard said when I first took his hand and told him my grief was still with me, but changing, he thought I was going to tell him I was ready to get another dog. I had to spell it out. I told him I was sure of my own thoughts, of what I wanted, but he had full veto power. For years, he'd given the same to me. We'd both lost our first child. If it would hurt him too much to try for another, I'd accept it.

"You're earning a good salary now," I said. "I'm just saying. If you decide yes, we could afford it."

He gave me a look. We both knew money wasn't the issue. If I got pregnant, I'd lose my job at the library, married or not. But Leonard had finished his internship and gotten a job in an emergency department. I'd worried that would be exactly the wrong place for him to work, but he said it was nothing like

Korea, because in the ER, he wasn't helpless. He didn't have to just watch people die.

"I don't know," he said. He looked as if I'd hit him with something heavy. Not pained, though. Just struck.

He said he needed time, at least a few weeks, to think.

On my last day at the library, the rest of the staff threw a little party for me, and they all went in on a sleeper stroller with a sunshade. The head librarian wheeled it in with a big red bow tied around the handle. There was a card for me, too, full of congratulations, and assurances that I would be a wonderful mother.

I wanted to ask *What makes you all say that, exactly?* But I knew they meant well.

Within a few weeks, I was wearing maternity clothes, and strangers on the street would smile at me, and rush over to hold open doors. Everyone at the obstetrician's office called me "Mrs. Lifton" or "Ma'am," always speaking to me politely. So compared to my first pregnancy, as far as how I was treated, it was night and day.

Some things were harder. In my seventh month, my ankles swelled up so much I could only wear flip-flops. And I was far more tired than I remembered being in New Jersey. Once, I went for a walk, and didn't get far from our apartment building before I got so worn out I sat down on a bench, thinking I just needed to rest my eyes. I woke to a woman tapping me on the shoulder. She told me she was about to call the police, as she'd worried I was on heroin, or that I was dead.

The nurse I saw wasn't worried. She said third-trimester fatigue was hardly unusual.

"Especially when the mother is a little older," she said. "Do you have anyone to help you when the baby comes? Is your mother nearby?"

She asked this brightly, just making conversation. I thought of Mae, so far away in Florida. She wouldn't be able to come out.

"My mother's dead," I said. I didn't say it to make her feel bad, but it seemed like she should have already learned not to assume. "I have friends here," I added. "And my husband."

"Sorry to hear about your mother." She turned her back to me, washing her hands. "What about your mother-in-law?"

I was silent. I didn't think of myself as having one. The nurse looked back at me, waiting.

"She's far away," I said. "In New York."

"Oh! Is that where you all are from? I love New York."

I told her no. She turned back to the sink.

"Well, I bet she'd come out if you asked her. Most people would fly to the moon to see a new grandchild."

"She's not most people," I said.

It wasn't completely a lie. Leonard's mother certainly wasn't most people, not to me, and not to him. But I knew I'd implied she wouldn't want to come out, and I knew that wasn't the truth.

People say that pregnancy softens your heart, and makes you

see all the world like a child in need of love. That's not what it was for me. When I'd been eighteen and pregnant, I'd had plenty of rage in my heart. The next time I was pregnant, at thirty-one, I had less reason to be angry, but I most certainly did not feel maternal love for everyone.

It was time, I think, that softened me. Time and thinking.

At dinner, Leonard told me about the people he'd seen at the ER that day: a woman on her second cardiac arrest who was still alive, a man who'd been stabbed in the back who wasn't, a toddler who just needed a nebulizer, a milkman who tripped on some stairs and bit off a chunk of his tongue. Even when I'd been working at the library, my stories could rarely compete. But he asked for details about my appointment with the obstetrician, and how my grocery shopping had gone. I told him everything except for what I'd been thinking about the most.

For that, I waited until after dishes, when we adjourned to the couch. We'd gotten into a routine of listening to a record while he gave my ankles what we called the World-Famous 8-Fingered Massage. It should have been world-famous, what Leonard could do for my swollen ankles, for all of me. I told him he was the only doctor I'd ever met with warm hands.

"What do you think of the name Jennifer?" He dug his expert thumb into the arch of my foot. "You don't hear that too often."

I told him I liked Jennifer fine. The week before, we'd decided on Diana for a girl. The week before that, Colleen. Our front-runner for a boy, Marcus, had held steady for over a month. Girl or boy, we both wanted something strong, and something people would spell right on the first try. But for a girl, we wanted a name that was a little unusual. We didn't know the name of our first child. We'd probably never know it. But still.

"Jennifer Lifton," he said. "Jennifer Lorraine Lifton." He kept working on my ankles, moving his head to the rhythm of the record. The previous year, the frostbite on his cheek had turned into skin cancer, and the surgery to remove the lesions had left scars. Sometimes, when I saw him in profile, when he didn't know I was looking, his eyes had a weary, wounded expression that disappeared when he faced me. There was no one I'd rather look at.

He pulled on my big toe. "Why'd you only paint the nail of this one?"

I told him it was the only one I could reach. He said he'd paint the others for me, after he got my ankles in better shape. I knew by then he might be mad at me, but he'd still do it.

"Leonard," I said. "I think you should write your mom back."

His hands lifted from my feet. The record kept playing, the snare drum steady. I pulled my feet from his lap and sat up as best I could.

"We should invite her out here. She should meet this grandchild."

"Where's this coming from?" He was breathing heavily, his neck starting to flush.

I pointed at my heart, and then at my head. I didn't know if he had her address, if he'd even saved one of her letters. If not, it seemed likely she'd write again.

"Have you been writing to her?" he asked.

"No," I said. "You're her son. You're the one she wants to hear from. You can say it's not my business. But it is, Leonard. Because I love you. And I think you miss her."

He ran his palm over the top of his head. "Why not my dad, while we're at it? Why not invite him, too? Have a big party for them."

"She's said she's sorry," I said. "She said she was sorry to me. I bet she's said it to you. That makes her different from your dad."

He was silent.

I sat up a little more. "I've been thinking about how you said she lost her courage around him. You told me that a long time ago, before you even went to Korea. Mae noticed it, too. She told me that after she and my father went over to meet them."

"You're saying she was his puppet?" He made a sour face. "No brain in her own head? She did it, too, Nora. She lied to your face. And she lied to me, again and again."

I nodded. All this I knew. But I also remembered the day I bicycled over and found her on her patio. She'd looked ill. She'd looked like she'd aged twenty years in two.

"She must have been out of her mind with worry, not knowing if you were dead or alive."

He looked at me. "What she did. What she took from us."

"Leonard. She was worn down like I was."

The one eyebrow went high and stayed high. "It's not the same," he said. "It's not the same at all. You didn't lie to me. You didn't lie to anyone."

"No," I said. "I just signed our child away. Goodbye. Good luck."

He shook his head. "Not the same."

But it was the same. I couldn't believe he couldn't see it, though for years, I hadn't seen it myself. She and I had both been scared and exhausted. And maybe Mr. Lifton could be just as relentless as Miss Berry, and just as certain about what should be done. I didn't know what Leonard's parents' marriage had been like, or why his mother had lost her nerve around him. But I did know that by the time she lied to me, she'd spent years—not days, not months, but years—not knowing if Leonard was dead or alive.

"She loved you," I said. "I didn't know your dad. I was hardly around him. But she loved you, Leonard. And she's sorry."

When he looked up, his eyes were dry. He didn't say anything, and I didn't either. At the end of the song, he went back to work on my ankles. Still, I knew he'd heard me.

The first time he wrote to her, he sent a postcard. Baby steps, I thought. She wrote back right away, and he replied with a proper letter. That Christmas he sent her a card with two pictures—one of Marcus in his baby Santa suit, and another of all three of us. We both signed it, and though I signed *With Love*, Leonard only signed *Merry Christmas.*

On her birthday, in July, he called her long distance, and she got to hear Marcus babble and say his first and favorite word, which was *Hi!* I was on the other side of the room, but I could hear her laughing and cooing, that same musical voice of hers. After she and Leonard had talked for a while, I got up and asked him to hand me the receiver. I wished her a happy birthday. That was all. But she said thank you. Thank you, Nora. Then she said it again.

She flew out to see us when Marcus was almost two, quick but unsteady on his feet, and able to shriek with delight and clap his hands whenever his appropriately favorite song, "Wild Thing," came on the radio. In preparation for the visit, Leonard and I spent time teaching him the word *Grandma* and pointing at the picture that she'd sent. The hope was that he wouldn't receive her as a stranger. I'd written to her that we were doing this, and the day she arrived, she was dressed exactly the same as in the picture—the same yellow bolero jacket, same pillbox hat, even the same earrings. The trick worked. As soon as Marcus saw her in baggage claim, he shouted out "Grandma!" as if I'd paid him to do it, and all the other people waiting for their bags turned and smiled. But Geneva—she'd asked me to call her Geneva—looked so nervous, and as I carried Marcus toward her, her eyes stayed focused on me. I kept smiling, trying to put her at ease. Leonard had said he'd pick her up, so she was likely caught off guard.

"Welcome!" I said, and went right in for a hug, my free arm encircling her waist. Even though I stood up on my toes, my chin didn't clear her shoulder. I heard her say, "Oh! Oh!" and she sounded happy enough, but when I leaned back, I saw Marcus had a hold of her hat, which was pinned to her hair. I got him to let go and apologized, then turned to tell him it wasn't nice to grab other people's hats. When I glanced back at her, her hat was askew, and she herself looked unsteady. Her nose was running, her eyes bright.

"He looks just like you," she said. She didn't seem displeased. She put her hand to her heart, just for a moment, then started to unpin her hat.

"Leonard got called in," I said. "But he'll be home tonight."

Fifteen years had passed since I last saw her, that day on her back patio, when she'd lied to me, and also hugged me, and told me I was captain of my ship. She'd put on weight, enough to not appear sickly, and once she'd freed herself from the hat, she looked as sophisticated as ever. Her long gloves were the same shade of beige as her shoes. Under the jacket she wore a sheath dress and a long chain necklace with a gold square for a pendant. When I offered to take her hat so she could hold Marcus, she tucked the pendant under her dress and opened her arms.

I don't think she saw me get out my camera, which worked out great. In the first shot, she and Marcus are nose to nose, wide-eyed, taking each other in. In the second, she's laughing, her head thrown back, and he's reaching for one of her earrings. In the third, he's laughing, and she's beaming love, and they're both turned to the camera, to me.

We had much to distract us at first: getting her bag; taking another picture of her, this time in front of the airport's UFO centerpiece; then traffic; then showing her the house and the guest room, which had a little closet I'd finished cleaning out exactly one hour before she'd arrived. She changed clothes so she could play with Marcus on the carpet while I made lunch. Even when we were eating, we mostly focused on him. She told me that Leonard, too, had been an early walker and a late talker. While I cleaned up, she put Marcus on her lap and sang "Yankee Doodle" to him, which he loved.

I knew that once he went down for his nap, it would be just the two of us in a quiet house. She knew it, too. When I came out of his room, I found her sitting on the carpet by Marcus's toys, looking nervous again.

"I want you to know . . ." she started.

"Don't," I said. "We covered all that." I didn't want another apology. It was like she kept handing me umbrellas. Now that I'd accepted one, I had no need for another.

"Okay." She looked down at her feet. "I keep wanting to apologize because it's all I can do. I didn't tell you this. Or Leonard. Because it came to nothing. No new information.

But last year, I hired a private investigator in New Jersey. I know the records are sealed, but I was hoping he could tell me something, something that would help."

I didn't know what to say to this. *Thank you* didn't seem right. But I wondered how much she'd spent on the investigator. It was my impression, and Leonard's, too, that his mother didn't have a lot of money. For the last few years, she'd been working as a receptionist for an undertaker in Queens. She'd written that she loved the work, which, according to her, was mostly about staying organized while also being kind to people stumbling through the first, raw days of grief. She shared an apartment with twin sisters, one widowed, one divorced. I never picked up that she had any regrets over leaving Leonard's father, but it seemed her country club days were behind her.

She raised her head. "Leonard said that was the hardest part. Worrying about her."

I told her that was right. But I also told her I didn't want her to hire another investigator.

"She's probably okay," I said. I was surprised, hearing these words in my own voice. These were Leonard's words. Mae's words. Janet's. The words of good friends who knew about her, including Carol. Even Shirley, at eight, had said as much. But I'd never let myself say them. I always felt like I was lying to myself to feel better. Saying them now, believing them, I felt as if a window opened inside me, one I hadn't even known was there.

"It's hard hoping, though," she said. "I know it's hard."

I knew that she knew.

"She's probably with people who love her," I said. "And people she loves." I spoke quickly, not wanting her to interrupt. "I could live my whole life convinced that she's unhappy or hurting or dead. And be wrong."

"That's right," she said. "That's exactly right."

"It won't change anything for her. It won't save her, my being unhappy."

"No," she said. "And I bet you're right. I bet she's happy. And Nora, I'll tell you something else. If she's anything like you, anything at all, I wish, so much, that I could know her."

She stopped to sniff and wipe her cheek, and I admit a tiny part of me thought, well, she's still an actress.

But in the end, I believed she meant it. I just did.

Our new house had a little backyard, the perimeter lined with crepe myrtle trees the previous owner must have planted when I was still a girl in Missouri. After Leonard came home, the four of us ate pizza out on the deck, and Geneva pointed out the beauty of the crepe myrtles, which were bright with fuchsia blooms. By then, Marcus felt comfortable enough with her to sit in her lap, though halfway through his first pizza slice, he slid down and toddled over to Leonard.

At first, despite their correspondence, Leonard and his mother were awkward with one another, speaking politely, as if they were strangers. Leonard asked about her flight, and about her job with the undertaker, and she asked him for all kinds of details about his work in the emergency room. Even as they talked to each other, they mostly looked at me or Marcus.

But when I stood and said it was time for me to give him a bath and put him to bed, only Marcus himself had a different opinion. I let him kiss his admirers good night, and then carried him off, knowing we were leaving Leonard and his mother to each other. I took my time. Marcus usually got two bedtime stories, but that night, I read him three. He had a little music box that played Brahms's "Lullaby," and I wound it up and played it for him. Even after he fell asleep, I stayed where I was, rocking him.

By the time I came back out, a waxing moon, almost full, hovered just above the crepe myrtles. Leonard had cleared the plates and brought out the fat candle in a hurricane holder that Carol had sent for my birthday. He and his mother both looked more relaxed, though I could tell they were glad to see me. I took the empty chair between them. I got the sense that neither of them wanted to go inside, but I felt no need to make conversation.

Apparently, they didn't either. The crickets were singing, pulsing in unison, unseen up in the trees. For a long while, the three of us sat together, listening.

ACKNOWLEDGMENTS

I'm indebted to Jon Wilson, author of *The Golden Era in St. Petersburg: Postwar Prosperity in The Sunshine City.* Wilson's book provided the year-by-year changes to the city that I needed, and his prose captures the optimism and excitement of the era without resorting to schmaltz or glossing over the cruelty of laws and customs that sought to exclude so many. Ann Fessler's *The Girls Who Went Away: The Hidden History of Women Who Surrendered Children for Adoption in the Decades Before Roe v. Wade* gave voice to dozens of women with stories that stayed with me for years after I first read them. Lewis H. Carlson's *Remembered Prisoners of a Forgotten War: An Oral History of Korean War POWs* is another collection of first-person accounts that I couldn't stop thinking about.

My mom grew up in Orlando, and she passed away, at the age of eighty-four, while I was working on this book. In the last years of her life, we talked nearly every day, sometimes about what it meant to lose her own mother when she was twelve, and about her memories of being a young woman at midcentury. This novel's story isn't about my mom, but when I asked her to imagine that it was, she helped me understand what Nora would have been up against. My mom got married and left Florida in her twenties, only returning home for visits. But she always spoke of Florida with such affection that it has long held a place in my imagination.

Thank you to the Hall Center at the University of Kansas. A fellowship gave me much-needed time away from teaching to research and begin work on this novel. Before 2020, I'd never been to St. Petersburg, but Wilson's book, mentioned above, made me sure that was where these characters would live, and after a particularly freezing week in Kansas, I decided I needed an immediate research trip. St. Pete has of course greatly increased in population since the era of this story, but through the city's effort and thoughtfulness, landmarks like the public library at Mirror Lake and the downtown's Open Air Post Office are still standing, still beautiful, and still in use. Thank you to Lynn and John for letting me stay at their place, and for letting me use their cruiser bike to get around town the same way Nora often does. And a big thank-you to Karen Roehm, who took time between school getting out and a faculty meeting to show me around the bright and architecturally stunning St. Petersburg High, where Nora and Leonard would meet.

ACKNOWLEDGMENTS

In 2021, I was diagnosed with an aggressive cancer in my right cheek. I want to thank the researchers, innovators, doctors, nurses, and support staff who contributed to my having a very different outcome than I would have had if I'd developed the same cancer just a few decades ago. If not for this army of people working and caring for patients right through the pandemic, this book wouldn't be here, because I wouldn't be here. But I am here. Thank you.

Thank you to all the smart people who read early and sometimes misguided drafts when I was still figuring out the story: Kelly Cannon, Alec Feather, Alice Lieberman, Anna Neill, Becky Mandelbaum, and Lucia Orth all gave me their time and valuable insight. Talking about the characters with Amy Devitt helped me articulate, even to myself, who they were and what they wanted. The wonderful Amy Persechini rounded up a bunch of readers for a very early draft, and though the final version might be unrecognizable to them, their thoughts were helpful and encouraging. So thank you to Amy and her friends: Cindy Bartel, Ellen Sommi, Sandy Suffian, Margaret Yrun, Christy L'Esperance, Marla Nelken, Linda Steigman, Teri Tankel, Kim Homolka, Rina McCormack, LoEva Eddington, Sue Stromm, Linda Zapulla, and Meg Sarnoff. Priti Lakhani and Colleen Morrissey read later drafts with care and made suggestions I gratefully took. Kara Northway also read a late draft, making smart suggestions that shaped the final manuscript. Kara and her husband, Bret Flanders, also helped me finally figure out a title that seemed right. Tracey Lien, a writer as generous as she is brilliant, read early, middle, and late drafts and never failed to nail exactly what could make the story stronger.

I have long felt fortunate that my literary agent is Margaret Riley King, who has acted with integrity, warmth, and wise support through all kinds of writer weather. My editor at Riverhead, Sarah McGrath, showed extraordinary patience with this novel, and when I finally had a draft to share, she responded with both encouragement and her characteristically discerning eye. Sarah has a great talent for both identifying and conveying where to cut, where to sharpen, and where to deepen. I'm grateful not only for her editorial acumen but also the empathy she brings to her work.

Alison Fairbrother, also at Riverhead, made thoughtful and convincing points that further improved the final manuscript. Corinne Leong kept me on track for publication. And I certainly want to thank Gabriel Levinson, Katie Hurley, and the other heroes of copyediting for reading every sentence with so much intelligence and care.

I know I'm lucky to have the inventive Jynne Dilling Martin in my publishing-and-marketing corner. Ashley Garland, Nora Alice Demick, and Bianca Flores impressed me from the start with their forward-thinking creativity and nimbleness. When a writer hopes that her book will be sent into the world in the best way, she's hoping to work with a crack team like this.

I want to thank the friends who never read a draft (likely because I wouldn't let them), but who bolstered my soul through the hard times and basked with me in the good. Thank you to my daughter, Vivian, for being as openhearted and perceptive as any heroine I'd want to read or write about, and for continuing to expand my heart and mind.

Finally, I want to thank Ben Eggleston, who read drafts, helped me strategize, and shoveled the driveway when I was in Florida. When I expressed discouragement, he argued against me with conviction. He slept in hospital rooms and drove me to appointments in KC and Cleveland, where he showed up with notebooks, organized. (This will surprise no one who knows him.) He googled surgeons and read their publications. When I couldn't talk, he got me to laugh, and he grew skilled at interpreting my scrawl on a whiteboard. He sat beside me when I got bad news, worse news, and mitigating news. When I got good news, then great news, he cheered as hard as I did. Ben, I hope we have a lot more good times ahead to celebrate together.